'Debut novelist Ray Celestin has based his beguiling crime thriller on the true story of a serial killer who terrorized New Orleans for more than a year after the First World War. Beautifully written, the evocative prose brings the jazz-filed, Mob-ruled "Big Easy" of pre-prohibition America to life in glorious effect with a story full of suspense and intrigue. Stunning'   *Sunday Express*

'*The Axeman's Jazz* manages to be both a fascinating portrait of a vibrant and volatile city and a riveting read'   *Guardian*

'Slavery's legacy haunts many characters in Ray Celestin's debut novel *The Axeman's Jazz* . . . Celestin smartly evokes the atmosphere of 1919 New Orleans, and a city dominated by music and the mob. Gripping'   *Sunday Times*

'Louis Armstrong is among those trying to track down a serial killer in the New Orleans of 1919 in Celestin's outstanding debut novel'   *Daily Telegraph*

'This thriller, which blends voodoo, gangsters and jazz into an intoxicating mix, is based on a true story'   *Sunday Mirror*

'An absolute must for true crime fanatics'   *Refinery29*

'A rewarding crime novel, swinging its way to a terrifying dénouement with all the panache of a New Orleans marching band . . . An excellent debut'   *The Times*

'Smart, thrilling and dripping with class. A very special debut'
Malcolm Mackay, author of *The Necessary Death of Lewis Winter*

'Utterly compelling, soaked in the unique intoxicating atmosphere of the New Orleans of the period. Marvellous, engaging characters and the writing is pretty much pitch perfect'   R. N. Morris

THE AXEMAN'S JAZZ

Ray Celestin is a novelist and screenwriter based in London. His debut novel, *The Axeman's Jazz*, won the CWA New Blood Dagger for best debut crime novel of the year, and was featured on numerous 'Books of the Year' lists. His follow-up, *Dead Man's Blues*, won the *Historia* Historical Thriller of the Year Award, and was shortlisted for a number of other awards, including the CWA Gold Dagger for best crime novel of the year. The novels are part of his City Blues series, which charts the twin histories of jazz and the Mob through the middle fifty years of the twentieth century.

Also by Ray Celestin

Dead Man's Blues
The Mobster's Lament

THE
AXEMAN'S
JAZZ

RAY CELESTIN

PAN BOOKS

First published 2014 by Mantle

First published in paperback 2015 by Pan Books

This paperback edition first published 2021 by Pan Books
an imprint of Pan Macmillan
The Smithson, 6 Briset Street, London EC1M 5NR
EU representative: Macmillan Publishers Ireland Limited, 1st Floor,
The Liffey Trust Centre, 117-126 Sheriff Street Upper, Dublin 1, DO1 YC43
Associated companies throughout the world
www.panmacmillan.com

ISBN 978-1-5290-6563-3

3 5 7 9 8 6 4

A CIP catalogue record for this book is available from the British Library.

Map artwork by HL Studios

Printed and bound by CPI Group (UK) Ltd, Croydon, CR0 4YY

Visit **www.panmacmillan.com** to read more about all our books
and to buy them. You will also find features, author interviews and
news of any author events, and you can sign up for e-newsletters
so that you're always first to hear about our new releases.

To Captain Alex and my godparents

This story is based on real events.
Between 1918 and 1919 the Axeman of New Orleans
killed six people.

The reprint of the Axeman's letter on pages 4–5 and 267–8
is a transcription of the original and is not the
work of the author.

'When I blow I think of times and things from outta the past that gives me an image of the tune. Like moving pictures passing in front of my eyes. A town, a chick somewhere back down the line, an old man you seen once in a place you don't remember.'

LOUIS ARMSTRONG

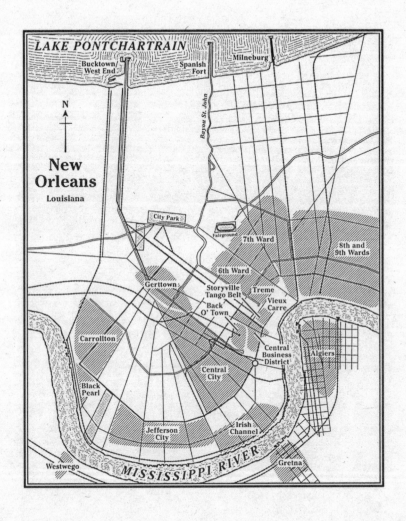

PROLOGUE

PROLOGUE

New Orleans, May 1919

John Riley stumbled into the offices of the New Orleans *Times–Picayune* an hour and a half after he was supposed to have started work. He sat at his desk, took a long slow breath, and raised his eyes to peer about the room. Even in his befuddled state he could see his colleagues stealing glances at him and he wondered exactly how unkempt he must look. He had been out the night before, at his usual spot on Elysian Fields Avenue, and he raised a hand to his face to make sure he wasn't still perspiring. When his fingers rubbed against a stubble at least two days old, he felt a pang of regret for not having sought out a mirror before his arrival.

He looked at his desk and his gaze landed on his typewriter. Its black metal frame, its crescent of type-bars, its levers and keys, all made the thing seem daunting somehow, cold and hard and otherworldly, and he realized he wasn't in a fit enough state to start writing just yet. He'd need a few coffees and a packet of cigarettes, and maybe a lunchtime brandy before he was ready to tackle anything requiring a fully functioning brain, so he decided to kill what was left of the morning with something that approximated work. He rose and stumbled over to the in-tray where the letters to the editor were kept. He grabbed as many as he could, cradling them against his chest, and returned to his seat.

There was the usual correspondence from irate residents, people with complaints, know-it-alls, and those who used the letters page as a forum for arguing with one another. He selected a few of the longer diatribes to print as they filled up the page more easily, then he sifted through the letters from people who claimed to have seen the Axeman. Since the killings had started a few months ago, the office had been inundated with letters from concerned residents who swore they had seen him on his way to some murder or other. Riley sighed and wondered why these people sent these things to the newspaper and not the Police Department. He lit a cigarette and picked up the last letter in the pile. It was an unusual-looking envelope, rice-paper thin, with no sender details, and the newspaper's address written on it in a spidery scrawl of badly splattered, rust-colored liquid he hoped was ink. He took a drag on his cigarette and opened it up with a fingernail.

Hell, May 6th, 1919

Esteemed Mortal:

They have never caught me and they never will. They have never seen me, for I am invisible, even as the ether that surrounds your earth. I am not a human being, but a spirit and a demon from the hottest hell. I am what you Orleanians and your foolish police call the Axeman.

When I see fit, I shall come and claim other victims. I alone know whom they shall be. I shall leave no clue except my bloody axe, besmeared with blood and brains of he whom I have sent below to keep me company.

If you wish you may tell the police to be careful not to rile me. Of course, I am a reasonable spirit. I take no offense at the way they have conducted their investigations in the past. In fact, they have been so utterly stupid as to not only amuse me, but His Satanic Majesty, Francis Josef, etc. But tell them to beware. Let them not try to discover what I am, for it were better that they were never born than to incur the wrath of the Axeman. I don't think there is any need of such a warning, for I feel sure the police will always dodge me, as they have in the past. They are wise and know how to keep away from all harm.

Undoubtedly, you Orleanians think of me as a most horrible murderer, which I am, but I could be much worse if I wanted to. If I wished, I could pay a visit to your city every night. At will I could slay thousands of your best citizens, for I am in close relationship with the Angel of Death.

Now, to be exact, at 12:15 (earthly time) on next Tuesday night, I am going to pass over New Orleans. In my infinite mercy, I am going to make a little proposition to you people. Here it is:

I am very fond of jazz music, and I swear by all the devils in the nether regions that every person shall be spared in whose home a jazz band is in full swing at the time I have just mentioned. If everyone has a jazz band going, well, then, so much the better for you people. One thing is certain and that is that some of your people who do not jazz it on Tuesday night (if there be any) will get the axe.

Well, as I am cold and crave the warmth of my native Tartarus, and it is about time I leave your earthly home, I will cease my discourse. Hoping that thou wilt publish this, that it may go well with thee, I have been, am and will be the worst spirit that ever existed either in fact or realm of fancy.

The Axeman

Riley took a drag on his cigarette, put the letter down and wondered if its author really was the Axeman, and if not, who the hell else would send something like that to the paper. Authentic or not, it'd be a sin not to print it. Riley grinned and rose, and his colleagues turned to look at him as he marched towards the editor's office. He didn't care to wonder if he should tell the authorities before going to press – in instances like this, it was better to ask for forgiveness than for permission. They'd print it, and the city would read it, and a chaos would descend, and New Orleans might well spiral into the greatest night it had ever seen.

PART ONE

1

To the west of the French Quarter, in the uptown slum the Orleanais referred to as the Battlefield, a Negro funeral procession lumbered through the granite sheen of a dawn fog. The mourners, dressed in dark suits and veils, their heads bowed, were reduced to shadows as they moved in and out of the mist, an effect which gave the procession a spectral feel, as if the parade in its entirety had somehow managed to wander into Hades.

The funeral had commenced just after dawn, when the coffin had been carried out of the vigil house and placed on the hearse and the mourners had assembled on the street. Once all was set, the Marshall had blown a shrill, lingering whistle, and the five brass bands employed for the day struck up a slow, haunting version of 'Nearer My God to Thee'.

The marshal, a somber-faced, regal old man dressed in a top hat, frock coat and bright-yellow gloves, turned on his heel and led the cortege through the grass-cracked streets. He was immediately followed by the hearse, horse-drawn and draped in satin, black feather plumes fluttering in the breeze. Then came the bereaved family, wailing into handkerchiefs, and after them the five brass bands, each musician top-hatted and tailed, their coats bedecked with epaulets and tassels. At the very rear, the cortege ended in a press of well-wishers, mourners, and ragged street-children known as the second line, urchins who had nothing better to do than follow parades across town all day, even if it meant being led as though by a Siren to one of the city's many graveyards.

The man being buried was a member of a number of Negro men's associations – the Zulu Aid and Pleasure Club; the Odd Fellows; the Diamond Swells; the Young Men Twenties; the Merry-go-Rounds – and on its way to the graveyard the procession had stopped at each of the association's assembly halls so the club's members could bid farewell to their brethren. Only then did the cortege move on to the cemetery, the songs becoming ever more melancholic as it made its way. When the hearse entered the grave-yard all the instruments died down except for the snare drum, which rattled out a desolate, lonely rhythm, the drumsticks muffled with a handkerchief to imitate the timbre of military kettledrums. And when the procession finally reached the tomb, the drum died out too, and for a brief moment, there was silence.

Then the preacher began the service, intoning against the sibilant wind, and when he had finished, the family threw soil onto the grave, one by one, a process that contained its own rhythm and beat. And after the last mourner had thrown his handful of earth, and the sods had thumped onto the coffin and trickled down its sides, the crowd turned expectantly to the marshal, who stood a few yards back from them, shivering on a stretch of uneven earth, the breeze flapping the cuffs of his trousers.

The old man greeted their stares with wide, milky eyes and after a few long seconds of wind-rustled silence, he nodded, lifted his hand to his chest, and turned over his sash to its parade-day side, a side of dazzlingly bright colors, an African scheme of checkered red, gold and green that shimmered through the fog. And almost in an instant, as if a spirit had taken control of the crowd, the funeral transformed. Club members flipped over their membership buttons, the band turned their jackets inside out, smiles broke, the marshal blew his whistle and before they knew it the band was playing dance music – a raunchy, loud and ironic selection: 'Oh Didn't He Ramble'. The horn players blared, the second line danced among the tombs, and the club members opened bottles of bourbon and beer to toast the deceased. A carnival atmosphere swept through the parade and carried it along as it snaked through the cemetery and back onto the streets, where more people joined the celebrations and the ever-increasing mass of revelers made its way back to the wake.

As the funeral procession had lumbered through the city, performing its well-rehearsed rite of music and movement, it was watched keenly by a 19-year-old slip of a girl in a red pimiento dress, who went by the name of Ida Davis. She hadn't had much difficulty finding the funeral – sound travelled without much obstruction in New Orleans, a flat, wooden city of low-lying buildings, open ground, rivers and lakes. Her father, himself a musician, had often remarked on the phenomenon, saying it was almost as if the city had been constructed as an instrument for the dispersal of music. When a band played – and New Orleans bands were especially loud – it could be heard all the way across town.

And so she had followed her ears and found the cortege, and now she watched it with a disapproving frown. It wasn't that she looked down on the drunken mourners, or the free-loaders, or even the ratty street-children in the second line. Rather, it was the irony of it all that she lamented. Louisiana was a place where Negroes were seldom allowed to express their culture openly, and a funeral provided a rare opportunity for public display, for the downtrodden to be treated with pomp, and it was this that made her frown, that the only time a Negro was allowed to be treated with grandeur was when he or she wasn't even alive to appreciate it.

She stepped off the sidewalk and made her way up the line of mourners, scanning the faces of the musicians, looking for her closest friend, possibly her only friend – a chubby-faced young horn-player on second cornet, who had not yet changed the pronunciation of his name to the French form *Louey*, and was still known to Ida and everyone else in the Battlefield as Lil' Lewis Armstrong.

She spotted him soon enough, at the head of the procession, playing along to an up-tempo rendition of 'High Society'. Lewis noticed her and raised his eyebrows; then, without breaking rhythm or key, he blew out a complicated flourish on the horn by way of a greeting. Some of the crowd nearby cheered drunkenly and Lewis handed his cornet to one of the second-liners, a gangly barefoot child in a frayed white shirt.

Lewis stepped out of the line and approached, his walk stymied by the too-small tuxedo trousers he was wearing. Lewis was almost nineteen, chubby and dark-skinned, with a round face that was a perfect cradle for a distinctive grin. Ida was his opposite in almost every respect – slender and deliberate, with skin just a touch darker than milk, and an almond-shaped face that made people turn. She was also a little introverted – a shyness born of being light-skinned enough to pass for white, a trait which made her few friends in the Battlefield.

Lewis tipped his hat and smiled. 'Hey, Ida,' he said, 'you good?'

His voice was fleecy and deep, rasped by tobacco and liquor, and she was surprised to hear that it betrayed no hint of awkward-ness or curiosity. She hadn't been down to see him in months, and now she had turned up in the Battlefield of all places, unannounced and feeling embarrassed.

'I'm good,' she said, smiling weakly. She had come to him for a favor, to ask for help with an investigation. But now she was with him, she didn't quite know how to make her request. It had been so long since she had seen him, and it was difficult to talk over the noise of the bands, who were reaching a raucous crescendo to their increasingly off-kilter rendition of 'High Society'.

Lewis peered at her with a puzzled look and she could tell he had guessed something was up.

'If you wanna talk,' he said, 'I can meet you back at the wake.'

Ida had been hoping to avoid the wake.

'Sure,' she replied, enunciating over the music. 'Where is it?'

Lewis grinned at her, a gleam in his eye. 'Just follow the band,' he said with a shrug, and before Ida knew it they were both chuck-ling. He tipped his hat at her and trotted back to the parade. The band struck up the opening to 'The Beer Barrel Polka' and Ida watched as the second-liner returned Lewis's cornet. Then her friend stepped back into position, merging into the dark-suited parade rolling drunkenly up the street, its blaze of music and noise fading once more into the mist.

2

A black landaulet police car flew through the fog-bound streets of Little Italy, the driver blaring the horn wildly in an attempt to avoid accidents. He swerved past market stalls and farm wagons and startled pedestrians and occasionally clipped the curbs and banquettes of the narrower roads. At the intersection of Upperline and Magnolia Streets, he veered the car through a sharp corner and screeched to a halt a half-block from a grocery store. In the rear of the vehicle, Detective Lieutenant Michael Talbot dropped back into his seat and breathed a sigh of relief.

'Nice driving, 'Rez,' he said.

'Thanks,' the driver replied, failing to notice the sarcasm. Through the glass partition that separated the two men, Michael saw the driver flip open a pocket watch and check the time.

'Seven minutes and twenty-five seconds,' said the driver, a round, swarthy man called Perez. 'That's gotta be a record,' he added, flashing a smile at Michael through the rearview mirror. Michael smiled back weakly, still feeling faintly nauseous.

Perez scrabbled around the dashboard for a notebook and with the stub of a pencil wrote down the time. The New Orleans Police Department had taken receipt of its first ever fleet of motorcars only a few months previously, and the drivers in the various precincts had, as far as Michael could tell, set up some kind of betting league on how fast they could drive their various routes. Three of the new cars had already been wrecked, one of them by Perez.

Michael let his stomach settle for a moment and arched his back to look out of the car's rear window. His eyes settled on the cheap corner-store grocery a little further down the street. It was typical of the stores Italian migrants were setting up all over the city – single-storied, a shop in the front, living quarters in the back, a yard for deliveries at the rear, and a sheet-metal sign teetering above the whole jerry-built mess, proudly displaying the owner's name. Michael sighed and rubbed his face, running his fingers along the scars that pitted his cheeks.

Outside the store, among the carriages from the Police Department and the Coroner's Office, a mob had gathered – Italian locals that a cordon of patrolmen was half-heartedly holding back. Michael could tell it wasn't the usual kind of crowd that always seemed to materialize at grisly crime scenes – the passers-by, the neighbors, the reporters, the street-corner habitués with nothing better to do. This crowd hadn't gathered out of macabre curiosity. It was there because it was scared, and Michael's heart tightened at the sight of it. From what he knew about human nature, it didn't take much for fearful mobs to turn violent.

'Into the madding crowd,' he mumbled to himself.

'Say what?' Perez asked, glancing up from the notebook with a frown and a dart of his eyes in the rearview mirror. But Michael had already opened the passenger-side door, flipped his homburg onto his head and stepped out into the street.

He strode towards the far end of the cordon, hoping to avoid being noticed by taking the longer route, but Michael was a lurching type, singular and easy to spot. He was a head taller than most other men, with gangly, awkward limbs, and a face razed red and bumpy by smallpox. As he approached the cordon, he pulled the homburg low, but a beady-eyed reporter happened to turn his way at just the wrong time. Michael saw him nudge one of his colleagues and whisper, and in an instant the crowd erupted. Cameras swung towards him and a riot of flashbulbs strobed and popped, sending little clouds of soot into the air that mottled the fog. The paper men shouted his name and bellowed out questions. Angry Italian phrases flew his way. He carried on pushing past the throng, and after a few seconds of jostling he made it to the cordon and through to the other side. He nodded hello to a few of the patrolmen that he recognized, stony-faced, annoyed-looking men, none of whom bothered to respond. A young, earnest beat cop in a starched blue uniform trotted down the front steps to greet him.

'Morning, sir. The victims are this way,' said the beat cop, a greenhorn called Dawson, freshly returned from the war and eager to prove his worth. He held his hand up to the storefront with a smile, and Michael thought there was something of the maître d' about the gesture. He nodded his thanks and Dawson led him up the front steps and into the dim interior of the grocery.

The store was lined on all sides with neat pinewood shelves crammed with tins of fish, meat and assorted Italian delicacies that Michael had never heard of. Drums of olive oil were piled high along one wall, and festooned from the rafters were upturned bunches of dried oregano that to Michael's mind lent the store a grotto-like air.

At the far end was a glass counter filled with breads and foul-smelling cheeses, and a Dutch meat-slicer, its cranks and disc-blade gleaming, a leg of pork still lying in the tray. The cash register stood next to it, and as Michael expected, it was completely undamaged. Beyond it was the door into the domestic part of the building. They approached, and Dawson held up his hand again. Michael, unsure of what to make of the boy, nodded and smiled. He took off his homburg and stepped through the door.

The living room was cramped, illuminated by a greasy light, and made smaller by the officials drudging away in it. Two patrolmen were taking an inventory, a doctor from the Coroner's Office was bent over one of the bodies, and a photographer, a Frenchman with a portrait studio in Milneburg, readied a new roll of nitrate for his camera.

Michael inspected the room – a dark wood table and a side-board filled most of the space, a window looked out onto the side of the neighbors' house, and at the back a door led into the kitchen. None of the furniture had been upset or overturned, and a gospel book still lay at one end of the table. The walls were covered in floral wallpaper, yellowing and ancient and spotted with mold. Photographs of somber old Sicilians competed for wall space with an accumulation of cheap religious images – crucifixes, Madonnas, postcards of cathedrals and pilgrimage sites. In the space that led into the kitchen were the bodies of the two victims, splayed out on the linoleum floor in a pool of dark, resinous blood.

Michael crossed the room and knelt next to the bodies. The wife was short and plump, with aged skin and salt-colored hair. Dried blood had glued her nightdress to the rolls of fat around her midriff, marking out the curve of her figure. Michael could make nothing of her face, which had been so viciously attacked with a sharp object that it resembled less a human head than some kind of crater, around the lip of which a handful of flies buzzed frenetically.

The husband was slumped by the window. Most of Michael's view was obscured by the doctor who was still examining the body, but he could see the man had wounds similar to his wife's. His right arm was outstretched and pointed towards the sideboard, whose lower drawers were streaked with finger-wide lines of blood.

Michael shook his head and took a last, sorry look at the two corpses. He had learned it was best not to dwell on the savagery his job confronted him with, so he crossed himself, a token gesture that somehow helped insulate him from it all, then he stood and stretched the tension out of his knees. Behind him the photographer took a snap and the flashbulb popped in the stillness.

Michael wiped the blood from the soles of his Florsheims onto an already ruined Persian rug, stepped over the wife's body and entered the kitchen. An axe had been left by a cupboard, propped up on its rough-hewn handle. Michael noticed fragments of bone speckled along the blood-encrusted blade. In the sink there was more blood and a few crumbs of mud. The door from the kitchen into the yard behind the house had been forced open from the outside, the frame around the lock an explosion of jagged wood. Michael stepped into the yard and the morning cold pressed itself against his face. On all three sides, high wooden fences cut off the view and gave the yard an eerie stillness. Next to the door was a haphazard pile of firewood, and beyond that, a barren space occupied solely by weeds and rusting metal trash. Michael looked around for a moment, then returned to the clammy warmth of the living room.

'Dawson? What have we gathered so far?' He pulled a chair from under the table, sat, and motioned for Dawson to do the same. Dawson sat and read from a polished leather notebook. 'Victims were Mr and Mrs Joseph Maggio. Fifty-eight and fifty-one years old respectively. Sicilian immigrants. Owned the store a couple of years. Neighbors said they moved in from somewhere in Gretna. I called headquarters – neither of them had any convictions.'

Michael nodded. Mr and Mrs Maggio fitted the profile – Sicilian shopkeepers with no criminal ties, seemingly picked at random. In the preceding attacks, the killer the press had dubbed the Axeman had entered the victims' residences at night and, as the name would suggest, dispatched them with an axe, showing considerable relish in what he was doing, and no interest whatsoever in burglary or molestation. Aside from the Maggios, the Axeman had already attacked three households, killing among others an infant and its mother. And with each attack the violence had increased, becoming more gruesome and crazed.

'The neighbors saw nothing unusual,' continued Dawson, 'no one arriving; no one leaving; no screams or shouts; no noise of a break-in.'

'Means of entry?'

'No clues whatsoever as to how he got in, or left. And here's the kicker, sir – the room was locked from the inside when the bodies were discovered.'

The killer had a habit of leaving rooms that way. Either he exited from windows which slid closed after him, or he picked locks shut from the outside after he'd finished. These explanations hadn't stopped the press from painting the Axeman as some kind of supernatural being with the ability to float through walls. New Orleans was a superstitious place at the best of times, and now a sizeable portion of the city believed they were under attack by some form of demon.

'Who kicked in the kitchen door?' Michael asked, remembering the scene at the back of the house.

'That'd be . . .' Dawson flicked through his notebook. 'Patrolman D. Hancock, sir. The wife's niece discovered the bodies. She helped out in the shop. No one was answering when she arrived this morning so she walked round the back. Spotted the wife's body from the window. Hancock was first to the scene.'

'Any tarot cards?' asked Michael.

Dawson nodded, reached over to the sideboard and handed Michael two bloodstained cards. Michael inspected them – the Justice card and the Judgment card. Like the ones they'd found on the previous victims, they were expensively made, hand-painted, bigger than normal playing cards, and rendered in lurid reds and purples, with outlines in black and gold ink. The Justice card portrayed a robed man sitting on a throne, sword in one hand, scales in the other. The Judgment card showed an angel flying high above a hellish, barren landscape, while a crowd of naked sinners pleaded to it from the ground. On the reverse was the usual intricate, monochrome pattern found on all playing cards, but this one had depictions of tiny animals weaved into the design. The animals seemed to be calling to each other, crying out against their geometric prison.

'Where were they found?' he asked, handing the cards back to Dawson.

'In the victims' heads, sir,' said Dawson bashfully. 'Inserted into the wounds.'

Michael nodded. He knew the Mafia sometimes left tarot cards at execution scenes, calling-cards to let people know what happened to those who didn't toe the line. But Michael also knew the Mafia didn't butcher grandmothers and children. And if the attack was an execution, what had a God-fearing elderly couple done to deserve it?

Most homicides were committed by people known to the victim, and in New Orleans every community stuck to their own. If a Sicilian had been killed, the most likely person to have done the killing was another Sicilian. And since the victims had all been shopkeepers, and Sicilian shopkeepers were invariably mixed up with the Mafia, it all pointed in one direction – the Family. But the savagery of the attacks and the scattering of tarot cards, with their links to voodou, had convinced half the city that the Axeman was a Negro – despite the fact that not a single person had actually seen the killer. In neighborhoods all across town, colored men were being chased through the streets by mobs. It was only a matter of time before there was a lynching.

The Axeman was stoking up distrust in a city already full of suspicion. Each of New Orleans's communities fenced itself off from its neighbors: the Creoles of color to the north; the Irish to the south; the Negroes to the west; the Italians in Little Italy in the center; with enclaves of other groups – Chinese, Greeks, Germans, Jews – scattered about like pawns on a chess board. Only in the very center of town, in the French Quarter, in Storyville, in the business district, was there any intermingling. The segregation caused suspicion, and the suspicion furthered the segregation. And now there was an Axeman lighting a flame under it all, causing all these closeted people to rub and spark against one another, and Michael was the man the city had entrusted to put a stop to it all.

From somewhere in the backyard, the noise of a woodpecker drilling its head into a tree floated into the room. The doctor stood at this point, groaning as he did. He was an old man with a rusty complexion and a portly physique. An elaborate white mustache adorned his upper lip, combed in the Victorian style into two great walrus arcs.

'Knees ain't what they used to be,' he said in a rough, cigar-smoker's voice. He tottered over to the table, slumped into a chair next to Michael and fumbled through his pockets for a three-pack of Fonsecas. He offered one to Michael, who refused with a wave of his hand.

'I've got my own,' he said, taking a silver cigarette case from his pocket. He opened it and took a Virginia Bright from inside. The doctor struck a match and the two men shared it.

'It's the same old story, son,' said the doctor, shaking the flame from the match and dropping it onto the table. 'Victims were dispatched by the usual means. I'd estimate the time of death as between eleven and one last night. No signs of rape. Can't say much more for now.' The doctor shrugged and took a long puff on his cigar. 'What do you say?' he asked Michael, raising his eyebrows. It was the same expectant look Michael had been seeing increasingly since the murders had started. He peered over to the two corpses lying on the floor, barely a yard from where he and the doctor were chatting.

'I'd say at about eleven or twelve o'clock last night the Maggios were sitting here in their living room. Wife was sitting over there, reading scripture.' Michael motioned to the gospel book on the far side of the table. 'Not sure what the husband was doing. Maybe she was reading it to him. Anyways, he was sat over here, near the sideboard. Killer entered the property from the backyard, because the front's on a main road, and from the back he just needs to climb the fence. He picked the lock of the kitchen door. What with the yard-fences being so high he could have taken his time. He grabbed the axe from the pile of firewood because I didn't see any axe there, and the man would have been a fool to carry a weapon with him when he knew there'd be one waiting. The wife heard a noise when the killer stepped through into the living room. She stood up because she's closest to the kitchen. See how she's lying on the floor?' He pointed to the wife's body. 'Killer attacked her first. The husband sees what's happening, tries to grab for something in the sideboard, maybe a gun, in the second drawer down. But he's too slow. He carries on trying to open the drawer while the killer attacks him, hence the blood on the sideboard. Killer took his time mutilating them. Then he goes to the kitchen and discards the evidence. Leaves the axe, and I guess he washes the blood off his hands and clothes and boots, because there's specks of blood and mud in the sink. He steps out into the backyard and locks the door from the outside with a pick. 'Course, that's just conjecture, on account of Patrolman D. Hancock obliterating a crucial piece of evidence in his rush to get in. The killer leaves the property with not a single piece of evidence on him. Not even a bloodstain on the underside of his boot. That's about the sum of it.'

Michael took a drag on his cigarette and stared at the two bodies again. 'What I can't figure out,' he said slowly, 'is how the killer got from the wife to the husband without either letting off a scream.'

'Maybe he struck the wife,' Dawson suggested, 'then threw the axe across the room at the husband, you know, Injun style.' Dawson mimicked what he thought the over-arm action of an Apache might be, to illustrate the point.

Michael and the doctor shared a look. 'Maybe,' said Michael. 'Whatever he did, he did it quick.'

He turned to the two officers who had been taking an inventory of the room but had stopped to listen to Michael's theory.

'You two checked the sideboard yet?' he asked.

'No, sir,' said one of the men.

'Well, let's see what Mr Maggio was grabbing for.'

He stepped over to the sideboard and opened the bottommost drawer to reveal two stacks of neatly folded linen. He frowned, rummaged around underneath the stacks and came out with a shoebox. He opened it to find a mound of papers – invoices, receipts, the couple's naturalization papers, and several wads of crisp five-dollar bills.

'Guess he was trying to buy the killer off,' said the doctor.

Michael flicked through one of the wads and frowned. The treasury seal was in red ink, a design used exclusively on Federal Reserve notes that hadn't been issued for nearly five years.

'These notes are unused,' said Michael. 'Crisp as the day they were printed.'

'So?' said the doctor with a shrug.

'So either Maggio got these out of the bank five years ago and they've been sitting here ever since, or they're counterfeits.'

Michael took the shoebox out of the drawer and handed it to Dawson.

'Get hold of someone from the Bureau of Engraving and Printing and check the serial numbers. No one keeps that much money in a sideboard for five years. Specially not in New Orleans.'

Dawson took hold of the shoebox and nodded. Michael lost himself in thought for a moment, and in the silence the sound of the woodpecker rose again to fill the room.

'What about the graffiti?' said the doctor.

'What graffiti?'

Dawson led Michael out to the back yard and round to the side of the building. Scrawled in foot-high spidery brown letters on the side wall of the store were the words:

MRS TENEBRE WILL SIT UP LIKE MRS MAGGIO WHEN I'M THROUGH.

Michael stared at the words and shook his head. Had the Axeman stopped to write them a message? Was he telling them who was next on his list? Was he goading the police for his own amusement, or trying to scare a future victim?

'Get the Frenchman to take some photos,' Michael said to Dawson, pointing at the graffiti, 'then drape something over it before any of the jackasses out front see it. Then get back to the precinct and run a search on every Tenebre in the city, male and female. I want a list on my desk by this afternoon.'

Dawson tipped his hat and rushed off. Michael stood for a moment, hands on hips, then turned around and scanned the yard for a second time. Trash was scattered everywhere: tin cans; newspapers; broken wood from packing crates; an outdoor grill rusted in a corner, warped and unused. All across the space, a carpet of weeds and bushes had grown tall and choked the ground. There was something sad and forlorn about the whole of it. The Maggios had failed to insulate themselves from the dirt of the streets. He thought of his own home briefly, of the crowd outside the store, of the weight of the city's expectations on his shoulders. Two more victims, and a foot-high message from the killer letting them know another was on the way. Michael shook his head, crossed himself once more, and stepped back inside.

3

Just to the north of New Orleans, in scrubland outside a farming town called Boutte, stood a handful of barnlike structures surrounded by rings of razor-wire fences and dust-bowl courtyards. The buildings were made of heavy wood and blacked-out windows and were used by the State of Louisiana as a halfway house – a stop-off point for convicts in transit. The prisoners' barracks were located at the compound's very center, and when the door of the building was swung open, a sharp clang reverberated across the labyrinth of huts, enclosures and fences.

Two men stepped out into the morning chill and shuffled single-file towards the edge of the courtyard, their shoes crunching a rhythm on the gravel underfoot. The first man was a convict on his way to freedom, having the night before completed a six-year sentence. His hands were cuffed in front of him and he was dressed in a crumpled, moth-eaten suit of sky-blue cotton. He had arrived at sunset the previous day, on the convict transport wagon that journeyed between Boutte and Angola, the Louisiana State Penitentiary a hundred and twenty miles northwest.

The convict had spent the night in the icy barracks, and had slept well despite the cold, tired as he was from the journey. The wagon took just over a day to travel from the isolated crook in the Mississippi where Angola was located, far up at the very edge of the state. Convicts were never transported after dark, so the Board of Control used the halfway houses as rest stations – this one being the very last link in the barbed-wire daisy-chain that led all the way to New Orleans.

A few minutes after dawn the convict was awoken by the jab of a nightstick in his guts, and now he was being shadowed as he walked by the nightstick's owner, an ominous man in a royal-blue warden's uniform, who stared at the prisoner with a slant in his eye. After traversing four courtyards and waiting four times for gateways in fences to be unlocked for them by the guards, they eventually arrived at the compound's front gate.

'Patterson!' shouted the warden.

A toothless streak of a man, with a shotgun slung over his shoulder, appeared in the doorway of a sentry hut and grinned at them. He sauntered out of the hut, approached the bars that lay across the front gate, and undid the locks that kept them in place. Then he heaved the bars back and swung open the gate, its lower edge scraping against the uneven clay of the road.

The warden tapped his nightstick on the prisoner's shoulder and the prisoner turned to face him. Luca D'Andrea was a slight, dark-haired man in his early fifties, with a face that was both handsome and hollow, brown eyes sparkling under a soft, sorrow-filled brow. The warden removed the cuffs with a jangle of keys, and Luca rubbed his wrists. Then he nodded, as if to say thanks to his captor, and stepped through the gate onto the road outside.

Boutte wasn't much to look at. The road was rutted and dusty, and on either side scrubland stretched to the horizon, barren save for a few stubby, crippled trees. If there was any point that marked Luca's transition from a prisoner to a free man, this was it, but he felt no joy, no sense of freedom, just a heavy, anxious uncertainty – the same feeling of dread that had racked him in the months leading up to his release.

During the years of his incarceration he had been given two square meals a day, a place to lay his head, and enough work to stop him pondering the sorry turns his life had taken. From dawn till dusk, six days a week, he had farmed the Manhattan-sized penitentiary estate for the profit of the prison board. Angola had been named after the plantation on which it had been built, and the plantation had been named after the mother country of the slaves that had first worked its land. A fact which led the inmates to muse that when it came to back-breaking regimes, shackles and chains, Angola's name wasn't the only fragment of its slaving past that echoed into the present.

Unlike most of the convicts, however, Luca hadn't begrudged the work. He experienced a serenity in the fields that he had never known before, an acceptance of his place in the world that calmed and reassured him. But now he had no work to keep him from dwelling on memories he'd rather forget, and his days stretched into the future as empty as the scrublands in front of him.

He peered down the road, and thought he could see New Orleans, just about visible on the horizon, dancing in and out of the shimmering mist that clung to the ground. He thought there was something vaguely feminine in the way the image moved through the haze, like a showgirl in a bar.

'It's a long way to the Big Easy,' said a sarcastic, adenoidal voice behind him.

Luca turned to see a thin, swarthy man leaning against the fence opposite, arms folded, smoking a cheap brand of cigarette. John Riley, a familiar but unwelcome face. During Luca's trial, Riley's newspaper had run a series of exposés on him, using editorials Riley had written to stoke up public outrage. The reporter smiled at him, reached into his pocket for a cigarette case of tarnished brass and proffered the contents to Luca. Luca peered at the cigarettes, picked one out, and Riley sparked a match for him.

Luca studied Riley's face and noticed how he had aged. Riley had always sported dark patches around his eyes, but now they were more noticeable, more ingrained, and they were accompanied by hollowness around the cheekbones, a stretched, almost mummified pallor. Riley was a man, thought Luca, who oozed decay.

'You don't look too happy, D'Andrea,' said Riley in his well-heeled staccato. 'In lieu of a welcoming committee of family and friends, you should be pleased to see me.'

Riley grinned a yellow-toothed grin and Luca took a long drag on his cigarette. Riley was wearing a cream-colored blazer and a straw boater with a red silk band wrapped around the crown. The clothes would have hinted of the Ivy League and rowing clubs and strong-jawed, northeastern families if they were on anyone but Riley. Instead they looked coarse, somehow, louche even, on the haggard, round-shouldered figure in front of him.

'I got a car coming,' continued Riley. 'Can give you a lift if you like.'

Luca gave the reporter a sideways glance. People like Riley didn't do favors without expecting something in return, and Luca was in no position to be striking bargains and making pacts.

'I was thinking I'd walk,' said Luca, who had been looking forward to strolling in a straight line for as long as he wanted, with no chains around his ankles or barbed-wire fences cutting him off, or gunmen trotting by his side.

'It's twenty miles plus to New Orleans,' said Riley with a frown.

Luca shrugged. 'What do you want?' he asked, and the reporter paused.

'You know how it is,' he said, his tone plaintive. 'I didn't particularly wanna come down here and spoil your big moment, but my editor asked me to get some quotes,' he explained, throwing his hands into the air, bemoaning the whims of fate.

'Still haven't been promoted, then?' said Luca flatly, and Riley laughed a short, contrived grunt of a laugh.

'Thanks for the smoke,' said Luca. He fixed the cigarette between his lips, put his hands in his pockets and started off down the road to New Orleans.

'Jesus, Luca. I came all this way,' said Riley, scampering along after him. 'C'mon, you were always good copy,' he pleaded.

'I was good copy when you were stitching me up,' said Luca. Riley grimaced and cast a look over Luca's face.

'I have to say, chum, you're looking good,' Riley said. 'Most folks age at twice the pace in Angola. You look just the same as the day you was sentenced.'

'Go to hell,' said Luca, taking another drag on his cigarette.

Luca hadn't been expecting his return to New Orleans to be an easy experience. He knew the city was no paradise; it was violent and unforgiving, awash with criminals and immigrant communities that treated one another with hostility and suspicion. But it was also a city with a beguiling energy to it, a bright and opulent charm. For all its segregation and spite, its shabby streets and faded glory, it was easy to become bewitched by the city of New Orleans. And so the whole time Luca was in Angola he couldn't help feeling that when he returned, he would be entering a better world. That the slime of the prison life would wash off him like some kind of amniotic fluid. But now, as he looked at Riley, he wondered if he wasn't just exchanging one kind of slime for another.

'Well, how's about that,' said Riley. 'I tell you what, on this day of new beginnings, let's turn over a new leaf? Start afresh?'

Luca was about to send another curse Riley's way when he stopped and sighed. Something about the prospect of new beginnings tugged at his conscience. Maybe if he gave Riley what he wanted the man would leave him in peace.

'What do you wanna know?' Luca said, and Riley's smile returned.

'Just the usual,' said the reporter. 'How was your time in Angola? How's it feel to be outta that convict garb? What's your view on the state's correctional facilities now you've seen them from the other side?'

Luca gave Riley a look. 'You didn't come down here to ask me that,' he said. 'Not even the Louisiana State Prison Board gives a shit about the state of its correctional facilities. Your readership sure as hell ain't gonna give a damn.'

Riley screwed up his face. 'Still sharp as a tack, huh, Luca?' he said. 'You know, some men get out and their brains've gone to mush. Not you, though.' Riley tipped his hat at Luca with a smirk. 'What's your view on the Axeman murders?' he said.

Luca frowned and peered at him. 'What Axeman murders?' he asked, and Riley nodded knowingly.

'Word didn't reach you during your sojourn at the state's expense? A crazy Zulu's been running around town killing Italian grocers. Six weeks since the first attack and your old pal Talbot, who's in charge of the case, is making no headway. Making a mess of it, in actual fact, and people are getting rightly upset.'

Luca noticed a light wind whipping dust along the road towards New Orleans. Times had changed, he thought: now it was Michael's turn to have his name dragged through the mud. Luca had tried to keep abreast of changes in the city. As inmates arrived in Angola they brought with them news of the outside world, and Luca had listened in earnest to these prison-yard dispatches. He'd heard of the Great War, of the Great Hurricane, of the Influenza Pandemic, of Storyville being closed down; he'd even heard of the new type of music that was, according to the Negro inmates, engulfing the city. He knew the Eighteenth Amendment had been passed and prohibition was just around the corner, and he wondered what it would do to the tinderbox of clashing interests that was New Orleans. But amidst all this news of upheaval and strife, Luca had heard nothing of the goings-on in the police force, or of his old protégé.

'What's it got to do with me?' he asked.

'Well, seeing as you got history with Talbot, the boss and I were hoping, in his hour of need, you'd supply the *Schadenfreude*. I mean, it's only because he squealed on you that he got promoted. If he's not fit for the job it's kinda funny you getting released just at the point people are beginning to notice.'

Riley breathed deeply, having trouble talking, smoking and keeping up with Luca's brisk pace all at the same time.

'Kinda like the chickens coming home to roost,' he wheezed. 'At least, that's the angle the ed wants. Ironic.'

He peered at Luca, waiting for an answer, but Luca stayed silent, his eyes fixed on the horizon, on the distant image of New

Orleans in the mist. He was trying to make out once again the dancer in the mirage, but all he could see now was a swirl of dust, sunrays and dew.

'No one cares what I think,' he said. 'People'll believe what they wanna believe. I learned that much during the trial.'

Riley nodded, and they strode on a little further without talking. Over the fields on either side of them a murder of crows angled and swooped, letting out piercing, nervy squawks.

'Don't you have anything you want to say?' said Riley after a while, his tone softer, pleading. 'It's because of Talbot you spent the last six years in a cell. I mean, he was supposed to be your protégé.'

Luca made a valiant effort not to let his spirits sink, and tried not to think of betrayal. He stopped and turned to face Riley, and Riley instinctively took a step back.

'Five years,' said Luca calmly. 'I got one off for good behavior.' He took a last drag on the cigarette, flicked it onto the road and swiped it out with his boot. 'Michael did the right thing,' he continued, 'I don't hold him no grudges. I just wanna start my life off again. No vendettas, no living in the past. All I wanna do now is get to New Orleans, eat some food that ain't half-rotten and covered in roaches, buy me a drink, and maybe buy me a woman. Put that in your paper.'

Luca turned and strode off down the road and Riley watched him go, a perplexed expression on his face.

'Luca, haven't you heard?' he shouted. 'You can't buy a woman no more! The Navy outlawed the brothels!'

Luca ignored him and carried on down the long, dusty road to New Orleans.

4

As Ida had expected, the wake was a raucous affair, the house bursting with an uproar of drunken, dancing people. Most of the neighborhood was there, the club members, the five bands, the street kids, the happy stragglers, and the deceased's family too. Music and noise blared through the thin walls of the house and out across the ward like a siren, promising good times that called yet more hopefuls to the party.

By noon the majority of the mourners were stumbling through the house, inebriated on cheap spirits and marijuana, heroin or cocaine, or else they had paired up to sweet-talk in quiet corners and nooks. A cutting contest between two of the bands was taking place in the yard, each band trying to outplay the other. The noisy and unforgiving crowd not only played judge, but joined in with the music too, clapping and shouting and crashing their feet onto the floor in a shuddering percussion that shook the ground.

To avoid the crush inside the house, people had spilled out onto the street, some passed out in pools of vomit, others lying on the grass drinking and smoking, still others leaning against fence posts, shooting the breeze.

On the porch steps of a house opposite, Ida and Lewis sat side by side, taking in the scene. Ida always felt uneasy in the midst of a party, never quite sure of what she was supposed to do, invariably looking for a corner to melt into. Lewis, catching on to her discomfort, had suggested they go outside and survey things from afar, and Ida had taken him up on the offer. She glanced at him as he watched the goings-on opposite. She noticed the puffy eyes, the weary look, the slump to his shoulders. Funerals were tough work

– the bands had to play all the way through the parade, the ceremony, and then the wake, which could continue well into the early hours.

Lewis looked her way and caught her inspecting him, and she smiled at him sheepishly.

'Whose funeral is it anyway?' she asked.

'I dunno,' said Lewis, 'some old-timer.'

Ida nodded and they lapsed into silence once again. She hadn't seen Lewis since the dog days of the previous summer, the longest they had gone in their six-year friendship without meeting up, and she hoped they weren't slipping away from each other for good.

'You sure you don't wanna beer or something?' said Lewis, noticing Ida's stiffness.

'No, I'm good, thanks,' she said, shaking her head.

A drunken mourner staggered past them, the collar of his shirt broken, his eyes watery. He recognized Lewis and nodded hello, then he stopped and stared at Ida, frowning, confused. She was used to these kinds of reactions from passers-by. People stared partly on account of her looks, but mainly because they were never quite sure what race she was. She stared at the ground, praying the man would leave without making a comment, and eventually he stumbled on. Lewis watched the man go then he peered at her.

'Ain't nothing you can't handle,' he said, trying to sound warm and reassuring. She smiled at him coyly, and looked across the road to the house opposite, at the man swaying up the stairs. 'Lewis, I'm sorry I ain't been coming around so much these days.' She wanted to follow up with an excuse, to say she had been just so busy lately, or that Gretna was so difficult to get to. The hiatus had coincided with her getting the job at the Pinkertons, the bottom-of-the-rung office job she hoped would lead to a detective's role one day. She could have used that as an excuse, but she couldn't lie to Lewis – they both knew the reason she had stopped coming around.

'How's Daisy?' she asked.

'She's good,' Lewis said, responding as if the question was

perfectly innocent, and Ida could tell by the way he answered that he was lying. Ida and Mayann, Lewis's mother, both agreed that Daisy was no proper match for him. The girl was a couple of years older than he was, querulous and prone to bouts of violence. She worked as a prostitute in the honky-tonks across the river, rough places full of levee workers and longshoremen, and it was in one such place, the Brickhouse, that Lewis had met her the previous spring. Although Mayann was in no position to criticize a working girl on account of her job, both she and Ida couldn't help but feel that Daisy was below Lewis, and worse yet, she made him miserable. Mayann had given her blessing begrudgingly, and a few months shy of Lewis's eighteenth birthday, he and Daisy had married at City Hall, less than five weeks after first meeting each other. Lewis had moved across the river to Gretna to be with her, and at first Ida paid them regular visits. But over the course of the year, as it became plain that Daisy thought Ida a snob, and Ida dropped every hint she thought Daisy ratty and coarse, Ida had visited Lewis less and less, until eventually the visits had petered out altogether.

'And how's Clarence?' Ida asked, smiling, trying to move the conversation to less sensitive subjects. Clarence was Lewis's 5-year-old cousin, who Lewis had taken in when the boy's mother had died after childbirth. Lewis had legally adopted the boy just after his marriage, and had moved him into the apartment he shared with Daisy, where the three of them made a peculiarly teenaged and hobbled-together family.

Lewis frowned when he heard Ida mention Clarence and a pained look crossed his face.

'You didn't hear?' he asked, and Ida shook her head, alarmed at the upset she could hear in his voice. Lewis peered at her, taking a moment before speaking again.

'He had a fall,' he said. 'Landed on his head. Doctors said he's gonna be slow.'

'Oh Lord!' Ida exclaimed. Her eyes widened and she clasped

her hand on Lewis's arm. 'I'm so sorry,' she said, her voice quavering, tears welling up in her eyes.

Lewis shrugged, forlorn, and spoke in a halting voice, explaining how on a rainy afternoon a few months back, Daisy and he were listening to records while Clarence played with his toys on the back gallery of the house. Then they heard screams and ran out to see Clarence lying in the courtyard below, a drop of twenty feet, blood all over his head, crying and anguished.

Ida stared at Lewis, realizing he blamed himself and that the slump she noticed about him was something much deeper than tiredness.

'Ain't your fault,' she said, shaking her head. He returned her look and then she took him in her arms and they hugged.

'I should have come to see you,' she said, cursing herself for letting Daisy get between them. 'I would have if I'd known.'

'It's OK. You're here now,' he said warmly.

They held each other for a while longer and then Lewis pulled a bottle of beer from one of his pockets. He opened the cap on the handrail of the stairs with a thump of his palm, and offered it to Ida, who took a birdlike sip. The beer was warm, frothy and watered-down and it left her mouth tangy and dry. She passed it back to Lewis, who took a long swig, and they stared at the goings-on at the party once more.

'So what's up with you?' he asked. 'Must be important if you coming into Back o' Town?'

Ida stared at him, embarrassed that she hadn't come down just to see how he was. 'Am I that obvious?' she asked.

Lewis smiled and shook his head. 'I've known you a long time,' he said.

Ida nodded and bit her lip. 'I need to interview someone,' she said, 'and I didn't really wanna do it on my own. I was hoping you'd come with me.'

'Sure,' said Lewis, 'you ain't going with Lefebvre?'

Lefebvre was Ida's boss at the detective agency, an obese white Creole, listless, slow-mannered and stricken by liquor.

'This is kinda . . . extracurricular,' she said. 'I been reading about the Axeman murders in the newspapers and I kinda noticed something.'

Lewis rummaged around his pockets, found a pack of cigarettes and offered one to Ida. The cigarettes were the cheap ones they sold in Back o' Town, the ones tobacco-pickers made themselves from stolen leaves. The tobacco was untreated and it burned the back of the throat like hell, but Ida took one anyway.

'At work we got this list of "non-contracted agents", which is company-speak for stoolies,' she explained. 'The Axeman victims from two weeks ago, the Romanos, well, the wife had a nurse. The nurse was who discovered the bodies – Millicent Hawkes. Well, her name came up on our stooley list. She turned up a few years ago trying to sell info to us on the Romanos, saying they were up to something. We get lots of folks coming in trying to do that, like we Marie Laveau or something. All the newspapers are talking about *innocent victims*, but that don't sound so innocent to me,' she said, shaking her head. 'I just wanna find out what she was trying to sell. See, Hess never bought it, but he left a record she came. Hess was like that. Kept records o' everything.'

'Hess?' asked Lewis, frowning.

'Hess was Lefebvre's old partner,' said Ida. 'Anyhow, I can't investigate officially, cuz the police ain't asked us for assistance, so, I was gonna do it on my own.'

'That's jake, Ida,' said Lewis, 'but why you want me to come with you? I ain't exactly hard-boiled.'

'I ain't never interviewed someone on my own before,' she said. 'I'm gonna feel kinda stupid turning up there, you know, I'm just a girl and all. I don't reckon she'll take me seriously.'

'Well, I can understand that,' said Lewis, his face suddenly somber. 'I don't take you seriously either.'

He grinned and Ida smiled and shook her head.

'Why you wanting to go stepping on the cops' toes anyway?' he asked. 'You getting bored already?'

Ida bit her lip again and thought for a moment. 'Kinda,' she said. Lefebvre had promised her fieldwork when she had first been hired, but the promise had proved hollow. She found herself spending her days answering letters, filing and running to the store to buy him rye. She deserved a break, a chance to prove herself. Ida had graduated top of her class in every subject and was better read than most of her teachers, and she didn't see why she should have to settle for a career at the bottom of the ladder, just because other people deemed her gender and the tint of her skin to be a hindrance.

Lewis peered at her and nodded. 'I'm free next week if you wanna go then,' he said. 'Any daytime's good. I got 'em open since I quit the coal carts.'

Ida stared at him and frowned. 'You quit the coal carts?' she asked. 'When?'

'Last year,' he said. 'Armistice Day. 'Bout thirty seconds after I heard the war was over.'

Ida frowned at him and he explained how the end of the war meant the nightclubs reopening and work for musicians becoming abundant once more. He told her of the upturn in his fortunes, how he had been recruited by Kid Ory to play with his band at the New Orleans Country Club every Saturday. And how a few months after that, at a gig in the Cooperator's Hall, Fate Marable had heard him and signed him up to play on the steamboats that took moonlight cruises up and down the Mississippi for the Streckfuss line.

'Lewis, that's great,' said Ida, grinning at him. 'Just wait till I tell Daddy. He's gonna be rightly proud.'

Ida's father, Peter Davis, was the reason the two of them had met. He had been Lewis's music teacher when Lewis was an inmate at the New Orleans Home for Colored Waifs, a Victorian correctional institution that Lewis was sent to when he was twelve.

Professor Davis had taken Lewis under his wing, and would occasionally ask him over to his house to play cornet while Ida accompanied him on the piano. Ida was never more than a passable pianist, but she obliged her father and, over time, the two lonely children became friends.

'Main thing is I'm learning,' said Lewis. 'Kid Ory's a step up, and Marable's band, they say that's like going to the *conservatoire*.' He finished the sentence in a sing-song, hoity-toity voice and the two of them chuckled. 'They all sight-read,' he continued, 'and they teaching me this and that. It ain't every uptown darky gets to play with the Creole bands.'

Lewis smiled awkwardly and Ida could tell he was both proud and bashful. He had always had a streak in him for self-improvement, for bettering himself, for learning everything he possibly could about music – traits that made him different from most of the stony-faced, cocksure Waifs' Home boys her father taught.

'So you reckon you can figure out this Axeman thing?' said Lewis, turning to look at her.

Ida stared at him and raised her eyebrows with mock seriousness.

'*There is no combination of events for which the wit of man cannot conceive an explanation,*' she said, before a Cheshire-cat grin broke out on her face. Ever since Lewis had met her, she had either been reading Conan Doyle books, or quoting them at him, and the thing had become a joke between the two of them.

'That Sherlock talking again?' asked Lewis, and Ida nodded.

'You need to stop reading those books, Ida. They stopping you from seeing the world right.'

Lewis tapped his finger against his temple and Ida shook her head at him. Then they smiled at each other and lapsed into silence, smoking and taking sips of the warm, frothy beer, watching the crowds opposite coming and going, stumbling and buzzing around the house like moths at a lamp.

5

The detective bureau was a bustling mess of noise, people and furniture that just about fitted into the second floor of the 1st Police Precinct. Over the years the bureau had swelled, pushed out the other occupants of the floor and spread itself contentedly across the entire story. It had been a haphazard expansion and it had turned the bureau into a dense, almost impassable place, brimming with desks, crates, partitions and cops. Tables jutted into corridors, filing cabinets blocked doorways and stacks of boxes that no one ever thought to look inside of gathered dust and obscured the light from windows.

Michael wound his way around these various obstructions on his return from the Maggios', and on past the different bureau teams – Vice, Juvenile, Robbery, the newly established Narcotics division, and his own team, Homicide. Some of the men were shouting to each other across the floor, others talking on phones or tapping out reports on typewriters. He passed a knot of detectives taking part in a meeting, horseshoed in front of a blackboard adorned with chalk diagrams, suspect photographs, and frayed copperplate maps of the city. Further on, a clutch of men sat in a rec area drinking coffee and chatting. Their conversation died down when they saw him pass. Wherever he went in the department, people stayed silent, partly to protect themselves, mainly to show him he wasn't wanted. It had been five years since he testified against Luca and still the enmity hadn't ebbed. Although recently he had noticed a change in the looks and silences that shadowed his steps – the distrust was giving way to pity.

He reached his desk, deposited his hat and coat on a stand and was about to sit when the door to the bureau captain's office opened and an iron-clad voice boomed his name out over the floor.

When Michael entered McPherson's office, the captain was sat behind his desk, palms pressed together prayer-like in front of his chin. There was something otherworldly about the captain's bearing that Michael could never quite get a handle on – the frosty blue eyes, the bony face. Michael thought McPherson would have made an excellent monk – his looks lending themselves as much to the cassock as to the bluecoat.

Michael sat and McPherson tossed a newspaper across the desk at him.

'Read that,' said the captain, his Scottish accent soft and cold. Michael took the paper in hand and turned to the front page.

'Last night some Spic thought the Axeman was in his house,' said McPherson, précising the story for Michael in a weary voice. 'So he went into the kitchen and shot what he believed to be an intruder. Turned the lights on and realized he'd killed his own wife. You can add her to the list of victims.'

McPherson stood, walked to the window and stared out onto the busy street below. Michael scanned the paper. The story was splashed across the front page, accompanied by a drawing of the Mexican man in question, above a caption which described him as 'hapless'. Michael contemplated the choice of words.

'What did you get from the crime scene?' asked McPherson, his voice betraying an almost personal concern that Michael hadn't noticed before.

'It's the same story, sir. No one sees anything. No one hears anything. The killer leaves no clues. Except for the tarot cards, of course. And this time there was some graffiti.'

'Graffiti?' McPherson turned from the window to face him. The sky outside was ghostly white and McPherson's frame looked faintly menacing outlined in front of it.

'It read like a threat. To a Mrs Tenebre,' said Michael, trying to ignore the effect. 'I've put a bluecoat on it.'

'Good,' said McPherson. 'There can't be too many Tenebres in the city. Anything else?'

'Might've found some counterfeits, too,' said Michael. 'They'll be checked out in a day or two.'

McPherson nodded and ran his fingers across the silver tie pin at his chest. 'Have you been through the latest-sightings file yet?'

'A little,' Michael replied, stifling a groan.

The sightings file was a weighty bound folder listing all the sightings the public had made of suspicious characters around the time of the attacks. The file was a disturbing look into the psychology of New Orleans's residents, or at least those residents who sent letters to the police. People wrote in to say they had seen Negro men flying through windows, eight-foot-tall Italians, Slavs with horned heads, dwarves, Chinamen, Creoles who disappeared in a puff of smoke, or banshees fluttering between rooftops. One letter that made a particular impression on Michael explained in disturbingly lucid language how its author had seen the devil himself promenading down Esplanade Avenue in a top hat and tails, twirling a cane in the moonlight. Michael had taken to reading the file on the tram home, more as a macabre distraction than anything else.

'The sighting file's full of cranks, sir. You can't trust what people see,' he said. 'The reward was a bad idea.'

The file was already thick before the mayor announced the reward, and now the tip-offs were coming in by the hundred.

'Tell the mayor,' said McPherson, the weariness returning to his voice. Michael let the comment hang in the silence.

'You know I have a soft spot for you, lad,' said the old man, his tone changing, becoming more fatherly, and Michael realized he was hearing the preamble to some bad news.

'You've proved your loyalty in the past. Made sacrifices. Heavy ones that we are fully appreciative of. But the longer this goes on for, the more the chance your . . .' McPherson paused to choose his next words carefully, 'personal life might come to the public's attention.'

Michael shifted in his seat, the Damoclean sword that was his personal life glinting momentarily in the corner of his eye.

'I know Behrman has some pull with the newspapers,' added the captain, 'but the leash is only so long.'

Michael frowned, puzzled as to why McPherson was making the threat now, after all these years. Was he trying to warn him of something? Michael stared at the old man, studying his eyes for some kind of clue.

'If it would help, sir,' said Michael, 'I'd resign the case.'

McPherson thought for a moment, then moved from the window, and sat on the edge of the desk.

'Resignation's not an option, lad. The mayor said that would smell like failure, and it'd only keep them at bay for so long.'

'So you've discussed the possibility?' said Michael, a little too quickly.

McPherson paused, embarrassed at having made the slip.

'We've discussed it,' he said flatly. Michael nodded, the news making him feel numb. His failure was getting him noticed in all the wrong places.

'I can't offer you much in the way of protection,' continued McPherson, 'but I thought you'd like to know. Like I said, I've a soft spot for you.'

'Thank you, sir,' said Michael.

The old man grew silent and Michael got the feeling there was more to come. He reached for his cigarettes, patting down his breast pockets before realizing he had left the silver case in his coat.

'Which is why I felt I should let you know about something else,' said McPherson. 'I had word from Angola. Luca D'Andrea's being released today.'

Michael felt a pang in his chest, as if he had been caught at some kind of wrongdoing. Luca coming back to the city was something

Michael was expecting, a vague, dark event looming on a far horizon, but the reality of it, the fact it had actually happened, caught him unaware, and he was surprised at how unsettled he felt.

'He got released early?'

'Early parole for good behavior.' The captain sighed. 'It seems the Family's grasp extends to the members of the parole board. Obviously we'll be keeping an eye on him, but I thought you'd like to know.'

Michael returned to his desk and slumped into his chair. He put a hand to his forehead and mulled over the news that Luca had been freed. A menacing image of him stalking the streets looped over and over in his head like a snatch of discordant music. He wondered what Luca was like now, if Angola had mellowed him, doused his energy. Or had he grown angry, ready to seek revenge on his protégé? In the years since the trial, Michael had not been bothered by Luca's associates – there had been no attempted hits, or beatings or threats, and although he thought this strange, he had become accustomed to it as the status quo. Perhaps Luca's associates had been instructed to leave Michael in peace, that the settling of scores was Luca's right alone?

He thought of McPherson's threat, too. Despite the fatherly advice, McPherson was hanging him out to dry. The whole department was making hay while the killer was at large – warrants had been made easier to obtain and the mayor had called for extra police on the streets, which meant overtime pay. Police squads had been raiding gambling joints, safe-houses, brothels, opium dens, stash-points – and all the while using the killings as a flimsy excuse for the crackdown. As long as Michael was failing, the rest of the department had what it needed to keep arrest rates at an all-time high. And that was the reason they wouldn't accept a resignation – the higher-ups had already picked Michael for their fall guy. His name would get dragged through the mud, then he'd be shipped out with a pat on the back and sad regrets.

Michael had to find the killer before McPherson and the higher-ups decided it was time to cut him off. If he failed, the twenty years he'd spent on the force would end in public humiliation and disgrace. And for a man in Michael's situation, it would be hard to find a job in New Orleans after being let go from the police. Failure could well lead to penury, and if what McPherson had hinted at came to pass, failure could possibly lead to prison. Michael couldn't help but feel it might all be punishment for his part in Luca's downfall, that the world was coming full circle.

He leaned back in his chair, fished the silver case from his coat, and lit a much-needed cigarette. He took a drag and spotted someone approaching his desk – a spindly, red-haired cadet in his late teens. As the boy made his way through the bustling floor, Michael saw he had been assigned a beat-cop's uniform too large for him, a mismatch which made him look awkward, a little clownish even. He reached Michael's desk, cleared his throat and spoke in a thick Irish brogue.

'Excuse me, sir. I know you're in charge o' the Axeman case,' he said, tumbling over his words. 'I found these in the records room. I thought they might be useful.'

He held out some tattered, dusty reports. Michael frowned, took them out of the boy's hand and motioned to the chair on the other side of the desk. He sat and Michael flicked through the reports – moldy pages and murder-scene photographs.

'What's your name, kid?' said Michael, scanning the files.

'Kerry, sir.'

Michael offered his cigarette case to the boy, who smiled and shook his head. He noticed the boy's pallid skin, a sea-sick tint of green he had seen in countless new arrivals. He had often wondered on the cause – the ocean-liner food, the lack of sunlight in the holds, the unhealthy air of the countries left behind, or simply the interminable rolling and pitching of the ships.

'You been in America long?' he asked.

'Six weeks, sir. I came over from Dublin.'

Michael nodded. 'My mother was from Dublin.' He stubbed out his cigarette in the ashtray on his desk, turning the butt methodically before emptying the ashtray into the wastebasket by his feet.

'So you thought you'd come to America and be a policeman?'

'To be honest, sir, I never saw myself as a cop, but . . . you were the only ones hiring Paddies.'

The boy grinned at the joke, or maybe at the truth of the situation, and Michael smiled back at him.

'Why are you bringing me these?'

'They're three unsolved murders, sir, from 1911. I thought they matched the Axeman murders.'

Michael studied the pages, flicking through them at speed. He noted the descriptions of the victims, their addresses, the means by which they had been killed, and his mind began to conjure up reasons for an eight-year hiatus.

'You found these in the records room?' he asked. 'In the basement?'

'Yes, sir,' mumbled Kerry.

'And what were you doing in the basement?'

'Well . . .' An embarrassed expression descended onto Kerry's face. 'Lodgings are hard to come by at the moment.'

Michael gave him a look, half-pitying, half-confused. Why wasn't he living with the other new recruits in the patrolmen's dormitories? And why was he spending his spare time going through old police reports?

'Thank you for bringing these to my attention,' Michael said.

'Thank you, sir. The supervising officer was Detective Hatener. I thought maybe—'

'Hatener?' repeated Michael, and he flicked back through the reports.

'I thought maybe—' But before the boy could finish Michael had risen from his desk and was marching across the bureau floor.

6

Luca D'Andrea tramped down the grand avenue of Canal Street in the midday sun. Trams, carriages and the occasional motorcar rattled past him in the middle of the street, and on the banquettes people bustled about the shops and stalls. He trudged past department stores, restaurants and diners, past praline-sellers and coffee-cart men. He breathed in the aromas wafting through the city, chicory and spices, cologne, manure, chartreuse and gumbo, exhaust fumes and sweat. When he passed the boys outside the saloons hawking newspapers in whiney yelps, his head began to ring. The cascade of people, the sights and the noises, made him feel queasy, and he wondered if he was feverish from the long walk or the lack of food.

He put a hand to his head and slowed his pace. It all seemed too much – the billboards, the glare of the sun, the eyes of the people rushing past, the buildings crowding together street after street. The things of the world in all their forms loomed into his mind, making him feverish and weak. He felt that everything was wrong in some indefinable way – that the world he'd been thrown back into was unfamiliar, malevolent. Claustrophobia rushed over him and the banquette swirled beneath his feet. He lurched backwards, reeling into the storefront of an oyster saloon, sending waves rippling dangerously across the sheet-glass window.

He struggled for breath and felt his heart rushing, a cold sweat breaking out across his chest. He closed his eyes and amid the darkness, an image shimmered into his mind – the lonesome, calming fields of Angola, the bulrushes swaying in the wind.

He breathed as deeply as he could and snapped his eyes open.

The world blurred in and out of focus, rolling and sharp, and came to rest on a little girl, standing on the street in front of him. She wore a summer dress of deep-blue cotton, and her mimosa-gold hair was held in place by rhinestone barrettes that glinted in the sunlight. She frowned, green eyes sparkling up at him.

'You OK, mister?' she asked, curious and concerned.

Luca heaved air into his lungs and nodded.

'Anna!' A man shouted in a hawkish voice, and Luca looked up to see a broad-chested Cajun standing a little further down the street, scowling at them. The girl gave Luca a last sympathetic smile, turned on the balls of her feet, and skittered off up the road.

Luca bent double and caught his breath. He wondered what the hell had happened to him – a palpitation, sunstroke, nerves? When he felt his heart beat a little slower, he pushed himself off the storefront, regained his balance, and stumbled on, perspiration dripping from his brow. The crowds eased as he reached the poorer end of the street, and the feeling of suffocation receded a touch. As he continued his journey, the shops lining the street became dingier and more decayed, the apartments above them sporting red velvet curtains and placards with gaudy adverts drawn on them for the 'voodou priestesses' whose parlors were housed within.

Luca remembered arresting a Haitian woman in one of those apartments years before. The woman had kicked and screamed and even bitten one of Luca's team in the neck, sending a blast of blood fountaining into the air. Luca had to hit her with his nightstick to restrain her, and the woman had spat in his face and cursed him. A voodou curse, the woman had sneered. At the time Luca had laughed, but now, as he returned to New Orleans, he wondered about the power of curses.

He turned left off Canal Street, slowly regaining his composure, the panic leaving his body, and he made his way southwards down the quieter back alleys beyond. The tall stone-clad department stores gave way to low-lying tenements and gloomy shops, all packed into narrow, shady streets. After a while, Little Italy crept up on him, along with a wistful nostalgia, the lonely kind, where the sadness of losing the past outweighs the consolation of memory.

He had returned to a city that considered him a pariah, and he realized with regret that he was hurtling towards old age with nothing to show for all his years – not a career, nor a family, nor any friends he could trust, nor even a penny in the bank. He had as much in the world as he did when he had first arrived at Carlo's thirty years before. He felt the anxiety from earlier return in a lesser form, but he breathed deeply and pushed hard to keep it out of his mind, and he surprised himself by managing to suppress it.

He carried on walking for a few minutes more and arrived at his destination, a three-story building set behind a sprawling walled garden. He knocked on a dark wooden gate and waited, and after a few seconds a panel in the gate slid open and a face peered out at him.

'*Luca! Luca, sei tornato!*' said a hoary voice, and the gate swung open.

He was back where he had started.

A few minutes later, Luca was sitting in a sparsely decorated reception room that had hardly changed in the five years since he'd last been in it. Old wood furniture and whitewashed walls, bare except for the occasional picture or photograph of a forebear. Light was slanting in from a row of windows on one side, beyond which was a meticulously tended vegetable garden.

In the stillness his mind drifted back to the first time he'd ever been in the house. Luca had arrived in New Orleans at the age of fourteen with his parents, two peasants from Monreale in north-western Sicily. Within a few months of their arrival both parents had died in a cholera epidemic and Luca was left penniless and completely alone. He did what all immigrants do when they are in need and have no one to call on: he sought out his countrymen, and managed to land work as an errand-boy for Carlo Matranga's family.

When he reached his eighteenth birthday, he was urged to join the police force, being one of the few Family employees who didn't yet have a criminal record. Luca worked his way into the detective bureau, and while solving crimes legitimately, he also helped out Carlo and the rest of the Matrangas. He leaked information, made evidence disappear, coerced his colleagues into taking bribes, and worst of all, framed innocent people for the Family's crimes. When Luca was indicted on Michael's evidence, the Family paid off the judge to ensure he was given the most lenient sentence possible. The last time Luca had seen Carlo was just before the trial, in this very room, where the two of them had eaten lunch with the judge.

Luca stood and paced the room. He noticed a mahogany table in a corner by the windows and approached it. On the table was a gramophone, the box made of cherry wood inlaid with pearl, the tulip-shaped horn painted sky blue and gold. Luca turned the disc on the platter and read the label – 'The Victor Talking Machine Company Presents Titta Ruffo & Enrico Caruso Singing Verdi's *Otello*'.

He smiled. He had heard Carlo play the record a hundred times. He thought about winding up the gramophone, putting the silver nautilus shell that housed the needle onto the record and listening to the bittersweet music. He had heard music while he was in Angola, the work-songs of the men, hard songs tinged with gospels and sweat and the clang of chains, but he hadn't heard real music, with violins and clarinets and the sonorous voices of his countrymen. He was about to wind up the machine when the door opened and Carlo hobbled in.

'Don Carlo,' said Luca, bowing his head. Carlo approached and Luca bent to kiss his hand, but before he had a chance the old man caught him in a hug. He smelled the washing powder on Carlo's clothes, the tang of aftershave on his neck, and for some reason, a little of his nausea returned. They broke apart and smiled at each other. Carlo Matranga was a slight man, with a soft, grandfatherly face and close-cropped hair that had turned a creamy white. Luca noticed with a pang of sadness that Carlo's dark, piercing eyes had dimmed, becoming milky and glazed, as if adjusting themselves already to the world beyond.

They sat on a pair of wicker chairs by the windows and a maid brought them water and wine and small plates of anchovies, olives and cheese, the richness of it all turning Luca's stomach. They spoke of Luca's time in prison and Carlo asked him what his plans were. Luca tried to gauge whether the old man was taking it for granted that he wanted to return to his old way of life, and Carlo, always astute, picked up on Luca's hesitation.

'You are welcome to come back and work for us,' said Carlo, 'if you want, that is.' There was no rising intonation to the remark, but Luca recognized it as a question, and he smiled awkwardly. He dreaded the idea of going back to the life he had previously lived. When he had lain on his bunk in Angola at night and thought of all the hurt he had caused, nervous pains seared through his gut, a folding over of his intestines that kept him awake. He thought of the phrase 'a broken man', and could not deny its appropriateness. He could admit none of this to his *padrino*, of course – he had obligations, dues to pay, expectations to fulfill. Extricating himself would be a delicate, fragile process.

'I had all my money in the bank,' said Luca, trying not to sound self-pitying, and Carlo nodded knowingly.

Before he had been convicted, Luca had liquidated all his assets and entrusted the money into the care of Ciro Poidomani, a corpulent old Neapolitan who acted as an under-the-counter banker for the city's criminal element. A few weeks before Luca was released, he discovered through the prison grapevine that Ciro had been arrested. Luca's life savings, as well as the money of half the criminals in New Orleans, had been seized by the police, with Ciro facing a string of money-laundering charges. If Luca had been let out just a few weeks earlier, he would still have his life's savings – something, at least, to show for all his years.

'Would you like money?' asked Carlo, studying Luca with an eagle's stare.

Luca shook his head. 'I'd like a job. Temporarily,' he said, 'I want to return to Monreale.'

Carlo paused for a moment, staring at Luca, then he laughed softly, indulgently.

'This is your home, Luca,' he said. 'There's nothing for you in Monreale. What would you do there?'

Luca shrugged. 'I could open a café, run a shop . . .' he said, suddenly feeling foolish.

Carlo peered at him, and realizing Luca's feelings were sincere, he softened his tone.

'You're a man of the world, you could never be a shopkeeper,' he said, shaking his head, as if admitting an unarguable truth.

Luca smiled. 'I don't want to die in America,' he said. 'If you can give me a job, I'll save enough for a ticket and to start a business when I get there.'

Carlo eyed him with something Luca guessed was disappointment, and he prepared himself for a refusal, to be reminded of the debt he owed the Family.

'After everything you have done for us,' Carlo said, 'I will give you this money. You don't have to work for it.'

Luca wondered if the old man was being sincere, or if his offer was a test. He smiled and shook his head.

'If you give me the money, then I'm nothing more than a beggar.'

Carlo nodded slowly. 'Always so proud,' he muttered, before turning to stare at Luca with a searching expression. 'And what of the unfinished business?' he asked.

Before Luca had gone to Angola, there was talk of retribution against Michael. It wouldn't have saved Luca from prison, but it was thought it should be done for the honor of the thing – the execution of traitors was expected. But Luca had vetoed the idea, saying that revenge was his to take alone, that he would deal with the matter on his return. The truth was he still cared about Michael.

'I think it can wait,' he said.

Carlo sighed and nodded, and Luca wondered again if the old man was disappointed in him.

'There is a job you can do for me,' Carlo said, and he motioned towards the garden.

Luca was not expecting him to acquiesce so readily and he wondered if he had made his terms clear. They stood and the old man put his sallow, flecked hand on Luca's shoulder. 'Come. We'll talk outside,' said Carlo. 'Tell me, Luca, have you heard of the Axeman?'

7

Ida left the wake a little after one and returned to the office on foot, journeying westwards through the Vieux Carré. The French Quarter was the postcard section of New Orleans, the part the tourists came to see, ancient buildings, shadowy courtyards, balconies of wrought iron finer than lace. With the deftness of a big-city dweller, she dodged the sightseers staring up at the buildings, and skirted past the hawkers that flooded into New Orleans daily, the fruit-sellers, the colporteurs, the rags-bottles-and-bones men, and the thousand and one other shades of huckster who sold their wares on the streets and announced themselves with ditties of their own invention, half-shouted, half-sung.

'My horse is white, my face is black, I sells my charcoal two bits a sack.'

Ahead of her the banquette was obstructed by an oyster-seller filling a bucket with his wares. Many of the houses in the quarter had buckets attached to their balconies. The buckets could be lowered to the street via a rope, so the ladies of the house could conduct business with the hawkers without ever leaving their apartments. Ida watched as the oysterman called out to a woman three stories above him and the bucket began to sway its way upwards. Ida crossed the street, aware that a slip of the woman's hand could result in a rain of seafood.

She turned a corner and entered the French Market. Rows of Negro women sat along the edge of the banquette, dressed in dazzlingly colored *tignons*, starched white aprons and skirts of blue calico, with fichus of intricate needlework draped over their shoulders. They sold breads and cakes and pralines from trays they placed on the street in front of them, fanning their wares with palmetto fans and joking with each other. In the center of the market the farmer's stalls were busy with customers, it being the middle of the lunch hour, and in the far distance an advertising wagon for a furniture sale made its way along an avenue, a jazz ensemble on the flatbed blaring out music to draw a crowd.

The music of the jazz band mingled with the songs of the hawkers and Ida wondered if other cities were like this, music forever making itself heard, either up close and brash, or soft and distant, haunting the streets. She thought of *gumbo ya-ya*, the Creole expression – *gumbo* meaning a mix, and *ya-ya* meaning 'to talk', the two words together meaning 'everybody talks at once'.

She passed the last of the market stalls, veered around the advertising wagon and its cargo of raggedy musicians, and trotted up the front steps of a tall, nondescript office building. She made her way to the third story and, traversing a long, echoing corridor, approached a glass-paneled door with the words *Pinkerton National Detective Agency* stenciled on it in faux-gold paint with black trim.

She opened the door gently and entered the lobby with soft, ballet-shoe steps. The blinds were down and the room was smothered in an inky blue half-light that caught the motes of dust suspended in the air. She tiptoed along the floorboards, past her desk, and snuck up to the opaque glass partition that separated the reception area from Lefebvre's office. She pressed her face against the frosted glass and peered into the room beyond. Lefebvre was where she expected him to be; in his chair, asleep, a solitary tumbler and an empty bottle of rye on the desk in front of him.

She crept towards the tabular wooden filing cabinets in the reception area, took some files out and returned with them to her desk. She sat and read through them, squinting in the darkness, copying information into a notebook. She looked up every few minutes, through the frosted glass, to make sure Lefebvre's broken image hadn't moved. Making copies of agency information was a sacking offence – not that Ida thought Lefebvre had it in him to get rid of her. The New Orleans bureau of the Pinkerton National Detective Agency only had two employees. Sacking Ida would have reduced the workforce by half, and hiring a replacement required time and effort, both of which would have got in the way of Lefebvre's drinking. And not even business got in the way of Lefebvre's drinking. So much so, that by the time Ida had been appointed, he had let the bureau slide into a terminal decline.

The Pinkertons had never really had much business in the South to begin with – during the War Between the States, they were employed by Lincoln as a de facto state security agency, and the connection still tainted their reputation. Although the lack of work had its advantages, Ida couldn't help but get frustrated at times. She had never really wanted to work for the Pinkertons; she'd wanted to join the police force, but she was doubly excluded, firstly on account of her sex, and secondly, under the only-one-drop rule, on account of her race as well. So the Pinkertons were her only viable option – she could lie about her race if she needed to, and her sex didn't matter, because the Pinkertons, unlike other agencies, employed females in detective roles. Ida had learned of this, years before, in one of the pulp detective magazines she collected assiduously.

So when she turned seventeen, she came down to the office and asked the ageing, corpulent Creole who ran the place if there were any jobs going. Lefebvre, with sincerest commiserations, told her there was nothing, but that in a few months their receptionist would be retiring, and if Ida could get her typing up to speed he would be happy to consider her, and from there, if she showed enough aptitude, she could progress on to fieldwork. Ida took Lefebvre up on his offer, happy to have a foot in the door, but the fieldwork was slow in coming, and meager when it did arrive, and she ended up spending her days doing tedious clerical work or running Lefebvre's personal errands.

So she'd decided to take matters into her own hands, to escape a suffocating existence of days wasted at a desk, of being trapped doing the same monotonous chores every day. She had fixed on the idea that solving a big case was the only way to get noticed, to prove to her superiors, and to herself, that she could do it. But the big cases didn't come along often at the Pinkertons' New Orleans bureau.

She heard a noise in Lefebvre's office, lifted herself up and peered through the partition – Lefebvre was still asleep but he was muttering something to himself, involved in some restless, dreamy conversation. She often wondered what had caused Lefebvre's slide into oblivion. He didn't just drink for the feeling, or to forget, she could tell that much. There was a haunted look to the man, a deathliness that followed him closer than a pickpocket.

She wondered if she would ever end up like him, if it was the lot of the detective to be alone, out of step with the rhythm of the world. She had already spent most of her life feeling like an outcast; her troublesome skin tone had made her the victim of school-ground bullies, and the object of leering men. She never really had a friend in the world until Lewis arrived at her house, and so she passed her time with books and pulp-fiction magazines, immersed in a world of cowboys and pirates, Arctic explorers, ghost-hunters and magicians, but most of all detectives. She had read in one of those mystery magazines years before that the best detectives floated between worlds, and she guessed that summed her up – she could go to places where blacks weren't allowed, and to places where whites wouldn't dare. And so she'd learned early on that being a detective was the best she could hope for.

She resumed her work – copying down everything about Millicent Hawkes she thought would be relevant, before returning the notebook to her handbag and the files to the cabinet. She stepped over to the front door and opened it slightly, waited a moment in the silence, then slammed it shut. She saw Lefebvre's image jolt up through the glass partition.

'Morning, Monsieur Lefebvre,' she shouted nonchalantly as she strode over to the windows and began pulling up the blinds, leaving a trail of sunshine in her wake.

8

Michael strode across the bureau floor, files in hand, riding a wave of indignation and annoyance, headed towards the desk of Detective Lieutenant Jake Hatener. Hatener was a fixture in the bureau, an obese man fifteen years Michael's senior, who carried with him an air of permanent irritation. He had been Luca's right-hand man in the days when Luca ran the bureau. During Michael's investigation of Luca and his clique, he had gathered enough evidence on Hatener to have him sent away for decades. But when the arraignments rolled around, the District Attorney had pressed no charges against him. His omission from the list of indictees left the rest of the police force, Michael included, wondering exactly what contortionist's trick Hatener had performed to escape scot-free. In the years since, Hatener had barely spared a look for Michael, and the two had fallen into the routine of silent enemies. When Michael approached, Hatener was just finishing off his lunch, the grease-paper wrappings of a sandwich splayed across his desk. Michael threw the police reports at him.

'Why the hell didn't you tell me?' he said.

Hatener stared at Michael, a frown breaking out across his heavy, sagging face. Then he composed himself, wiped the grease of the po'boy sandwich from his chin, and picked up the reports.

'What are you talking about?' he muttered, flicking through the pages.

'They're the same as the Axeman. You investigated.'

Hatener read the reports a moment, and Michael studied the emotions flickering across his face, from confusion to understanding to concern. Hatener stared up at Michael. 'Where'd you find these?' he asked.

'You should have told me,' said Michael, noticing out of the corner of his eye people around the bureau stopping to watch the exchange.

'I forgot,' said Hatener, the hint of a grin on his lips. 'These were nothing like the Axeman anyways. Just a bunch o' dumb guineas that didn't know any better.'

'You buried the reports!'

'What the hell's going on?' Michael turned to see McPherson standing behind him. It was only then that he noticed the silence, that the whole floor was staring at them. Michael swiped the reports from Hatener and passed them to McPherson.

'Hatener was withholding information relating to the Axeman,' he said.

Hatener stared at him bitterly. 'Just like you to go squealing to the boss, huh, Michael?'

McPherson glared at them both.

'In my office, now,' he hissed.

McPherson made a show of slamming the door behind them, then he seated himself at his desk and flicked through the reports.

'Well, don't just stand there like idiots,' he said without looking up.

Michael and Hatener sat on the two chairs opposite and eventually McPherson put down the reports and rubbed his forehead. 'What was your evaluation at the time?' he asked, turning to Hatener.

'Counterfeiters,' Hatener replied, and Michael and McPherson caught each other's gaze. 'The Matrangas were using grocers to distribute. Word was the three victims got greedy.' Hatener shrugged, and Michael and the captain inferred his meaning. The victims had been killed by the Family so there wasn't any point investigating. Hatener and his partner had let the cases grow cold.

'Sure, they were grocers and they got killed with an axe,' Hatener continued, 'but it wasn't related to the Axeman. No tarot cards left. No women and children killed.'

'Did anyone get fingered?' asked McPherson.

'A few names got bandied about,' said Hatener, shrugging again.

'Regardless of any dissimilarities,' said Michael, 'I think it's worth investigating. Discreetly. If the press gets a hold of this, we need something on record. If it is the same perpetrator, I'd say the only things to have kept him quiet for eight years would be Angola and the state insane asylum.'

McPherson nodded.

'I'll assign a few bluecoats to go through the records, find anyone whose incarceration and release coincides with the hiatus,' said the captain. 'Jake, go back and revisit the witnesses. Don't mention the Axeman, make up something about a standard eight-year check-up on unsolved murders.'

Hatener gave the captain an annoyed look and shook his head.

'You screwed up, Jake, and now you're gonna put in the leg-work.'

As Michael returned to his desk, he mulled over what Hatener had said. If the Axeman was responsible for the earlier killings then he finally had a lead to pursue, a means of whittling down the infinite list of possible killers to a manageable handful. For the first time since he had started his beleaguered investigation, he could see some light at the end of the tunnel. He smiled at the thought of a victory, no matter how distant.

He got back to his desk and was surprised to see Kerry still milling about.

'I'm sorry, Detective Talbot, I didn't mean to cause a ruck.'

'That wasn't a ruck, son, and it's not your fault.' Michael leaned back in his chair and grinned. 'Thank you for bringing the files to my attention. I'll be sure to mention it to your CO.'

Kerry returned his grin and nodded his thanks, but he made no move to leave, and Michael wondered what else the boy could want.

'Listen, kid,' he said. 'You might not know this on account of you being a greenhorn around here and all, but I am, without a doubt, the least liked person in this precinct. Probably in the whole New Orleans PD. You ain't doing yourself any favors being seen about my desk, so if you got something to ask me I'd advise you do it quickly.'

Kerry nodded and tried to smile, but Michael could see the confidence draining from the boy's face. He had hurt Kerry's feelings, and he felt a twinge of guilt. He peered at the boy again and guessed by the look on his face that he was plucking up the courage to make some kind of request.

'It's just, well, I'd like to help out on the Axeman case, sir. Help you solve it, you know,' said Kerry. 'I work hard, and, without meaning to sound big-headed, I think I'm clever enough. I guess I'm just asking for a chance, sir.'

Michael lit a cigarette and stared at the boy through the smoke. He thought about having someone around him to help out, someone he could mentor, and he was surprised to find that he actually quite liked the idea. His mind flashed back to his relationship with Luca, how Luca had taken him under his wing, had shown him the intricacies of the job. Perhaps he could make amends by doing the same for the boy.

'You sure?' he said. 'Working with me'll make you public enemy number two in here.'

Kerry shrugged. 'I was an outsider back home, sir. I'm used to it.'

Michael smiled and held out his hand and Kerry shook it, his grip firmer than Michael had expected.

9

Carlo's garden was an anomaly in squalid Little Italy, being spacious and open and brimming with myriad plants, bushes and trees. Luca and the old man strolled through an orchard at the far end of the garden, near the longest of the high whitewashed walls that surrounded the property. Luca could hear the sound of carts running along the street on the other side, the shouts and screams of urchins playing stickball. They passed a clutch of vines, stunted and sickly in the foreign soil. It was well into spring but they showed no signs of budding, their sinewy, brown tangles lofted into the air as free of green as the trellises of wood and wire that supported them.

'I can understand you wanting to go home,' said Carlo, images of a far-off, sun-drenched land flitting across his eyes. 'Remember the wine in Monreale? We've been trying to grow our own here, but the soil . . .' Carlo shook his head ruefully. 'America isn't a land for wine,' he muttered. As they strolled, the old man held out a hand to the vines, touching the branches, testing the trellises, as if they were all in an attritional battle against the unforgiving American land.

'So you've heard about the Axeman?' he said, casting a sideways glance at Luca.

Luca nodded. 'A little.'

'He's been making things difficult for us,' said Carlo. 'The police are using it as an excuse to close things down, and we don't have Mayor Behrman's protection anymore. The raid on Ciro's bank would never have happened in the old days.' Carlo paused for a moment to rue the loss of better times.

'Of course, it's not just the police,' he continued. 'The people are looking to me for help. Everybody pays us protection, but we can't protect them from this.'

He lifted his hands into the air as if to indicate some kind of malevolent ether. 'The killer is making us look weak. We need to find him. Make him an example.'

Luca nodded, understanding what Carlo was asking him to do.

'You used to be a detective,' he said, his voice soft. 'Deliver him to us, and I'll give you the money you need to go back to Monreale.'

Luca smiled. 'When I was a detective, I had the whole department to help me. I'm rusty. Older.' He shrugged as if to suggest he was nothing special, that he wasn't the right man for the job.

'I understand,' said the old man. 'We'll give you all the help you need.'

Carlo stared at Luca with the expression of a man who was accustomed to being obeyed, and with that look, Luca realized that he had already been chosen for the task, and there was no way he could refuse. It wasn't the work he had been expecting. He had hoped to be given a simple job – driving, collecting envelopes, book-keeping. He had dreaded a job that involved being violent, inflicting pain and sorrow. An investigation, he reasoned, was neither a simple job nor a violent one. After forty years in America all he wanted now was peace, the freedom to go back home and find somewhere quiet to rest. If one last case was the means to get to that peace, he'd do it. But then he thought of Michael, of being put on a collision course with the man he wanted to avoid. The best he could hope for was to run the investigation and not get caught, and to finish it to Carlo's satisfaction, because he knew what would happen if he failed. Luca had expressed a desire to walk away, and no one was ever allowed to walk away. He had to pray the old man wouldn't renege on his promise.

He turned to Carlo and they smiled and shook hands. He was

back in the world of men, of people with agendas and bargains to be made. They turned and ambled back towards the house.

'It'll be good to have you around again,' said Carlo, as if there had been no hint of coercion in Luca's return. 'One of the old faces. The young ones, they don't understand the proper ways. They call us *zips*, as if we should be ashamed we were born in Sicily.'

Luca nodded somberly. 'America does strange things to people,' he replied.

They passed through a row of lemon trees and the smell of citrus wafted into Luca's nose.

'Where will you stay?' asked Carlo. 'I'd offer you a bed here but for the restrictions of your parole.'

'Do you still have an interest in the hotel?' asked Luca. 'The old one in the business district?'

The hotel was outside Carlo's stomping ground, in a busy area close to the mainline stations. If anything went wrong, Luca reasoned, he could skip town a lot easier than he could from Little Italy. Carlo frowned at him, and Luca sensed he had made the old man suspicious.

'Yes,' said Carlo, his eyes fixed on Luca, ready to pick up on any emotions that might flicker across his face. 'But there are nicer places you could choose.'

'That'll be fine, thank you,' said Luca trying to keep his expression fixed. 'I've been in a prison all these years, it's too soon for a home. A hotel will help me readjust.' Carlo continued to stare at him, then eventually he nodded, either believing the lie, or choosing to ignore it, or most likely making a note of it for later use. They smiled at each other and continued on their way. As they approached the doors to the house, Luca saw the gas-lamps had been lit and the first hints of dusk were darkening the sky. The house looked warm and inviting, speaking of the family Luca had never really known.

'Well, how about you stay for some food?' said Carlo. 'Giulietta is making *spaghetti alla carrettiera*.'

'I'd be honored,' said Luca.

He noticed someone had set the gramophone off; the sound of Verdi and Caruso floated through the open terrace doors. Luca knew the characters were singing about betrayal, about swearing a pact of loyalty to each other, *by the marble of heaven*. The strings and horns seemed to hover in the air, the voices floating above them, enchanting and faraway. They stood for a moment in the twilight and listened to the music, then Carlo turned to Luca, the glow of the lamps shining on his face.

'We have to find him before the police do, Luca. Otherwise we can't use him as an example.'

Luca nodded. 'I'll get to him before anyone else.'

Carlo put his hand on Luca's shoulder, and they stepped back into the warmth of the house.

10

John Riley sat in the lecture room in Gibson Hall and scanned the rows of smiling undergraduates, and the vision induced in him a mouth-drying, bilious nausea. He prayed the mayor would keep his speech short; he prayed he could get out of the hall before anyone accosted him; he prayed the streetcar would come on time and he could make it across town to Elysian Fields Avenue before he started to vomit.

He had wasted his day catching the bus out to Boutte, speaking to D'Andrea, catching the bus back. And now he was going to waste his evening reporting on the mayor's annual talk to the graduating class of the Tulane University Law School, a talk that was deemed newsworthy by no one in the city except his fool of an editor, himself a graduate of the Tulane University Law School.

Riley was a Tulane alumnus too, but the university held no great place in his heart. Whenever he approached the Romanesque buildings on St Charles Avenue, his thoughts invariably drifted to thwarted ambitions. He had been accepted by Harvard to study Comparative Literature and Philosophy, but a downturn in his parents' fortunes forced him to study locally, provincially, and thus his dreams of a literary life in the salons and publishing houses of New York and Boston had withered and died.

The door at the front of the room opened and the mayor stepped in with some of the university administrators. The undergraduates clapped politely and the mayor smiled and waved a hand. Mayor Behrman was a round, stocky man, with a balding head and a bushy mustache. He'd dressed in a tweed suit and a bow tie in a vain attempt to paint himself as the somber, Deep South Democrat he thought it expedient to be. Riley took his pad and pencil from his pocket. He licked the pencil and realized how dry his mouth was – sticky and tasting faintly of iron. He probably didn't need the notes, he had reported on the mayor's speech for the past four years and it had never changed – a numbing list of platitudes about the city was all he could offer.

'New Orleans, the Big Easy, the City That Care Forgot, the Crescent City, Paris on the Mississippi, the Most Un-American of American Cities. Why does our hometown have so many names?' the mayor asked in a booming voice. 'Built on a marsh, six feet below sea level, between a river and a lake, the existence of New Orleans is both a miracle and a testament to the tenacious nature of man. This is how our city earned its sobriquets.'

Whenever Riley was faced with such an event, where thinking wasn't really required, he split his intelligence between the job at hand and dreaming up names for the literary journal it was his ambition to found, a journal that he envisioned would become the cultural diary of the city, where he could publish his criticism and the essays of other great minds. But the journal was forever being put on hold by the demands of his job, by a lack of funds, by his nightly trips to Elysian Fields.

'In our short but illustrious history,' continued the mayor, and Riley wrote down his words in an automatic shorthand, 'we have had to face over fifty major floods and over fifty hurricanes; in fact a hurricane heads our way roughly every two-and-a-half years. Faced with such destructive and constant force, is it any wonder we have gained a reputation for enjoying a good time?'

The mayor paused for a beat while the students laughed, and Riley stifled a groan. He had originally thought of naming his journal *The Stylus*, in honor of his hero, Edgar Allan Poe. But as the years dragged on he became worried that, like his hero, he might die prematurely, before he ever got his journal off the ground, and so he used his spare moments to search for a name with less morbid associations.

'We've had to deal with epidemics of malaria, smallpox, yellow fever and cholera. And just last year the Spanish Influenza that took so many of our fellow citizens from us,' said the mayor. 'And the swamps that surround our beautiful city are home to alligators, bears, cougars and coyotes, a variety of venomous snakes and spiders, and –' the mayor paused for comic effect '– Republicans.'

The students laughed once more and the mayor continued. 'Such is the fortitude of New Orleans that it has managed to survive this hostile environment, and not just survive, but flourish. In the battle between man and nature, New Orleans stands as a testament to what can be achieved by small groups of men, properly united by a common goal and a resilience of thought.'

Riley stopped his daydreaming to wonder about the battle between man and nature. New Orleans flooded every couple of years, and storms and fires destroyed its landmarks just as often, the marshy land caused the streets to crack and the buildings to subside, the high groundwater level meant they couldn't even bury their dead properly. If New Orleans was anything, he thought, it was a symbol of man's weakness in the face of nature, and he wondered from where exactly the mayor got his optimism.

'We have been ruled by the Indians, the French, the Spanish and the Americans, and if it wasn't for the help of a ragtag band of soldiers and pirates, we'd have been ruled by the British too. It is perhaps this mixed history that has given rise to our reputation as a place where . . .' the mayor paused again, 'things are a little different.' The students tittered, but Riley couldn't help but agree. New Orleans was different – it was the dark side of the country. Its Francophone population, its blurring of racial boundaries, its tropical climate – the rest of America thought New Orleans an exotic, foreign enclave, hidden away in the heart of the Deep South. A place that had more in common with the murky, steamy ports of the Caribbean and Brazil than the cities of the puritan north.

'Everything's different in New Orleans,' continued the mayor.

'It's an American city, sure enough, but it's an American city named after a French Duke, in a state named after a French King. We drink our coffee different, cook our food different, play our music different. We name our squares after African countries, and our streets after Greek myths. We bury our dead aboveground, but build our city below sea level. We celebrate Mardi Gras, not Shrove Tuesday, we have parishes not counties, we don't ban vice, we legalize it. We've been different since a handful of French traders came here and decided, against the good advice of their Indian guides, to build a city on a marsh.'

The mayor droned on and Riley returned to daydreaming about journal names: *The Southern Review? The Artist? The Reader?* As he dreamed and copied down the mayor's dawdling speech, a drop of sweat fell from his brow onto his notepad. And then another. He put his hand to his face and realized he was not only soaked in sweat, but that his hand was shaking too.

Eventually the students were on their feet, applauding, and the mayor was smiling at them and waving regally. Riley thanked God, pocketed his notebook and jostled his way through the crowd. He exited the hall to see the streetcar approaching along St Charles. He sprinted to the stop and waved his hand at the driver, and he thanked God a second time when the streetcar slowed down and he hopped aboard. He'd be in the Vieux Carré soon enough, and from there he could walk to Elysian Fields.

He took a seat at the front and as the streetcar sped him through the city, he thought about the lecture. The mayor was just repeating to the students the stories New Orleans told itself, stories about its past, about its character. Stories told so many times the place was in danger of crumbling into a myth of its own making, into a past that never was. If the city was a person, thought Riley, it would be an ageing whore. Smeared in rouge and yellow smiles, affecting airs and graces, wrapping herself in faded French silks. Coquetry and frills concealing decay.

He got off the streetcar at Decatur Street, stalked through the

Vieux Carré and arrived at Faubourg Marigny. He thought about the mayor's idea that New Orleans was some kind of beacon, fighting the proud fight for mankind against marshes and fires and diseases. And he thought about the Axeman and the chaos he was bringing to the city. Riley knew more about the Axeman than he should. He knew more than the police and more than the Matrangas. He came into so much information through his work it would be impossible not to find out something. And as he walked he wondered, as he had been wondering for the last few weeks, what he should do with that information. What could he do that was honorable but didn't put him in harm's way?

He turned right off Chartres Street and onto Elysian Fields. The avenue was the widest in New Orleans and connected the Mississippi with Lake Pontchartrain to the north. Bernard de Marigny had envisioned the avenue as a French-style boulevard with shrubbery and landscaping and a waterway down its center filled with swan-boats. He had named the street after the Champs-Élysées in Paris, which itself was named after the Elysian Fields, the Ancient Greek name for heaven. Riley relished the aptness of the city's Chinese laundries being located on the road to heaven. But thanks to a protracted streak of bad luck, de Maringy's plans never came to fruition and the thoroughfare was eventually leased to the Pontchartrain Railroad Company, which built a railway for belching, noisy trains down the center of the avenue, in the exact place where the French nobleman had dreamed of gilded swan-boats.

After a few minutes Riley approached the Jiang Launderette. He opened the door and stepped inside and the girl at the counter recognized him. She smiled and nodded to a door by a row of steaming vats. Riley smiled back and went through into a long dingy corridor, then he stepped through a second door into an even longer room, dimly lit and heavy with smoke. The room was decorated with drapes and rows of mattresses, each one separated from the next by squat latticework screens. Along the walls were badly painted Chinese landscapes – endless seas and fantastic mountains, dotted by tiny, faceless figures.

Jiang, the proprietor, a slight man with a ready smile and a wispy mustache, saw Riley and cast a quick glance at the sweat on Riley's face, at his paleness, and Riley guessed from the man's expression that he was perturbed by what he saw. Jiang raised his hand and led Riley through the room, past the other patrons lying on their mattresses, past the latticework screens and the other pieces of cheap chinoiserie that littered the place. They reached an empty mattress and Jiang stopped and bowed, and Riley nodded, took off his coat and lay down. Jiang disappeared, and it was only when he was alone that Riley noticed the music – Chinese flutes and nameless stringed instruments playing foggy, empty chords. He had never heard music in the laundry before; he looked about him and saw a gramophone in a corner, and slumped next to it a Chinese girl in a traditional robe, her hair dangling over her face as she swayed to the music.

Presently Jiang returned and laid a tray next to Riley's mattress, before smiling and retreating to the shadows at the front of the room. Riley had known the man for seven years but he couldn't say if Jiang was his first name or his last. He peered down at the tray, at the lacquered wood and fake mother-of-pearl inlay. Laid out on top of it was an oil-lamp, a ceramic bowl and a pipe stem made of bamboo, a foot long and stamped with a pattern of twisting dragons. Next to that was a long metal needle, a book of matches and a lacquer box. Riley opened the box and took the two porcelain bowls from it.

He lit the lamp with a shaking hand and scraped the resin from the bowl with the needle. He transferred a pea-sized amount into the second bowl and mixed it with the *yen pox* within. As he prepared the mix, Riley looked around the room at the people gathered there from all over the city, the Chinamen and the whites strewn around their mattresses, sleepwalkers in search of a dream. He had been noticing a lot more white men since the end of the war, young, strong-looking men with shell-shocked eyes, soldiers lost and fallen into the poppy's sour embrace.

Once the mixture was ready, Riley prepared the pipe. He screwed the pipe stem onto the bowl, placed the mixture in the bowl, placed the bowl over the oil-lamp, waited for the vapor to form, and inhaled.

He sucked the acrid fumes into his lungs and as he waited for the hit, he noticed he had stopped sweating, that he had stopped shaking, that his mind was no longer panicked. He gazed at the Chinese landscapes on the wall. The artist had left the space between the mountains and clouds untouched, and the untouched paper became, by inference, the sky. The sea was painted in a similar way, the boats floating on empty paper. Nothingness, turned into matter and given meaning solely by Riley's brain. The mountains and seas seemed to overpower the figures, making them tiny, insignificant. Riley heard echoes of the mayor's speech, of man against nature, and he guessed the view of the artist was more in keeping with his own – that man was too small to ever win such a battle, no matter how noble the intentions. Build a city, Riley thought, and eventually some agent of chaos would come along and destroy it, be it a hurricane or a fire or a flood. Or an Axeman.

Suddenly a thought occurred to him: the mayor had forgotten an item in his list of names for New Orleans, an old name, a reference to the waterlogged expanses the city was built on – *the Floating Land*. He liked the name, with its hints of *Yoshiwara*, of enchantment and magical realms. It felt appropriate as he looked around his dim surroundings, the girl swaying to the music, the sleepwalkers floating in their dreams.

PART TWO

PART TWO

The Times-Picayune

Saturday 12th April, 1919

Local News

Anger Grows As Latest Axe Victims Buried

'Who'll be next?' is the question being asked by the Italian citizens of New Orleans, as the latest victims of the elusive slayer were buried this week. Resentment at the police's handling of the case was high as the bodies of Mr and Mrs Joseph Maggio were laid at rest, Friday afternoon, in the same vault in St Louis Cemetery, No.3 Esplanade Avenue.

Mourners crowded the mortuary parlor of Valenti & Bonnet on Toulouse Street, and later, at St Mary's Italian Church, where the caskets were carried by members of the Cefalutana Benevolent Association. The crowd reached such proportions it overflowed into the street, blocking traffic during the services.

Although the officiating priest, Father Scamuzza, made no mention of the murders during his oration, the Axeman was high on the minds of the mourners we spoke to at the funeral. Many were frustrated by the police's lack of progress in the case, and annoyed that the Police Department seemed to be directing their energies towards questioning members of the Italian community, when the prevailing belief among the residents of Little Italy is that the crimes are the work of a crazed Negro.

The Police are allegedly directing their inquiries in such fashion on the orders of Det. Lieut. Michael Talbot, orders which have naturally caused anger among the law-abiding Italians of the Quarter, with some going so far as to call the Police's tactics harassment. One man at the funeral, who wished to remain anonymous, said: 'I've known the Maggios for years. Suggesting they were involved with the Mafia is not only wrong, it's insulting. The Mafia doesn't kill women and children.'

As the sad scenes unfold and anger grows there is yet more unsettling news for the embattled lawman. Luca D'Andrea, the former Bureau Detective who was imprisoned in 1914 on corruption charges, was freed from prison a few days ago.

Readers may remember that it was Det. Talbot who was the main witness against his former mentor D'Andrea in the corruption trial which rocked the Police Department some five years ago. The return of the erstwhile lawman just as Talbot is under pressure to solve the Axeman case is synchronous to say the least. D'Andrea spoke to our reporters as he left a secret halfway house outside the city.

'I'm not surprised Talbot is making no headway into the case,' said the former detective. 'He only got where he is because he squealed. It's the chickens coming home to roost. If the Department really wants to solve this, they should give the case to someone who reached the level of Lieutenant Detective on merit.'

11

A few days after Ida and Lewis had met at the funeral, the two friends found themselves standing outside a cheerless tumbledown house on the northern edge of the Battlefield. Ida was fidgeting with the clasp of her handbag, snapping it open and closed, open and closed, for no good reason at all. Lewis glanced her way, and was about to say something when a stout middle-aged colored woman opened the door a crack. The woman, who was of the opinion that an unsolicited knock at the door only ever meant trouble, eyed them with a suspicious glare.

'Mrs Millicent Hawkes?' Ida asked in the sweetest tone she could manage.

'Yeah. Who's asking?' said the woman.

'My name is Ida Davis, and this is my associate, Lewis,' said Ida, gesturing towards Lewis, who tipped his Stetson at the woman.

'We'd like to talk to you about Mr and Mrs Romano,' said Ida. 'We're private investigators.'

'Private investigators?' said the woman, putting a fist on her hip. 'You barely out of diapers, girl. I already told the police what I had to say, I ain't wasting my breath on you.'

She took a step back and moved to close the door.

'It'd be in your interests,' said Ida quickly, and the woman stopped the door mid-swing. 'You paying?' she asked.

'Kinda,' said Ida.

'Kinda how?'

'We know a few years back you tried to sell information on your old employers to a detective agency,' said Ida. 'Talk to us, and we'll make sure the police don't find out.'

The woman narrowed her eyes.

'You blackmailing me, girl?'

'I believe I am,' said Ida, smiling back at her.

Lewis caught the riled-up look on the woman's face and wondered if she might not take a swing at Ida.

'Shit,' said the woman eventually, 'I always knew going to the Pinkertons was a bad idea.' She nodded to herself, as if confirming the assertion, then swung her arm from the doorjamb. 'I guess you better come in.'

The woman stomped back into the house and Ida turned to Lewis and beamed. The woman led them along a dim corridor and into a cramped kitchen lit by a solitary window that looked out onto next-door's brick wall. Freshly used dishes and pans were peeking above a high lather in the sink, lending the room an aroma of soap powder, onions and fried fish. Mrs Hawkes took a seat at a table by the window and gestured for Ida and Lewis to do the same. They sat opposite the woman and as Ida took her notepad and pen from her bag, Mrs Hawkes stared at her with a curled lip.

'What the hell are you anyway?' she asked, and Ida caught her meaning.

'I'm the same as you,' she replied, meaning she was colored, too.

'Oh yeah?' said Mrs Hawkes, looking her up and down. 'Last time I looked in the mirror, I weren't high yella,' she said, using the derogatory term for a light-skinned person, 'and I weren't dicty to boot.'

The two women stared at each other, and Lewis could feel the atmosphere thicken. He'd heard people call Ida *dicty* plenty of times, meaning they thought she put on airs and graces, that she thought herself better than the average Negro. Lewis knew the insult always caused his friend to spin off into a bout of frustrated introspection, trying to find a reason why people thought that about her – was it her bearing, the way she spoke, the way she appeared a little cold to people, or was it just the way she looked?

'I'm sorry if I offended you, ma'am,' Ida said. 'We just came cuz we wanted to know what it was you tried to sell the detective agency.'

'Pay me and I'll tell ya,' said Mrs Hawkes. 'That was the deal then, and that's the deal now.'

'I understand that, ma'am,' said Ida. 'But things are different now – you're involved in a murder investigation.'

The woman got that same haughty look in her face that Lewis had noticed on the doorstep, and something in the expression reminded him of his mother, the fragile pride of those who have nothing.

'How do I know what I tell you ain't gonna end up on some police report?' said the woman, rubbing her neck at the collar of her tuck blouse.

'You can trust us. It's not in our interests to tell the police,' Ida replied. 'I can guarantee whatever you say goes no further.'

Mrs Hawkes thought for a moment, drumming her fingernails against the table.

'OK,' she said when she had finished her deliberations. 'I'll tell you. On condition that after this little chin-wag, I never see either o' you again.'

She looked from Ida to Lewis and back, and Ida nodded.

'What's up with him?' the woman said, shaking a finger at Lewis. 'He don't talk?'

Lewis smiled. 'Whatever you say is in the strictest confidence,' he said, in what he hoped was his warmest pulpit voice.

'OK,' said Mrs Hawkes, folding her arms over her considerable chest. 'Romano was involved with some counterfeiters. Used his cash register to palm off fake notes to his customers. That's what I tried to sell to the detective.'

'And how long was that going on for?' asked Ida.

'Few years,' said Mrs Hawkes airily.

'And who did he get the notes from?'

Mrs Hawkes shrugged.

'I dunno,' she said, 'a couple o' dagos. Never caught their names, but I figured they were Black Hand. Used to come by the store every Monday, leave a wad of cash. All the cops had to do was turn up and check the till.'

'And Romano was working for these counterfeiters right up till he died?' asked Ida.

Mrs Hawkes paused for a moment.

'No. I think he stopped doing it a while back.' Lewis peered at Ida, who was staring into space and tapping her pen against her chin.

'Mrs Hawkes,' Ida said, 'I was wondering how the Romanos could afford a nurse. I mean, they were just grocers and all.'

'They were broker than the ten commandments most of the time,' replied Mrs Hawkes with a grunt. 'The insurance company paid my wage. On account of Mrs Romano's accident.'

Ida frowned.

'Mrs Romano used to work in a garment factory,' Mrs Hawkes explained. 'One day the machine she was working on broke up and took her eyes out, so she could only see shadows. That's how I come to work for them. The union arranged a cost-of-care stipend.'

Ida frowned once more, and Lewis got the impression she wasn't entirely convinced.

'And how long were you working for them?' asked Ida.

'Five years coming up September.'

'And what were they like? Decent folks?'

Mrs Hawkes shrugged. 'Decent enough,' she said. 'Mrs Romano could scream the house down when she hadn't had her fix, but other than that they was fine.'

'Her fix?' asked Ida.

'Heroin,' said Mrs Hawkes, sighing. 'Woman was fixed on it since the accident. Got hooked after the doctors gave it to her in the hospital. Had to go pick up those little bottles Bayer used to sell from Katz and Besthoff on Canal. Three bottles a week. Apart from that they were just normal folks. Like I told the police.'

Ida smiled and nodded. 'And is there anything you didn't tell the police?' she asked, and Mrs Hawkes paused for a moment.

'There's one thing I didn't tell 'em. And it ain't cuz I hid it neither – I'm a law-abiding citizen,' she said, her tone a little uppity. 'The night after I'd spoke to the police, I went back to the house. See, I had a few bits 'n' pieces I left over there – work things, you know – and I went back to get 'em. I let myself in and gets my things as fast as I could. The place felt creepy, you know. They took away the bodies but the blood was still there. Lord knows what they went through. Anyway, as I'm walking back down the street, I see this ratty, lil' white kid hanging 'bout outside. Looked like a dope fiend – all jittery and leery looking, you know. Well, he gave me an odd kinda look as I walked past him, kinda like he was waiting for me to go.'

'What did he look like?' asked Ida.

'I can't say, it was kinda dark – tall, skinny, white,' she said, shrugging. 'I turns the corner and gets to thinking how strange the whole thing is, and maybe I'm going crazy on account of recent events. So I stop, and I peek back around, and I see this kid walk right on up to the house, jimmy the door, and go inside. Now I know this ain't right, so I hang 'bout outside to see what happens. He's in there for a good half-hour, then he comes back out and hauls hips down the street.'

'A burglar?' asked Lewis, frowning.

'That's what I couldn't figure out,' said Mrs Hawkes. 'He walked outta there empty-handed, no bags, no bulges in his jacket. Nothing.'

Ida jotted down the last of Mrs Hawkes's comments in her notepad, tapped the end of the pen against her chin thoughtfully, then looked up and smiled.

'Thank you, Mrs Hawkes, you've been most helpful,' she said brightly.

Mrs Hawkes led them out of the house, and after she'd

closed the door on them, Ida turned to peer at Lewis with a pleased look.

'Well, that was the biggest pack o' lies I heard all year,' she said with a smile, before descending the front steps at a clip, and striding into the street.

12

Of the three leads Michael had to follow, two petered out within a few days. The search through the city records for people with the name from the graffiti came up blank. They located fifteen residents called Tenebre, seven of them women. Only three of them were *Mrs* and none of them were employed as grocers. A team of five detectives had interviewed all of them anyway, and raked through their histories. None of them had any connections with the previous victims or could explain why a madman might target them. Michael had spent a whole day double-checking the reports himself, and could find nothing to spark a connection in his mind. The seven women were put under armed guard, just in case.

A day later he heard back from the Bureau of Engraving and Printing. A message had arrived on thin, slippery rice-paper, fresh from an underling's office in Washington, stating in telegram type that the currency found at the Maggios' was authentic. The revelation left Michael confused as to why two shopkeepers had had so much fresh money in their house for so long. It pointed to some kind of illicit activity, but Michael wasn't sure what kind.

The only lead left was the eight-year hiatus between the current crop of killings and those Kerry had uncovered from 1911. McPherson had recruited a trio of bluecoats to sift through the prison records, while Michael had divided the folders from the state insane asylum between Kerry and himself. The trawl through the asylum records was unsettling. Each commitment entry had a ruled box next to it with the cursory remarks of the doctor approving the committal, and Michael felt inevitably drawn to read the comments:

William Kernig, male, white, single, 32 yrs. old, native of
N.O. La., recommended his committal to the S-I-A at Jackson,
on Sept. 17th '11, finding him insane, suffering from Chronic
Mania.

    This man is in rags, barefooted and bareheaded. Says
his name is Duke. Replies foolishly to some questions and
cunningly and correctly to others. He has been insane for over
two years, with lucid intervals. Suspect a syphilitic affection of
the brain.

Name after name of Orleanais who had lost their minds while living in the city. A creeping idea had formed in Michael's head that in some way it was the city itself that had driven these people mad. Someone once told him New Orleans was the kind of city that made gluttons out of monks, and murderers out of saints, and now he wondered if it wasn't also a place that made lunatics out of the sane. He had noticed a pattern while reviewing the files – many of the city residents committed were not native Orleanais; it was the newcomers the city was turning insane.

People arrived in New Orleans in their thousands every month, mostly from the countryside, mostly poor, mostly Negroes, all of them looking for a better life. He guessed they didn't realize until it was too late that all they were doing was swapping one form of poverty for another, trading in shacks and barren earth for tenements and street violence. Over the years, Michael had thickened his skin against the city. He knew it to be perilous and dirty, a place where the most dangerous people brushed past him every day. But he had externalized the danger, built a wall. New Orleans and all its ills had become an abstract, something he likened to the city fog: he passed through it daily, and in some sense it was real, but it left no mark on him whatsoever. Perhaps it was inevitable that people arriving fresh from the countryside took leave of their sanity, brought low by slums, poverty and the everyday violence of city-living.

Mary Cecilia, female, colored, married, 48 years old, native of N.O. La. Recommended her committal to the S-I-A at Jackson on Sept. 18th '11, finding her insane, suffering from Hallucinations with Delirium of Persecutions.

Claims she is being poisoned by the Mayor. Her left leg is amputated above the knee.

Michael looked over to the desk where Kerry was at work. A task lamp was shining a cone of light onto the boy's shoulders, casting his face into high relief. Michael wondered what was so bad about Ireland that made Kerry seek a new life in New Orleans, and what the Big Easy had in store for the boy. Glutton, murderer or loon? The boy had done well in the short time he had been working for Michael – he was literate, diligent and clever, more than Michael could say for the majority of the Police Department. He had arranged for a proper uniform to be assigned to the boy, and had even offered him money so he could move into the officer's barracks until he found a place of his own. But the boy said he preferred sleeping in the camp beds in the basement that the night shift used.

Claudette Robicheaux, female, Creole (col.), married, 59 yrs. old, native of N.O. La., recommended her committal to the S-I-A at Jackson, on Sept. 18th '11, finding her insane, suffering from delusions and Chronic Paranoia.

The woman cries repeatedly for her 'children' yet has never given birth. Threatened her Doctor with a knife and accused him of killing her 'babies'. Recommend isolation.

Michael closed the folder and checked the time. It was gone ten thirty. He looked around and noticed the bureau had emptied while he'd been working. The place was silent except for the buzzing of the lights overhead, illuminating pools of the floor in a sharp, burnt-out yellow. He stood and stretched and wondered where the day had gone. As he put his hat and coat on, he noticed Kerry was still bent over his desk, squinting his way through his files.

'Call it a night, son,' said Michael.

Kerry peered at him, bleary-eyed from the paperwork, then he smiled and nodded at Michael, wishing him a good night. Michael tipped his hat back at the boy and made his way towards the exit.

As he snaked his way around the floor he noticed Jake Hatener was, unusually for him, working late as well. The old man was slumped in a chair in the rec area, his considerable belly almost pinning him to the seat. He had a coffee in hand and some kind of witness statement on his lap. Their eyes met and Michael nodded without breaking stride. As he turned the corner into the stairwell, he caught a glimpse of Hatener in the distance, lazily scratching his great belly.

The tram came within a quarter of an hour, and Michael took a seat near the front, glad to get out of the wind blowing through the street. The car was empty save for a few other tired-looking men, returning home after a long day of work, staring out of the windows at the storefronts and lights speeding past.

When the streetcar reached his stop Michael rang the bell, descended and ambled up the quiet avenue of colonial houses where he lived. He noticed a man pacing about in the shadows outside his house, flicking in and out of the darkness beneath one of the sprawling oaks that lined the sidewalk. Michael slowed his pace, sizing the man up. He was too well-dressed to be a stick-up kid, but something about his slouch suggested he was waiting for someone, and he had been waiting for a while. When Michael got closer and realized who it was, he stifled a grimace – John Riley, the reporter from the *Picayune*. Riley exuded a smugness that grated on Michael, a sense that the reporter thought dealing with the work-a-day world was somehow beneath him.

Riley caught sight of Michael and grinned. He detached himself from the shadows under the tree and approached.

'Good evening, Detective. You're a very hard man to get ahold of.'

'You should have tried the precinct.' Michael brushed past Riley to the front steps to his house.

'I guess you heard about D'Andrea getting released,' the reporter continued. 'What's your view on that, by the way?'

Michael turned and looked down at Riley. Hollow-faced and wearing a sand-colored sports jacket he'd long ago grown too thin for, he had something of the scarecrow to him, a meager scraping-together of cloth, flesh and bone. Michael noted the darkness around the eyes, the oily skin, and he thought of the emaciated Chinamen he saw getting dragged through the precinct every now and then.

'My view is if you're gonna make up quotes, at least make 'em believable.'

Riley smiled. 'I've something you might be interested in,' he said. He took a packet of cigarettes from his pocket, flipped one into his mouth with practiced nonchalance, and offered one to Michael.

'I got my own, thanks,' Michael said, on seeing the brand Riley was smoking.

Riley shrugged, struck a lucifer against the heel of his shoe and lit the cigarette. He exhaled leisurely before flicking the match onto the sidewalk.

'I heard Mayor Behrman and Captain McPherson were happy to leave you out in the cold on this Axeman business. The sacrificial lamb has already been anointed, and you're it. Or is the term "scapegoat"? I get confused by these animal metaphors.' Riley shrugged again, acting playful, and Michael stared at him with what he hoped was a blank look. 'I also heard they might let your, uh, domestic arrangements,' said Riley, nodding towards Michael's house, 'put you in an awkward situation.'

Riley was repeating McPherson's threat from a few days before. Michael's heart jumped and he stared at Riley.

'I heard the same,' he said, making no effort to hide his concern.

'So it looks like you could use an ally. I'd like to propose an agreement. How about it, Talbot?' said Riley, his tone plain and free of his usual sarcasm.

'The *Picayune*'s been dragging my name through the mud for the last six weeks,' Michael retorted. 'Why in the hell would I wanna buddy up with you?'

'Because it looks to me like the only hope you got for your career is solving this case. You fail and you lose your job, everyone finds out about you-know-what, and the only work you'll be getting is as a security guard. If you're lucky.' Riley paused. 'I don't wanna see that happen. I'd like to help you. In return, you feed me a few scraps, let me know when you're making the arrests.' Riley smiled. 'We've had some pretty good mileage with the Axeman, be a shame if we weren't there all the way to the end.'

Michael eyed Riley. 'And what do I get?'

'A tip-off,' said the reporter. 'Something to help you on your way.'

He took a business card from his jacket and held it up. Michael deliberated, feeling he was being tempted into making some tawdry, Faustian pact. But in the cold night air, on the porch of his house, the card seemed like a life raft of sorts. He walked back down the steps and accepted it.

'I'll see what I can do. If, and only if, the tip pans out.'

'It'll pan out,' Riley replied with a smile. He flicked his cigarette into the empty street and the two men watched it for a moment as it bounced and sparked against the asphalt.

'Ermanno Lombardi. Look him up.' The reporter winked and smiled. 'Have a good night, Detective,' he said, before turning and sauntering off down the street. Michael watched him go, the wind flapping at his jacket, the man's figure dissolving into the grain of night.

He inspected the business card and wondered how Riley knew the Police Department was going to ship him out when the case was over. Michael would run a check on the name first thing in the morning, and if nothing came up, he'd haul Riley in for another chat.

He put the card in his pocket and entered his house. He proceeded along a hallway and through a door at its far end, into a high-ceilinged room which occupied most of the first floor. On one side was the kitchen area and, connected to it on the near side by a wide arch, the living room. The lights were on, and a fire glowed orange in the hearth. The apartment had been decorated simply but with warmth and care, carpets lay scattered across the floor, two couches and an armchair snug by a fireplace.

Michael strode through the room with a smile on his lips. He was home, and despite Riley propositioning him outside, he felt like he was safe, away from the grime of the city and his job. He walked through the arch and entered the kitchen. Sitting at the kitchen table, darning a child's jacket, was a slender black woman roughly the same age as Michael. Her hair was pulled back, and she wore a simple gray skirt and a white lace blouse. She worked at the stitching in her hand with an easy concentration.

'Annette.'

The woman smiled without looking up.

'You're late.'

Michael approached her and she put down her work. They smiled and shared a tender kiss, then Michael sat opposite her, took his hat off and tossed it onto the table. Annette yawned, then stood and stretched her arms out catlike.

'You eaten?' she asked, her voice sleepy.

Michael shook his head.

'I'll heat up the stew.'

She made her way to the heavy copper stove in the corner and hauled a casserole dish onto one of the open hobs. Michael leaned back in his chair and peered into the living room. On one of the couches by the fireplace, curled into the cushions, two children were sleeping, a boy and a girl.

'They wanted to stay up till their daddy got home,' Annette said, and they shared a smile.

13

Detective Jake Hatener sat in a booth in a gloomy late-night diner mopping up the last dregs of cream sauce from a steak au poivre with the corner-end of a baguette. He had planned on waiting for his friend before ordering but boredom overcame him. Food had always distracted Hatener, stopped him from brooding on a life whose unfolding had become dull, predictable and irksome. At some point in middle age he had grown tired of the things that as a young man gave his days an edge – the alcohol and narcotics, the freebies from the whores on his protection route, the sudden, searing bursts of violence. He was reaching the last stretch of service before retirement, had seen everything imaginable, and somehow had lost what it was that made it all enjoyable.

He had stayed late in the precinct, waiting for Talbot to leave, and then he made his way to the beanery through the wind that had picked up that night. The diner was abandoned apart from a forlorn-looking waitress sitting on a stool at the counter, filing her nails and occasionally glancing at the door. Hatener called her over and ordered two coffees. She picked up the plates, wiped the table and slunk off towards the kitchen.

The front door opened and Luca sauntered in. He grinned as he approached the table and Hatener stood and the two men hugged.

'Good to see ya again,' said Hatener, slapping Luca on the back. They sat and the waitress brought them their coffees. Hatener was surprised at how well Luca looked. He had always had an ageless quality to him – when they were cadets Luca had the air of someone much older, commanding and knowledgeable. Now he was in his fifties, he somehow still looked boyish.

'You look better than I expected,' said Hatener, who had known younger men than Luca leave Angola with crooked postures and the sun-burnt, leathery skin of old farmers.

'How's Mary?' asked Luca.

'She's good,' Hatener lied. 'Sorry you couldn't come by the house.'

Luca waved away the apology and they set about catching up. Luca spoke to Hatener about his time in Angola, about the beatings, the guards, the insect-infested food that left him half-delirious. He told him about the stench of the place, a rancid mix of sweat and mold and excrement that no amount of scrubbing could dislodge from his clothes and hair. Hatener listened and in return he told Luca his own stories, about changes in the city and the Police Department, about the young men who went off to the war in Europe and had flooded back into the city, jobless, bitter and shell-shocked. He told Luca about his own son, who had gone to the war and never returned, obliterated by a German shell in a field outside Reims. Not even a casket for them to bury him in, Hatener lamented, just a pair of dog-tags and a typewritten letter from the government. Hatener had never really spoken to anyone about his son in the year since they had received the letter. He even told Luca about the rift that had developed between him and Mary since their son's death, about Mary's silent spells and endless weeping.

The two men looked at each other, contemplating the tricks life had played on them. Hatener called the waitress over for refills, and it was only then that he noticed Luca hadn't finished his coffee.

Hatener gestured to the cup and Luca rubbed his stomach by way of an explanation. 'Something I picked up in Angola.' Hatener nodded. Most of the men who returned from Angola came back with ulcers or twisted guts or other stomach complaints. When the waitress arrived at the booth, Hatener ordered a coffee for himself and a hot milk for Luca. He watched the waitress leave then he slid a dossier across the table.

'I need 'em back first thing,' he said.

Luca smiled, picked up the dossier and flicked through the pages. It had been five years since he had really read anything, and he realized with a panicky sense of loss that his eyesight had deteriorated.

'What do you want them for?' asked Hatener.

'Carlo asked me to look into it,' said Luca flatly, and Hatener frowned at him.

'You only been out a few days.'

Luca shrugged. 'My savings were in Ciro's bank.'

'Ah,' Hatener nodded, 'we woulda given Ciro a tip-off if we knew, but the orders came from up high.'

Luca made an expression to suggest there was no point dwelling on the thing, and then he turned his attention to the dossier in his hands. Hatener peered at him, finding it sad that his friend was already back at work for the Matrangas.

'You need some money?' he asked, and Luca looked up and shook his head.

'I'm good,' he said, and returned to the files – every report Michael had on the Axeman case, swiped from the precinct for the night by Hatener: witness statements, coroner's statements, scene-of-crime reports, photographs, newspaper clippings – enough from each attack to get Luca started. Luca spotted Riley's name on one of the newspaper clippings and a memory surfaced.

'Heard they made the District illegal,' he said, referring to Storyville, the licensed prostitution district that had for years made New Orleans the tourist center of the South.

'Sure,' Hatener replied with a grimace, 'for all the good it did.'

Towards the end of 1917, the War Department's Commission on Training Camp Activities forced Mayor Behrman to close down the District on account of the large numbers of Navy men from nearby training camps who were contracting venereal diseases there. The mayor's administration fought the War Department all the way to Washington to keep the District open, but amidst claims that Mayor Behrman was undermining the war effort, Storyville was reluctantly closed in November 1917, another victim of the Great War.

'Wasn't the only thing,' said Hatener. 'They made mary-jane illegal too, and the *babania*, and now they're doing the same for booze. Imagine that, can't buy a woman, a beer or a smoke anymore. Call that America?'

Luca smiled. 'So what's going on in the old district now? Ghost town?' he asked.

Hatener smiled and shook his head. 'Everything's going on exactly the same. 'Cept maybe the runners gotta pay a bit more protection. Behrman wasn't too keen on the idea anyway, so he lets things slide. You hear about the night with his car?'

Luca shook his head and Hatener told him an anecdote about the mayor's car being stolen during a Sarah Bernhardt performance at the Dauphin. As he told the story the two men settled into their old rhythm, and for a few minutes they stopped feeling like old men and became instead the youngsters they were years ago, when they were strong and carefree and life had none of its current weight. When Hatener got to the end of the story, they laughed and lapsed into a warm silence. Hatener stared about the diner and noticed the waitress had fallen asleep on her stool, her head canting dangerously towards the bar in front of her.

'I'm glad you're back,' said Hatener, still grinning. 'Things ain't the same at the bureau. Specially since this Axeman thing. We're running backwards and forwards between McPherson's office and the Family trying to get warnings out.'

Hatener shook his head, and Luca nodded, acknowledging that times had indeed changed for the worse. He flicked through the dossier again and came across an envelope, opened it up and took out a handful of bloodstained, ghoulish-looking tarot cards.

'The killer leaves 'em at the scenes,' explained Hatener. 'That's one of the reasons why Talbot's pushing the Family angle.'

Luca flipped the cards over and held them close to his eye, inspecting them minutely.

'These cards aren't Italian,' he said.

'You sure?' replied Hatener.

Luca nodded. 'My mother used to read the *tarocchi* in Italy. You only get these animal designs on French cards,' he said.

'A Creole?' suggested Hatener.

'Maybe,' said Luca, putting the cards back in the envelope. He had seen similar *tarocchi* cards years before, when he had arrested the Haitian priestess on Canal Street, after her boyfriend had been caught shaking down her customers' houses while they were with her. A man whom nobody knew was killing Italian grocers and leaving French tarot cards at the scenes. Either the killer was a Creole with a grudge, or somebody trying to make it look like a Creole with a grudge.

Luca took a cigarette from his pack and lit it.

'Thanks for the files, Jake,' he said. 'I'll have 'em back to you first thing tomorrow morning.'

The two friends smiled at each other, clinked cups and downed the last of their drinks. Hatener put some bills down on the table and they left the diner. The waitress was still sleeping when they walked past her, her head lilting as if to the music of her dream.

On the street outside they hugged and arranged a six o'clock meeting the next morning and then they said their goodbyes. Luca sauntered off up the windy street, and as Hatener buttoned up his coat against the chill he watched the retreating figure of his old friend, and couldn't stop himself from thinking what a shame it was that Luca D'Andrea cut such a lonely figure.

14

A brittle wind blew down Magnolia Street, swaying the shop signs and shooing a tin can along the road like a clanging, rusty tumbleweed. In a spot opposite the Maggios' store, just a couple of yards from where Patrolman Perez had parked a few days previously, Ida and Lewis huddled in the moonlight shadows of an abandoned half-built house. Little Italy was littered with such unfinished buildings, pinewood remnants of interrupted dreams. Immigrants who had scrimped together the paltriest of savings would buy a cheap plot of land and begin construction of a family home. But these newcomers' financial situations were ever-precarious, and more often than not circumstances changed for the worse, and projects had to be abandoned, leaving Little Italy scattered with weed-choked shells of houses.

Ida had found the place when she'd scouted the area the day after they'd talked with Millicent Hawkes. She'd reasoned that if someone had searched a previous crime scene, they would probably search the most recent one, too. So she'd looked around the neighborhood for an appropriate spot from which to conduct a stakeout, and after not too long she had found what would have been, in better times, the homestead of some ambitious family or other. The building had walls, a floor, roof beams that segmented the moonlight, and most importantly, an unobstructed view of the Maggios' store. And although the place didn't keep the cold out, it stopped them from being seen, and gave them somewhere to sit.

Ida had guessed from what Hawkes had told them that the last break-in occurred three or four days after the preceding set of murders, so Ida had let the same amount of time elapse, and had come down to the house for the first night of surveillance the previous evening. She had come alone that time as Lewis was booked for a gig, and she had sat on her own, in what she guessed was supposed to be the living room of the dream house. From just before midnight to just after dawn she'd kept watch, leaving as soon as it was light to grab a few hours' sleep before work. Although she was a little disappointed that nothing had happened during the first night's watch, she was also relieved that she wasn't called into action without Lewis there to help.

She had met him earlier that evening in the French Quarter, noting he looked a little sheepish, and that he was hiding a bruise under his hat. When she had asked him about it on the walk over, Lewis had eventually admitted the bruise was an embarrassing trophy from his latest argument with Daisy. Ida had guessed the situation at the house in Gretna was getting steadily worse, but she hadn't realized it had descended into violence. She tried to talk to Lewis about it, but he acted bashful and she gathered he didn't want to discuss it, so they sat in the empty, roofless house in silence, Lewis mulling over his personal life, Ida fighting off her sleepiness.

'Why did you think the woman we interviewed was lying?' Lewis asked abruptly, breaking a fifteen-minute spell of silence. Ida turned to look at him, frowned, and then shrugged.

'A bunch of things, I guess,' she said. 'Hawkes said she got employed cuz Mrs Romano's union helped 'em out. But I checked up. Mrs Romano weren't on no union lists I could find. The factory owner was paying them off for some other reason.

'Then she said the Romanos were flat broke. But that didn't make sense either, cuz they were slinging counterfeits,' she continued. 'Then she said she went back to get her stuff from the house at night. Why'd she go back at night? If your boss just been murdered, you really gonna go get your stuff from the crime scene in the middle o' the night?' As Ida talked and she warmed to the subject, her sleepiness wore off and she began to speak faster and faster. 'Why didn't she go in the day? Also, why'd she wait so long before going? Then she said the guy she saw breaking in had a funny look in his eye, and he walked right past her. But when I asked her to describe him, she said she only saw him from a distance.'

'Ida,' interrupted Lewis, 'if everything she said was a lie, why are we sitting in a derelict house in the middle o' the night?'

'Not everything she said was a lie, just most of it. Here's how I reckon it happened,' and Ida began to spell out her theory in a Gatling-gun staccato. 'Hawkes didn't go back to *get her things* from the house. She went back to get money. Counterfeit money. I don't reckon the Romanos ever stopped distributing counterfeits like she said. Otherwise, how else they pay for the wife's heroin bottles? If they were still distributing, then there was still fake money in the house, and I don't mean in the till like Hawkes said, I mean somewhere where the police would never find it. She figured after the police had cleared out, she could go back and collect it for herself. That's why she waited a few days before going back. That's why she went back in the nighttime. And that's why she told us the Romanos were broke and they stopped counterfeiting.'

'OK,' said Lewis, 'but if she was trying to keep all this secret, then why'd she tell us she went back at all?'

'Because she wasn't sure what we knew – which is why the bit about seeing the kid breaking in is true. She went back that night and got the money, but on the way out she sees someone else breaking in. Naturally she assumes it's one of the counterfeiters looking for what she just took.'

'Naturally,' echoed Lewis, with a sarcastic grin, and Ida gave him a sideways look before continuing.

'Then we turn up on her doorstep, and she's wondering if we've been sent by the counterfeiters to see if she took the money. So she feeds us the story about "collecting her things".'

Lewis frowned. 'Then why'd she tell us she saw the kid? If she thought we were counterfeiters, that's just asking for trouble.'

'I know,' said Ida. 'I still can't figure that one out either. We ain't exactly the kind counterfeiters would employ, and she didn't ask us how comes we knew about her selling info to the Pinkertons.'

Lewis thought for a moment. 'You sure the kid she saw wasn't just a porch-climber?' he asked. 'Some sap-head that heard the Romanos' was empty on account of the murders?'

'Hawkes said he left the building without a bag. If he was a thief then how comes he didn't steal nothing?' said Ida. 'And Hawkes said he was in the house a half-hour – you ever hear of a second-story man taking a half-hour to shake down a house? He was searching the place. Here's how I see it. All the victims are in a counterfeiting gang. Something goes wrong, I dunno what, and they fall out. So someone goes round 'em all getting revenge. Then someone else figures he needs something from the victims' houses, so he pays some sap to go and check the crime scenes after the police have gone, and Hawkes stumbled into it all.'

Lewis mulled over Ida's theory and in the silence the sound of alley-cats caterwauling rose up in the distance and continued for a few minutes. Lewis was about to speak when he spotted, a block further down the road, a sticklike figure loping towards the Maggios' store. He nudged Ida in the ribs and she turned to see the figure too. As he got closer they saw him more clearly – a wiry, stooped boy barely out of his teens, clad in poor stuff, a flat-cap pulled low over his brow. He approached the Maggios', looked around him, then trotted up the front steps. Half-hidden in the shadow of the lintel, he removed some kind of tool from his jacket and set to work on the door. After a few seconds, he slid the door open and entered the store.

'He ain't no Axeman,' whispered Lewis. 'Boy's so thin I can count his ribs.'

Ida nodded in agreement and watched as a faint light arched through the Maggios' for a few moments before it faded out completely. Half an hour later the faint light reappeared briefly then died out, and the boy emerged through the shadows of the porch. He looked about him and skulked off up the street, shoulders hunched, pace quick. Ida and Lewis waited till he was a block away, then they stepped out of the house, and followed him at what they gauged was a discreet enough distance.

The boy took them on a snaking walk out of Little Italy and through the city center, towards the industrial yards by the docks. The roads around the area were empty and silent, many of them without any lighting whatsoever, and the dank smell of the Mississippi hung heavy in the air. After leading them through a labyrinth of alleys, the boy made his way down a narrow footpath and approached a high double-gated wooden fence. He banged on the gate, and after a few moments it was hauled back with a metallic groan and the boy stepped through the opening and into the yard beyond. Ida and Lewis caught a glimpse of the building inside before the gate shut again – a sprawling Victorian warehouse slumbering in the shadows of a wide, empty yard.

'So what do we do now?' asked Lewis.

'Let's take a look around,' Ida replied.

They turned and began to wind their way around the perimeter. On a street that backed onto a brewery opposite, they found a place where some barrels had been piled up next to the fence. With a strong jump from the barrels, a hand-hold onto the top of the fence was possible.

Lewis went first and he hauled Ida up after him. They sat on the top of the fence and peered into the yard below. Lewis pointed to something moving on the far side of the yard, and after a few seconds Ida realized what it was – two guard dogs, wide-jawed hulking Dobermans, lolling about in the shadow of a wooden enclosure. Ida looked around some more and noticed a light shining from a set of windows on the far side of the warehouse. The windows were at a spot where the yard-fence curved around close to the building, and Ida suggested they walk around the perimeter a little further and see if they could look in.

They hopped down off the fence and continued along the road

until they reached the point where the warehouse light was shining out of the windows. There were no barrels this time to allow them to jump onto the fence, so they peered through the gaps between the fence-panels instead. This afforded them a sliver of a view across the yard to the warehouse and its illuminated windows, through which they could see a work area full of boxes and sewing machines. Fur coats on hangers lined one side of the space and in the middle were tables overflowing with pelts, furs and wraps in various stages of creation. In one corner, by a davenport, was a safe, and a table where the boy they had been following was sitting. In the light they could make him out properly – a drawn face, a dope-head's complexion. On either side of the boy were two swarthy-looking men in gabardine suits, with square, stony builds and dark eyes.

After a few minutes, a towering broad-chested man with a bushy red beard strode into the room. The man unbuttoned the heavy fox-fur coat he was wearing, clipped a safe key onto the ring hanging from his belt and approached the table. He put his thumbs through his belt-loops, puffed out his chest and stared down at the boy. The boy seemed to wither under the man's glare, looking small and befuddled. They began a conversation, which Ida and Lewis couldn't hear, but the gesticulations of the boy, and the imposing way the man towered over him, left them certain that the man was the boy's paymaster, and he was questioning him about that night's break-in. Eventually the man nodded at something the boy said, pulled a few bills from his pocket and handed them to the boy, who took the money with a grateful smile and a subservient bow of his head. Then the bearded man nodded to the men in suits and all four of them stood and seemed to be getting ready to close the place up for the night.

Ida and Lewis stood back from the fence and shared a look.

'Let's head back around to the front,' said Ida. 'Watch 'em leave.'

They made their way towards the front gate, hanging back in the shadows of a building opposite, and after a quarter of an hour the front gate was yanked back noisily, and a gleaming black Type 55 Cadillac purred out into the road. One of the men in suits, and the boy they had followed, sauntered out after the car. The suited man locked the gate shut while the car was idling, and the boy stood by the car. The bearded man, who was in the passenger seat, leaned out of the window and addressed him.

'See you at the usual time tomorrow, Johnson,' the man said in a Cajun accent, the syllables sliding into each other in a glissando tinged with French.

'Yes, sir,' said the boy, his voice frail and cracked. He touched a finger to his cap then ambled off up the street, vanishing into the darkness. Then the suited man was had locked the gate jumped into the car and it drove off in the opposite direction.

'What do you reckon the time is?' Ida asked after they had watched the car disappear over the brow of the road.

'Dunno,' replied Lewis. 'Steeple said two thirty 'bout ten minutes before we got here – must be around three by now.'

They trudged back the way they came, smoking cigarettes and hunching their shoulders against the chill. Ida had been right about the boy visiting the latest crime scene, and he'd led them straight to his taskmaster, the man who was paying him to search the victims' houses. Finding out the name of the big Cajun in the fox-fur coat was the next step. Her thoughts were interrupted by the screech of a night-owl echoing through the empty street. Ida looked up and shared a look with Lewis – local folklore deemed the sound an omen of a death to come. Then she shrugged, as if to dismiss the superstition, and they returned to their silent trek.

When they reached the center of town, Lewis helped Ida into a cab, before he made his own long journey back to Gretna, and, Ida guessed, another argument with Daisy. She rubbed her eyes and looked about her as the cab drove through the streets. The first fingers of dawn were already stretching out over the horizon. The cab turned south, and with the Mississippi to its side, headed into the roaring fire of sunrise.

15

When he heard the rapping at the front door Michael was at the kitchen table eating breakfast. He had been half-reading the newspaper, half-watching Annette with a fascinated eye as she readied Thomas and Mae for school. He studied her as she knelt in front of their son, trying to tug a coat onto his resisting arms. She stopped when she heard the knock, flashed Michael a wary look, and they slipped into a familiar routine, like firemen at the ringing of a bell.

Under Annette's watchful gaze, Michael rose from the table and approached the door. He hadn't told Annette of McPherson's threat, or of Riley repeating it the night before. He had originally decided no good could come of startling her, but now he questioned his decision. Had McPherson called in the threat already? Michael had been expecting to have at least a few weeks' grace – enough time to arrange for Annette, Thomas and Mae to leave the state and settle somewhere out of the way.

He padded softly through the living room and when he reached the doorway he turned to look at Annette and the children, and lifted a finger to his lips. His son and daughter mimicked the gesture with grins on their faces, as if playing a game, and Michael smiled back at them before stepping out into the corridor.

Their cover-story was that Annette was his maid; a cowardly pretense he only went along with at her insistence. It was, as she pointed out, the most believable of all the lies they could have told. They had concocted the story at the start of their relationship, just after Michael had returned home from the smallpox ward and Annette had moved in to nurse him. It had worked well enough until their son came along and forced their hand. One look at the children from an ill-disposed cop was enough to have them convicted, but even so, they kept their little routines, and a separate bedroom for show, and left the house clear of family photographs, school certificates and the thousand other trinkets that attest to the life of a family.

There were no wedding photographs to hide. When Annette had first realized she was pregnant, they made a decision to travel to Kansas City – the closest place they knew of where the laws were in their favor. They had spent the long, dusty journey across the endless mid-western plains separated from each other, in segregated cars, on segregated platforms, and eating alone in the partitioned areas of station-side diners. And all the while Annette was coming on with her sickness, dizzy from her condition and the heat.

They made it all the way to Kansas City and found the preacher they had heard about, a man who was sympathetic to Southerners in their situation. They wed in a small out-of-the-way chapel, and began the return journey later the same day. Although their relationship was sanctified, it left them in a legal limbo when they returned to New Orleans, and they waited daily for the knock that might send them both to prison. So after McPherson and Riley had made their threats, Michael was especially riddled with angst as he stood before the front door and cleared his throat.

'Who is it?'

As he waited for a response, a heavy stillness seemed to stretch time. He heard the wispy sounds of children playing somewhere distant.

'It's Kerry, sir,' said a muffled voice outside.

Michael relaxed and opened the door. Kerry was standing on the front step, his green eyes bright with the morning light.

'Sorry to bother you, sir. The duty officer sent me. There's been another murder.'

*

Half an hour later Michael was standing in a kitchen in Gretna, inspecting the corpses of the latest victims while gagging sounds emanated from the toilet next door. Michael was impressed Kerry had made it all the way to the bathroom before being sick. The victims were another married couple, Edvard and Anna Schneider. No one had been able to figure out what nationality they were just yet, but they sure as hell weren't Italian, and Schneider wasn't a grocer, he was a lawyer. The pattern established in the earlier attacks had been well and truly broken.

From what Michael could tell of the remains, the Schneiders were a stocky, middle-aged couple. The wife with pale, freckled skin and hazel hair, the husband with a porcine face and a bristling ginger mustache. They were laid out in the kitchen, the husband slumped against the foot of the sink, the wife in the middle of the room. While the husband had only a single slash wound to the head, the wounds inflicted on the wife were much more grotesque. The killer had placed the woman flat on the floor and had cut chunks from her flesh which he had left in a pile in the sink. Her head had been attacked with such ferocity that it was now no more than a splash of red against the floor.

Most bizarrely of all, the killer had traced lines with his fingertips through the bloody pool surrounding the woman's body. Revealing the white floor-tiles underneath, the lines had dried and created an effect like a photographic negative or a woodblock print. The lines formed crude drawings of what Michael guessed were straw dolls, nightmarish things with screaming mouths and crying eyes. They had a frantic quality to them, but also a childishness, a playfulness which made them all the more revolting. Michael wondered if the Axeman had planned to make the drawings, or if the decision was spontaneous, a sudden burst of inspiration when the killer looked down at the fresh pool of blood in front of him. Michael turned away from the bodies, crossed himself and walked out of the kitchen.

He slumped onto a couch in the living room, sighed, and lit a cigarette. He had planned on spending the morning chasing up Riley's tip. Ermanno Lombardi. Checking for the name in the records, trying to find an address or a KA. Instead he had to deal with yet another killing. He ran his fingers over the scars on his cheeks and looked around the room. The place was close with people – officers were going through the couple's possessions, the Frenchman was taking photographs, a sergeant was collating the reports that were arriving from the neighbors. The doctor emerged from the kitchen and sat opposite Michael on an armchair. They stared at each other in silence, then the older man shook his head.

'Probably happened between midnight and two,' said the doctor. 'He hit the husband with a single stroke to the head and let him bleed to death – probably took a good while for the man to lose consciousness. Then he did that to the wife. I'm assuming it is the wife, of course, there's no actual way of identifying her just yet.' The doctor took a puff on his cigar and sighed. 'Seems to me he planned it all out. He disables the husband and then forces him to watch while he tortures his wife. The last thing the poor man saw was the butchering of his nearest and dearest.'

A bluecoat entered from the kitchen and handed Michael two tarot cards.

'We found them by the sink, sir,' said the bluecoat. Michael thanked the man and inspected the cards – the Magician and the Hanged Man. The Magician card showed a robed figure standing in front of an altar, holding aloft some bizarrely fashioned metal tool. On the altar were swords, daggers and strange symbols. The Hanged Man card depicted a man in a tunic hanging upside down from a crucifix, a chilling smile playing on his lips. They were of the same style and type as the other cards, with a hellish quality that he couldn't attribute to any of the specific elements – the colors, the lines, the faces of the characters portrayed – but only to all these elements in combination.

The door to the bathroom swung open and Kerry stepped into the room, wiping his hand against his mouth.

'Feeling better, son?' Michael asked, looking up from the cards.
'Not really.'

The boy looked green, paler than he usually did. Michael
smiled, motioned for Kerry to sit opposite him on the sofa, and they
went over the information they'd gathered from the beat-cops.

Two hours earlier the neighbors in the downstairs apartment
had noticed a pool of blood staining the carpet in their living room.
Realizing the blood was dripping down through the ormolu of a
chandelier, they'd alerted the building's superintendent, who in
turn called the police. The front door was locked from the inside
when the officers had first entered, and Schneider's keys were found
in the drawer of a sideboard. Uniformed officers were currently
taking statements from all the other tenants in the building and
from residents of the neighboring blocks, but as yet no one had
reported anything meaningful.

In contravention of the new housing regulations, the building
had not been fitted with external fire escapes, so entry or exit from
anything other than the front door was impossible. Yet the front
door was locked from the inside. The Axeman must have picked the
lock shut while he knelt in the building's corridor – a huge and
needless risk. Michael imagined the headlines – *Axeman Slays Two
in Fourth-floor Apartment, Door Found Locked from the Inside*.

'The killer must have cased the building before entering,'
Michael said, 'then he must have spent a bit of time gaining entry
from the street. Once he was in the apartment building he went up
the stairs, and must have spent, what, fifteen minutes or so picking
the lock to the Schneiders' front door? Doing it in complete silence,
too, or Schneider would have grabbed the gun we found under his
pillow.'

'He could have knocked on the door and asked himself in on a
pretext,' Kerry suggested.

'That's possible, but if Schneider kept a gun under his pillow,
I doubt he'd have let a stranger in on a ruse. And none of the
neighbors heard a scream.'

Michael lit another cigarette and rubbed his face. It was the shifts in the man's behavior that made no sense to him. He planned his attacks meticulously, then he killed in a frenzy, then he calmly washed himself down, then he took stupid risks like picking doors shut from the outside.

Michael stood and paced the room, noticing with a grimace that a butcher's smell from the kitchen was steadily making its way into the living room.

'The first three attacks were similar – the victims were all Sicilian, all took place in the same neighborhood, and the victims were all grocers and shopkeepers. But this one – it's in a different part of town, the victim is a lawyer, reasonably well-to-do and—' Michael paused and scratched his head. 'Has anyone figured out where they were from yet?' he asked loudly.

'The wife was German, sir,' said one of the officers taking an inventory of the room. 'We found her naturalization papers.'

'The husband?'

'We're still not sure. One of the neighbors said he might be Dutch.'

Michael sighed and took a drag on his cigarette. 'Maybe Schneider was the lawyer for the three grocers,' said Kerry.

Michael smiled, glad the boy had made the suggestion, even if it was an obvious one.

'I've already sent a couple of men to check at his workplace,' Michael said. 'We'll know soon enough. Now, say the Axeman was just attacking people at random, moving neighborhoods would make sense – most of the patrols are taking place in Little Italy now. But, why pick this apartment? In a building complex, four floors up? If he was just choosing people at random, he could have picked an easier mark. He made this so difficult for himself, it implies he's targeting specific people. Which would make these murders planned, and not the random slayings of a lunatic.'

He put his hands on his hips and thought. The tarot cards, the warning scrawled on the side of the Maggios' house. Specific victims but exaggerated violence. The only thing he could think of that reconciled it all was retribution, vengeance. But what had the victims done to deserve revenge attacks so savage?

'Kerry, I want you to run an errand for me. Get back to the precinct and run a search on an Ermanno Lombardi,' said Michael. 'And don't tell anybody you're doing it, OK?'

'Sure,' said Kerry, smiling. He stood and straightened his uniform, then flipped his cap onto his head and exited the apartment.

Michael watched the boy go then crossed over to the windows on the far side of the room. He peered into the street below, and was seized for an instant by a ridiculous fear that he might see Luca standing on the sidewalk four stories down, staring up at him with narrow eyes. But all he saw were the police cars, and the cordon, and a gaggle of reporters scurrying about trying to interview the locals. For a moment he felt a strange kind of warmth, as if being removed from the world below made him untouchable, safe. And then he remembered the two mutilated bodies in the next room.

16

When Lewis looked back on the first six years of his life, the years he spent living with his grandmother in the house on James Alley, his memories were suffused with the glow of security, of feeling wanted and loved. The images of that time which had tumbled down through the years into his adult mind – images of his grandmother washing laundry in the backyard, of the streets in the Battlefield where the house was located, of the stream of relatives and callers that came by for visits – for some reason, all of them had faded in comparison to the images of the sprawling chinaball tree that haunted the backyard of the house on James Alley.

The tree was no taller than the bungalow, but it made its presence felt. In summer, clusters of lilac flowers speckled the tree and released a fragrance that wafted through the garden and permeated the house, scenting the washing Lewis's grandmother strung out to dry. And in winter the tree's marble-sized fruits made the garden loud with the calls of the songbirds that flocked there to feast on the sticky yellow orbs that dropped to the ground and formed a slick, tarry carpet. When Lewis had been bad his grandmother made him cut switches from the branches, and when he had been good, he was allowed to climb into its canopy and play. And on the day it all came to an end, it was there that Lewis happened to be, unaware he was about to experience the first great wrenching of his life.

When he heard his grandmother's call, he noticed her voice sounded a little more strained than it normally did, with a little more weight in the tone. But Lewis was only six years old, and he hadn't yet grasped the importance of subtleties, so he paid it no heed as he rushed into the house to see what was up.

He trotted into the lounge, and was surprised to see his grand-mother perched on the sofa with a haughty, stern-looking woman he had never seen before. Both of them wore grave expressions, and his grandmother asked him to sit. He hauled himself up into an armchair and peered at the two of them. His grandmother, a washerwoman and an emancipated slave, a follower of both Catholicism and voodou, had always taken Lewis everywhere with her, even to the houses of the rich folk she worked for, where Lewis would play hide-and-go-seek with the white children who lived there, while she laundered their parents' linen. So Lewis thought he knew all her acquaintances, which made the mystery of the inscrutable woman sitting next to her all the deeper.

His grandmother took a moment, and then explained in lan-guage tailored for his six-year-old self, that his mother, living out in Black Storyville, had contracted an illness after giving birth to his new baby sister, and that Lewis's father had abandoned her once more. Then she explained that Lewis had to move to his mother's house to care for her, and the woman sitting next to his grandmother was going to take him there. Lewis looked from his grandmother to the stranger, and back again, and promptly burst into tears.

As his grandmother dressed him in his best clothes – a white Lord Fauntleroy suit – and packed his case, she tried to soothe him as best she could, then after he had said a tearful goodbye, the stern-looking woman led Lewis out of the house.

When they got to the tram stop at Tulane Avenue, the woman, exasperated by Lewis's bawling, knelt down next to him and spoke to him for the first time, in a voice that was surprisingly warm.

'Lewis,' she said, 'you know what that place is behind the stop?'

Lewis followed her finger to the doleful red-brick building on the other side of the road – the House of Detention. Lewis nodded and wiped the tears from his eyes.

'It's where the bad people go,' he said, and the woman nodded at him and smiled.

'Now, if you don't shut the hell up, that's where you gonna end up, too,' she hissed.

Lewis felt like bursting into tears once again, but he did everything he could to stay quiet and not sob. He wiped the tears from his eyes and resolved not to look at the woman again, in case her hard, stranger's face caused him to bawl once more.

Presently the streetcar arrived. Lewis had never ridden the streetcar before. He stepped onto the tram after the woman, nodded hello at the driver, and sat in the first row of seats, where there was a window free for him to look out of. The driver rang the bell, and the tram sped off, and Lewis smiled as he watched the houses go by. And then he heard the woman shout his name. He turned to see her sitting all the way at the back of the tram with a vexed expression on her face.

'Boy!' she shouted. 'Get back here where you belong!'

Lewis, thinking she was joking, turned back around and carried on staring out of the window. Until he felt a hand grab his arm and yank him out of the seat. He stumbled to the floor, grazing his knee, and the woman dragged him by the elbow all the way down to the end of the tram, past rows of wide-eyed passengers watching the spectacle the pair were making of themselves. She threw him onto the back-row and pointed at the sign on the rear of the seat in front: FOR COLORED FOLKS ONLY.

'You wanna get us lynched?'

'I ain't never been on the streetcar before,' Lewis said, and peered at her, confused and upset.

When the tram reached the corner of Tulane and Liberty, they descended and crossed the two blocks to Mayann's on foot, the woman dragging Lewis by the wrist. They approached a rickety wooden door set into one of the houses by the intersection of Liberty and Perdido and, without knocking or needing the use of a key, the woman pushed the door open with a robust shove. The room they stepped into was dim and joyless, and Lewis had to squint to make anything out. Amidst the rattletrap floorboards and bare walls, the space was taken up by an imposing iron-frame bed, a rudimentary kitchen along one wall, and a second door opening out onto a back courtyard which provided the only source of light. Through the open doorway Lewis could glimpse a view of the tumbledown houses opposite, and the clotheslines arcing through the yard. He scanned the rest of the room, amazed at how small it was, how dingy and close, and he wondered where the other rooms were.

After a few moments his mother sat up in the iron-frame bed, rubbed her eyes and smiled weakly at Lewis, who did his best to smile back. Then he noticed that sleeping next to her was the baby sister he had never met, a wrinkled bean of a thing, tiny and smothered in rough cotton cloths. His mother turned her gaze from the baby to Lewis and Lewis saw she looked ill, eyes puffy and full of water. Lewis had only met his mother on a few previous occasions, when she had paid visits to him and her mother-in-law at the house in James Alley, occasions when she'd made an effort and had arrived well turned out in her Sunday best.

'I thought maybe your grandma wouldn't let you come.' She spoke quietly, her voice so weak and delirious that Lewis thought she might be talking to herself.

'Lewis,' she continued, 'I ain't done right by you in the past. But I'm gonna try and make it up to you.' He looked at her and suppressed an urge to cry. He wanted to go back to his grandmother's, to the sunlit house in James Alley, with its jumble of rooms, and its garden, and its chinaball tree. How could this single dingy room have suddenly become his home? A room so poor-looking it seemed to have been robbed of its light. A room in a faraway part of town, with its two trembling strangers, weak and in need.

Now, twelve years later, Lewis was once more hauling his life's possessions up Perdido Street in the direction of his mother's apartment. But this time he was the adult. And as he looked down to Clarence, who was stumbling along by his side, he realized with a heavy sense of history repeating, that his adopted son was about the same age he himself had been when he was dragged, terrified, across town by the nameless woman.

The pair of them cut pitiable figures. Lewis had bloodstains on his shirt and a scab forming on his lip that was beginning to itch. He had a burlap sack flung over one shoulder with their clothes in it, and his cornet case slung over his other shoulder. In his hands he had the painfully heavy Victrola windup record player that, aside from his horn, was his prize possession, and on top of it a stack of records – the Original Dixieland Jazz Band, Enrico Caruso, Luisa Tetrazzini, Henry Burr – all tied together by a flimsy length of twine. Next to Lewis, Clarence groaned under the weight of a canvas bag full of his toys.

'We nearly there, boy,' said Lewis, with a smile, and Clarence grimaced.

'I'll tell you a ghost story if you want? About Jean Lafitte.'

But Clarence shook his head and turned his gaze to the street in front of him, and Lewis felt guilty once again that he had put the boy through the unsettling and painful process of moving out to Gretna and back again.

They crossed Liberty Street and approached the apartment. He put the Victrola and the records down with a groan, knocked on the door and rubbed the small of his back while he waited. After a few seconds the door swung open and Mayann Armstrong appeared, still wearing her blue-and-white maid's uniform. She was a stocky, robust woman, but a life of toil and stress had taken its toll and she had aged well beyond her thirty-three years. She peered at the two sorry figures in front of her with a frown, stared at Lewis's busted face, then at the belongings on the floor, and shook her head, then without a word wandered back into the apartment. Lewis nodded at Clarence and they picked up their things and shuffled in after her.

Inside the apartment the back door was open and from the

courtyard Lewis could hear the sound of women chatting, and children playing hopscotch. They put their things down and Clarence scrabbled about the floor settling his toys into their new home. Mayann leaned against the kitchen counter and stared at Lewis, her arms folded over her chest.

'What happened, boy?' she asked, some tenderness and concern entering her voice.

'I couldn't take it anymore,' said Lewis, and he told her about the increasingly quarrelsome atmosphere in the house in Gretna. The arguments had always included Daisy throwing something at him – shoes, records, toys, even bricks picked up from the street on one occasion. And Clarence would be in tears, clinging to their legs as they shouted at each other. Then Daisy had taken to swinging punches at his mouth, knowing it was his weak-spot. A busted lip meant he couldn't earn a living, and before long Lewis had decided to pack his things and head back across the river, choosing love of music over love of a woman.

While Lewis talked and Clarence knelt by their bags unpacking things haphazardly, Mayann listened to her son with a stony face. When he had finished, she didn't remind him she had been against the match with Daisy from the start, that she had fully expected something like this to happen. She held out her arms, and hugged him.

'You best get over to Mrs Parker's and see if you can borrow a mattress. And I guess we're gonna need some extra food.'

'I'll head on over to Zatterman's and Stahle's,' said Lewis, putting his hat back on his head. 'Red beans and a pound o' rice?' he asked with a smile, and Mayann smiled back at him and nodded.

Lewis walked to the door and opened it, but before he left he stopped and turned back to his mother, as if forgetting something. Mayann stared at him, and Lewis grinned. 'Thanks, Mama,' he said sheepishly, and Mayann shook her head. Then they heard a whirling noise and looked down to see Clarence had unpacked the records, had placed one on the platter of the Victrola, and was spinning the gramophone's handle like a top. As Lewis stepped out, the music from the Victrola started up, an aria from *The Barber of Seville*. The sound of Tetrazzini's voice floated past him and out onto the street, where it mixed with the jazz blaring out of the honky-tonks across the road. A few of the hustlers lounging about outside turned to see where the opera music was coming from and they caught Lewis's gaze. He smiled, tipped his hat at them, and ambled off in the direction of Rampart Street, picking at the scab on his lip.

17

Morning sunshine beamed through the gaps in a wooden fence and sliced through a yard brimming with clotheslines. The lines were stretched and doubled back across every available inch of space, and from them hung a sea of white sheets that flapped and danced briskly in the wind. In the center of the yard, in the middle of the swinging walls of laundry, sat a dark-skinned, emaciated Creole by the name of Bechet. He sat at a scrubbing board working soap into wet linen with long, wiry fingers, mumbling a folk song to himself under his breath. He heard a noise, stopped singing and peered upwards with a frown. A shape moved between the washing lines, a shadow of a man. A sheet was pulled back and the shape revealed itself to be Luca D'Andrea.

A grin broke out on Bechet's face and he spoke in a broken French accent. 'Luca! *Longtemps!* For a minute there, I thought you were a ghost.' Bechet chuckled to himself and Luca smiled back at him. The old Creole was a spindly man, with sun-cracked skin, and a near-perpetual smile. Luca peered at him sitting at his board in the center of his washman's yard, and he had the impression of a spider perched at the center of its web.

'How's life?' Bechet asked, his tone warm.

'Life's good,' replied Luca. 'How's the laundry trade?'

'Ah,' Bechet shrugged, 'linen gets dirty, linen gets clean.'

He peered up at Luca, squinting his eyes against the sun, his hands scouring out a slow, metallic rhythm on the scrubbing board.

'I assume this isn't a courtesy call,' said the old man, and Luca shook his head.

'I need information on the Axeman.'

Bechet stopped his scrubbing and a look of dismay crossed his face. 'The Axeman? Now why you wanna go chasing him?'

Luca frowned at him and shrugged. 'Why shouldn't I be chasing him?' he asked, and Bechet narrowed his eyes and lifted an index finger in his direction. 'Because it seems like to me,' the old man said, his finger wagging, soapsuds curling round the underside of his hand, 'the Axeman's a demon.'

Bechet burst into a loud, raucous cackle and moved his hands to his chest.

'You chasing a demon,' he said. 'A homegrown, New Orleans demon.'

Luca grimaced and gave Bechet a dismissive look. He had been buying information from the old man for nearly two decades, and although Bechet had always struck him as eccentric – it did take a certain type of character to run the risk of being an informer – in all those years, Luca had never known him to cackle and rant about demons. Luca had been seeking out all his old informants and associates since his release. Those who were still alive, and still lucid enough to talk, all told him the same thing – no one in the whole city knew anything about the Axeman, it was as if he didn't exist. And now Bechet was calling the killer a demon.

'I was thinking it might be a Creole,' said Luca, trying to get the conversation back on track. 'You hear of any Creoles with a taste for axes and a grudge?'

Bechet's laughing settled down and he shook his head.

'Plenty o' folks got grudges in New Orleans,' he said. Then he stared at Luca and held up the soap-bar he had been using on the sheets. 'You put all these poor folks together and squeeze 'em tight,' he said, squeezing the soap in his knotted, gangly hands. 'And you've molded a demon.' He opened his hand. 'A demon in the shape of New Orleans,' he continued, his eyes unusually cold. The old man shifted his gaze to the misshapen soap in his hands, then tutted to himself, as if having witnessed a sin, and he set about his work once more.

Luca frowned and wondered how those bony old fingers had the strength to crush a rock-hard bar of soap.

'This Creole hunt,' said Bechet, 'it ain't one of your frame-up jobs? Angola didn't teach you nothing?'

Luca shook his head. 'This ain't a frame-up,' he said, 'I think this might be voodou.'

'Voodou?' Bechet looked up at him with a bemused expression. 'Maybe. If you wanna know about this kinda stuff, I know a lady can help. I'll get you the details, but the price, it's gone up while you were away. What it was, plus ten.'

Luca shrugged, indicating money wasn't a problem, and Bechet grinned at him.

'Inflation, *mon ami*. This girl can help you out. In more ways than one,' he said, raising his eyebrows. He stood, wiped his hands on his trousers and stretched out the creaking armature of his back. Luca noticed a copper wire wrapped around Bechet's ankle, a slave charm to ward off consumption. Luca thought it strange – the old man was from Haiti, an island of freemen. Bechet resumed humming the folksong he had been singing to himself and ambled away, disappearing behind the lines of hanging sheets.

Luca looked around the yard while he waited. He felt strangely at home with the sheets dancing about in front of him, their shifting planes like a crisp, geometric fog. He had been out of prison long enough, but he still found himself craving enclosed spaces, nooks and crannies, holing himself up in his hotel room most nights. During his time in prison he didn't have to worry about where to go, what to eat, when to wash and sleep. Freedom meant concerning himself once more with the realm of weight, matter and consequence. It made him feel like a ghost re-entering the world. And he still had the feeling that somehow the world he had returned to was not quite the one he had left, or at least not the one he remembered. In Angola he had remade the outside into a pristine, sparkling place. And now he found he couldn't quite cope with the actuality of New Orleans, a polluted city of refuse and foul smells. Bechet's yard of sheets so white they glinted in the sun was the first place he had been since his release that actually felt clean. It gave him a sense of hope, that the slime and stench of Angola might, given enough time, be washed off him for good.

He took a cigarette from his packet and lit it. He had been smoking incessantly since his release, mainly because he hadn't really been eating. Whatever it was that had happened to his stomach in Angola didn't sit well with rich food, coffee or liquor. And so cigarettes had become the least painful option.

Eventually Bechet reappeared, hobbling back through the sheets, carrying with him a scrap of paper and two battered metal cups.

'No smoking here, Luca. Laundry gotta smell fresh,' he said, taking a deep breath of the morning air, tapping his chest with his palm. Luca flicked his cigarette onto the ground and stubbed it out with a swipe of his boot.

Bechet handed him the slip of paper and one of the cups. '*Bierre du pays*,' said Bechet. A Creole beer brewed from pineapples. Luca used to enjoy the tangy taste of the drink, but now he wondered what the beer would do to his stomach. Bechet held his cup up to toast the transaction, and Luca, out of politeness, clinked his cup against Bechet's and drank. Then he gave Bechet the money he had asked for and Bechet checked the notes before putting them into his shirt pocket and sitting back down on his stool.

'You know, this whole Axeman thing makes me laugh,' Bechet said. 'If you look at it from a Negro point of view. You haven't exactly been a friend to people o' color. You and all the police. Setting 'em up, beating 'em down, framing 'em, taking their money. Now some darkie's running round town killing whites, and everybody wonderin' who gonna be next.' Bechet shrugged. 'It was always gonna happen.'

Luca stared at the old man and nodded.

'I think you got a point there, old friend,' he said, tipping his hat at Bechet. '*Au revoir, mon ami.*'

He was about to turn and leave when Bechet spoke again.

'You know, we have a saying back in Haiti. *Complot plis fort passe ouanga.*'

Luca frowned. He had lived in New Orleans long enough to have picked up a decent French vocabulary, but the myriad dialects and turns of phrase of the Creoles and Cajuns still remained a mystery. Bechet picked up on his confusion and smiled.

'It means "conspiracy is greater than witchcraft".'

Luca smiled back. 'I'll keep that in mind,' he said. Then he turned and walked away from the old man, disappearing through the shifting white sheets.

18

When Michael looked back on his life, he felt its path had for the most part been directed by two, and only two, large and fateful decisions. The first of these was choosing to start a family with a colored woman, the second concerned the death of a book-keeper named Reginald Abner.

At the time of what came to be known as the Abner affair, Michael was partnered with a more experienced detective called Jeremiah Toby Wilson. The two men had been assigned to transfer a suspect, Reginald Abner, from the precinct to the courthouse and then on to the city jail. Transfers were not generally the work of detectives, but Abner was a special case. He had been arrested the day before on a murder charge, and in an attempt to get his sentence reduced, he had informed the bureau that he was willing to turn over evidence he claimed he had against Carlo Matranga, which could see the man electrocuted. The captain of the bureau at the time, although not completely convinced of Abner's story, assigned two detectives to babysit the transfer just in case. Michael and Wilson were considered among the most trustworthy of the bureau members, Michael on account of his youth, Wilson on account of his age.

But Wilson didn't show for work that day, and in his absence Luca was given the job of overseeing the transfer. Michael had heard the stories about Luca, and he knew of the rumors that linked him to the Matrangas. So the fact that the captain had chosen Luca to oversee the transfer made Michael uneasy.

The two of them met in the bureau and headed down the stairs that led into the yard. The yard was a dusty, open space that housed the precinct stables and its wagons, and was surrounded by high brick walls. It was sunny when they entered, the day falling in the sweet spot between the foggy season and the height of summer. The wagon assigned for the transfer was already horsed and waiting for them, standing just in front of the bolted iron gates that led out onto the street. Luca ordered Michael to ride up top with the driver, while he accompanied Abner in the back. One of the stable hands opened the heavy, squealing gates and the driver leashed the horses out onto the street.

They rode without incident for a quarter of an hour, slowly threading their way through the morning traffic. The sun beat down on them, making the wagon's buckles and running-boards gleam and the horses' bodies glisten with sweat. As they reached the edge of the business district, where the thoroughfares became a little wider and unencumbered, they were halted by a blockage in the street ahead of them – a market man's stall had overturned in the road. Vegetables and fruits had spilled along the manure-strewn street, and a crowd of people had formed, some trying to help the owner right the stall, others surreptitiously helping themselves to the produce.

The driver halted the wagon behind another two carriages that had been gridlocked by the blockage and, crossing the reins over his knees, let out a sigh. Among the crowd, Michael heard the wail of a watermelon man. 'Watermelon! Watermelon! Red to the rind! If you don't believe me just pull down your blind!'

Then he heard a metallic noise to his side. He turned and peered down at the wagon door. Against all regulations, Luca had gotten out of the back of the wagon and was approaching the blockage, leaving Abner unaccompanied, and, to Michael's amazement, he had left the door unlocked.

Michael moved to get down off the top of the wagon, but the driver grabbed his shoulder in a strong, farm-hand's grip.

'Where you going, son?' he asked.

'Going to keep an eye on the prisoner,' Michael replied.

'Stay here.' The driver clamped his hand firmly on Michael's shoulder.

He should have noticed the driver's tone – that he was issuing advice not an order, but Michael grimaced, pulled away and jumped off the top of the wagon.

'Goddamit!' yelled the driver after him.

Michael was stepping round the side of the wagon when Luca happened to turn his way. Luca froze when he saw Michael, then he sprinted forwards. Michael heard people in the crowd screaming and he saw Luca shouting at him, but he couldn't make out what he was saying.

Confused, Michael scanned his surroundings – he could see the open door of the carriage, and Luca running towards him, his face fixed in a shriek, and he could feel the uproar in the crowd, and then he saw them dispersing in a wave. Three men, red bandanas over their faces, guns gleaming in their hands, were running through the crowd, knocking people to the ground.

Michael rushed forward to get the door locked before the men reached it, even as they were raising their weapons towards him. But something heavy grabbed him from behind and knocked him to the floor. The men reached the wagon and swung the door back. Michael heard Abner's horrified screams then the crack of gunshots, shrill and bursting in his ears. The bullets ripped into Abner and the man collapsed onto the carriage floor. The men fired countless rounds into the body, then they turned to make their escape, sprinting through the now emptied road, disappearing round a corner.

The whole episode only took a few seconds, but to Michael it felt like an eternity, a long and silent shadow play he was too shocked to understand. He remembered where he was – pinned to the ground next to the wagon he was supposed to be protecting. The men were gone, but Luca was still holding onto him. Blood from the wagon was dripping out of the door, pooling on the grimy street. The crowd had come out of hiding, raising up a chorus of wails through which Luca hissed into Michael's ear.

'You tell them I knocked you over to save your life. You tell them they jimmied the door.'

Michael said nothing, still too shocked to speak.

'Got it?'

Luca's breath was hot on his ear and the back of his neck. He could smell cigarettes and the ferrous tang of blood. Michael nodded and Luca got off him. The crowd watched them as they both stood. Luca dusted himself down and went to speak to the driver.

Michael glanced about him, dazed, head spinning. He stared into the wagon, at Abner's slumped form, half his head sprayed across the interior. The crowd came closer, peering at Michael and the wagon. Michael suddenly felt claustrophobic and he started hyperventilating, feeling like he might fall to the floor again. He put a hand against the side of the wagon and breathed deeply and slow. He peered up and caught the eye of a teenage girl in the crowd.

'He stopped you,' she said flatly, nodding towards Luca.

'I know.'

Later that day, still dazed by what had happened, Michael found himself sitting in a waiting room in the judicial buildings that housed the District Attorney's offices. A secretary, of the type Michael had only ever read about in magazines, swung her hips into the waiting room and ushered him into a west-facing office that was filled with the glare of the afternoon sun. Three men sat behind a table in front of a long bank of windows, their features dimmed by the blazing light behind them. Michael recognized one of the men instantly – the Deputy Inspector of Police. Another he knew to be an official from the District Attorney's office, but the third man he had never seen before, and no one took the time to introduce him. Michael got the impression from the man's dress and the authority he seemed to have over the other two that he was either from the administration in Baton Rouge, or from an agency further north.

Michael took a seat and the official, a bespectacled, birdlike man, asked after his health, if he had suffered any ill effects from the day's events. Michael answered that it was still too early to tell and the response caused the three men to smile awkwardly. Then the DI cleared his throat and addressed Michael in a fatherly tone, stern but with a little warmth.

'Son, we read your report and we're not buying it. Witnesses came forward. We know they didn't jimmy the door. We know D'Andrea held you back. If you continue protesting that's what happened we'll charge you with accessory to murder, along with D'Andrea, and you'll wind up in Angola with the three animals that actually fired the bullets.'

Michael suddenly noticed a dryness in his throat, a feeling of broken glass when he swallowed. He peered up at the men, but the light blazing in from the windows behind them hurt his eyes, and he had to put his hand up to his head.

'D'Andrea being put in charge of that transfer wasn't an accident, son,' the DI said. 'We planned it. We gave him enough rope to hang himself and, well, he's hanged himself. In the most spectacular fashion imaginable.'

The DI smiled and leaned over the table towards Michael, something silhouetted in his hand. Michael realized he was offering him a cigarette. He took one from the pack and nodded his thanks.

'We know you're honest, an exemplary record and so on, that's why we partnered you with D'Andrea today. We'd like to make you an offer.'

Michael lit the cigarette and took a drag and the smoke felt like rubble in his throat. The glare of the sun was making his head pound, and he was straining his eyes to make out the silhouettes of the three men. He assumed the alignment of the table in front of the window and the afternoon sun was deliberate.

'We'd all like to see an end to D'Andrea and his cabal,' the DI continued. 'We could bring him down on charges for today's little incident, but that would only sever one of the hydra's heads. What we'd really like to do is get the lot of them, and to do that we need someone on the inside. That's the offer we'd like to make to you, son. Gain D'Andrea's confidence, become a part of his group, document the goings-on, and then we can take down the whole sorry lot of them. So what do you say, son? Would you like to help safeguard the integrity and reputation of the bureau?'

Michael looked about him for an ashtray and he realized that although he had offered him the cigarette, the DI himself wasn't smoking. He needed a painkiller and a dark room to lie down in. He squinted his eyes against the burning windows. Would they really charge him with accessory to murder for what had happened?

'I, uh, I don't know D'Andrea at all, sir,' he said. 'I don't see how I could infiltrate his clique.'

At this the third man leaned forward and smiled at him. 'That's perfectly fine,' he said, his voice unruffled. 'We've already planned that out for you.'

19

The day after Ida and Lewis followed the house-breaker to the docks, Ida attempted to retrace their steps, hoping to find the warehouse the boy had met the Cajun in before the breadcrumb trail of her memories disappeared once and for all. She'd been surprised to learn that the man paying the boy to search the crime scenes was a Cajun. What business did a Cajun furrier have with a group of Italian grocers? If she could find the warehouse, she could find out who owned it and put a name to the face, and she cursed herself for not getting the details the previous night.

In the couple of hours she had managed to sleep, she had dreamed a memory of the night's events, somehow mixed with a recollection of Sherlock Holmes's nocturnal search among the docks of London in *The Sign of Four*, a search which, she remembered with a pang of panic on waking, had proved unsuccessful. She didn't bother to eat breakfast, instead drinking a glass of milk before making her way down to the docks with a sting in her eyes and a light head from lack of sleep.

She only realized after she arrived that the docks were not a fit place for a person made clumsy by sleep deprivation. Coal barges, freight ships, tugboats and ocean liners jostled for space in the harbor, a forest of sails, masts and funnels swelling on the water. And on the wharves, carts, wagons and people shifted about endlessly. Cranes swung freight from the bowels of ships onto the dockside, building up stacks of cargo boxes that towered into the sky like giant anthills, which were dismantled just as soon by an army of stevedores and loaded onto wagons headed for the train depot.

The workers were Negroes for the most part, roustabouts who

couldn't read or write, so the movement of cargo was arranged by the use of a system of colored flags, hundreds of which, in myriad schemes and colors, fluttered over the cargo areas, ships' hulls, train wagons and wharves, and lent the docks a festive, jaunty air. The workers were anything but: they were hard, taciturn and weather-beaten men, but on seeing Ida some of them changed their demeanor, declaring undying love for her with grins and elbows in their coworkers' ribs. Ida ignored them and bumped past knots of businessmen and shipping clerks with inkstained fingers, who were attempting to impose some kind of order on the chaos, and she staggered past bleary-eyed passengers from Liverpool, Lisbon and Le Havre disgorged by the giant transatlantic ocean liners that brooded silently in their berths. She fell in with the flow of people, aimlessly pushed along the wharves, only hearing vaguely the blasts of ships' whistles, the gull squawks, the crash of machinery, the slap of the yellow river against the banks and the constant work-songs of the men.

At some point she arrived at a jetty where a crowd had gathered in a hushed cluster. They were standing by the edge of some planks that overhung the waters, circled around some activity that Ida couldn't make out. The atmosphere was solemn and expectant, like the mood outside the newspaper offices when crowds gathered to hear the election results. She stopped to see what was going on, but couldn't get a good view. She slid through the press to get closer to the center and managed to catch a look at three stevedores, muscled Negroes in dirty shirts and jeans, fishing at something in the water with a pole. Two policemen stood next to them, directing oper-ations with barks and gesticulations. Something had been found entangled in the mooring posts off the jetty and the crowd whis-pered at what it might be.

After a few minutes, the two larger stevedores took control of the pole they had extended into the waters, and with a back-bending heave they hoisted something onto the jetty. It took Ida a few seconds to realize what it was – the decomposing corpse of a naked young girl. The crowd gasped, and the policemen attempted to form a cordon around their doleful catch. Ida stepped back in shock, casting her gaze as quickly as she could from the girl's dripping body, from the lifeless green eyes, the blackened nails, the mess of blonde hair.

A taste of vomit rose into her mouth and she lumbered backwards, out of the throng. She raised a hand to her head and only vaguely heard the crowd as it murmured and prayed for the unfortunate soul. Ida stumbled on, trying to get the image out of her head, feeling like she might be sick at any moment. She let herself be taken up again by the movement of the people and she lost track of time. She wasn't sure how long she drifted among the crowds, but at one point, far from the center of the docks, she realized the crowds had thinned out and she found herself alone on an almost empty wharf, standing in front of a tin-shack café. She wandered in and ordered a tea, a drink she only ever consumed when ill. She sat for a while cradling the steaming cup, taking sips and trying her hardest not to vomit. The café was quiet, and looked out onto the wharf, where some longshoremen were loading sacks of grain onto a wagon. They had set the sacks on a raised platform to stop the wharf-rats – the vagrants who lived under the docks – from running knives between the gaps in the planks of the wharf and siphoning off the contents of the sacks. Ida was close enough to hear the longshoremen's work-songs and she listened to them singing as she finished her drink.

> *Got the riverfront blues and I'm blue as can be*
> *That ole Mississippi sure makes a fool outta me . . .*

The song had much of the river to it, a soothing sound, lullaby-like, a lilting, back-and-forth rhythm, soft like the tide, or the slap of waves against the docks.

> *My baby is there when the man gives me my check*
> *But when I looks at the river I feel like cuttin' my neck*

Ida left a nickel on the counter and stepped out onto the wharf. A flock of gulls flew about above her head, excited and arcing around in circles – a sign of bad weather to come. A couple of pan ladies walked past her, vendors of hot pies, sandwiches and candies carried in cloth-covered trays at their waists. The women looked at Ida, then one of them said something to the other, and they laughed. Ida watched them for a moment, then she buttoned up her coat and left the docks, the serenade of the river and its workers softening as she walked.

> *Up every morning when the clock strikes five*
> *And I don't know if I'm even comin' back alive*

She made her way along the spider's web of streets and alleyways that radiated from the ancient wharves like Amsterdam canals, checking for landmarks and paths from the previous night. Eventually, as dusk was approaching, and quite by chance, she found the warehouse. Circling it, she came to the entrance gate, and next to it a sign listing its owner and occupier – a fur-trading and garment-manufacturing company owned by a man named John Morval. Even in her half-dazed state, she recognized the name, and realized with a sinking feeling that her theories about the killer might well be all wrong, and the answer might not lie in the goings-on of a counterfeiting gang. Morval was the man who owned the garment company Mrs Romano had worked for – the company that had mysteriously paid the Axeman's victim a monthly allowance after she was blinded at work.

20

Luca walked from Bechet's house in the 7th Ward to Florida Avenue and caught the streetcar westwards, all the way to the City Park, where he got off and continued the journey on foot, heading north up Bayou St John. Before it fell into disuse, the bayou was the main transportation route between Lake Pontchartrain and the Mississippi. Now it collected weeds. As Luca journeyed north along its bank, he noticed that rich people had built picturesque summer houses on the stretches nearest the city, where the grasses and reeds had been cut back to give the bayou a tame, contrived beauty. Further away, the summer houses gave way to the dwellings of poorer families, who had set up homes on the bayou itself, in slipshod, leaky riverboats.

Addresses didn't mean much out in the bayou, so the paper Bechet had given Luca contained instead a set of directions and a name. Luca journeyed northwards till he was about halfway between the lake and the city before turning west and heading into the maze of paths that snaked through the swamps between the bayou and Metairie. The swamps were a desolate, secluded place, an empty half-world of water and land that had an unsettling effect on Luca. The more he trekked into the mangroves the more eerie he felt the landscape become; twisting tree roots rose up out of the water, snaking around bulrushes, water-lilies, tamaracks and a hundred other plants whose names he didn't know. Above him willow trees, cypresses and palmettos linked their branches over the pathways, clustering so thickly that Luca felt as if he was journeying through a rabbit hole. This impression was heightened by the Spanish moss that blanketed the trees like teal-colored snow, hanging off branches, smoothing the edges of the world until the landscape lost its sharpness and everything merged into a single bewildering shape, indistinct and otherworldly.

Occasionally he came across a shack, set back from the path, solitary and scrabbled together from discarded wood, sheets of tin and reclaimed advertising signs. The effect made the buildings look like scrap-book collages, with multi-colored advertising logos and slogans cut up and woven haphazardly into the walls. Some of the shacks were still lived in, others abandoned. The swamps were home to a shifting population of disparate, disenfranchised people, mainly small communities of Negroes or Cajuns, who lived in shanty villages and fished the waterways, or trapped animals for their fur. When Luca happened to pass them, they stared at him with suspicious, unwelcoming eyes.

As he journeyed he wondered why a voodou priestess was living among the chaos of the mangroves, and not in some gaudy consulting room on Canal Street. The time of the priestesses had long since passed, their halcyon days having been in the middle of the previous century, when the great and good of New Orleans consulted them on all manner of problems. The priestesses, dressed in colorful *tignons* and flowing robes, conjured spells for society ladies in Haitian or Congolese, or prepared ointments and potions, or divined the future through the casting of chicken bones, or contacted the spirits of the dead in ghoulish séances. The whites paid them handsomely and held them in such high esteem that the most famous priestesses were regular attendees at society functions, at a time when other colored people were treated no better than cattle.

But the customers didn't realize the industry was a sham, built on a network of messengers and connections. The colored servants of the rich would collect information about the goings-on in their employers' households and sell it to whichever priestess their masters were consulting. When the clients arrived for a consultation the priestesses knew, as if by magic, all their intimacies. The pantomime the priestesses performed – a mix of the occult,

Catholicism and African magic – held its charm for well over a century, but eventually the priestesses fell from grace. Their presence ebbed, from the gilded ballrooms of New Orleans to the cheap apartments of Canal Street, and now, it seemed, even all the way to swamps outside of town.

Presently Luca came to a group of shacks and cabins on the edge of a small lake hemmed in by trees and bushes. He checked the directions again and guessed he was at his destination. The lake emitted a stagnant humidity and strange animal calls rose up from the mangroves on its far side. Luca put the paper back in his pocket and was trudging along the dirt track that connected the shacks when he heard a girl's scream tear through the sky. He dashed along the path until he came to the source of the scream, a cabin on the near side of the lake, and swung open the door.

In the corner of the single room, an overweight colored woman in a blue smock sat in a chair, crying into a handkerchief. On a table in the middle of the space sat a teenage colored girl, her legs spread apart, and kneeling in front of her was a Creole woman tending to the girl's crotch – sewing up some kind of wound while the girl yelped and writhed in pain. Blood sullied the girl's skirt and dripped down the edges of the table, pooling on the warped floorboards below.

When Luca opened the door the three women turned to look at him, and instantly turned back to the matter in hand. The Creole woman spoke to the girl, who couldn't have been more than fifteen years old, in smooth, French-accented tones, and the girl wailed and clenched her hands to the side of the table. The Creole woman brought a thread up from the girl's crotch and broke it off, carefully knotting it a few times.

'All done now. Just need to clean you up,' she said, in a warm, coaxing voice, then she stood and stared at Luca.

'Wait outside,' she said dismissively, taking a bucket and cloth from the kitchen counter and returning to the girl.

*

Luca sat on the steps outside the cabin for a half-hour or so, smoking cigarettes while he waited. Around the building was a yard of sorts, delineated by a half-collapsed wire fence, inside of which a handful of underfed chickens strutted around, pecking food from the grasses and weeds. There were a couple of barrels of rainwater in one corner of the yard and a smoke pit in the other. Luca noticed two basil plants placed either side of the front door, one male, one female – an old slave superstition to ward off bad spirits.

Beyond the yard was the desolate lake on whose opposite bank, amid the mangroves, stood a few other, lonely shacks, and beyond them, the bayou. When the wind whistled through the mangroves a perturbing whine rose into the air, soared into a crescendo, then died down again to nothingness. Luca became aware of a lyrical quality to the noise, and he wondered if what he was hearing was the wind, or the call of some unknown creature, or if the noise was the sound of the mangrove itself, lamenting its own mournful existence.

His thoughts were interrupted by the door opening. The girl limped out, resting one hand on the older woman's shoulder, and gripping a roughly-hewn crutch with the other. They gave Luca strange, embarrassed looks as they hobbled past him and down the steps. They made their way along the dirt track, their progress slow, and Luca wondered if he should offer to help. But he was unsure if he could help, or even if they wanted his assistance, so he did nothing but tip his hat at them and hope they didn't have far to travel.

He realized the Creole woman was standing behind him, also watching the pair depart. Seeing her up close, Luca noticed she was only a little younger than him, and she was unusually beautiful. Burnt almond skin and high cheekbones and a fragile depth to her eyes. Her hair was pulled back from her face and was onyx-black except for a few gray strands at her temples. Luca peered at her a moment, and she met his gaze with an open, forthright look.

'What happened to her?' Luca asked, gesturing towards the retreating figures. The Creole woman frowned at him, as if she didn't believe his interest was genuine, then she nodded towards the dirt track.

'She got pregnant. Her mama took her to a back-room quack to get rid of it. Same old story,' she said, her accent a lilting mix of French and diphthong-rich New Orleans. 'The quack took her money and got rid of the baby, but he pretty much destroyed her womb. She would've bled to death if she hadn't come to me.'

Luca frowned, then returned his gaze to the track to look at the forlorn mother and daughter once more, but they had already disappeared from view.

'Is she gonna be OK?' he asked.

The Creole woman shrugged.

'She'll live. That's the main thing,' she said. 'But she don't ever have to worry about getting pregnant again.'

She stepped forward and sat on the porch next to Luca, and Luca noticed the fragrance of rosewater on her skin, the scent of coconut oil in her hair. He realized he hadn't been this close to a woman since before Angola, and something about her closeness, her scent, made his freedom seem more real.

He smiled and offered her a cigarette, and she accepted. As Luca leaned over to light it for her, he noticed the bloodstains on her arms and dress.

'My name's Simone,' she said after thanking him and taking a deep draw of smoke.

'Luca,' he responded, shaking the flame from the lucifer in his fingers.

'Italian?' she asked with a frown, and Luca nodded.

She looked at him for a moment and Luca got the feeling she was weighing him up. Then she turned from him and grabbed a bucket of water that was sitting on the porch. With the cigarette clenched between her teeth, she rolled up her sleeves and washed the blood from her arms.

'What can I do for you?' she asked, her tone suddenly cold and distant.

'I heard you're a *voodouienne*,' said Luca, feeling a little foolish.

'And who've you been talking to to hear that?' she asked.

Luca shrugged. 'A friend of mine in the city,' he said.

She stared at him again, the same far-off, guarded look. Then she smiled to herself and Luca got the feeling she was mocking him in some elaborate, personal way.

'I'm not a priestess,' she said, 'but if you tell me what your problem is, I'll tell you if I can help.'

Luca tried to judge the best way to approach her. He'd composed a line of inquiry on the journey there, a convoluted story that the average person might buy, but now he wasn't sure it would work on her.

'If you don't tell me what's wrong, I can't help you.' She took her hands out of the bucket and dried them on the apron around her waist.

'What's the matter?' She took a drag of her cigarette. 'Need a love potion? Want me to smite someone? If you want that there's a hundred fake "spiritualists" in town. Just take a walk down Canal Street and stop wasting my time.'

She had her head cocked to one side as she spoke and Luca caught the full glare of her eyes, a deep, distracting hazelnut brown tinted with flecks of green.

'Is that what people come to you for?' he asked.

'The stupid ones. Most just come here when they can't afford a doctor. Like the girl and her mother,' she said, nodding towards the dirt track.

Luca paused and wondered why Bechet had sent him here. The woman was some kind of country medic, a midwife and nurse; she probably had as little in common with the priestesses on Canal Street as the average surgeon did.

'I'm investigating the Axeman murders,' he said. 'I'm not a policeman, I'm a private detective, and—'

'Why are you asking me?' she interrupted.

Luca shrugged. 'The killer's been leaving tarot cards at the crime scenes. French cards. The type I know are used in voodou rituals.'

She stared at him with a half-suspicious, unsettling look that made Luca feel guilty for some reason.

'You can buy those tarot cards in any dime store in town. I wouldn't think them important. Voodou's not demons and blood and witches and crazy people running around with axes. It's just medicine for poor folks. Slave masters got scared of it and made up a bunch o' horror stories. How'd you know it's not a white man, making it look like it was a Creole? Leave a few tarot cards behind to prove the point. Police are quick to blame a colored man for anything.'

Luca nodded. The cards could be a red herring, left by the killer to throw the police off the scent. But they felt like something more to Luca, they felt like a message.

'These aren't normal cards,' he said. 'They're expensive. Hand-painted with gold ink, they're about so big.' He held up his hands to indicate the size, and Simone stared at him with a frown. 'You know where someone would get ahold of cards like that?'

'Sure,' said Simone. 'The voodou priestess department store, just off Canal.'

Luca frowned, then turned to look at her and saw a girlish grin had crossed her face. He smiled at her, surprised she had made the joke. She had struck him as a serious type, taciturn and aloof, but the joke had made her seem softer, down-to-earth, easier to warm to. But as quickly as the grin had appeared it was replaced by a mournful look, as if she regretted the intimacy the joke had brought about.

'I've seen cards like that before,' she said, her tone serious once more. 'Years ago. I don't think you can buy 'em in New Orleans. Ones I saw, a Frenchman brought over from Marseilles. I guess you'd could call 'em collectors' items. Maybe you should be looking for rich Europeans.'

She turned to peer at him and he smiled back at her. Rich Europeans weren't exactly what he'd had in mind. He nodded and Simone shrugged, and the two of them stared into the distance.

'If you don't mind me asking,' Luca said, 'how'd you get into this?'

Simone smiled, remembering a long-distant memory. 'My mother,' she said, her voice heavy with nostalgia.

Luca smiled back at her. 'My mother used to read the *tarocchi* back in Italy,' he said.

She nodded and they lapsed into silence once more. When they'd finished their cigarettes she surprised Luca by asking him if he would like some tea. Luca, who had been expecting her to send him on his way, accepted with a smile, and she made the tea and they sat on the porch drinking it, talking of this and that, both of them happy to watch the day go past. It had been years since Luca had spent time with a woman, but he seemed to regain his charm with her, settling into the easy manner he was known for before his fall. In their conversation he caught a glimpse of what his life might be like when he left New Orleans behind — a life of sitting in the open and talking of nothing, whiling away the time, free from worrying about unatoned-for sins.

As they talked the wind murmured through the trees and whistled through the cracks in the wood-paneled cabin, making it moan and strain.

'It's been blowing a gale two days now,' she said. 'There's a storm coming.'

Luca glanced around him — dusk had firmly settled on the handful of buildings scattered around the dirt track, and the sky was gathering dark. Simone stood and made her way into the yard. She grabbed a bail of juniper branches speckled with berries and threw it into the smoke pit. They lit the bail so the smoke from the berries would keep the mosquitoes away and they watched the fire a little, before Simone nodded to the swamps behind the yard.

'Spook-lights,' she said, and Luca followed her gaze. In distant patches all across the swamps flickering blue flames glowed and danced about on the ground, methane bubbling up through the earth and catching the light.

'Jack o' lanterns, we call them,' said Luca, 'or will o' the wisps.' They watched the ghostly phosphorescence for a few moments, sweeping across the black ground like some stunted, earthbound northern lights, then they returned to their place on the porch. A few of the bayou-dwellers had lit juniper fires too, and their houses glowed orange in the gloom. One of the neighbors on the far side of the lake picked out a song on a mandolin, minor chords that floated across the water and twisted about the mangroves with the whining of the wind.

Luca felt there was a heaviness to the backwaters, a mournful quality, as if they were on the edge of something more than just the bayou; the place felt deathly and hellish.

'You're not gonna get back to New Orleans before night,' Simone said, turning to peer at him with a smile, the orange of the juniper fires flickering in her eyes.

REPORT OF HOMICIDE
Department of Police

First Precinct, New Orleans	Sat. April 12th 1919
Name of Person Killed:	Unknown
Residence:	Unknown
Business:	Unknown
Name of accused:	Unknown
Residence:	Unknown
Business:	Unknown
Location of homicide:	Unknown
Day, date, hour committed:	bet. Thu. April 10th & Fri. April 11th (Coroner's Clerk initial estimate, see below)
By whom reported:	Harry Majest (colored), 1827 Chippewa Street
To whom reported:	Corporal Bernard Yeager
Time reported:	11 o'clock A.M. Sat. April 12th
If arrested, by whom:	Still At Large
Where arrested:	N/A
If escaped, in what manner:	N/A
Witnesses:	Harry Majest (colored), # 1827 Chippewa Street Jonas Mouney (colored), # 1232 Perdido Street

Detailed Report

Capt. Paul Coman reports that at 11 o'clock this A.M. Wed. 9th April, Harry Majest (Negro), residing at # 1827 Chippewa Street and a man-of-all-work in the employ of the Audubon Zoo came to this station and informed Corporal Bernard Yeagar that a body had been discovered in Audubon Park. Corporal Yeager and Patrolman James A. Burns immediately proceeded to the above place in the Precinct Wagon and on arrival there discovered the body, partially buried in the center of a clump of oaks in a secluded section to the south of the park.

With the help of Mr Majest and another worker at the Zoo (see attached witness reports, Majest H. #1-2698-1919, Mouney J. #1-2699-1919), Corporal Yeager and Patrolman Burns successfully unearthed the body. They thereupon noticed two bullet wounds in the victim's forehead, roughly an inch apart, an inch and a half above the right eyebrow. Also extensive lacerations and bruising around the face and rear cranium. The victim's hands were tied together behind him with twine.

As of writing of this report the body is yet to be identified. Cursory Bertillon statistics reported at scene by Corporal Yeagar: male, Caucasian, mid 20s, crop-cut red hair, blue eyes, no distinguishing marks. For a full description, see attached, Initial Coroner's Report, Hunter J. # c-8733-1919.

Corporal Yeagar notified by telephone Your Office at 12.55 P.M., Patrolman Peter Styles, and also the Coroner's office, Clerk John Gazave. Whereupon Mr John Hunter, Clerk to the Coroner's Office, arrived up on the scene circa 1.35 P.M.

By order of Mr Hunter the body was removed to the Morgue at the Charity Hospital in the First Precinct Patrol Wagon, in charge, Driver William Godfrey and Patrolman Peter Styles.

Mr Hunter's initial report (see attached, *ibid.*) was that judging from the levels of decomposition, the man had been killed no more than two days previously, and had been buried immediately upon death.

Victim's clothes (one brown tweed sports jacket, white cotton shirt, black cotton trousers, and undergarments) were removed to the Coroner's Office. Also possessions: one silk handkerchief (found breast pocket of jacket), one return train ticket to Baton Rouge, 2nd class, purchase date 1st April (found left jacket pocket).

Carbon copies of this report, attached Witness Statements, and Initial Coroner's Report have been sent to the Detective Bureau at the First Precinct Station.

> Very respectfully,
> Capt. Paul Coman
> Captain Comd'g Prec't
> W.D. Watson, Clerk

21

Raindrops tapped a metal rhythm on the roof of Lewis's room. The rhythm became music and as he slept, the music entered his dream; the dream of a memory from when he was seven years old, the first time he lived with Mayann. Mayann was twenty-two at the time, and she had a new man who, looking to impress, took her and Lewis to a riverbank outside the city for a Sunday afternoon picnic. After they'd laid down the blanket and eaten the food, Mayann and the man got to drinking and sent Lewis out to explore.

Lewis wandered off, through riverside undergrowth and clumps of trees, until he reached an open sun-baked field, where he heard a strange noise, faint and wailing, carried on the breeze. The noise twisted and doubled back on itself like an ampersand snaking through the air, music of a type Lewis could never have imagined, notes which slurred into each other like a soft, sorrowful voice. He followed the music all the way to its source – a copse on the far side of a fresh-cut field, where an ageing dark-skinned man with matted hair, ragged clothes and a wild look played a Kress horn, a dented tube of tin two feet long. The man saw Lewis and he stopped playing and smiled, crooked yellow teeth standing out defiantly against the gaps in his gums. Lewis halted and stared at the man.

'What you playing?'

'You ain't never heard it before?' The man spoke in a hard, broken accent, and Lewis shook his head.

'I'm playing the blues.'

The man grinned and started playing again. The same mournful talking sound. Percussion began to accompany him, soft at first, then louder, a steady thumping, a knocking at the door.

Lewis woke, wiped the sleep from his eyes and opened the door to a rain-sodden Ida. She came inside without a word and they sat on the bed and Lewis gave her a rag to dry herself off.

'Dammit, my hair's gonna kink,' she said as she wiped the rag about her head.

Lewis would have liked to offer her some food and drink, but all he had in the house was a pail of water and some leftover catfish heads. He poured two cups of water from the pail and proffered a cigarette in lieu of food, which Ida accepted. As they smoked, she filled him in on what she had been up to since they last met – the trip to the docks, finding out the name of the garment factory owner, and the background checks she had performed to find out as much as she could about the man. She had followed the protocol Lefebvre had taught her for researching a suspect. She'd been through the Pinkertons' own records first, and finding nothing, she moved on to the publicly available records in City Hall, and then the musty back issues of local newspapers in the library. She gave Lefebvre the excuse that she was updating the Pinkertons' files, killing the downtime between jobs with tedious clerical work that Lefebvre was only too happy not to get involved in.

She then mosaicked the pieces of information into a picture of the man who had been paying someone to search the crime scenes. Most of what she found related to Morval's business, the fur-trading company he had run for over twenty years, which had made him, as she found out, one of the richest men in the city. In addition to trading furs, he had expanded into making other types of clothing and hit gold about ten years previously when he was awarded the contract to make the uniforms for a roster of local government agencies – most notably the police. Morval's main supplier of textiles was a man named Sam Carolla, someone the Pinkertons did have files on. Carolla was a Mafioso. Ida noted the irony: the boys in blue were wearing clothes supplied by the Black Hand.

In the court records Ida dredged through she found the lead she was looking for – Morval's former business partner, a man named Elliot Hudson. Just before Morval landed his government contracts, he bought Hudson out of his side of the business. A few weeks later, Hudson filed a suit against Morval claiming coercion in the sale. A week after that, Hudson abruptly withdrew the suit. It all pointed to a bitter falling out, which was probably followed by Morval threatening Hudson into giving up the legal action. Ida had figured if she could convince Hudson that it was safe to talk to her, and if the man still harbored a grudge against Morval, she could use him to find out what she needed to know.

'John Morval must've been the guy in the fox-fur coat, the one we saw questioning the kid that broke into the Maggios',' she said, recalling the bearlike man they had spied on in the warehouse.

'Just because he was in there and calling the shots, doesn't mean he's the owner of the place,' said Lewis.

'No,' Ida agreed, 'but remember there was a safe in the corner of the warehouse, and the fox-fur guy clipped a safe-key onto his belt. Only the owner or the manager's gonna have the key to the safe.'

Lewis gave her a look and Ida smiled. *It is my business to know things*, she thought, quoting from 'A Case of Identity'. *I have trained myself to see what others overlook.*

'I wanna interview Hudson,' she went on. 'He'll tell us more about Morval, about his deal with the Black Hand. I'm thinking if Morval works with the Black Hand and he's involved in the killings, the Black Hand's probably involved too.'

'How you so sure this guy's gonna talk to us anyway?' asked Lewis.

'Morval screwed him out of his half of the company. Anyway, I sent him a telegram and offered him some money. I got the feeling he was on the broke side.'

Lewis peered at her quizzically. 'And where'd you get the money from?'

Ida bit her bottom lip and smiled at him.

'We got a fund at the office for paying informants. I dipped into it. Lefebvre ain't gonna notice. He's skimming money out of it himself.'

Lewis stared at her and play-acted being shocked. 'I never thought I'd see the day,' he said with mock indignation. 'How much you take?'

'Twenty-five,' she said sheepishly and they both grinned.

Elliot Hudson lived in a boarding house in the Irish Channel, a low-rent blue-collar neighborhood populated mostly by Irish immigrants. Ida knocked at the boarding-house door and a blocky woman in an apron and a shapeless dress answered.

'Hello. We're here to see Mr Hudson, please,' Ida said, flashing her best smile.

'Third floor,' said the woman, jabbing her thumb backwards. She stood aside to let Ida through, but as Lewis tried to pass her, the woman held up her hand.

'No Negroes,' she said with a single shake of the head.

Ida and Lewis stopped and looked at each other.

'Ma'am,' said Ida, turning to face the woman, 'we're here to see Mr Hudson on business.'

The woman stared at Ida. 'I don't make the rules, miss,' she said, her voice harsh and sullen, 'so I ain't in no position to change 'em.'

She glared at Ida and Ida glared back.

'It's fine,' said Lewis. 'I'll stay outside.'

'In the rain?'

'It's fine. Just go on up,' said Lewis, his voice soft, his eyes projecting a knowing fear – *We're in the Irish channel, Ida. Don't cause a fuss*.

Ida frowned at him for a moment and then she nodded, realizing his concern. She grimaced at the woman and stomped into the building. The woman watched her go, and without a word slammed the door in Lewis's face.

*

Ida ascended the stairs three flights and knocked on the door with Hudson's name on it. The door swung open and a sleepy man with a two-day stubble peered at her. He wore a vest and a pair of stained trousers held up by a cord belt, and nothing on his feet.

'Mr Hudson? I'm Miss Davis. We corresponded by telegram.'

'Ah, Miss Davis. Come in,' he said, his voice strained.

It was a one-bedroom apartment that smelled of dust and the bed-sheets of a man just woken up. A stove, a wardrobe and a bed took up most of the room, leaving just enough space for a tiny table and two chairs by a solitary window. Hudson gestured for Ida to take a seat at the table and he ambled over to the stove, scratching his face as he went. Ida sat and noticed a foul-smelling bucket at the foot of the table.

'You'll have to excuse me,' said Hudson, 'I just woke up. Coffee?'

'Thank you,' said Ida, peering at the bucket, which was filled with tarry brown spit.

'I hope you don't mind Turkish,' said Hudson as he spooned ground coffee beans into a pan.

'That's fine,' Ida said, looking up from the bucket, not really sure what Turkish coffee tasted like.

'You never mentioned which detective agency you work for, Miss Davis. You're not from the Pinkertons, I hope?'

'No, sir. I'm from the Thiele Agency up in St Louis,' she said after a moment, hoping Hudson didn't notice the hesitation, or the quiver in her voice.

'Never heard of them.' He turned around and stared at Ida. 'If you don't mind the crudeness of the question,' he said, a smile playing on his lips, 'how much exactly does the Thiele Detective Agency of St Louis pay for information?'

The man had asked the question breezily, but Ida could tell the easy tone was forced, that he was trying to hide some financial desperation.

'That depends on the information, sir,' she said with a smile.

'Well, that's a businessman's answer if ever I heard one.' Hudson chuckled and turned back to the stove. He stood over the pan for a few moments then he poured the coffee into two tiny cups of chipped, yellowing china and shuffled over to the table. He set the cups down and sat opposite Ida. As she took the cup in her fingers she noticed Hudson was staring at her, scanning her face for something or other.

'You got black in you?' he asked, frowning, the tone of his voice more surprised than suspicious, as if he had just noticed that there might be something not completely European to her.

'No, sir,' said Ida, the confrontation with the landlady fresh in her mind.

Hudson stared at her a moment longer, and then he nodded, believing her lie. He picked up a packet of Piper Heidsieck lying on the table, lifted its sky-blue lid and took a pinch of the flaky chewing tobacco from inside.

'So what exactly is it you wanna ask me?' he said, rolling the tobacco between his fingers.

Ida took her notebook out of her bag and flicked through a few pages.

'Am I right in assuming – and sorry if I'm being forward here, Mr Hudson – that John Morval forced you to sell your side of the business to him?'

Hudson smiled. 'That's one way to put it.'

Ida smiled back. 'Would you mind telling me what happened?'

Hudson peered at her again with the same searching look, as if he was making a judgment of her character.

'This is strictly between us and the agency,' he said, his tone serious. 'My name doesn't get mentioned anywhere.'

Ida nodded.

'OK then,' he said, smiling. He tossed the pinch of tobacco into his mouth and began to chew.

'John had some associates of an Italian disposition, if you get my meaning. And one of these associates had bought someone in the mayor's administration, a high-binder responsible for handing out government contracts for the procurement of uniforms for municipal workers. John's associate, the one who bought the contracts, had a criminal history.'

'Sorry, Mr Hudson,' Ida interrupted, 'would this associate be Sam Carolla?'

'Possibly,' said Hudson with a smile. 'Now, it didn't look right for a government contract to go out to someone with a criminal history. So John came up with a proposition – he'd graft the government contracts himself, and in return John would make the Italians his main suppliers of textiles. I had a compunction against working with those kinds of people. So he forced me out.'

Ida smiled and took a sip of the grainy, bitter coffee. She rolled the liquid around her mouth a moment and decided she quite enjoyed the taste.

'Is Morval still involved with these associates?'

'I shouldn't see why not.'

'And was Morval ever involved in any counterfeiting that you know of?'

Hudson frowned and shook his head, then leaned forward and spat a stream of tarry saliva into the bucket.

'Never heard he did anything like that,' he said. 'John's involved in a hundred and one underhand things, but I don't believe that's one of them.'

Hudson picked up his cup for the first time and without taking the wad of tobacco from his mouth, took a sip.

'Are you aware of a Mrs Romano?' asked Ida. 'She was a worker in Morval's factory.'

'Can't say that I am.'

'Mr Hudson, would you say Morval had it in him to kill?'

Hudson stopped his chewing for a moment and raised his eyebrows. 'You investigating a murder?'

Ida smiled and stayed quiet, and Hudson nodded to himself.

'John could kill a man as easy as buy him a drink,' he said, his eyes narrowing. He paused and Ida noticed a solemnity in his demeanor. 'He's the closest thing to evil I've ever come across. A dark, vicious thing, Miss Davis.' He paused again and stared at her, his face cold and stony. 'I've known the man since we were children. We grew up in the same village, out north of Lake Borgne. Morval Senior was a trapper, too. Used to take John out with him from when he was a child, showed him how to kill animals, how to skin them. You gotta understand what seeing that much blood so young can do to a man. It changes his appetites, if you know what I mean.'

Hudson said the last with a snide, knowing intonation that unsettled Ida. 'If someone's wound up dead, Miss Davis,' he continued, 'and John's one of the suspects? I'd put him top of the list. Now, I think I've given you about enough of my time. How's about that money we were talking about beforehand?'

By the time Ida exited the house, Lewis had been standing on the street for the best part of twenty minutes, and it was never a good idea for a colored man to be standing on a street in the Irish Channel for that long. The city's Irish and Negroes were competing for work on the riverfront just two blocks away, and the Negroes were winning, something that made people like Lewis even less welcome than usual. So when Ida made her way out of the building, Lewis heaved a sigh of relief, waved away her apology and started off down the road as quickly as he could.

They walked in silence along an avenue lined with orange trees and huddled-together houses bordered by overflowing gardens, before turning onto Tchoupitoulas Street. They passed by the river and along the levee which had been planted with willows that swayed in the rain, and eventually they reached St Mary Street, home to the neighborhood cattle pens and slaughterhouses, where the stench of livestock, manure and pig's blood filled their noses. As they arrived at the last of the pens, Lewis noticed four urchins taking shelter from the rain under the eaves of one of the abattoirs.

They were young, with red hair, string belts, and trousers ragged at the ankles.

Ida caught on that Lewis had seen something and followed his gaze, and the urchins noticed them in turn, and spoke to each other in quick whispers. They moved out from under the eaves and stood in the center of the walkway. Lewis scanned the surroundings – they were completely alone, in an open area of mud and ditches, the river on one side, the butcheries on the other. As they approached, two of the boys stepped aside to let them through, all of them leering at Ida. When they had gone a few paces forward, he heard one of the boys behind him shout in a nasal voice, 'Aintcha ashamed!'

Before Lewis knew what had happened he was stumbling forward and falling to the floor, a sharp pain in his back. He heard only scratches of noise as the ground spun around in front of him, Ida screaming, the boys shouting.

He tried to stand, but something on his back was pressing him down. Then kicks starting pummeling him, cracking into his sides, his ribs, his hipbones and kidneys. He heard Ida crying, the abrasive sounds of a tussle. He flailed an arm out to his side and somehow managed to grab hold of a foot. He pulled as hard as he could and one of the attackers fell to the ground with a thump and rolled about, clasping his knee. The tallest of the boys was on top of him now, swinging punches, while the other two were dragging Ida into a storm-water ditch. Lewis lurched upwards, knocking the tall one to the side, getting in a blow to the face, dropping him to the floor.

Lewis watched the boy writhe in the mud for a second then ran over to the ditch – the two remaining boys had pinned Ida to its muddy bottom; one held her wrists, the other was pulling at the waist of her skirt. Lewis jumped on them, knocking one over. The second one swung a punch his way and hit Lewis square in the jaw. Lewis stumbled and collapsed and as he reeled about in the mud, he caught a glimpse of Ida creeping up on her two attackers, a rock in her hand. Lewis heard two cracking sounds and then he felt something in his hand – Ida's fingers, slippery with blood and rainwater. She pulled him up, and as they climbed out of the ditch, Lewis cast a look back. He saw the two boys sprawled out on the ground, their heads coated in blood.

They ran down the road till the panic burnt off, checking behind them through the rain as they went. Lewis was the first to stop, a five-minute eternity later. Despite the fact that his ribs seared with pain every time he breathed, he leaned against a fence and hyperventilated.

'They're gone,' he said between heavy, rasping gulps.

He looked up at Ida for the first time. She was crying, fear and shock distorting her face. She looked at him with a confused, terrified expression and he didn't know what to do except push off the fence and hug her. He felt the weight of her body heaving against him as they held each other under the darkening sky, the two of them trapped in the wires of rain.

22

While Captain McPherson stood at the front of the third-floor meeting room and addressed the crowd of policemen gathered there, Michael leaned against a table next to him, his arms folded, barely listening to what was being said. Instead he stared out of the windows, watching the rain shimmy stupidly down the panes, his mood dark. The meeting had been called because the previous afternoon the officers trawling through the prison records had completed their work. Lists had been compiled. And now the department needed a troop of men to cover the city to try to find all those who had been in prison or the insane asylum during the eight-year gap between the killings in 1911 and the current murders.

The meeting room was too small to comfortably house the pack of beat-cops and detectives gathered there, so tables had been stacked against the walls, and the windows had been opened to let out the heavy air of too many men. Anyone whose lieutenant had agreed they could be spared had turned up, happy to have a day away from their usual duties, and so the meeting had the jokey atmosphere of a classroom on the morning of a school trip. Something which annoyed Michael further.

After the Schneider murders, Michael had been called in for yet another dressing down from McPherson. He didn't mention Riley's tip-off to his boss, and when the meeting was over, Michael had met Kerry and the two of them completed the search for the name Riley had given him. Everything came up blank. Ermanno Lombardi had no convictions, no KAs, no mentions on any of the bureau's lists of informers. They left the name with the housing department in the hope they'd come up with an address; if they didn't, as humiliating as it was, Michael would have to go back to Riley and press him for more information. So now their only hope was that the 1911 killings and the current crop had been committed by the same person. And Michael was not entirely convinced this was the case.

McPherson had started the meeting by hooking his thumbs under the lapels of his jacket and scanning the faces of the men with his frosty blue eyes.

'OK, gentlemen,' he began. 'As you all know, we've been going through the records from the state prison and the S.I.A. We've tallied the results and we've got just over eighty suspects that fit the bill. Sixty or so are parolees, the rest were let go from the loony bin. Thanks to the efforts of the parole board and the medical commission, we've managed to obtain addresses for most of them. Each two-man team will have four suspects to question. Pick up a list as you leave the room. I want you all out on the streets by ten hundred hours and reports handed in by noon tomorrow. Any questions?'

No one spoke.

'Good, you're all dismissed. Happy hunting, gentlemen.'

McPherson nodded at the men and strode out of the room. Michael put the lists on the front table and stepped back as the men stood and exited, picking up lists as they went. A bottleneck formed at the door where Michael stood, and as the men waited in a loose huddle, he half-heard a whisper and an echo of snickers on its tail.

Nigger-lover.

The voice was soft, cold and laced with derision. It was self-righteous, too, as if the speaker was voicing a long-held grievance, or felt he was righting a wrong. It took a moment for Michael to realize what had been said, and another moment to realize that it had been directed at him, and when he did, a tense, tightening anger exploded inside. He jerked his head up and glared at the lines of policemen in front of him, swinging a scowl back and forth, hoping to find the culprit. But the men's faces were all impassive, or turned away from him in conversation, their eyes tracing lines in every direction but his. He thought of how the men would act once they were outside, laughing at what they had done, congratulating themselves with pats on the back, and he grew steadily angrier. But it was a frustrated, swallowed anger, a hopeless fury he could do nothing with. He wanted to defend his wife, but his enemies were invisible, snipers on a distant horizon.

A half-hour later, as he strode out of the precinct with Kerry beside him, Michael was still stewing in impotent rage. A cloudy gloom had descended on the street, and a steady drizzle was prickling the mud in the center of the road. He turned his collar up against the rain, and handed a list of suspects to Kerry.

'First suspect goes by the name of Breuer, sir,' said Kerry. 'Address looks like an apartment on Robertson.'

Kerry smiled at Michael, and Michael noticed how eager he was – Kerry's excited, boy-scout adventurousness at odds with his own self-pitying mood.

'What about the other addresses?' he asked, scanning the surroundings. Officers from the meeting were trotting down the precinct steps, heading out into the city. Their waxed raincoats and dickersons prompted Michael to examine his own shoes – rainwater was already seeping inside them, darkening the tan leather.

'Ah, two in the French Quarter and one in Little Italy,' said Kerry. Michael nodded and thought a moment.

'I'm assuming the suspect in Little Italy is Italian?' Michael asked.

Kerry checked the list and nodded. 'Umigliani. The other two are called Steiner and Stevens.' He folded the paper into quarters and slipped it into his jacket.

'OK, I guess we'll go to Storyville first and check out Breuer,' Michael said, 'then the two in the French Quarter, then we'll finish off over in Little Italy.'

Kerry nodded and they turned and trudged up the street in

silence. Despite the drizzle the roads were busy with hawkers, pedestrians and streetcars. They avoided the banquettes to keep clear of the shoppers and maintain their pace, traipsing instead through the manure-strewn carriageway in the center of the road. But when they reached Basin Street the traffic was so heavy they had no choice but to step onto the banquette, making slow progress as the wood was slippery from the rain. They crossed the tram-lines and turned right onto Bienville, heading into the heart of the District.

'What was Breuer sent down for?' Michael asked, as they passed a gaggle of cleaners brushing mud from the entrance to a hotel.

Kerry scrabbled the list from his pocket. 'Theft by deception,' he said, frowning.

'Seven years for that? Must have been one hell of a con. How old is he?'

Kerry peered at the list again. 'Sixty-two,' he said wearily. 'I get the feeling this guy probably isn't the Axeman.'

Michael nodded. A sixty-two-year-old confidence trickster was not the type they were looking for. Yet Michael's interest was piqued – he wondered why the man had received such an un-usually lengthy sentence, and also why he lived in an apartment on probably the worst street in the red-light district. The Axeman had displayed a Ripper-like willingness to attack women, and Breuer had chosen to live among the prostitutes of Robertson Street, the most destitute working girls in the city. There could be a connection. Michael lit a Virginia Bright and brought to mind the forlorn image of Robertson Street, poverty-stricken, fogbound and insalubrious. It didn't seem too dissimilar to the accounts he'd read of Victorian London's East End.

Storyville hadn't always been such a bleak prospect, however. The District had come into being in the 1890s, when a group of reformers in City Hall thought they could curb the spread of vice by making it a crime for prostitutes to live anywhere in the city except a designated area in the very center of New Orleans – the twenty blocks contained in the square formed by Basin Street, Canal Street, Claiborne Avenue and St Louis. The legislation had been written in part by an alderman called Sidney Story, and much to the man's annoyance, the area ended up being named after him – Storyville.

Entrepreneurs relocated there with a fervor to rival the Gold Rush, transforming the streets of what was a working-class neighborhood of Negroes, Creoles and whites, into a pleasure quarter flooded with the bright lights of bordellos, cabarets, hotels and saloons. Money flowed in and people made fortunes. During the District's halcyon days, the twenty square blocks of Storyville were home to over two thousand prostitutes, from those who worked in the grand *maisons* to those who plied their trade alone from hovel-like cribs.

Michael remembered Luca taking him around the District when they had first started working together, back in Storyville's heyday. There was an air of abandon to the place, a carefree energy and a joy that was at once sordid and innocent, playful and knowing. Storyville was by no means a paradise – there was violence, death and disease there. There was exploitation and a grim, brutal side to the operations that the tourists never saw. But despite all that, Michael found it hard not to remember it as a lantern in the night – bright, cheerful and warm.

The District was officially closed down in 1917, and although what was referred to as 'the sporting business' still continued there, it was a lot more discreet. Except for the occasional hints and clues scattered across the buildings – a red-curtained window, an open doorway, a sign advertising a cabaret or a show, the profusion and variety of 'hotels' – the District could have been any one of a number of shabby gray Orleanais neighborhoods.

As they crossed the final few blocks to their destination, the state of the buildings steadily deteriorated, until they arrived at the nadir, Robertson Street. On one side of the road was a row of crumbling, somber buildings, home to a warren of sporting women's cribs, and on the other side, the larger of the St Louis Cemeteries. Michael mused on the area's bleak mix of poverty, sex and death.

They made their way to a set of derelict red-brick tenements opposite the cemetery and Kerry nodded to Michael that this was the place. The rain had covered the tenements in a moist sheen that seeped into the brickwork and consumed the light, making the buildings look unusually dark. They found the front door of Breuer's building unlocked and made their way inside.

Michael sparked a new match at every flight of stairs, but the meager glow did little to dispel the darkness as they ascended. What light they did have revealed scorch marks and smoke stains covering crumbling brick walls, marking the places where tenants had left candles burning. There was a disconcerting smell of mold and gas, and through the darkness they could hear rats running about the walls, and the sound of a crying baby. Michael thought what easy prey the tenants of these building must be – all a robber had to do was walk in off the street, hide in one of these pitch-black corridors and wait for the right person to stumble by.

They reached the fourth floor, found the door to Breuer's apartment and knocked, but no one answered. They waited for a few minutes, listening for any sounds of movement behind the door, and when they heard nothing, they descended the stairs into the basement, and knocked on the door of the superintendent's room.

After a few seconds the super opened up. He was a towering man who held his chin high and his head back, preferring, Michael gathered, to look down on the world. The super informed them that Breuer had died three days earlier of a heart complication, and before that he had been in the Charity Hospital for a month. They asked to check his room on the off-chance, and the super, grumbling and muttering, led them back up to Breuer's room with the aid of a gas-lamp.

Michael and Kerry searched the place while the super leaned against the doorjamb and watched sullenly. The room was clean and nearly empty and after a few minutes they were sure it contained nothing of importance. They thanked the super and went on their way. Michael judged the man was telling the truth about Breuer – only fools lied about things so easy to disprove – but he told Kerry to double-check with the hospital authorities just in case.

He was glad to get back onto the street and out of the tenement and its stifling, heavy air. They trudged along Robertson for a couple of blocks, passing the St Louis Cemetery on their left. Because of its high groundwater level, New Orleans buried its dead aboveground, encasing them in highly elaborate tombs – a section for the Protestants, another for the Catholics, another for the whites, another for the Negroes – and it was the pinnacles of these tombs that Michael and Kerry could see above the cemetery wall, scattered across the sky.

They turned right down Conti Street and eventually reached the Vieux Carré. The next two names on their list also proved to be dead ends. Joachim Steiner, forty-seven, had been released from Angola four months previously, after serving a seven-year sentence for assault. He had smashed a man over the head with a bottle in a bar-room brawl that had, with depressing predictability, been caused by an argument over a spilt drink. On finding the man, they discovered he had been crippled during his stay in Angola and didn't have the use of his legs anymore. They crossed him off the list.

The next name was Barry Stevens, thirty years old, released after eight years in Angola, also on an assault charge, gained in this instance for an episode in which he brain-damaged his wife. At some point Stevens had found God, and now spent his time caring for his spouse and helping out at the local church. His priest confirmed he had been working in the church for two of the nights on which the murders occurred.

It was past noon by the time they arrived in Little Italy. They had stayed silent for most of their slog across the city. Michael got the feeling Kerry had picked up on his mood and was leaving him alone. But over the course of the walk Michael's mood had lifted, their journey through the city streets providing a therapy of sorts. He knew the city was gloomy and rough, but it was also some-where in which he could immerse himself – the market stalls, the shops, the miscellany of buildings and people, the shouts and the smells, and the hum of a million lives intersecting. He suggested they stop for lunch at a delicatessen he knew, and Kerry readily accepted. The place was bright and lively, bustling with workers on their lunch breaks, and housewives and maids shopping for groceries. They found two seats at the end of the counter and let the heat warm them up a little. Michael bought them both coffees and hot po'boy sandwiches. They took sips of the coffee and after a couple of minutes the sandwiches arrived – two long baguettes cut in half, overflowing with slices of beef shoulder, pork and bacon, and salad dressed with mayonnaise, dill pickle and Creole mustard. Kerry looked at the plate in front of him with a dis-trustful, startled frown.

'It's enough to feed a family,' he said eventually, before turning to Michael and grinning.

'How is it?' asked Michael after they had taken a few bites.

'Grand,' said Kerry, his voice muffled by the food in his mouth. 'We don't have anything like this back home.' Michael noted the boy's grin and that the color seemed to be returning to his face, and he experienced something of the fatherly contentment that came over him when he watched his own children eat.

'You only get food like this in New Orleans,' said Michael, who, although no gourmand, was proud of his city's culinary tradition. French, African, Spanish and Italian influences had been brought together by generations of Orleanais cooks, and the result was a unique and exuberant cuisine.

'Shame all the suspects have come up blank,' Kerry replied, and

Michael noticed a seriousness in the boy's voice; he didn't have the heart to tell the boy that they might well be involved in a wild-goose chase.

'It's the way of police work,' he replied. 'I get the feeling we'll probably have more luck with the next one.'

'On account of his being Italian?' Kerry asked.

Michael nodded and took another bite from his po'boy. He stared out of the windows that ran across the front of the store. Between the warmth of the people inside and the cold rain on the street, a thick condensation had formed over the glass, making the world beyond seem nebulous and soft.

'If you don't mind me asking, sir, you seem pretty sure the killer's Italian.'

'Let's say it's an inclination,' Michael said, turning his gaze from the window.

'How so?' asked Kerry, frowning.

Michael thought for a moment, suddenly realizing the answer he was about to give Kerry was nearly identical to something Luca had taught him years before. He had the sense of a chain spanning an unfathomable darkness, and the idea that he was a link in this chain somehow reassured him. He felt the need to explain to the boy what Luca had taught him over the years of their relationship – that the best solutions to any mystery were the simplest ones, because simplicity was the source of nature's elegance, and mysteries were nothing more than nature unilluminated. The idea wasn't something that could be taught as though from a textbook, it was a *sense*, an approach that was nurtured over years on the job. And Michael realized that by taking the boy under his wing, he had somehow committed to a lifelong undertaking. The realization was quickly followed by a pang of guilt – Luca had no doubt felt the same way when he had taken Michael under his wing, and Michael had repaid him with betrayal.

'You know what Occam's razor is?' he asked, and Kerry shook his head. 'Simplest explanations are normally the best.

Most murderers are known to the victim, and in a town like New Orleans, where everyone sticks to their own, Occam's razor suggests if an Italian's dead, he was killed by another Italian. Italians kill Italians, Negroes kill Negroes, Jews kill Jews. That's the way it works round here, barring a few exceptions.'

'But Schneider wasn't Italian.'

'That's the part I haven't figured out yet,' replied Michael. 'But even Schneider had tarot cards found on him. You ever heard people talk about the Black Hand?'

'Sure, it's another name for the Mafia,' said Kerry.

'It's an old name for the Mafia,' said Michael. 'Back then, when the Mafia killed someone or sent an extortion note, they'd leave a small card with a drawing of a black hand on it, to let people know who was responsible. Hence the name. Sometimes they didn't leave cards with black hands on them, they left tarot cards. Saved them having to draw the thing themselves.'

Kerry nodded and they lapsed into silence as they finished off their food, and Michael noticed the delicatessen's noise, heavy with the clatter of cutlery on plates, people talking and the hiss of grills and percolators. They ordered more coffees and sipped them as the lunch-break crowd headed back to work and the delicatessen grew quiet. The staff began cleaning up after the rush with a resigned weariness. Michael pushed his plate away and lit a cigarette.

'You know New Orleans was the first city in America to have the Mafia?' he said.

'No, sir.'

'It's a dubious honor, but one we hold nonetheless. Up north, in New York and Chicago, the Mafia's from all different parts of Sicily – Palermo; Catania; Messina; Siracusa. That's why they're always killing each other. Not in New Orleans. There's never been a real war between families here, at least not one that's spilled out into open bloodshed. It's because here they're all from the same little town in Sicily – Monreale. And they stick together like glue.

No fighting, no vendettas. They're organized and they get on with their business.'

Kerry frowned. 'How comes you know so much about the Mafia?' he asked, and Michael paused for a moment and shrugged. He had spent years in the company of Mafiosi while he was under Luca's tutelage, and he knew the history and character of the families better than any detective in the bureau. It was a strange position to be in, and one that he had never quite gotten used to — a white cop of Irish descent, married to a colored woman, working for a Sicilian crime family. It would never have come about had it not been for the meticulousness of his handlers at the District Attorney's office, who had arranged for him to infiltrate Luca's gang.

After the Abner affair, Michael was demoted to beat duty for six months. Then the men arranged for a consignment of fur coats to come into his possession. Michael approached Luca with the coats, and claimed they were from a cousin in St Louis, a hijacker, who was looking to get rid of them out of town. Luca took the coats and sold them on, and a month and a half later Michael was given a set of gold watches which he passed on to Luca, too. Over the next year, the stolen goods kept coming, cigarettes, whiskey, jewelry, ammunition, designer dresses. Luca took them all off Michael's hands and, as the two grew close, Michael was accepted into Luca's gang.

The gang was involved in everything the Family was involved in — extortion, hijacking, fencing, gambling, prostitution, loan-sharking, counterfeiting. Michael learned about the deals they had with the mayor's administration; he met Carlo Matranga on a number of occasions; he heard the rumors about the torture squad that Hatener operated; he even participated when they were framing people. In the time Michael served as Luca's protégé, he was, by his own count, involved in sending as many as fourteen innocent men to Angola on false evidence. He kept a ledger on every one, and each time a new man fell victim to the gang, he was told by his handlers that the man would be retried and acquitted once Michael's undercover duties were over. But when the investigation finished and Luca was indicted, the bosses refused to reopen the cases, something that left Michael with a searing sense of guilt.

They finished their coffees and Michael stood. He picked up the bill and took it to the cashier, who tried not to stare at the scars on his face as she counted out his change. Michael was used to people staring and it wasn't something that ever bothered him. The smallpox had led him to the smallpox ward, and it was there that he had met Annette, the only nurse on the staff who didn't seem to pity him. So as much as the scars marred his looks, they were also a reminder of the means by which he had found his wife. People could stare if they wanted.

When they stepped back out into the street, the rain and wind bristled against their skin and they hurried the few blocks to the last address on their list. Paolo Umigliani lived in a hostel for bachelors on a narrow street at the edge of Little Italy. They found the place above a dusty, glum shop that sold Singer sewing machines and spools of thread whose rainbow colors had long since faded. The hostel was reached by a cramped, low-ceilinged staircase that smelled of disinfectant and tobacco. The old man who ran the hostel told them in a disdainful voice that Umigliani wasn't in, but he could normally be found at a barber's shop a block to the south, 'with the rest of the *Unione Siciliana*,' he added sarcastically, spitting out the words.

The barber's was located in a corner building on a road of shabby shops and market stalls huddled underneath waxed sheets. Despite the rain, a few ragged children were running up and down the street, splashing mud at each other and playing catch. Michael paused as they got close to the barber's and took a step behind one of the stalls, motioning for Kerry to do the same. He peered round the corner, through the large sheet-glass window that fronted the barber's, where a group of burly Italian men lounged about. Michael recognized a few of the faces from his days with Luca, especially a swaggering man a few years younger than him who looked like he was holding court in the waiting area at the front of the shop.

'You see the big guy in the fur?'

Kerry peered across the street at the shop and nodded.

'That's Silvestro "Sam" Carolla,' said Michael. 'He's Don Carlo's underboss. The number two Mafioso in the city.'

Michael had met Silvestro countless times, mainly at meetings Luca had organized. Silvestro was Don Carlo's nephew and despite being loudmouthed and unpopular, he had risen up the ranks to the level of heir apparent. People thought of Luca as the natural successor to Carlo – sharp, well-liked, charming – everything Silvestro wasn't. But because of family ties and family history, Silvestro had ended up being number two. It was obvious Carlo had reservations about passing on his empire to a man as brash and egotistical as his nephew, so Silvestro lived life as a perpetual deputy, frustrated and humiliated. And now he had cropped up in the middle of the Axeman investigation.

'I'm gonna go in. You wanna stay here and keep an eye out?' Michael asked, offering Kerry an excuse not to enter the barber's. Kerry thought for a moment, and Michael could see a hint of trepidation on his face.

'No. I'll come,' he said, eventually.

Michael smiled and they stepped out from behind the stall and strode across the muddy street into the barber's. A bell rang as Michael entered and Silvestro and a few of the men sitting around the coffee table by the front door turned his way and the room went quiet.

Michael saw that apart from a little extra weight, Silvestro hadn't changed much. Macassared hair slicked back from a sneering face, a jailbird scar across one cheek, coal-nugget eyes and a hooked nose so prominent it made the rest of his features look as if they were receding.

They stared at each other, Michael with a cold, earthy grimace,

Silvestro with an expression of unrestrained surprise, as if a man he knew to be on the other side of the world had just stepped into the shop. He frowned and the surprise was replaced by a lean, bloodless smile.

'Hello, Mikey,' he said, using an abbreviation he knew Michael disliked. 'You here for a haircut?'

Silvestro's pronunciation was slow and nasal. Michael noticed he hadn't lost his Italian accent over the years, but it had been subdued, strangled by a heavy Southern drawl.

'I'm looking for Paolo Umigliani,' Michael said, peering around the room in an attempt to look casual. The place was long and narrow, receding like a corridor into the distance. Two barbers were at work, and in the far depths, a group of younger men loitered in the shadows. Michael guessed if Umigliani was in the shop, he would be among this group, but with the length of the room and the lack of light, he couldn't make any of them out clearly.

Silvestro smiled and fingered the diamond-encrusted pin that held his necktie in place. Michael had seen the pin, or one like it, on sale in the jewelry department at D. H. Holmes and he remembered the price worked out to about half his annual salary. Carolla had always compensated for his battered looks with an expensive wardrobe, and Michael wondered at the cost of the man's black fur coat and the gold rings smattered across his fingers.

'Why ya asking after Paolo?' said Silvestro, the smile disappearing.

Michael shrugged. 'You know, the usual.'

He noticed the barbers had stopped their work to gawp. The ageing one closest to them had all but frozen, the foam-clotted razor in his hand dangling in the air next to his customer's neck.

'Who's the kid?' Silvestro asked Michael, gesturing in Kerry's direction. 'Got a new sweetheart?'

The rest of the men burst into laughter laced with sycophancy and a kind of relief. Silvestro smiled again, and made eye contact with Kerry.

'Don't stick with him too long, kid. You'll probably end up in prison with the rest of the PD.'

Some of the others snickered and Silvestro grinned.

'So, is Umigliani here? Or do I have to ask you all for ID?' Michael asked, rocking on his heels. Silvestro glared at him, and they held each other's gaze long enough for everyone in the room to get uncomfortable. In the corner of his vision Michael could see Silvestro's cohorts getting tense, their hands moving slowly towards the weapons concealed in their pockets, and he wondered if he hadn't miscalculated the situation. He decided to go for broke and bluff some more.

'I ain't got all day,' he said in a singsong voice.

He could feel Kerry looking about the room at the barbers and the menacing suits, and he could hear the muffled sound of rain beating against the windows. He made a show of sweeping his eyes over the place. On the counter underneath the mirrors were razors and packets of pomade, blue china cups holding brushes, and glass cabinets filled with ointments, disinfectant, and folded, steam-pressed towels.

Without shifting his gaze, Silvestro waved his men down, then he turned and peered into the depths of the shop to the group of younger men.

'Paolo!' he shouted.

In the distance, a gaunt and sallow-eyed young man stood up.

'*Sì, capo,*' he said in a weak, reedy voice.

'*Vieni qui.*'

The man sloped to the front of the shop, passing a row of poster-size advertisements on the back wall for hair tonic, Beaumont soap and Colgate's Ribbon Dental Cream. When he reached Silvestro, he stopped and bowed his head as if he was a crucifer in mass.

'*Va' con il cafone,*' said Silvestro, nodding his head towards

Michael, who knew enough Italian to recognize the insult. '*E ritorna presto.*'

The man frowned at Silvestro in an antsy, schoolboyish way.

'*Ma, capo—*' he pleaded.

'*Sbrigati!*' Silvestro shouted, showing anger for the first time. A look of panic crossed the young man's face, then he bowed his head again and took a railroad jacket and a black homburg from the stand next to the door. Silvestro turned back to look at Michael.

'Paolo'll help you out,' he said.

'Much obliged,' said Michael. 'See you 'round, Sam.' He tipped his hat at Silvestro and turned towards the exit.

'You're supposed to be investigating the Axeman, aren't ya?' said Silvestro, a vague irritation in his voice.

Michael paused, turned to face Silvestro again and nodded.

'Then why ya coming round here? Ya should be in Back o' Town. Looking for niggers.' He spat the final word, and Michael tensed up yet again. 'Seems like everyone in New Orleans knows what color o' skin the Axeman got, 'cept you,' Silvestro said, before shrugging theatrically.

'Yeah, how you so sure about it?' asked Michael.

Silvestro grinned at him.

'I asked your *wife.*'

At this the room burst into laughter again, and Michael felt foolish for walking straight into Silvestro's trap. A nauseous feeling knotted his stomach and he tried his hardest not to let his emotions show.

The laughter continued for a few seconds longer, then the same edged silence returned.

Michael turned to Kerry.

'Come on. We got what we came here for,' he said, failing to stop the dolor seeping into his voice. Kerry nodded and took Umigliani by the elbow, and Michael turned to walk back out onto the street. As he stepped into the entranceway, he caught a glimpse of himself reflected in the glass panel inset in the door – a pale, tired face, warped by smallpox, spectral and translucent against the image of the rainy street beyond. The reflection staring back at him seemed strange, at odds with the self-image he carried around in his head, and Michael realized with a sinking feeling how he must look to Silvestro and his men. He turned the handle and swung the door wide.

'Hey, Michael,' Silvestro shouted over the sound of the rain pouring away in the street, 'you ain't never gonna find the Axeman. Ya chasing a ghost.'

But Michael was already outside. Kerry and Umigliani followed him, and Umigliani shivered at the cold before putting the black homburg onto his head.

'Let's find somewhere quiet,' Michael said, without looking either of them in the eye.

They made their way down the street until they came to an empty alleyway. It was narrow, nothing more than a mud track between two tenements, where some broken guttering above was splashing rainwater onto a clump of garbage cans. They turned into the alley, and found a recess in one of the walls where a set of coal-delivery doors had been boarded up. Under the recess was a dry, covered space and they sheltered there to keep from the downpour.

Michael peered at Umigliani, inspecting him up close for the first time. He had a sorry, hollow face, and his downturned open mouth made him look a little simple. The homburg he was wearing was too big for him and sloped to one side of his head. Michael wondered if Umigliani had picked up the wrong hat, so badly did it fit him, its smartness so incongruous with the rest of his scruffy, frayed outfit. This man was no killer, but he was in Carolla's clique, and he might have useful information.

'We checked your record, Umigliani,' Michael said. 'Date you got released is about the time the Axeman started killing people. And now we find you in the company of known criminals. It doesn't look good.'

Umigliani shifted his gaze between Kerry and Michael, and Michael noticed the blackness around his eyes, the slack, quivering jaw.

'I . . . I not the Axeman,' he said in a stutter, speaking too fast and tripping over his words. He had an Italian accent, stronger than Silvestro's, and the poor grammar made him sound childlike.

'Kerry, check his pockets, please.'

Kerry hesitated for a moment, then stood in front of Umigliani and asked him to raise his arms. Umigliani did so and Kerry patted him down. With his arms outstretched and his mismatched hat and railroad jacket, Umigliani reminded Michael of a scarecrow come to life, moth-eaten and blank-faced.

Michael thought of something Luca had once told him – that street-gangs would occasionally take local mentally backward boys under their protection. They'd act the friend and keep the boys around as entertainment, butts for their jokes and as gofers to fetch things from the local store. The boys were usually lonely and ostra-cized and enjoyed the camaraderie, even if it occasionally turned harsh. But at some point the gang would set the boy up for a job committed by someone else. The boys were rarely in a position to defend themselves and so they worked out as the perfect patsies. Michael looked at the empty expression on Umigliani's face and wondered about his seven years in Angola.

Kerry fished through the man's pockets and found a bundled-up cloth in the breast pocket of his jacket. He frowned, unfolded the cloth and found inside a fistful of dark-green marijuana. It was a compacted lump, dry and fragrant against the moldy scent of the alleyway.

Kerry and Michael looked at each other and an expression of dismay came over Umigliani's face. He started muttering to himself softly, but with speed and concern.

'That's not yours, is it?' Michael asked.

Umigliani shook his head and stared at his feet.

'You know this got made illegal, right? While you were in

prison?' Michael said. Umigliani nodded and looked like he was about to start crying. Michael didn't have the heart to arrest him. Umigliani was just another dupe – exploited by his friends, being set up for sorrows further down the line. Michael could see the man had a future filled with bad fortune and he wasn't going to add to it just now.

'I'm not gonna arrest you for this, Paolo,' he said, adopting a tone he used when explaining things to children. 'But you gotta promise to stop doing favors like this for your friends back there, OK?' he continued, holding up the marijuana. 'You don't wanna end up back in Angola.'

'No, no.' Umigliani shook his head and continued muttering to himself.

Michael nodded at Kerry and Kerry wrapped up the cloth and handed it back to Umigliani, who took it and bowed his head in a servile, cowed way.

'Th-thank you,' he said.

'No problem, Paolo,' said Michael, and then he turned to Kerry. 'C'mon, let's get out of here. He ain't no Axeman.' Kerry nodded and they stepped out into the rain. Four suspects and a wet and wasted day. They took a couple of steps through the miry alleyway before they heard the voice stuttering behind them.

'I . . . I tell you about the Axeman.'

They stopped and turned to see Umigliani standing in the rain, smiling at them. 'To . . . to say thank you,' he added.

Michael shared a look with Kerry then turned back to face Umigliani.

'What do you know?' asked Michael.

'Mm, everybody asking who . . . who is the Axeman?' said Umigliani, in his broken English. 'No one know, but I know s-something.'

Michael nodded at Umigliani to continue.

'My cousin, he . . . he knows a man. He said he knew who the . . . the Axeman was. And then . . . he wasn't there anymore.'

'You mean the man disappeared?' Michael asked.

'*Si*,' said Umigliani. 'Dis . . . appeared.'

Umigliani took off his hat and wiped the rain from his brow with a shivering hand and Michael caught a glimpse of dirty nails chewed to the nub.

'What's his name?' asked Michael. 'The name of the man your cousin knows?'

Umigliani smiled.

''Manno. 'Manno Lo . . . Lombardi.'

At the mention of the name, Kerry and Michael stared at each other – Riley's tip-off.

'You know where I can find him, Paolo?' asked Michael.

'Mmm. No. He dis-disappeared.'

'How about where he lived?'

Umigliani shook his head. 'I know where he worked . . . the Vieux Ca . . . Carré,' he said, mispronouncing the French. 'He fixes cars for . . . O'Neil.'

'O'Neil's auto-shop? In the French Quarter?' Michael asked, coaxing.

'*Si, si*. You find him there. He knows the Axeman,' Umigliani said, the rain splattering about his flimsy smile.

23

The next morning Luca woke to the sound of rain dripping into the cabin through the myriad cracks in the wooden roof. Puddles had formed on the floorboards and the rain tapped into dented pots and pans spread across the floor. He lifted his head from the pillow, looked around and realized he was alone. He felt tired and sleepy, but in a good way – he'd spent the night with a beautiful woman and the tiredness was refreshing, proof that he was back in the real world. He rolled himself over to the side of the bed, stood and let out a long, body-stretching yawn.

He could make out the inside of the cabin better now than he could the previous night. The interior consisted of a large single room that had been broken up into smaller sections by hangings and panels and folding screens. The place was brimming with houseplants and flowers lined up in pots and jars across the floor and on every available surface. The plants gave the cabin a soft, homely feeling that it lacked in other respects – there were no photos of family, no paintings, no decorations of any kind except for a crucifix on one wall and a picture of St Luke on another.

Luca picked up his shirt and trousers from a chair next to the bed, put them on and sauntered into the kitchen. The table had been scrubbed clean, the caustic smell of disinfectant wafting from the still damp wood. Something was bubbling away in a large battered pan on the stove, and when Luca lifted the lid a plume of steam from the broth inside floated into the air. Next to the stove, nailed into the wall, were rows of shelves stacked high with jars of herbs, liquids and spices. Luca ran his eye across them; all the jars were carefully labeled in French, all sparklingly clean and free of dust.

In another corner was an overflowing bookcase. The books were mainly in French, and mainly on medicinal subjects, as well as some anthropological works on the folk religions of Africa and the Caribbean. On one of the shelves a carved wooden statuette was being used as a bookend. Luca stared at the blank, impassive face with its thin lips, and noticed on the base an inscription identifying the figure as Bulul, the Philippine god of rice.

The door opened and Simone stepped in – a cloth over her head to protect her hair from the rain.

'You hungry?' she said, a smile on her lips. She was holding up the hem of her apron with one hand and she lowered it to reveal, nestling in the fold, a half-dozen freshly laid eggs. She set them down and poured the broth from the pan into cups, handing one to Luca.

'What is it?' asked Luca after he took the cup.

'*Teane*. Creole tea. It's good for you.'

Luca tasted it – slightly bitter, herbal and warming.

Simone took sips from her cup while getting pans from the kitchen and placing them under the remaining leaks.

'You need someone to fix the roof?' asked Luca.

'I'll do it myself,' she said.

She prepared the eggs by frying them in oil, melting cheese on top of them and sprinkling them with lemon juice and oregano. She sliced some stale brown bread on the table top, spread clotted butter over the slices, and then they ate, drinking the remaining *teane* between bites.

Simone didn't seem to be bothered by the silence; she ate with the same grace and poise that was her way in everything else, and he wondered how she'd ended up living like an outcast in the middle of the bayou. She looked up at him and caught his gaze and smiled.

'What do you do all day?' Luca asked, smiling back.

'This and that,' she replied, shrugging. 'Look after the chickens. Treat anyone that comes my way.'

'You see a lot of people?'

'Enough to get by,' she said, downing the last of her *teane*. 'What do you do all day?'

Luca thought. In the past that was easy to answer, but now? His days now had an empty, loose quality to them, despite the fact that he had tried to maintain his prison routine to help him adjust. He woke at dawn as he had in Angola, bought the paper and read it in a diner while he ate breakfast, and he was back at the hotel by 9 p.m. for lights out. What he did in between, he wasn't quite sure.

'This and that,' he said with a grin.

He ate the last of his food and downed what remained of the tea in a gulp, and it was only then he realized he had eaten a whole meal without shooting pains searing through his gut. He stared at the empty cup and guessed she was right when she said the *teane* was healthy.

'Thank you,' he said.

She smiled, picked up his plate and took it to the sink, pouring water from a bucket over it. Luca stood and went back to the bed. He put on his boots, slung his jacket over his shoulders and tried to decide on the least awkward way to say his goodbyes. He suddenly realized that she might be expecting money. Everything had seemed genuine to him at the time, natural even – the conversation, the lovemaking, cooking breakfast and eating, but now he wasn't so sure. Luca had never wanted for female company in the past. He'd had a string of *comares*, mistresses with a taste for the high life, and then there were the girls from Monreale the Matrangas had sent his way when Carlo's wife got it into her head to play match-maker, and he never had any trouble picking up drunk girls in the cabarets along the Tango Belt. But none of them had ever cooked him breakfast afterwards, or acted so nonchalant about what had happened the night before.

'Thank you for everything,' he said a little awkwardly as he returned to the kitchen. She turned from scrubbing the plates and smiled at him. He stood and waited. But she said nothing – just smiled at him some more.

'Are we going to do this again?' he asked.

'If I feel lonely again,' she replied, a coquettish glint in her eye. Luca smiled, tipped his hat and set off back to New Orleans.

By the time he returned to his hotel room he was soaked through. He took off his wet clothes, washed, and put warm socks on his cold feet. On his second day back in New Orleans he had gone shopping for clothes – he had bought two suits, both dark blue, a trench coat, a handful of shirts and thick woolen fisherman's jumpers, a flat-cap and a fedora. All chosen because they were nondescript, allowing him to blend into a crowd, to go unnoticed. He changed into one of the suits and the jumpers, slung the flat-cap on his head and went out to buy the latest editions of all the papers. He returned to his room and read the reports of the Schneiders' deaths. A series of Sicilian grocers and now a German lawyer? Luca had yet to meet a lawyer who was totally straight. If there was anything that linked all the victims, it had to be something the lawyer had been working on.

Luca hopped off his bed, crossed the room and slid open the bottom drawer of the dresser that stood by the window. Inside were the necessities he had requested from Carlo before he had started the investigation: a wad of cash, a gun and a case containing a set of tools for picking locks. He took some of the money and the velvet-covered case and left the hotel at once, catching a cab to City Hall to get Schneider's business address from the commerce register.

An hour later he was standing outside a grocer's downtown. To one side of the storefront was a doorway leading up to the apartments above the store. He checked the list of names next to the buzzers and saw Schneider listed as a tenant on the second floor. He stepped back from the doorway and crossed the street. Looking up at the second floor he tried to see if any police were still searching the place, but he couldn't make anything out from the low angle. He ambled a little further down the road, leaned against a lamppost and lit a cigarette. The street was too busy to use the picks on the door – he'd have to wait.

He finished the cigarette and saw a coffee-seller's cart at the intersection a few yards away. He sauntered over and bought a cup. The seller was Italian so they spoke for a little while, the usual talk that occurs between immigrants, and the seller offered to top up Luca's coffee with some grappa, 'to keep you warm in this goddamn rain'. Luca refused politely, the seller shrugged and went on his way, and Luca returned to his spot opposite Schneider's.

An hour later, after he had been thoroughly drenched in the rain and was beginning to wonder if he would catch a fever, the door to the apartments opened and an old lady stepped out. He trotted to the door as quickly and nonchalantly as he could, and as the old woman stepped into the street, Luca slipped his hand into the door frame to stop the door locking shut. The old lady peered at him and Luca tipped his hat at her. She glared at him, opened her umbrella and hobbled off down the street.

Luca breathed a sigh of relief and stepped into the building. He ran up to the second floor and found the door to Schneider's office. He looked around him, put his gloves on and took the small velvet-covered case from his pocket. He opened the case and took first one then another of the thin metal tools from inside it and began to work the lock. He was disappointed at how rusty he had gotten – it took him as long as twenty minutes to get the holds in place. But eventually he was able to slide open the door and step inside.

The office was cramped but tidy, and furnished with a row of filing cabinets, a safe, a desk and a swivel chair. Schneider's diploma hung from the wall, alongside a pair of landscapes in overly ornate faux-gold frames. He found signs that the police had already been there: they'd dusted for fingerprints and there were muddy foot-prints – police-issue boots – on the carpet and floorboards. Luca sat in Schneider's chair and went through the papers in the desk drawers, hoping to find something incriminating or illegal – anything that would spark against the evidence in his head and form a connection, no matter how fragile. But he found nothing in the desk drawers except a receipt for a batch of ephedrine bought from a Chinese apothecary, and a business card for a John Lefebvre, Pinkerton National Detective Agency. Luca smiled – he hadn't heard the name in years, and he decided to pay his old acquaintance a visit.

The rain pattered down all afternoon on the office's single grimy window as Luca checked the documents in the filing cabinet. From the nature of Schneider's papers it looked as if he specialized in property law, drawing up deeds, filing claims, working with clients involved in boundary disputes and planning negotiations. His clients were all white-collar – small businessmen, plantation-owners; no criminals that were known to Luca.

He set to work on the safe. It was an English design, a 1900 Chubb & Son rotary; it had, thankfully, notoriously loud disks compared to the newer designs. It took him just under the hour and a half he had predicted to crack it, and he felt a delicate, satisfied pride when the safe opened. Except for a layering of scuffed dust from the police fingerprinters, the safe was empty.

Luca sat on the floor and sighed. He lit a cigarette and closed his eyes, leaning his head back against the wall. The afternoon had turned to dusk, then into night, and he hadn't stopped the whole time except to draw the blinds over the window and light the lamp, covering the upper half of the shade with his coat to prevent too much light seeping out into the street. His clothes were still damp from the rain and he was exhausted.

It was only because he was sitting on the floor and the lamp was casting oblique shadows onto the floorboards that he noticed, when he opened his eyes, the scratches in the far corner of the room. They were on the edges of two adjacent floorboards – the kind of scratches made by someone levering up the boards with a tool.

He moved to the corner to have a better look. The scratches were not many, but they were deep, and the dust around the nails in the boards had been displaced. He found a letter opener on the desk, slid it in between the boards and slowly levered them up. He moved the boards out of the way, lowered the lamp into the floor cavity and leaned his head into the dusty, grimy space below. Just next to the lamp was a small metal strongbox. He reached in and lifted it out. He put the floorboards back in their place and then he heard a noise in the street below. He blew out the lamp and approached the window.

When he moved the blind to the side and looked into the street he saw the old lady he had passed when he came in. She was talking to two uniformed policeman, pointing up to Schneider's office. He jerked himself away from the window. Visions of Angola flooded into his mind and he cursed himself for being so stupid and so rusty. He moved as quickly as he could, motivated by a dread fear of being sent back to prison so soon. He set the catch on the door to close after him and padded out of the office. Peering down the staircase, he could see the cops already in the hallway below. He leapt up the stairs, and the cops, alerted by his footsteps, burst into a run.

He prayed there was a fire escape on the top floor, some means of getting onto the roof, but when he got there he was faced with just two doors, both of them locked. He could hear the footsteps of the policemen on the wooden stairs, heavy and getting louder. He glanced around and saw a storage cupboard set into one of the walls. He opened it. It was barely big enough to fit a child and was full to the brim with cleaning equipment – brushes, dustpans, mops, canisters of bleach.

He took Schneider's strongbox and placed it in the back of the cupboard, swinging the door shut as the cops rounded the last flight of stairs.

'Freeze!' they screamed, their faces contorted, flushed and angry. Luca raised his hands into the air but they knocked him to the floor anyway, smashing his head into the boards, and before he knew it he felt cold metal squeezing painfully against his wrists.

24

O'Neil's auto-repair shop was not so much a building as a collection of corrugated-iron sheets thrown together at the end of an alleyway. It was located in the industrial section of the Vieux Carré, just at the top of the bend in the river opposite Algiers. The alleyway backed onto a towering textiles factory, and despite the rain the air was heavy with the acrid, burning smell of cotton bleach.

An hour earlier Michael had called the precinct from a payphone in a post office in Little Italy, and the precinct had searched out the address for him. It was dusk by the time they arrived and they almost missed the shop in the gloom. But Kerry happened to catch sight of a tiny sign with O'Neil's name daubed across it, hanging above the metal shutter entrance.

He banged on the shutter with the underside of his fist and the movement sent noisy waves rolling across its surface. After a short wait they heard footsteps approaching and a muffled voice from the other side.

'We're closed,' the voice said, more weary than annoyed.

'It's the police,' replied Kerry.

For a moment there was quiet then the shutter shook and slid upwards to reveal a heavy-set Irishman with a bald head and a thick brown beard. He stared at them myopically for a moment, then leaned against the shutter and burst into a coughing fit so violent it bent him over and flushed his face red. Eventually he took a rag from his back pocket and spat into it, then he shook his head, turned and limped back inside the dimly lit shop.

Michael and Kerry shared a look then followed him in. They

were mole-eyed in the darkness until the man turned a knob at the base of a gas-lamp, and the room flooded with orange light. The workshop had three bays, one housing a Packard Victoria, the second a Stears-Knight, and running along the far end was a worktop cluttered with tools and machine parts. But it was the gleaming black Type 55 Cadillac jacked up in the nearest bay that caught Michael and Kerry's attention. It was an opulent, agile-looking car and it sparkled in the gaslight like a curved slab of pristine onyx. Michael thought it looked almost otherworldly in its sleekness, encased as it was by the dirty, ramshackle womb of the workshop.

The man leaned against the counter at the far end of the space, crossed his arms and watched them with a bleary-eyed look, an expression that made Michael wonder if they hadn't woken him from an early evening nap.

'Sorry to have bothered you,' he said. 'You O'Neil?'

'Sure,' the man replied easily, scratching his beard.

Michael noticed the wall behind him was plastered with photographs of pin-ups torn from magazines. He recognized a few of the faces – Belle Bennett, Colleen Moore, Betty Compson, waiflike young actresses of the silver screen – fragile and sultry. They had all been shot in the same way – backlit and soft-focused against hazy studio backdrops, dressed in chiffon and lace, reclining on chaise longues, smoking cigarettes and gazing soulfully into the distance.

The man looked over at Kerry, who was still standing in front of the car with a smile on his face, studying it like a museum exhibit.

'You like the boat, kid?' said O'Neil.

Kerry nodded. 'I ain't never seen a Cadillac up close,' he said, almost awestruck by the car.

'Runs like a top when it's working,' said O'Neil. 'Cannonball Baker drove from LA to New York in a Type 51 last year. Took him seven days. Reckon a 55 could do it in six.'

Kerry smiled, reluctantly pulled his gaze away from the car and sauntered over to the two men. 'You hear that, sir?' he said to Michael. 'From one end o' the country to the other in six days.'

O'Neil burst into a coughing fit again and while they waited for him to stop, Michael noticed the smell of bleach from the factory opposite had permeated the inside of the draughty workshop, and he wondered if the chemicals in the air weren't the cause of the man's breathing difficulties.

'I assume you didn't come here to talk about Cadillacs,' O'Neil said ruefully, his voice raspy. 'Or watch me cough my lungs out.'

Michael shook his head. 'You employ a man by the name of Lombardi?' he asked.

''Manno? I used to. Haven't seen him in a week.'

'How so?'

'He just stopped showing up. I guessed he got sick of being here. That's what you get when you hire dagoes. Unreliable. Like the car.' O'Neil nodded at the Cadillac, then rummaged around the pockets of his overalls for a cigarette. 'You know where we can find him?' Michael asked.

'He's got a pad over in the Seventh Ward. A boarding house. That's all I know. Why you looking for him?'

'The usual. You notice him acting strange the last few days?'

'Can't say as I did. He always struck me as a little queer anyway, if you get my drift.'

Michael nodded and handed O'Neil a contact card.

'If he comes back – tell him we're looking for him.'

'Will do.'

Michael tipped his hat at O'Neil and trudged out of the shop. Kerry smiled and followed him, taking a long last look at the Cadillac as he went.

Night had settled on the alleyway outside, and as there were no streetlamps they made their way to the main road in darkness. Two people had mentioned Lombardi in connection with the Axeman, and two people had mentioned he had disappeared after shooting his mouth off. It was a tenuous lead, but something to show for the day's work at least. If the Housing Department hadn't come up with an address by tomorrow, Michael would have to go through all the boarding houses in the 7th Ward himself, or go hat in hand to Riley.

They turned the corner onto Decatur Street and were suddenly surrounded by lights and noise and the evening rush. Factory workers and secretaries from the harbor-side businesses were heading home along the sidewalks or boarding streetcars bound for the suburbs. The commercial districts were emptying, just as the residential districts and pleasure quarters were beginning to fill. New Orleans was pumping people through its neighborhoods like a giant heart. But Michael didn't feel like merging into the crowd just yet. He needed some time to unwind.

'Spot you a drink, son,' he said to Kerry.

'I'd be much obliged.'

Michael hailed a cab and they drove against the traffic towards Esplanade Avenue, then along Bourbon Street till they reached the intersection with Bienville. It was still raining and the wind had picked up, making the gas-lamps lining the French Quarter flicker in their glass boxes. Michael paid the driver and they got in front of an ancient, two-story building with a black wrought-iron balcony that was overflowing with ferns, hanging flower baskets and potted shrubs. The shutters and awnings had been painted a bright lime green, and the sign on the front declared it to be *Jean Lafitte's Old Absinthe House*. Michael often came here, although he rarely ordered the absinthe. It was only every now and again he felt the urge for what the patrons of the Absinthe House liked to call the green muse.

'Absinthe?' Kerry was peering at the sign as they strode across the banquette towards the bar. 'I thought it's illegal.'

'It was banned four years ago,' Michael replied, smiling. 'But that's a very loose term in New Orleans.'

He swung the door open and they stepped into a warm,

intimate bar packed with workers who'd stopped in on their way home and out-of-towners who were already far too drunk. They sat at a table in the corner and the waitress came over and Michael ordered two glasses of green, the code word locals used to make themselves known. The waitress eyed Kerry's uniform and was about to remark on it when a bartender who knew Michael nodded to the girl and she smiled and headed off to get their order.

'Why's there a pirate behind the bar?' Kerry asked, nodding towards a giant papier-mâché bust that had been hung above the bar on a flimsy-looking wire.

'It's Jean Lafitte. From the Battle of New Orleans,' said Michael, and Kerry looked at him blankly. 'The British tried to invade New Orleans in 1815. We didn't have enough defenses so we roped in Lafitte to help out. He was a pirate and a smuggler but he had guns and boats. He signed his agreement with General Jackson in the room upstairs.' Michael gestured to a rickety-looking staircase that curved around itself and upwards to the second floor.

'If it wasn't for that pirate,' he continued, 'we might be speaking English now.'

They both chuckled and Michael followed Kerry's gaze to the bust – a swarthy French-looking man with a huge mustache, gold earrings and a red cap. The artist had done a bad job and the face had a garish, amateurish quality to it, making it look like a Mardi Gras mask.

The waitress returned and placed two drinks on the table. The Absinthe House Frappe had been the bar's specialty for decades, but in the last four years it could only be ordered covertly, mixed behind the bar and served in metal cups to hide its distinctive color. Before the ban the frappe was made in squat marble fountains that dripped water slowly onto the sugar cubes that sweetened the liquor. Now the liquor was prepared with the secrecy of an opium house.

Kerry peered suspiciously at the green liquid over the brim of the cup, but when Michael lifted his own drink and toasted in Gaelic, Kerry responded and they both took long sips.

'It's sweet,' Kerry said, and Michael nodded. He wondered if he would ever be able to sit in a bar with his own son this way, free from looks and worry and insinuations, and a guilty feeling came upon him, the notion that he might be using Kerry as a proxy.

'Why New Orleans?' he asked the boy.

'Sir?'

'Most Irish go up to Boston or New York these days.'

Kerry hesitated and peered into the cup in his hand.

'Well, I didn't really see the point of moving countries to go somewhere just as cold and shitty as Dublin.'

Michael smiled, but he got the feeling the joke was forced. Kerry returned to studying his cup, lightly swilling the absinthe around itself. 'Most Irish go where they got family,' he added.

'And you don't?' asked Michael.

'I was raised by priests, sir,' said Kerry, not meeting Michael's gaze. A sadness seemed to descend on the boy, and he took a gulp of the drink as if to ward it off, and Michael suddenly understood that the fragility he had seen in Kerry had deep roots.

'Must be tough not having a family,' he said. Michael had himself lost all links to his own family a decade earlier, when his parents and siblings disowned him.

'You don't miss what you've never had,' Kerry replied. 'The orphanage was OK, but you're out on your ear at eighteen. I didn't fancy staying on and becoming a priest, so I got a job on a coal cart till I saved enough for a steamer ticket.'

'You didn't have the faith to become a priest?'

'Sometimes I have faith,' Kerry said, becoming easy with the subject. 'I just didn't wanna end up like the priests at the orphanage. Most of them had been orphans themselves and I guessed it worked out as a bad life. I don't think there's any joy in being a priest when you've been forced into it by poverty. What about you, sir?' Kerry asked, perking up, forcing his voice to sound upbeat. 'What brought you to New Orleans?'

Michael slid his cigarette case from his pocket.

'I was born here,' he said, taking out a Virginia Bright and lighting it. 'Though most of the time I wish I hadn't been.'

He inhaled deeply on the cigarette and looked towards one of the street entrances where he saw Patrolman Dawson and his impeccably starched uniform hurrying inside. He scanned the room, spotted Michael, and made directly for his table.

'Sorry to disturb you, sir,' said Dawson, a little out of breath. 'We've been looking all over town. Luca D'Andrea was arrested earlier this evening, breaking into Schneider's office. He's at the precinct now.'

25

Sheets of rain plummeted through the night sky and into the Mississippi, where a tramp steamer, the *Dixie Belle*, fought her way up the angry river. The boat's beacons twinkled like fairy lights through the downpour, and over the noise of crashing water the sounds of a party emanated dully from her interior.

In the main hall, underneath fixed chandeliers, men in evening dress and women in ball-gowns danced to the music of Fate Marable and his Jazz Maniacs, who were performing flat, tepid versions of the latest standards. The band looked uncomfortable and confined in their tuxedos, especially the youngest member, who was still recovering from the shock of the fight he had been in that afternoon.

Lewis had almost been barred from the stage by Captain Joe, the line's owner, who took an unusual amount of interest in the musicians who entertained his guests. On seeing Lewis's left eye – an unsightly purple cauliflower of a bruise – and the cut on the side of his cheek, he had remarked that the boy looked like a hoodlum, and hoodlums had no place on the stage of the *Dixie Belle*. But one of the stewardesses, a girl with ambitions to work as a makeup artist in one of the city's theatres, had taken the matter in hand. She camouflaged the bruise with a dark powdery paste of her own concoction and covered the cut with camphor ice. Once Captain Joe saw that Lewis looked less like a ruffian, he was allowed to take his place with the other musicians.

Like any New Orleans band worth its salt, the Jazz Maniacs were musical polyglots, able to play the same song in myriad ways, tailored for the varying tastes of whites, Creoles, Negroes and even for the crowds of poor, ratty types that thronged the city's honky-tonks. Tonight they were taking it easy as Captain Joe wasn't standing at the back of the hall as he usually did, staring at his stopwatch, checking to see if the band was hitting the right tempo – seventy beats per minute for foxtrots and ninety for one-steps. There was a rumor that Captain Joe had sacked bandleaders on the spot for getting the tempo off, but that night, Lewis assumed, he must have had business elsewhere.

They finished the waltz they were playing – every fourth song was a waltz – and the audience applauded while the band sat, taking a break, and a fat, ruddy master of ceremonies in a swallowtail coat strolled onto the stage.

'Ladies and gentlemen. Thank you for braving the inclement weather to be with us tonight, in Captain Joe Streckfus's beautiful paddle steamer, the *Dixie Bell*. It's true when they say that nothing stops a New Orleans crowd from partying.'

There was appreciative laughter and applause from the crowd, and the MC puffed himself up and continued.

'We would like to extend a special thank-you to Mayor Martin Behrman for being with us tonight . . .'

Another wave of applause rose up from the crowd, and at the very front of the hall the mayor acknowledged his mention with an awkward wave of the hand. Lewis had never seen the mayor before, and on any other night he would have been excited, ready to run home and tell Mayann. The mayor looked to Lewis a little smaller than a mayor ought to be, a little more plain and ordinary, his looks chiming more with those of a bank clerk than a man who had run the city for the past sixteen years.

As the MC continued with his speech, the day's events ran through Lewis's mind. After the attack he had consoled Ida, taken her home and thanked God that her mother wasn't in to see the bloodstains, and her ripped, muddy skirt. When he was sure she was OK he had made his way home, changed into his tux and made it to the boat. He had progressed from the brothels and honky-tonks of Back o' Town to the Streckfuss Line steamboats and the New Orleans Country Club. He was supporting four members of his family, earning in a week what most laborers earned in a month, and still he could be attacked simply for being the wrong color in the wrong part of town. He loved New Orleans, but was under no illusion that the city was disgustingly segregated and prejudiced. He was playing on a steamboat for white folks, but there'd be gasps and anger if ever he stepped over the railing onto the dance floor.

He played for another hour before the band took their first proper break. Lewis managed to sneak a coffee from one of the waiters and sipped it in the storeroom where the band was confined when not on stage. Marable and the others dug into complimentary beers, a bottle each, and leftover food from the dinner.

Fate Marable's Jazz Maniacs were seven men from differing backgrounds, some of them Negro, some of them Creole, a racial mix that was unheard of in any band just a few years previously. Like Lewis, they had all been handpicked from the music halls of New Orleans by Marable himself, a pianist and calliope player from Paducah, Kentucky. Marable was a red-haired Negro, light-skinned enough to pass as white, who when asked, lied about his origins and claimed he was an Orleanais Creole. He'd encountered jazz on one of his visits to the city a few years earlier and had convinced Captain Joe to allow him to play a watered-down version of the new sound in his ships. Marable had plans to take the music into the interior, to spread the gospel all along the Mississippi, a dangerous enterprise as the whites thereabouts were known to be scandalized by Negro music and were prone to starting riots.

Lewis noticed Johnny Dodds peering at him from across the room. 'Dots' was the group's clarinetist and the older brother of their drummer, Baby, and he looked out for Lewis in the same big-brotherly way he did for his sibling. He crossed the room and nodded at Lewis's broken face.

'How'd you catch the beating, Lil' Lewis?' he asked with a sideways smile.

Lewis sighed, took a cigarette from his pack and offered one to Dots.

'Got jumped by a few po' whites out in the Irish Channel,' Lewis said. Dots gave him a puzzled look and took a cigarette from the pack.

'What the hell were you doing out there, boy?' he asked. 'Ain't no good ever come of a black man going to the Irish Channel.'

Lewis shook his head and made a face to suggest he didn't want to talk about it. He lit the cigarettes with a lucifer and they both inhaled.

'Hey, Dots, you ever heard of a cat called Morval?' asked Lewis. 'Cajun. Slings furs?'

'Sure, everyone's heard of Morval.'

'I haven't,' said Lewis, and Dots grinned at him.

'That's because you're not everyone,' he replied, raising his eyebrows.

'And what's that supposed to mean?'

'It means you're a rare bird, Lewis,' said Dots, and Lewis wasn't sure if this was a compliment or an insult.

'So what's he like?' asked Lewis.

'He's harder than a pawn-broker. Officially he's a fur-trader. Got a line on every fur store in town. Unofficially, he used to be big in Storyville.'

Lewis frowned. He hadn't expected Morval to be mixed up with the sporting business. Ida had painted a picture of him as a corrupt businessman, someone with political and Mafia connections. The idea that he ran girls, too, seemed odd to Lewis.

'But I heard he retired after the District got made illegal,' continued Dots. 'Why you asking, Lil' Lewis? You fiending for a fur?'

Lewis shrugged and shook his head.

'Nah, no reason,' he said. 'I heard someone mention his name is all.'

Dots gave him a look. He could spot very easily when Lewis

was lying.

'You get into any monkey-business with Morval and you'll regret it, Lewis. Man's a devil,' he said.

'Ain't nothing,' said Lewis, trying to act relaxed, smiling a little. If Morval was a pimp, Lewis knew exactly how to find out what he was up to.

PART THREE

PART THREE

26

Kerry opened the door to the surveillance room and stepped inside, praying his presence wouldn't be noticed. The surveillance room was a dimly lit airless box with wooden chairs scattered about it and a long one-way mirror that snooped into the interview room on its opposite side. The room had the murky, furtive atmosphere of a backstreet revue, and as it was packed with men from the graveyard shift, all excited at the distraction, the air was heavy with cigarettes, paper-cup coffee and sweat. Detective Hatener was there with two other detectives – Jones and Gregson, men Kerry had seen about the bureau, wise-cracking, wiry members of Hatener's team. The three of them turned to look at Kerry as he pushed through the throng and made his way to the front of the room. He smiled at them, and they nodded coldly in response. Then they turned their attention back to the one-way and stared through it with the concerned expressions of demolition men before a blast.

Kerry had heard the stories about D'Andrea, wistful stories about how he used to hold sway in the bureau, about a brilliant mind gone awry. The general consensus was that the bureau worked better under D'Andrea than it did now, that the men got paid on time, there were more kickbacks to go around, and it was all Michael's fault things had slid inexorably downhill since. Kerry gauged the atmosphere in the room and came to the conclusion that the men were universally rooting for D'Andrea. He found a spot near the mirror, pressed himself against the wall, and got his first glimpse of the man through the tinted glass.

D'Andrea was sitting in the interview room alone, arms folded, leaning back in his chair. He was not what Kerry had been expecting – he was good-looking and there was a relaxed confidence, almost an arrogance, in the way he leaned back. But Kerry also noticed he looked weary, that beneath the reassured veneer there was something else, a deep-seated loneliness he couldn't hide.

D'Andrea was wearing a fisherman's jumper and his hair was plastered against his face from the rain, and under the searing lights of the interview room he looked scruffy and lined, by no means the dapper tomcat of precinct folklore. Kerry noted that D'Andrea had no cuffs on, and on the table in front of him was a fresh packet of cigarettes and a coffee – the accoutrements of a man getting the royal treatment. There were no lawyers present, and Kerry thought it strange that D'Andrea hadn't requested one. He stole a glance at Hatener and saw he was still staring at D'Andrea with the same fatherly concern, leaning forward with his forearm against the glass.

Presently Michael and a stenographer entered the interview room, and everyone in the surveillance room quieted down and focused on the one-way with a hush like a cinema audience at the start of a feature bill. Michael moved briskly, papers in hand, sat opposite Luca and laid the papers out carefully on the table. It was only then that he looked up at D'Andrea and they made eye contact. When they looked at each other both their faces seemed suddenly wiped clean of emotion, as if by the cloth of an over-zealous maid. Michael nodded and D'Andrea nodded back, then Michael looked at the stenographer and the stenographer indicated with raised eyebrows that he was ready to start. The exchanges reminded Kerry of a tableau of miniature clockwork card-players he had once seen in a fairground diorama of a Wild West Saloon.

'Good evening, Luca,' said Michael, his tone hollow, trying hard to figure out what his opening gambit would be. He was normally good at interviews, but there was too much going on in his head to focus. He had been wondering during the trip back to the precinct how to speak to Luca, how to find out why he had been in Schneider's building. It couldn't be a mere coincidence; Luca must have been there for a reason, and the only reason Michael could think of was that Luca had been sent by Carlo, because Carlo wanted something incriminating removed from Schneider's office. But Carlo could call on a million kids to break into an office – why choose Luca?

Michael tried to straighten things out in his mind, but the ordering of details and evidence into plausible, coherent sequences – a process that normally came so naturally to him – was being thrown askew by feelings he had spent five years trying to suppress. The last time he had spoken to Luca face to face was before the indictment, when they were ostensibly still friends, and now he felt like a prodigal son, brimming with justifications.

'Good evening, Michael,' Luca said, before turning to the one-way mirror. 'Boys,' he added, with a nod of his chin and a glint of a smile, and Michael thought he could hear laughter coming from the surveillance room on the other side.

'I guess we can dispense with the pleasantries,' he said. 'Breaking and entering, burglary, possible obstruction of a murder investigation. And all while you're on parole,' Michael continued, keeping his tone as flat as he could manage. 'What were you doing there?'

Luca smiled and made a face to indicate that Michael's question was too inconsequential to bother with. As Michael looked at him he was glad to see that Luca hadn't aged so much, the boyish charm was still there, the devil-may-care grin.

'I got lost,' Luca said, 'thought it was my building. These things happen when you get to my age.'

Then he shrugged and Michael wondered if he had heard an edge in Luca's voice, a barely audible contempt.

'Three parole violations in one scoop,' he said. 'If you don't tell me what happened and let me see what I can do, you're going straight back to Angola.' He spoke in a neutral fashion, trying to make it sound like he was stating a fact, that he didn't care one way or the other.

'The most you can do me for is trespass. That's if the landlord wants to prosecute. Six months, tops.'

'Why'd Carlo send you to Schneider's office?'

Luca frowned and shook his head. 'Carlo's got nothing to do with this,' he said. 'Like I told you, I got the buildings mixed up. I only just moved in.'

Was there any point in putting pressure on Luca? He knew the way things worked as well as anyone. If it wasn't for the crowd in the surveillance room, Michael would have leveled with him, spoken to him plainly instead of going through with the charade. He sighed and retreated to the safety of procedure.

'You were breaking into Schneider's office,' he said. 'We found a lock-picking kit on you. And once we get the fingerprints back they'll prove you were in there, too.'

'Did someone break into Schneider's office?' Luca said with a frown. 'You won't find my prints inside. You've no witnesses who saw me in there. No signs of a forced entry, none of Schneider's possessions were found on me. All you got is a guy who got confused and walked into the wrong building. Not even a parole violation. Fish all you want. The most, the *very* most, you can scare me with is trespass.'

Michael noticed a certain gleam in Luca's eye, the look of a man who assumed he was untouchable. Luca took a cigarette from the packet in front of him and lit it with a match. He inhaled deeply and grinned, then he tossed the match into the ashtray and watched it for a moment as the flame died. He peered up at Michael, then, very deliberately, offered him one of his cigarettes as a joke.

In the surveillance room some of the officers snickered and laughed. Gregson smiled and turned to look at Hatener, but Hatener's stare remained grimly fixed on the one-way. Kerry glanced from Hatener back to the interview room. He could see D'Andrea's charm now, the breeziness with which he answered the questions, the ready nonchalance. Kerry had felt the weight in the room shift somehow, and he worried Michael might in some way be made a fool of.

The laughter from the surveillance room floated through the one-way and when Luca heard it, he wondered which of the men were in there, and if they were buying his act, or if they could tell how weary he felt. He smoked his cigarette casually, tapped it against the side of the ashtray, peered at Michael through the smoke. He had noticed from the moment Michael had entered the room that he looked older. Not more aged, because it was hard to tell how Michael aged, with all the scars across his face, but he looked more in command, more knowledgeable and comfortable in himself. Luca found it hard not to feel proud of his protégé.

He watched Michael take a cigarette from his silver case and light it with the matches on the table. Luca peered at the case and remembered buying it for Michael years before as a present, congratulations for some milestone reached, he forgot what exactly.

'If we link Carlo to these killings,' Michael said quietly, 'then you're not going down for trespass, you're going down for conspiracy. Carlo's put you right in the middle of it. Think about it – you're the perfect person: corrupt cop; fresh out of prison; and you've already taken the rap once and kept your mouth shut. How did he convince you to get involved in it all? He must have spun you one hell of a story.'

Luca smiled. Michael was doing what he expected him to, trying to cast doubt on his relationship with Carlo, open up cracks. Luca regretted having to keep his guard up, having to act cold and aloof. He guessed if they had met on the street or in a bar things would have been different, he would have told him he bore him no grudge. But under these circumstances, when the one person standing between him and going back to Angola was Michael, he had to play the role that gave him an edge.

'I was in prison for the first few murders,' said Luca. 'How are you going to swing a jury on that?'

'I don't have to for a conspiracy charge. I thought you would've been smart enough to see that Carlo's using you. You think Ciro's bank getting raided was an accident? All your money gone just as you get released?'

For the first time Luca felt a pang of nerves. He paused, peered at Michael and wondered if he had betrayed himself, if he had made some gesture which showed Michael had got to him. He hadn't thought to link what happened to Ciro with Carlo. Ciro getting raided had made sense in the context of the police clampdown, but now Michael's suggestion seemed to make sense too.

'Don't you think Carlo could have stopped the raid if he'd wanted to?' Michael said, hammering home the point. 'Then just a few weeks later Carlo pressures the parole board into having you released early.'

Luca stared at Michael and took a long drag on his cigarette, his mind drifting back to his first conversation with Carlo after his release, when he had asked to walk away from the Family and, to his surprise, Carlo had agreed so readily.

'Here's how I see it,' Michael continued. 'We let you out of here and Carlo's gonna think you cut a deal. We charge you with parole violation and you're back inside. It's Angola or a *paesano* hired by Carlo to take you out.'

Michael kept his tone flat, his face stony and impenetrable, but Luca thought he could see a pleading look in his eye, as if he wanted to make amends.

'Only way out for you,' Michael continued, 'is if we send you to court on a trespass charge, have a friendly word to the prosecutor. I'll guarantee you bail and a convenient court date.'

Luca needed to talk to Michael alone, away from the horde on the other side of the mirror. He darted his eyes to the one-way then back to Michael in a quicksilver arc. Michael's face didn't move but Luca sensed some kind of acknowledgment.

'I'd like to speak to my lawyer,' Luca said, not taking his eyes off Michael. The mention of a lawyer would mean holding off on the interview, a return to his cell, time away. He hoped Michael would seize the opportunity.

'We'll resume the interview in a little while.' Michael stubbed out his cigarette while two uniformed officers shuffled into the room and ushered Luca towards the door. As he exited, Luca caught a glimpse of himself in the one-way mirror and felt the presence of the grim-faced men lurking on the other side.

A quarter of an hour later Luca was sitting on his own in a solitary-confinement cell reserved for violent prisoners. Inside the narrow room was a creaking fold-down bed and a bucket, and above him a greasy air-vent and a single naked light-bulb. The brick walls were crumbling and upholstered in mold, and the sound of water dripping onto stone emanated from one of the corners. The whole effect made Luca think of dungeons, of treason, of the executioner's block.

The door opened and Michael stepped in, and the two men stared at each other. Behind Michael, someone closed the door with an echoing clang and turned the lock. Michael sat on the bunk next to Luca. He offered him a cigarette from his case and Luca accepted and they both lit up. Luca wondered if Michael remembered who had given him the case. Maybe it was significant only to him. Michael slipped the case back into his pocket and Luca got the feeling he was being pushed into the past.

'You look well,' Michael said finally, and Luca waved away the pleasantry. 'I'm not well. I'm old and rusty. If I wasn't I wouldn't be in this cell.'

Michael stared at Luca with something approaching pity. Now that the two of them were alone, Luca's front had melted away to reveal a tired, confounded old man. In a way, Michael felt glad that Luca was being honest with him; he hoped the candor was a sign of closeness, of good regard.

'I meant what I said up there,' he said. 'You cooperate and I'll do everything I can to help you.'

'I guess you do owe me something.' Luca turned his gaze to the floor and took a long drag on his cigarette.

'After I got let out, I went to see Carlo for a job. You were right about my money being with Ciro. Carlo asked me to look into the Axeman. He said it was costing him money and respect. Schneider's office was the natural place to start.'

Michael nodded. The story made sense, and more importantly he had the feeling Luca was telling the truth. In the silence he noticed the moldy, basement smell, the scent of ore and stagnant water, of having hit rock-bottom.

'He could be setting you up,' he said.

'The thought had crossed my mind,' Luca replied, 'but I doubt it. Everyone I've spoken to says the same thing, no one's got a clue who the Axeman is. If Carlo was involved, people would know.'

Michael had no choice but to agree.

'I got a deal that could work out for both of us,' Luca said, and Michael made a gesture to indicate he was willing to hear more.

'Let me carry on with my investigation,' he continued. 'Stick a couple of tailgaters on me, which you were gonna do anyhow. If I am involved you get to build up a nice body of evidence, if I'm not, and I find out who's doing the killings, I've handed him to you on a plate. It'll be like the both of us working on the case, but you're guaranteed all the plaudits. Another medal for your cabinet and we both walk away happy.'

Michael wondered if the last was a dig at him, but Luca betrayed no hint of it, and was instead peering at him keenly, waiting for an answer.

'If you let me have him,' said Michael, 'you'll still have to deal with Carlo.'

'I know. I'll worry about that another time.'

Michael stared at Luca through the cigarette smoke.

'I know this is going to sound like a stupid question coming from me,' he said, 'but how do I know I can trust you?'

Luca looked at him for a moment, then a grin broadened across his face and Michael couldn't help but smile, too. For the briefest instant their ill-fated friendship and the twists of fortune that had sent them both spiraling downwards became nothing more than a joke laid on by the universe for their sole enjoyment.

'You can trust me,' said Luca, 'because neither of us have a choice.'

'I'll speak to the DA's office about your prosecutor. You'll make bail and we'll schedule the case for a month's time.'

They smiled at each other again and Michael wanted to tell Luca he was sorry for everything that had happened to him. But something stopped him from speaking. There didn't seem to be any point in it – he got the feeling Luca already knew.

27

The next morning Luca sat in the dock of a sleepy courtroom tucked away somewhere in the recesses of the courthouse. He scanned the gallery for reporters or slack-jawed spectators but the place was near empty – confirmation that he was indeed yesterday's news. On the bench behind him a gray-haired, gaunt Sicilian met his gaze, Alessandro Sandoval, Carlo's lawyer and *consigliere*. Sandoval was flanked by two bodyguards, bored-looking dish-faced men in gray suits. Sandoval smiled and Luca smiled back, happy to see a familiar face.

He turned back around and waited for the judge to arrive and his mind drifted back to the meeting in the cell the previous night. Michael had looked so repentant, so eager to make amends. Luca wondered if he should have told him he no longer bore him a grudge.

There was a bustle of noise and Luca looked up to see the judge enter the court. He rose along with everyone else, then he sat down again and the tiresome legal proceedings began. The prosecutor stuck to the line Michael had agreed: trespass; no demand to send Luca back to prison for a parole violation until the trial. The judge set bail at a hundred dollars, Sandoval agreed the payment, and an hour later Luca was in the bustling lobby of the courthouse. He watched the rain-soaked attorneys and clerks entering from the street, crossing the slippery black-and-white-tiled floor. Police officers and men in suits lounged about on the wooden benches that lined the walls, or stood in groups discussing their cases. Luca felt distanced from it all, half-asleep, as he stood alone by the draughty main doors. The place brought back bad memories. He had managed to dodge Angola a second time and he felt a dull relief as he stared at the people buzzing about the hall.

Presently Sandoval approached with the two buttons and he and Luca hugged each other. They exchanged greetings, then consolations that they should be meeting again under such circumstances, as they strolled out of the lobby and down the glistening front steps, pulling up collars against the rain. They got into a Silver Ghost limousine that was waiting for them outside, and shook off the damp. Luca peered about the plush interior of the car, at the gray velvet upholstery, the mahogany panels.

'Carlo's new toy,' said Sandoval with a wry smile, and Luca smiled back. Then Sandoval's expression changed, becoming somber.

'I'm sorry, Luca. Carlo's calling you in.' He said it in a regretful tone, and Luca made a face to show he had been expecting such a thing to happen. Sandoval tapped the back of the seat in front of him, and the driver pulled the car out into the road. Luca inspected Sandoval, his thin frame, his face frail and aged. He was approaching seventy and was well past the point of running errands for the Matrangas.

'I thought you would have retired by now,' Luca said.

Sandoval inhaled, letting the air whistle through his teeth. 'You know how Carlo is,' he replied. 'Finds it hard to trust the new generation.'

Luca nodded. He and Sandoval had got on well together in the past – Sandoval was one of the many men in the Family who had mentored Luca over the years. He was never really a Mafioso, not in terms of character; he was a good man who somehow got dragged into the life. They looked at each other with a mutual weariness, two men broken by the Family, trapped in the back of a gilded car.

'I need you to do something for me,' Luca said. 'Get a kid to break into Schneider's office. There's a cupboard on the staircase, on the top floor. I left a box in there and I need it delivered to me. And Alessandro,' he added, 'don't tell Carlo about it.'

Sandoval eyed Luca suspiciously for a moment, and then he nodded. 'Sure,' he said, stony-faced. He turned to his side, pulled the blind down and closed his eyes, evidently trying to catch up on some rest. Luca turned and gazed out of the window, watching the rainy streets speed past.

'Boss,' the driver said to Sandoval, 'there's a brown sedan behind us. Been there since we left the courthouse.'

Sandoval opened his eyes and he and Luca turned to look behind them. They saw the car a little further down the road, two men who looked like police officers in the front seats, trying hard not to look like police officers.

'Talbot's tailing me,' Luca said.

Sandoval nodded and shrugged.

'It's to be expected,' he said, turning back round and closing his eyes.

Half an hour later Luca was back at Carlo's house, sitting in a chair next to the old man while he berated Luca for slipping up. No drinks or food were offered this time, just a cold formality, a getting down to business.

'You've directly implicated me in this,' Carlo said. 'I'm worse off now than I was before you got involved. What did you tell them?'

Luca shrugged. 'I told them nothing. They have no proof I was even in the office.'

'And your charge is what?'

'Trespass.'

Carlo eyed him doubtfully and Luca could tell what he was thinking – trespass was too light a charge. He drummed his fingers against the arm of the chair and peered at Luca.

'We'll speak to the landlord,' he said finally, 'get him to drop any charges.'

'Thank you,' Luca nodded, acknowledging the chastisement. Carlo glared at him then shook his head.

'And don't be so stupid next time,' he said, heaving himself out of his chair and exiting the room with a shake of the head.

Luca sighed to himself and stood. For all Carlo's fatherly warmth he could turn in an instant and make Luca go from feeling like a member of the family to feeling like an unwanted stray. He walked over to the window that looked out onto the garden. The rain was pelting the lawn and, a little further away, the bare vines, twisted and contorted, swayed in the plummeting rain. Luca wondered if keeping him on the case might be a ruse to make him lower his guard. Maybe a hit was already being arranged. He prayed Sandoval hadn't told Carlo about the box, and thought of the brown sedan that must be parked in front of the house. He remembered there was a gate at the back of the garden that opened out onto a different street. He crossed to the terrace doors and stepped out into the rain, closed the door after him, and made his way through the muddy paths to the very rear. He had time to kill and he knew exactly how to kill it, but first he needed to make a trip to a liquor store.

An hour later Luca was rapping his knuckles on the glass-paneled door of the Pinkerton National Detective Agency. A distinctly female voice asked him to come in and he entered the office to see a beautiful girl in her late teens or early twenties sitting behind the front desk. Beautiful except for a bruised eye and a cut on her forehead. Something about the girl reminded him of Simone, the upright posture, the litheness, the depth in her eyes. She turned her head slightly and met his gaze, and he could tell straight away she thought him suspicious.

'Hello, sir, how may I help?' She spoke in a silky voice, and Luca got the impression the girl was shaken, a little scared maybe.

'Is Lefebvre in?' Luca asked, pulling the flat-cap from his head.

'I'll just see if he's free. Who may I say is calling?'

'Tell him it's an old friend.'

The girl nodded, got up and straightened her skirt with the palm of her hand, then disappeared into the adjoining room. She reappeared a few seconds later and ushered him into Lefebvre's office.

The old man peered up and smiled at Luca as he entered. Lefebvre had aged ten years in the five Luca had been away. More blotches on his skin, more yellow in his eyes – the man was a slow-motion suicide suspended in alcohol. He gestured at the chair opposite and Luca sat and pulled from his pocket the bottle of rye he'd purchased at the liquor store. He held it in his palm a moment, as if checking the weight, then he placed it on the desk next to the bottle Lefebvre already had open.

'For the collection,' Luca said.

Lefebvre gave him a look, then bent to his right to rummage about a drawer in his desk, the rolls of fat around his midriff straining against his shirt.

'I heard you got out,' he said, returning to an upright position with two glasses in his hand. 'I heard you're back working for Carlo. In an unusual capacity.'

Luca stayed silent and Lefebvre poured them both double measures. They raised their glasses and drank, Luca knowing he'd regret it when the pains started shooting through his gut.

'To what do I owe the honor?'

'I came to ask you about a man named Schneider,' Luca said. 'I heard you two did a little business not too long ago.'

'I tell you about that, you tell me how you found out,' Lefebvre countered, raising an eyebrow.

Luca nodded and Lefebvre took another sip from his glass.

'He came to see me about some protection. Told me he was worried someone was after him and he wanted to hire a bodyguard. I told him we didn't really do that kind of thing anymore, but for a small fee I could give him a name. So he paid me a small fee and

I gave him a name.' Lefebvre lifted his hands into the air to signal the end of the story.

'When was this?' asked Luca.

'A couple of weeks before he got killed.'

Luca nodded. 'Seems like the name you gave him didn't work out too well for old Schneider.'

'Didn't work out too well for the name either,' said Lefebvre. 'The cops found him pushing up daisies in the Audubon Park last Saturday week. Two bullet holes in his head.'

Luca nodded again, sifting through the angles. Schneider had been expecting the killer. He had seen the grocers getting killed and had gone out to hire a bodyguard.

'Did you tell anyone about Schneider's visit?' he asked.

Lefebvre took another sip of the rye. 'Not a soul,' he said. 'Although the police came visiting yesterday. I told them what I told you, except I said to them I told Schneider I couldn't help him and that was that.' Lefebvre sighed melodramatically and shook his head. 'Things ain't like they used to be,' he said ruefully, resting his hands on the wide expanse of his stomach. 'That old bond between us and the police. It don't exist no more. Times have changed for the worse.'

Luca wasn't sure who exactly Lefebvre meant by *us,* but he nodded in token agreement. The Creoles were always bemoaning the passing of better times. They saw the history of New Orleans as nothing but a steady decline from the pinnacle of French rule, a slow, vulgar Americanization that had first marginalized and then dismantled their culture. Lefebvre, like many of the other white Creoles Luca had met, spent his time lamenting the loss of a gilded age that, as far as Luca could tell, was only ever a myth in the first place.

'So who was the name?' he asked.

'You don't know him. Some kid from Baton Rouge. Schneider wanted an out-of-towner,' Lefebvre shrugged. 'You know, a ghost.'

'And did Schneider tell you why he thought someone was after him?'

'What do you think?' said Lefebvre. Luca nodded and thought for a moment. Before Luca had been convicted, Lefebvre was an informer for the detective bureau; client confidentiality meant nothing to him. But when Lefebvre's old partner Hess found out what he was up to, and threatened to tell Pinkerton headquarters and the District Attorney's office, Lefebvre had ordered a hit on him, and Luca had helped arrange it. It was then that Lefebvre had scurried into a bottle, pickling himself in guilt. Back then Luca thought the whole affair pathetic, and didn't waste a second thought on it. But now he couldn't help but feel sorry for the regret-stricken mess of a man sitting in front of him. The really sad thing was Lefebvre didn't have the guts to end it all quickly. A shotgun would have been kinder and quicker than the bottle.

'Well, it's been good to see you again,' he said, running the edge of his flat-cap through his fingers. He put the half-drunk glass of rye on the desk and stood.

'You gonna tell me who tipped you off?' asked Lefebvre.

'Nothing to tell, old friend,' Luca replied with a grin. 'I found one of your business cards in Schneider's office. You need to be more careful who you hand those things to.'

'Sonofabitch.'

Luca grinned and sauntered out of the room. He nodded goodbye to the girl in the reception area, trotted down the stairs and through the ground-floor lobby. He stood under the building's portico while he buttoned up his coat and noticed a tall, heavy-set colored man staring at him from the other side of the road, his image flickering through the gaps in the traffic that sped between them. Luca frowned, trying to place the man's face, an angry, hurt-looking face that he'd seen somewhere before – Angola, maybe? He turned his collar up and stepped into the street, heading north towards the nearest tram stop.

When he reached the stop he lit a cigarette and turned to see if the tram was on its way. As he peered down the avenue he noticed the heavy-set man had followed him and was waiting at the stop, too. Luca wondered about the man – if he did indeed recognize the face, or if paranoia was getting the better of him.

The tram arrived a few minutes later and Luca hopped aboard. He cast a look after him as the tram pulled off – the man was still at the stop, waiting for a car on a different route. Luca relaxed a little and took a seat by the window. He watched the world go by all the way until the City Park, where he got off and took the long muddy path up Bayou St John, mulling over the case as he went. Schneider was onto something and he'd hired a bodyguard. His insistence on a bodyguard from out of town meant whoever he was scared of had links to the New Orleans underworld. And then the bodyguard was executed. Professionally. Either the Axeman was also good with a gun, or there were other people involved, clearing the way for him. Again Michael's insinuations about Carlo forced themselves to the front of Luca's thoughts, and he prayed that Sandoval would keep his word and deliver the box to him without telling anyone.

28

Against his better judgment Michael had gone to the courthouse that morning to watch Luca's case be heard. He wasn't sure why he had gone – everything had been arranged with the District Attorney and the judge in the small hours, but he felt as if he might miss something important. He didn't think his old mentor had seen him; he had arrived late, sat on the very last row of the gallery and left as soon as the bail had been confirmed. Luca had struck him as old and frail in the prison cell, on the back foot. But in the courthouse he looked assured, smiling with Sandoval and lying back in his seat with a cockiness that brought back memories of his trial five years previously. The display had made Michael wonder if it had been the right decision to let him go so easily. He ran through all the angles in his mind as he made his way back to the precinct. Was Luca really looking into the killings for Carlo? If he was, then Michael was wrong about the Family being involved – or was Carlo duping Luca, setting him up for something down the line?

When Michael got to his desk at the bureau, a bleary-eyed Kerry was waiting for him. They sat at his desk and Kerry went through the wad of papers in his hand.

'Jones and Shippey are on first watch at the courthouse,' he said, reading from a message at the top of the stack.

'Good. Search reports?' Michael asked, lighting a cigarette.

Kerry fumbled through the papers.

'Detective Hessel did the search on Schneider's office, two days ago. Came up with nothing incriminating. Except this . . .'

Kerry handed Michael a couple of clipped sheets of paper.

'Hessel wrote them up yesterday while we were out.'

Michael scanned the papers – Hessel had found a business card in Schneider's office for the Pinkerton Detective Agency. He had followed it up and the man at the agency claimed Schneider had been in there hunting for a bodyguard and had left empty-handed.

'Lefebvre,' Michael said to himself. He remembered the man, an associate of Luca's, a tremendously fat Creole, drunk and crushed by worries. It didn't make sense that he'd turn away a job as easy as finding someone a bodyguard. Michael thought of the gun they had found under Schneider's pillow, and now it turned out he had been looking for a bodyguard. If Schneider had told the Creole why he wanted the protection, and if Michael could make him talk, he would be one step closer to finding a reason for the killings.

'Ask him to come in for a chat,' Michael said.

'Yes, sir,' said Kerry. 'Detective Jones checked Schneider's filings at City Hall for the last five years. No cases involving known Family associates or any of the victims. Carter did a re-search last night. Found nothing, too, and there didn't seem to be anything missing.'

Michael thought for a moment, and rubbed his fingers across his face. As each new clue presented itself, it just as soon proved worthless. Maybe when the reports from the manhunt came in that afternoon a new lead might spark into life, but Michael didn't feel too optimistic about it.

He looked up and noticed Kerry was smiling at him.

'What's to smile at, son?' he asked.

Kerry held up a telegram triumphantly.

'From the housing department. Ermanno Lombardi's address.'

Lombardi's lodgings were in a slender, Creole town-house on an oak-lined avenue in the 7th Ward. The building was wrapped in pastel-colored stucco and set behind a tiny garden of night-blooming jasmine and persimmon trees. The street itself was quiet except for a few old Creole women who were busy cleaning their porches.

Michael and Kerry trotted up the path to Lombardi's lodging and rang the bell. A chubby old Creole woman, dark-skinned and wearing an apron, opened the door and looked them up and down through the mosquito screen. The women of the 7th Ward had a reputation for being house-proud and fastidious, the matrons of a black middle-class that was over a century old. The appearance of policemen on one of their doorsteps was as shocking to them as it would be to a society belle.

'Yes?' The woman's voice was wary and soft.

'We're from the Police Department, ma'am,' Michael said. 'We'd like to speak to Ermanno Lombardi.'

The woman frowned and a look of concern crossed her face.

'I haven't seen him for days,' she said in a thick French accent. 'He does this sometimes.'

'May we check his room?' Michael asked.

'For sure,' she said with a shrug.

She wiped her hands on her heavily starched apron and pushed open the screen door.

'Your feet,' she said, stern and haughty.

They wiped the mud from their shoes onto a tawny-colored welcome mat just inside the door and filed through the porch. The house was spotless and well-decorated with houseplants, paintings and rosewood *étagères* holding china vases, porcelain statuettes and other *objets d'art*. The aroma of mint julep wafted through the air. The woman smiled at them proudly and led them up a creaking carpet-covered staircase.

They approached a door on the fourth story and a disconcerting smell of decay caused the woman to grimace as she took a key from her apron pocket and turned the lock. When she swung open the door the smell wafted towards them in a much stronger form, a putrid, excremental stench. They caught a glimpse of

Lombardi splayed out on the bed, naked, a garrote wire around his neck, brown stains on the white linen.

The woman shrieked and backed away from the door, a hand over her face. Michael pulled a handkerchief from his pocket, covered his nose and mouth and stepped into the room. He approached the body and inspected it. The dead man had a look of anguish on his face, the muscles in his neck contorted, pulling his chin downwards, making it look as if he were smiling. His fists were balled up, clenching the sheets in frozen knots. Michael turned to Kerry and told him to call in the murder. Kerry took a last look at the body, turned and hurried down the stairs, leaving Michael alone with the remains of Ermanno Lombardi.

Half an hour later the house was bustling with people. In the room itself, a squad of policemen was busying itself with the usual crime-scene duties. The doctor had arrived and after a brief examination had estimated the time of death as at least a week beforehand. Lombardi was the sole lodger on the top floor and the landlady had a bad leg, so she rarely went up there to check on him. She claimed he often disappeared for days at a time, and she had put his final absence down to this.

Her character statement fitted what Michael had heard from O'Neil – Lombardi was quiet and anxious and kept to himself, and the only complaint she had about him was that male visitors came knocking for him a little too frequently. She said one man visited him more than any of the others, but could only give a vague description – a big Italian-looking man in his thirties.

There was no sign of a struggle in the room and the landlady said the last time she had heard Lombardi come in was the previous Monday, and that he might have been accompanied by someone, but she wasn't sure. Michael thought of the naked body and checked with the doctor, who confirmed there had been intercourse shortly before the death. Michael reconstructed the chain of events: Lombardi had been talking about the Axeman, and to shut him up, a man had been paid to kill him. The man had picked him up, taken him back to his lodgings, and after they'd had sex and Lombardi had fallen asleep, the man had wrapped a garrote wire round his neck.

When the men had removed Lombardi's body from the room and the windows had been opened to let out the fetid air, Michael looked through Lombardi's possessions. There was nothing suspicious in the room – no guns or stacks of money or bags of contraband, no ledgers written in code, or even a diary. In a chest at the bottom of the bed, however, he found Lombardi's washbag, a Twinplex razor, a bottle of macassar oil, another of Guerlain Mitsouko, a folding Brownie snapshot camera, and lastly envelopes full of photographs stamped by the Eastman Kodak Co of Rochester, New York.

Michael sat on the bed and went through them all. There were no photographs of family, just pictures of Lombardi's friends, and occasionally of the man himself. The same few faces kept reappearing in the photographs, five or six men, all athletic-looking, fresh-faced. There were holiday snaps from days at the Lake, from a picnic, a bandstand, some of inebriated gatherings in people's houses. The photographs had an intimacy to them and Michael felt as if he was trespassing when he looked at them.

He came to a photograph of Lombardi and a second man, a medium shot taken somewhere by the river, he guessed. The two men had their arms over each other's shoulders, smiling at the camera, the wind whipping their hair about.

Michael took the snapshot into the downstairs living room. The landlady had called her friends around for support, and was now in the midst of a gaggle of old Creole women consoling each other and lamenting the state of the world, one talking over the other in a wailing wall of prayers and sorrow. *Gumbo ya-ya*, he thought, and shouted to make himself heard.

When he had their attention, he showed the landlady the photograph and she confirmed what he had been thinking – the man in the snap with Lombardi was the man who visited him more than all the others. The man must know enough about Lombardi to give Michael a clue as to why he had been killed. Michael took the photograph back into the bedroom and he and Kerry went through the envelopes all over again, finding every photograph in which the man appeared. They laid them on the floor in a crooked, topsy-turvy grid, and when they had completed it they stepped back and studied the black-and-white mosaic in front of them.

Michael picked up the photograph he had shown to the landlady and inspected the stranger with his arm around Lombardi. Short nails. Right hand markedly bigger than the left. The left hand with cuts all over it. The man worked in a job where he used a knife. A butcher or a chef? He scanned through the other photographs and found one that showed a group of men at a gathering in someone's house. The stranger was seated at a table at the back of the room. He had a peacoat on and underneath it some grimy work overalls. On the breast of the overalls was a patch with a word that could only be partially seen under the shadow of the coat. Michael guessed at the word from only the first few letters: *Normanson's*. A fish-processing factory over in the docks.

29

Ida waited until D'Andrea had left before sneaking a peek into Lefebvre's office. He had the phone to his ear, drumming his chubby fingers on the desk, and Ida guessed he was waiting for an operator to connect him. She had heard snatches of the conversation between her boss and D'Andrea, including the name Schneider, and she guessed whoever Lefebvre was calling now was somehow involved in the thing. She approached her desk and hovered her hand over the phone, gunslinger-like, raising herself onto tiptoes so she could see Lefebvre's form through the glass partition.

'Monsieur Lefebvre?' she called. She saw Lefebvre move the phone away from his ear, and Ida picked up the receiver at her end.

'Yeah?' he shouted.

'I might go for lunch in a few minutes,' she said, a little unconvincingly.

'Sure,' said Lefebvre, shaking his head and returning the phone to his ear.

Ida sat at her desk and listened in while the operator connected him.

'John? It's Lefebvre,' she heard him say through the phone.

'Hello, Lefebvre.'

Ida recognized the voice on the other end, and realized why the Pinkertons didn't have any records on John Morval.

'We need to talk,' Lefebvre said, his tone brisk and businesslike. 'I just had a visit from Luca D'Andrea.'

There was silence for a moment, and in the background of the connection, Ida heard noises, typewriters, conversations, footsteps.

'What did he want?'

'Take a guess,' Lefebvre said sarcastically.

The other man sighed. 'Can you come to me?' he asked.

'Sure,' Lefebvre said. 'Be there as soon as I can.'

Ida waited till Lefebvre had put down the receiver at his end before she hung up. She grabbed her bag and coat, left the building and took up a position on the opposite side of the road where she hoped Lefebvre wouldn't see her. Two businessmen walked past her in the rain, suited and smiling underneath their umbrellas. They turned to look at her with the same expression that had been worn by the man she now knew to be D'Andrea, when he'd sauntered into the office. Lefebvre hadn't even noticed, he was too drunk, but now she raised a hand to the black eye and the cut disfiguring her face, as if to hide them from view. She was used to people staring at her, but not like this.

The same repeating images of the attack flashed before her mind's eye once more, and the terror of it all shook her nerves yet again. She remembered how frightened she had been, how she had picked up the rock instinctively but also with a searing anger, how she had hit the two boys, how they had lain like bloodied corpses in the muddy ditch. How seriously had she injured them? Would they seek her out? She felt once again the touch of her skirt as it slipped down her waist, her struggling uselessly as if in a nightmare, the weight of the rock in her hand. She remembered the abuse they had hurled at her and she wondered if they would still have attacked her had she been on her own, without Lewis.

On top of everything else she felt like a fool, that the whole thing was her fault. She had been playing at being a detective, and she had dragged herself and Lewis into danger because of it. Maybe being a secretary was all she was good for, something to pretty up the office. Wasn't that why Lefebvre had given her the job in the first place?

And yet, when she'd realized earlier on what Lefebvre and

D'Andrea were talking about, she hadn't hesitated to listen in, or to snoop on Lefebvre's phone call, or to come out here and spy on him, to follow him wherever he would take her. She got the feeling that while she was in her shocked state, something else had taken control and seen her through, and she realized she was more resilient than she had previously thought. This new awareness provided her with a new measure of confidence, and determination. She had no choice but to continue.

Lefebvre emerged a few minutes later, blinking in the daylight. He slanted his hat onto his head and trudged up the street, his immense weight and the alcohol in his blood making him unsteady on his feet. Ida followed him through the rain until a few blocks later, he turned off the road and entered a towering office building.

She hung about outside for a few minutes and when she was sure he had gone up to whatever floor Morval was on, she entered the reception area. She ignored the prim receptionist sitting behind a gold-trim counter and approached the building directory, which was pinned to a board by a dazzlingly green fern. There was an entry for a *John Morval & Co Garment-Makers* – which had leased the entirety of the fourth floor. Ida turned, nodded at the receptionist, and left the building.

She waited on the opposite side of the road again, under a shop awning this time, to keep out of the rain. Lefebvre's meeting lasted twenty minutes. He exited the building in a rush, looking anxious, and paced as quickly as he could up the street to a tram stop. Ida crossed back over to the same side of the road and waited. When Lefebvre's tram arrived and he had gotten on, she hopped onto it via the entrance at the back, hoping he didn't turn his head until she was seated. When she reached the partition screen that was moved backwards and forwards depending on how many Negroes happened to be in the designated places at the back, she slid into a seat, moving her body down the varnished wood until she was hidden from view.

The tram rode out of the business district, heading southwest into the long green residential neighborhoods that sprawled out of the city in a farrago of well-tended gardens and tree-lined boulevards. They passed by the quads of Tulane University and skirted past Audubon Park, and when they reached Perrier Street, Lefebvre rang the bell and Ida watched him waddle off the tram. At the next stop, she descended too, and traced her way backwards, catching up with Lefebvre as he turned onto Henry Clay Avenue. She followed him as he crossed Coliseum Street and watched him enter an ominous, sprawling building that looked like some kind of bloated French château. Ida could tell by the building's location, its size, the bars across the windows, and the fact that it was set behind a towering brick wall, that the place was a psychiatric hospital.

Once she was sure he was inside, she approached the gates to the building, and read the sign outside: *The Louisiana Retreat for the Feeble-Minded*. She had heard of the place, a hospital used by New Orleans's richest families. She watched people come and go through the main entrance, the nuns who ran the hospital dashing through the rainy courtyards with their hands to their veils. Ida walked around to the rear of the building, where she guessed the staff entrance would be. She found a gate giving onto the gardens, stepped inside and sat on a bench that was sheltered from the rain by a flimsy wooden pavilion.

After half an hour or so, a Negro girl a couple of years younger than Ida exited the building and sat on the veranda that ran across the rear wall. She was chubby and wore a navy-blue maid's uniform, her hair pulled back under a white cotton cap. She took a boudin sandwich from a metal lunchbox in her lap and ate it with slow, birdlike bites. Ida left the shelter of the pavilion and approached her. The girl frowned when she saw Ida nearing her. Ida smiled, noticing the sharp smell of disinfectant on the girl's clothes.

'Hey. You work here?' Ida asked.

The girl nodded and stared suspiciously at Ida's bruised face. Ida sat next to her and smiled again.

'You do me a favor, I'll give you some cash,' she said.

The girl stopped eating and frowned at her.

'What kinda favor?' she asked in a heavy Uptown accent.

'Man came in here about a half-hour ago called Lefebvre. You look in the visitor book and tell me who he went to see and I'll give you a dollar.'

The girl peered at Ida, weighing her up.

'Why you wanna know?' she asked, giving Ida the slant-eyed stare of a street-girl who knew something was afoot.

'I can't tell you that,' Ida said, trying to sound regretful.

The girl stayed silent and continued to stare at her.

'Two dollars,' she said eventually. 'Gonna have to give one to the receptionist.'

'OK,' Ida said, knowing full well the girl was lying. The girl smiled for the first time, happy to have got one over on Ida. She returned her sandwich to the lunchbox, brushed the crumbs from her dress, and re-entered the building.

Ten minutes later, Ida was on the return tram back to the city. Lefebvre had visited a patient called Samuel Kline Junior. Ida had heard the name before, but couldn't quite remember where. After she finished work, she went to the library and searched for the name in the local newspapers. She found it in a weight of articles. Brigadier General Samuel Kline Junior was from an old-money family, a war hero who had fought in Cuba and the Philippines. He had returned from active duty and entered politics, becoming a member of the Behrman administration, overseeing the committee that administered licensing in Storyville. Most of the articles, though, concerned a court case a few years before; he had been accused of indecency with a minor. He'd stepped down, been diagnosed with a nervous disorder and sent to live in the sanatorium by a friendly judge. D'Andrea had been to see Lefebvre about the

Axeman, and Lefebvre had then been to see a member of one of the oldest families in New Orleans. The people involved were getting more powerful and connected, and worryingly for Ida, her boss seemed to be at the heart of it all.

30

The rain had waterlogged the paths through the bayou, making each step a slow pull against the suction of the mud. Luca was a few minutes from Simone's, in a desolate stretch of the trail, when he heard footsteps thumping behind him. He turned to see the heavy-set man from the tram stop charging towards him, knocking into him with his shoulder. Before he knew it, Luca was on the ground. Blows smashed into his face with the force of piston pumps, slamming into his jaw, shattering his teeth.

'Eight years, motherfucker!' screamed the man between blows, and Luca realized through his daze where he knew him from – a decade ago, an assault in a saloon. The man happened to be nearby and had previous convictions. Eight years in Angola on Luca's falsified evidence.

He knew there was no point in trying to fight back – all he could do was keep his guard up and try to ward off the blows. He was old, weak and tired and his assailant had every advantage. As the man struck him again and again, on his head and arms and torso, Luca became delirious, his thoughts scattering, and something inside him stirred, withdrawing him from the world. The punches became dull impacts, painless and distant, as if it was someone else being hit. He had a premonition of his fate – a descent into the dark warm waters of the bayou, a descent that was in some way also a return, a restoration – and somehow the vision made him feel calm. He let his arms drop to his sides and he closed his eyes. The man carried on pummeling him, his fists like blocks of cement. Then the flurry of punches petered out, dwindling to a stop like a switched-off engine. There was silence except for the rain, then Luca heard the man sobbing.

'Eight years,' mumbled the man, his voice choked with emotion. 'Eight years.' Luca felt the man pick him up and drag him to the edge of the path, and he opened his eyes briefly to see mud crumbling into the waters of the bayou. He felt himself being lifted up and guessed the man was about to hurl him in. He was never sure why he did it, possibly it was some kind of primordial impulse, but as the man threw him over the water, Luca grabbed hold of the man's shirt, and they tumbled into the bayou together.

Luca had heard about drowning people, how once they'd surrendered to their fate a beautiful peace descended on them. He had always wondered how it was possible for anyone to know this, and whether it was not just a tale told to soothe the hearts of drowned sailor's widows. But now he felt himself succumbing to something, the descent of an eternal calm. He felt a kind of slime dissipate from his body, and his mind skittered back to images of church ceremonies, white-robed figures, heads dunked under water, the soothing lilt of hymns.

He burst above the surface and gasped for air. The water suddenly felt cold, stinging his cuts and bruises. He saw he was not too far from the bank. He scrabbled about and his hands made purchase on the mud. He breathed heavily, feeling something sharp in his lungs each time he inhaled. He mustered everything he could and rolled himself onto the bank and breathed deep, exhausting breaths. The pain of the bruises, cuts and fractured bones materialized in his body like a warm glow. He stared at the rain clouds high above him, the edges of the trees, the leaves dancing in the raindrops, caressing the sky.

He heard splashing and cries, and turned his head towards the water – the man was there, thrashing about, panic-stricken. He bobbed down under the water, broke the surface and screamed. Luca would be a fool to fish him out of the bayou, but he stumbled to his feet anyway, saw a low-hanging tree near the water and approached it. He had hardly any strength left, so he collapsed all his weight onto a branch where it forked off from the trunk. The other end of the branch dipped towards the water, and with a few thrashes the man reached it, got a hand on it, and pulled himself to safety.

Luca stared at the man as he coughed water, bent double; then Luca closed his eyes, and after a moment, he collapsed.

When he came to, the sky was darker and he was alone, folded up over the tree-branch. He searched about for the man but found no trace of him. With some effort he managed to get to his feet, and he limped in a daze towards Simone's cabin. He could barely see through the blood in his eyes, but he managed to get there somehow, collapsing on the path in front of her shack, sending the chickens into a squawking frenzy.

31

Normanson's factory was a draughty building of dark clammy wood perched on the very edge of the dock. Aside from a partitioned office by the entrance it was a colossal open-plan area with fifty or so tables spread across it in rows. At each table a worker in blood-smeared overalls and rubber boots processed barrels of fish.

Kerry and Michael spoke to the duty manager, a serious type in a bow tie, a one-dollar suit from the Sears catalogue, and equally cheap Porkony shoes. They showed him the photograph they had found in Lombardi's apartment and the man nodded solemnly in recognition. He led them across the floor, past the rows of tables, and explained the process to them: fish guts went to the slurry house; fillets to the canned-fish suppliers; oil to the apothecaries; and bones to the glue-makers. The factory was heavy with the oozy smell of brine and dead fish and Michael noticed Kerry was holding a hand to his nose to stop himself retching.

They approached a table where a burly, good-looking Italian was cutting up fish with an over-sized knife, throwing the different parts into colored trays. There was a grace and speed to the man's movements that didn't really sit with his bulk, the blade dancing in and out of heads, trunks and tails with a mercurial, ruby shimmer.

'Rocco, police is here to see you,' the duty manager shouted over the clatter of a hundred knives echoing against the walls.

Rocco looked up at them and nodded and Michael recognized his face from the photographs they had found. It was a stony face, hard and pitted, hollow under the cheekbones.

'After they're done, come by the office,' the manager hissed in a suspicious tone.

'Sure thing, boss.' Rocco spoke dismissively, without looking the man in the eye or breaking his rhythm. The manager gave him a withering look, turned and snaked his way back through the tables.

'Rocco, I'm Detective Talbot, this is Officer Kerry.'

Rocco glanced at them, a flash of cobalt under thick, feminine lashes.

'Whadaya want?'

'We wanna talk to you about Lombardi. You hear what happened to him, right?'

'No. What happened? He got killed?' Rocco asked, wiping the sweat from his brow with a hefty forearm. The casual tone made Michael pause, and he wondered if he had misunderstood the relationship between the two men.

'Yeah. He got killed,' he said eventually, trying to deliver the news with some kind of sobriety.

'I told him as much.' Rocco sped up his cutting, driving through the fish in irate swipes.

He picked up various pieces of bone and flesh with the side of the knife and tossed them into the trays. Michael caught sight of a perfectly cleaned spine, shining yellow. Rocco wiped the cutting board with a brush, dropping entrails into the gut-bucket at his feet.

'Well, it don't look too good for you,' Michael said.

'Yeah, how so?' Rocco had a hint of menace in his voice.

'We know why Lombardi got killed, shooting his mouth off about the Axeman. If whoever killed him knew he was talking, then they probably knew he was talking to you.'

For the first time in the encounter Rocco stopped working. He thought for a moment, the realization that he too might be in danger dawning slowly on his craggy features. He stared at them, then jabbed the point of the knife into the wooden table, where it quivered briefly on its blade. He picked up a rag from the side of the table, wiped his hands and nodded to a door in the far wall of the building.

'Let's talk outside.'

He led them across the work area, past men and women still drudging away at their tables while casting sly glances at Rocco and the two police officers. They stepped out through a door onto a covered jetty suspended over the dock-water. The industrial clatter of the factory dimmed to nothing as the door closed behind them, and was replaced by the sound of rain on the river, the blasts of distant foghorns. There were a few chairs scattered about, covered by the mossy beams overhead, and a carpet of cigarette butts lay on the floor.

They sat and Rocco stared out over the dock. 'What do you wanna know?' he said, taking a cigarette from a pack in his breast pocket and lighting it.

'Word is Lombardi—'

'*Ermanno,*' Rocco interrupted, 'his name was Ermanno. Calling him Lombardi makes it sound like he's dead.' The sudden sadness in the man's voice made Michael pause. There was sorrow in the brute sitting next to him after all.

'Sure,' Michael said gently. 'Word is Ermanno got whacked for talking about the Axeman. We wanna know what he told you about it.'

Rocco sighed and shook his head, and gazed out over the polluted waters in front of him. Two seagulls squawked in the rafters of the factory.

'This is off the record, OK? I ain't going in front o' no judge.'

'Sure,' Michael said, 'you're not under arrest.'

Rocco stared at him for a moment longer, then he ran an anxious hand through his hair and started talking.

'Well, I guess it goes back a few months. 'Manno got a telegram from an uncle up north – Boston. Runs a lumberyard. Asked him if he wanted to go up and work there. Money's good, so 'Manno says sure and starts getting ready to leave town, but then he gets asked to do a job. See, 'Manno used to run jobs for some hoods when he was strapped for cash; scare a guy here, collect some money there. Small shit. So just before he's leaving he gets asked to do a dope drop, out in the bayou somewhere. 'Manno says sure and takes a bundle out to where he's supposed to. But he gets suspicious, the bundle's too light for dope, and who the hell drops off dope in the bayou, right? So he thinks maybe he's being set up. He was kinda smart like that, you know.

'So he gets somewhere quiet and opens it up. No dope in there, just rags, newspaper pages, padding. He looks in the middle and finds a piece o' paper, some kinda letter, but it's written in French and he don't understand what it's saying. But in the middle of the letter is a list, a bunch o' names and addresses, right? He can understand that bit. So he ties the bundle back up and takes it to the drop-spot.

'But no one shows. Story was, if no one showed he had to leave the bundle by the side o' the road. So he waits around a few hours, and he gets the feeling someone's watching him, but no one shows. So he leaves the bundle in some ditch like he got told to and he heads back home.'

'Where was the drop-spot?' asked Michael.

Rocco shook his head. 'I dunno no specifics. Some road leading off one of the bayous, that's all he said.' He shrugged and took a drag of his cigarette, looking out over the dock.

'OK. Go on,' said Michael, leaning back in his chair.

'So he gets back and he's getting his things ready to head up north when he gets another telegram; the uncle with the lumber-yard dies in a fire. Yard gets burned to the ground, so no more job for 'Manno and he has to stay in New Orleans. This is about the time the Axeman killings start, and after . . . I dunno, maybe the third one, 'Manno realizes something: the guys' names that were on that list are the same guys getting whacked by the Axeman.'

'How many names were on the list?'

'I dunno. A few.' Rocco shrugged. 'More than have been killed, I think.'

'And what did he say about the names on the list, Rocco?' Michael pressed.

'What do you mean?'

'Were the names Italian? Were they men? What neighborhoods?'

Rocco shook his head again.

'I dunno, I can't remember. He just said they were names. He didn't say what kind. Just names and addresses,' said Rocco, a little agitated now.

'OK, go on,' said Michael, and Rocco resumed his story.

'So 'Manno twigs the whole thing was a set-up, like; he only got given the job because they thought he was leaving town, and now he's staying, maybe he's gonna get whacked to make sure he don't go stool-pigeon. So he starts getting money together to leave town, because he needs some money if he's gonna go on the lam, but, well, you know the rest.'

Rocco shrugged and looked out over the water; the bloodied bodies of discarded fish floated along the dock, sodden greasepaper, tin cans.

'How'd they do it?' he asked softly, turning towards Michael.

'Garrote. In his apartment.' Michael tried to keep his tone gentle.

Rocco nodded and stared at his feet. He swiped away a few of the cigarette butts with the toe of his boot.

'I tried to tell him to get away, but he wouldn't leave without money.' He sighed. 'When'd he die?'

Michael peered at the man — surprised at the depth of feeling. Another strange love, he thought.

'A few days ago. When's the last time you saw him?'

'About a week ago. We had an argument.'

Michael let the comment hang. He listened to the sound of the rain beating against the roof and the oily water in front of them, making the waste on the surface bob and roll. He took his cigarette case from his pocket, lit up and leaned in close to the man.

'Listen, Rocco. This is really important. Who'd he get the job from?'

Rocco turned to look at him and frowned, weighing up the pain of his heartbreak against the idiocy of informing on the Family.

'I ain't going to court. This is all off-record.'

Michael nodded.

'A guy named Pietro. I don't know nothing about him. All Manno ever said was he was an empty suit looking to get made.'

'What's he look like?'

'Small guy, Italian, greased-back hair. Maybe the same height as the kid,' said Rocco, motioning towards Kerry.

'Age?'

'Late thirties, I guess. I only ever saw him once,' Rocco shrugged.

Michael nodded and smiled. The two gulls above them burst out of the rafters and flapped across the open river, pushing hard against the falling rain. They watched the birds disappear into the distance.

'Any idea where we can catch up with him?'

Rocco shook his head.

'Manno used to meet him in some dive in the business district to get his jobs. Tito's, I think.'

Michael smiled again. 'Thanks, Rocco.'

He stood and Kerry followed suit.

'Hey. You serious about maybe I'm next?' Rocco asked.

'Maybe.'

'So what do I do?'

'If you think someone's after you, gimme a call.'

Michael handed Rocco a card, tipped his hat and strode back into the factory with Kerry.

They passed through the processing floor and out into the street. Michael's mind raced – Lombardo's list had had more names on it than those of the victims so far. There were more killings to come.

32

Lewis opened his umbrella against the rain and strolled along Perdido Street, stopping every few minutes to exchange greetings with acquaintances he hadn't seen since his return. It was strange being back in his old neighborhood, back among the people he had grown up with. As much as Lewis cared for them, he couldn't stop himself feeling downbeat when he passed by them on the street, the switch-blade wielders, the gamblers, the dope fiends, the pimps and their whores, all of them sleepwalking their way through their slum-dwellers' existence. Lives that were frittered and short, with no plans, or ambitions, or thoughts for tomorrow.

Lewis knew he was lucky to have a talent and a trade, something to save him from the poverty he grew up in. Things had changed from when he first moved to Mayann's when he was six, when his life was a miscellany of odd jobs, scavenging and making ends meet. Mayann had enrolled him in the Fisk School for Boys, but he spent most of his time trying to keep the family in food. He sold newspapers in Front o' Town or sung for nickels and dimes in a street-corner quartet or worked on a coal-cart, making deliveries to the cribs of the sporting women in Storyville. And when no work was forthcoming, he would go scavenging – sifting through the waste at the Silver City dump, or going down to the docks with his friends and waiting for the coal barges to be unloaded, then jumping into the empty hulls and collecting coal dust to sell around Back o' Town at five cents a bucket. The worst of it was when he rifled through the bins by the restaurants in the Tango Belt, bringing the discarded food he found home to Mayann, who would cut out the spoiled sections so he could return to the restaurants later and sell the food back to them for whatever the proprietors were willing to pay.

All this, along with Mayann's domestic-help job and the steady stream of men that passed through the apartment, meant there was always food on the table, but it was not a life he wanted for his own children, Clarence included. Lewis would always feel guilty about the boy's accident, and would indulge him as much as he could. He saved money each week to pay for doctors and a specialist school for slow children. He prayed he could make enough money to cure Clarence, to prove the doctors wrong. And if he couldn't prove the doctors wrong, he would make sure Clarence wanted for nothing.

Before Lewis had left the house that evening, Clarence had asked him to tell him a bedtime story when he returned. 'A new one,' Clarence had said. Lewis tried to think of a new ghost story to tell the boy but for the life of him he couldn't conjure one up. He'd been through the complete roster of Louisiana folk-ghosts in his attempts to sate Clarence's appetite. He'd told him about the *loup-garou*, the French werewolves that roamed the swamps and were scared of nothing except frogs. He had told him of Bras Coupe, the runaway slave and his renegade band, who attacked plantations and were immune to death. He'd told him of the needle men, the white medical students from the Charity Hospital who came into Back o' Town at night, armed with syringes full of sleeping liquid, ready to steal away black folks to use in experiments. He'd even told him of the *mystères*, the voodou skeletons that dressed in top hats and tuxedos, and were named after French aristocrats Baron Kriminel, Baron La Croix and Baron Samedi.

But Clarence's favorite stories were about the Pirate Jean Lafitte, who each time he buried treasure in the bayous killed a shipmate so his spirit would guard the hoard. The spirits were said to manifest themselves as the jack o' lanterns and will o' the wisps that were seen in the bayous after dark, the lights that receded as they were approached and drew travelers off the safe paths.

Lewis turned a corner onto Bienville Street and approached his destination – the Mahogany Hall, a whitewashed colonial building set behind a tiny well-kept garden. He stepped onto the porch, happy to be out of the rain, and knocked on the door. It opened to reveal a beautiful light-skinned girl of his own age. He explained who he was and she led him into an airy, well-decorated hall where he took a seat on a red leather button-back armchair.

Lewis glanced around the room – Persian carpets lay on the parquet floor, tacky gold chandeliers hung from a high, arched ceiling, and a grand piano stood in a corner. On the chaises longues and sofas strewn around the parlor, girls in lingerie relaxed and chatted, odalisque-like and weary. All of them were young and attractive, and most importantly, light-skinned, because the Mahogany Hall only hired octoroons – girls who were one-eighth black, seven-eighths white – what was considered the most desirable mix of blood by the Caucasian men who made up the Tenderloin district clientele.

It was still early in the night and the room was relatively quiet – the only customer in the parlor was at the bar, buying drinks. He happened to turn and noticed Lewis staring at him, and he was obviously surprised to see a young Negro sitting in the parlor like a client. Black men weren't allowed in any of the Storyville parlors, at least not as customers, a restriction that led to the rise of Black Storyville, the red-light district for Negroes a little further uptown, where Mayann had worked and Lewis had been raised. The customer shook his head and returned to a chaise longue, where a smiling young girl waited for him, feet tucked underneath her, a finger twirling her hair. The girl glanced at Lewis as the man returned and passed her a champagne flute. There was something embarrassed in the way she looked at Lewis, and despite her beauty Lewis felt sorry for her.

Some of the other girls milling about the lounge cast him glances, too, wondering why he was there. The girls reminded him of Ida. Not just in their looks – light-skinned, pretty and young – but also because they possessed the same rootless, distrustful air he had noticed in his friend. They had the sadness of exiles about them. Cast adrift by both races, they had washed ashore in the bordellos of New Orleans, where they took what society told them was their defining characteristic and turned it into a commodity, a taste of the exotic, which they sold back at hourly rates to the men who had orchestrated their exile.

Lewis smiled back at the girls, who, depending on their character, smiled back or turned to look the other way with haughty swings of their eyes. He didn't recognize any of them from the time when he'd worked at the establishment years before, when the Mahogany Hall was located on Basin Street. The old Hall was a four-story building decorated with herringbone floorboards and Tiffany's stained-glass windows brought all the way from New York. Jelly Roll Morton used to lead the house band there, but when he left to seek his fortune up north, Kid Ory was hired to replace him, and Lewis landed a job with the new group.

The doors to a back parlor swung open and an immaculately dressed light-skinned woman came over to Lewis.

'Lil' Louey!' she exclaimed in a thick French accent. Lewis stood and the woman embraced him, squashing his face against her bosom.

'Hello, ma'am,' said Lewis, talking directly into Lulu White's breasts. 'I can't breathe.'

Lulu unclasped him, stared at him, and smiled. She was a handsome woman, middle-aged and stout, with short hair and wide hips. Lulu was the owner of the Mahogany Hall, and had been since Storyville's heyday. In the blue books – the tourist guides to the District, which listed the reputable brothels and catalogued the girls by beauty, race and open-mindedness – Lulu had advertised the Hall as the 'Octoroon Parlor', where all the girls were, like Lulu herself, one-eighth black. She promoted herself as the 'diamond queen of the demimonde', and the promotion worked – she spent forty thousand dollars on building the Hall, and covered her costs within a couple of years. When the Navy forced the closure of the

District, Lulu moved to these new, shabbier premises. Gone were the Tiffany stained-glass windows, but there was still something to the place, a last remnant of *la belle époque*.

Lulu took Lewis through to a private parlor and ordered two cups of hot chocolate topped with peppermint schnapps. They chatted briefly about what they had both been up to in the few months since they had last seen each other, and then Lewis turned the conversation to the subject of Morval. He told her about the Axeman, and that Morval had been snooping around the crime scenes, and the theory he and Ida had about his involvement. He felt a little foolish explaining things to Lulu, but as he talked he realized how much they had uncovered, how close they were to figuring something out.

'What I couldn't understand,' Lewis said, 'was Dots said Morval was a pimp, but I never heard of him when I was working Storyville.'

'That's because Morval never worked in the District,' Lulu said. 'He was private. Had a stable of kids he sent out on demand. And his clientele were big-wigs. All very . . . hush-hush.'

'Kids?' Lewis repeated, to make sure he had understood her, and Lulu nodded. 'Anything a few years either side of puberty,' she explained flatly. Then she gave Lewis a look and a shrug, as if to say she'd long ago come to terms with the barbarity of her fellow humans. Lewis pondered the news for a moment, and remembered Dots telling him Morval was a devil. They looked at each other, then Lulu drained what was left of her drink, and ordered two more cups from a serving girl.

'I'm not sure how much of this – Morval's stable, I mean,' she continued, 'would have to do with the Axeman. Morval closed shop about the time the District got made illegal. The mayor removed his protection and Morval moved on to other business.'

'Ida said Morval worked with the Black Hand,' Lewis said. 'You think that had anything to do with Morval shutting up shop?'

'Maybe,' she replied. 'Matranga and Mayor Behrman fell out when the new ordinance came in, too. It could be related to that.'

Lewis nodded. He knew the story. When the Navy closed down the District, Carlo Matranga ignored the new ordinance and carried on running brothels regardless, something which landed Mayor Behrman in trouble with the War Commission; but Behrman couldn't do anything to stop Carlo as his own affairs were so intertwined with those of the Matrangas.

'I've met Morval a few times, you know,' Lulu said, 'and he gives off a feeling, something dead in his eyes. Makes you scared just to be around him.' Lulu waved her hand – the extent of Morval's nastiness was beyond words.

'You know anyone that knows Morval? Someone friendly I could talk to?' asked Lewis, and Lulu smiled. 'For sure,' she said, 'I'll go get you the address.'

Lewis left Lulu's as the clock turned towards eight. Evening had descended on Storyville and the lights of the bars, saloons and revues were shining neon against the inky night. Wispy music escaped from the cabarets, laughter and boozy chitchat, and the streets were thronging with people – tourists, johns, street-walkers, drunks, and advertising men trying to coax customers into their clubs with bawdy rhymes and wisecracks. The sporting business was still going on, but it wasn't the same as before. Lewis could sense a difference, something was missing, an emptiness at the heart of it all. He thought about Lulu and the new Mahogany Hall and he had the same sense that something had been lost. Storyville was beginning to feel like a remnant of another time, like the ghost-pirates out in the bayou, clinging on to a world they no longer belonged to, searching for treasures that had long since disappeared.

Lewis pushed against the flow of the gathering crowd, heading towards Back o' Town. In his pocket, he rolled the piece of paper Lulu had given him through his fingers, hoping the rain wouldn't get onto it. As he turned a corner, he heard the sound of church music wafting over the noise of the street, solemn music, earnest and lilting. He moved a little further up the road and came upon its source – a handful of women, middle-aged and stony-faced, standing in a semicircle at an intersection. They held tasseled banners and handed out leaflets to passersby, who for the most part strode past with shakes of the head and stares fixed in the opposite direction.

Lewis stopped to read the banners – 'Lips that touch liquor shall not touch ours'; 'Dry or Die'; 'Beware the first drink'. One of the women approached him, smiled and handed him a leaflet.

'Thank you, ma'am,' said Lewis. He tipped his hat at the woman and peered at the leaflet. At the top was a cartoon depicting something called the drunkard's progress and underneath a list of benefits the Temperance Movement would bring to the country.

The Eighteenth Amendment had been ratified earlier that year, and it was just a matter of time before prohibition came into effect. Lewis hadn't really thought about it too much, but he guessed prohibition wouldn't make much of a difference in New Orleans. The government had already banned the District, but there it was, still going on. He had a feeling the alcohol ban would go the same way, at least in the Big Easy. New Orleans rarely did what the government told it to.

As much as he hated the harsh realities of being a Negro in New Orleans, something about the city's disregard for other people's authority, for the rest of the world, seemed right to him. A well-mannered rebelliousness that chimed with his own personality. He wrapped the note he got from Lulu into the leaflet and put it in his pocket, and he smiled to himself as he pushed past the crowds and headed home. Now all he had to do was think up a ghost story to tell Clarence.

33

Kerry stepped out of the precinct with the letter gripped tightly in his hand and his hand thrust firmly into the depths of his pocket. He could have posted the letter via the internal mail, or dropped it in at the post office a block from the precinct, but the letter was important and he thought the act of posting it should be afforded some kind of ceremony. So he decided to go for an evening stroll, up through Storyville and on to the Tango Belt, and mail the letter at the post office there.

He crossed over the road, dodging the slow-moving early evening traffic, and thought how hard it was for a man with no friends and family to mark a milestone with anything more than the hollowest of rituals. Although he had made one friend in the city, he couldn't really tell Detective Talbot what he was up to. He couldn't tell him about his search, about the real reason he had been rooting through the police files when he'd found the old Axeman cases. Kerry had lied to him when they first met, but only because he was a stranger, and now they were close, it was difficult to tell him the truth. But then again, the detective was keeping his own secrets, too. Kerry had heard the rumors, the ones that said Talbot kept a Negro woman at his house, that he had fathered children by her and kept them locked up and out of sight. Some of the men had even hinted the woman was kept locked up, too, that there was a hint of sadism to the affair. Kerry wasn't sure about that — Detective Talbot wasn't the kind of man to inflict pain on anyone. He knew that much. Perhaps if all went well, Kerry resolved, he'd let Detective Talbot know.

He made his way to Storyville. He liked the old red-light

district – it had a character and a brashness to it unlike anywhere in Dublin. At an intersection he heard church music, and thinking this incongruous, he followed it to its source – a group of middle-aged women, Salvation Army types, holding a temperance rally. He stopped and watched the group for a while as they sang and shook their banners. Kerry had come to realize that everything in New Orleans was accompanied by music, from rallies to funeral parades to advertising wagons to the hawking of produce on street corners. It was as if the residents weren't happy unless they were singing some kind of song.

He watched as one of the women gave a leaflet to a chubby Negro boy in a suit, who smiled and thanked her profusely. Another thumped the Bible in her hand as she lectured to the people rushing up and down the avenues. Kerry rued his luck – he had arrived in America just as alcohol was being made illegal. He shook his head and carried on with his walk, soaking in the atmosphere, knowing it would make him feel less alone. He wondered what he would do with the rest of the evening, once he had posted the letter. He didn't want to stay up drinking with the night shift again, and he didn't want to spend the evening lying on his camp-bed, reading in the bad light of the basement. He thought he might go to the picture house and watch a movie, the new Fatty Arbuckle was out.

Kerry arrived at the post office and made his way to the letter-boxes by the building's marble steps, where a huge stone eagle looked down on the entrance like a guardian. He was surprised to see that a smattering of offices on the upper floors still had their lights on, a mosaic of orange windows glowing across the building's facade. When he reached the letterboxes he smiled. He took the letter out of his pocket, unfolded it, pressed it flat with the palm of his hand, and after taking a long breath, dropped it through the slot.

The job was over. Now all he could do was wait. He turned on his heel and strolled through the dark, wet city, heading towards the warmth and anonymity of the picture house. It was still early and as he traversed Canal Street he watched the people coming and going. Smiling couples were making their way to theatres and restaurants, the women in furs and pearls, the men in suits, smoking cigarettes. Others were returning from shopping expeditions, laden with bags. Kerry watched them all with a smile on his lips, as their forms swayed in and out of glaring shop-lights, their feet stepping in black puddles filled with electric neon from the adverts high above.

34

Luca relaxed in a dented and tarnished copper bath that Simone kept hidden behind a muslin drape in the corner of the cabin. She'd done a good job of washing his bruises and cleaning him up, applying ointments from the jars on the shelves to disinfect the wounds. She had asked who had beaten him, and when he said he didn't know and he didn't care she took the hint and pressed no more. They'd spent the night in her bed, and when they woke in the morning he'd suggested the bath, against her advice, because bruises needed cold water not hot, but Luca had insisted.

He watched her approach with a heavy saucepan and pour more steaming water into the bath. Then she put the pan down, took her robe off and stepped in, tiptoes breaking the surface. Luca sat up to make room for her and they lay in silence for a while. He looked about the room and noticed the absence of the pots and other vessels she'd scattered about the floor the last time he was there.

'You fixed the roof?'

'For now,' she replied with a shrug.

Luca nodded, leaned his head back and watched the steam from the bath rise up to the rafters, where it condensed on the wooden planks and dropped back down to the floor in cold, clean raindrops.

'You mind me asking a question?' he asked, turning to look at her. She peered at him and shrugged again in response.

'How comes you never married?'

She didn't answer right away, taking some time to weigh up her words.

'You know "Pauvre Petite Mam'zelle Zizi"?' she asked, and Luca shook his head.

'It's an old Creole song. About the dangers of falling in love.' She spoke softly, nostalgically, as if the reference to the song was answer enough.

'How comes *you're* not married?' she asked.

Luca paused. He'd asked himself the question often enough but had yet to form an answer he was entirely sure was right.

'There were girls,' he said, 'but never anyone I liked enough.' The answer was partly true, at least to his own mind. 'Sometimes I think maybe I've left it too late.' She stared at him, the slightest frown contracting her brow.

'It's never too late,' she said flatly, shaking her head. And with that she closed her eyes and the silence resumed. Luca looked down at his naked torso, shimmering beneath the water, a litany of bruises and cuts spread across his stomach and chest. Then he closed his eyes, too, edged himself a little into the warmth of the bath, and together they listened to the muffled sound of the rain outside.

He left a couple of hours later and didn't get back to his hotel till well into the afternoon. The attack hadn't hurt his legs, but the bruises on his abdomen, and what Simone suspected was a fractured rib, made any movement difficult. He spotted the two plainclothes policemen outside the shop across the street and wondered if Sandoval had managed to get the box to him. As he entered, the concierge, an old Sicilian, chubby and lined, whispered to him in Italian.

'*Signore*. Something was delivered to you last night. I left it under your bed.'

'Thank you, Paolo,' said Luca.

The concierge peered at him myopically and nodded towards his face. 'What happened to you?'

'Kids,' said Luca and made his way up the stairs. When he got to his room he eased himself onto the floor and slid the box out from where the concierge had stashed it. It was made of thin metal painted black and had a clasp-lock holding the top shut. Luca prized it open easily enough with a knife and peered through the contents – dusty banknotes and a few legal papers. He took the papers out and examined them – a notary's letter, drafted by Schneider, confirming a land sale, and a deed of sale itself for the Belle Terre Estate in Lafourche Parish, by a company called Tenebre Holdings. The name was familiar. Luca sifted his memories. His mind wandered through reams of newspaper print, brown letters with paint dripping off them, wooden slats – a crime-scene photograph from Michael's files. The graffiti scrawled on the back of the Maggios' house.

Mrs Tenebre will sit up like Mrs Maggio when I'm through.

Luca thought for a moment, folded up the notary's letter and slid it into his back pocket. He put everything else back in the box, wiped it clean of prints, and took it downstairs, telling the concierge to hide it somewhere safe. Then he stepped out into the rain and hailed a cab.

Fifteen minutes later he was at City Hall, talking to a spinster in the records room. He guarded his tongue, knowing that whatever he said would be relayed to the policemen following him.

He was directed to the register of companies and, after making sure the spinster had shuffled back to her desk, he looked through the cards in the file system. He found the details for Tenebre Holdings, registered in Orleans Parish in 1888. Its only filed transactions involved the purchase of the Belle Terre Estate, Lafourche Parish. The company was dissolved nine months later by a board of trustees. The sole owner of the company while it operated was a woman named Mrs Maria Tenebre, of Belle Terre, Lafourche Parish.

He placed the card back in the drawer carefully, making sure it didn't stand out from the others, and headed back to the spinster at the reception desk. She peered at him over her glasses as he hobbled towards her, a faintly annoyed expression on her face.

'Excuse me, ma'am,' he said. 'If I was looking for a land register for a parish outside Orleans, how'd I go about it?'

She eyed the bruises and cuts on his face, the black eye, her glare dripping with reproach.

'Land registers are kept in two places,' she answered primly. 'In the seat of the parish where the land is registered, or at Baton Rouge. Documents in both places are publicly available, although if you'd like to see the Baton Rouge register, you have to make a request in writing beforehand.'

Luca tapped his fingers against the registrar's desk and the spinster peered down at the scabs on his knuckles.

'Thank you, ma'am, you been very helpful,' he said with a smile, flipping his hat on and heading towards the exit. The victims must be linked somehow to Maria Tenebre of Lafourche Parish. Find her, thought Luca, and I'll find out why they've all been killed.

35

The Church of the Immaculate Conception was a towering Jesuit folly built in 1857 at the northern end of the business district. It possessed none of the austerity for which its founders were renowned, but was rather an opulent, dizzying building, a tangle of Byzantine mosaics, Moorish domes, Venetian pillars and Gothic arches that soared flamboyantly into the sky. Sitting in the last row of the pews and staring up at the onion-domed altar, Michael got the feeling he wasn't so much in a church as a vast majestic theatre-set designed to resemble a sorcerer's lair.

Michael wasn't a religious man, but a few years previously Annette had started taking Thomas and Mae to a Baptist church uptown every Sunday morning, and Michael, left alone in the house feeling bored, listless and antsy, had started to fill the time with great walks around the city. One wintry morning he had taken refuge from the inclement weather in a church, and for the first time since he was a child he had sat to the end of the Mass and found he had enjoyed the experience. It didn't incite any religious feelings in him, but he liked the warmth and the smiles that broke out at the end of the service, and even the sunbeams that shone through the stained-glass windows and bathed the marble floors in glowing pools of colored light.

At the altar, the priest was finishing the recital of the *Agnus Dei* and the congregation readied themselves to receive the communion. There was an expectant bustle about the church, which woke Michael up a little. He never bothered to go up to the altar, preferring instead to watch the people shuffle back and forth, the grandmothers, the children, the somber-faced women and crotchety old men.

Sitting alone in the pews, his mind inevitably drifted to Annette and the children, who were at that moment sitting in different pews, uptown, in a ramshackle church, separated from him by half a city and a skin-color, and perhaps by a God, too. Annette had the good sense to know they didn't have to keep living a divided life. She had dreams of heading north, to a bigger, more liberal city. She had even mentioned the rumors that circulated about Paris, of black servicemen who had stayed there after the end of the war, seeing a better future for themselves in a foreign country on a distant shore than in the hate-soaked Cotton States.

The talk of escapes and new homes had been just one of many shadows cast over their relationship, but the idea of actually moving had always seemed unreal to Michael, distant and dream-like. The publicity and the stress of the last few months, however, was bringing him round to Annette's way of thinking. He was increasingly feeling that he was reaching the end of something, and the Axeman was involved, forcing his hand.

The congregation stood for the prayer after communion and, the service concluded, the people sauntered out of the church. Michael made his way past the Alhambra-style columns and arches and out through the Moorish doors onto Baronne Street. He put his hat on and watched the parishioners talking to each other, catching up and exchanging gossip. Annette and the children would be getting home soon. Annette would prepare a hot lunch and they'd sit and enjoy the meal, and afterwards Michael would play with the children or read the paper. And when the children had gone to bed, he and Annette would lie down on the sofa and wrap themselves up in front of the fire.

He smiled, lit a cigarette and stepped out into the rain. The business district was dead on a Sunday, the roads empty except for the occasional car or tram splashing its way up the street. He walked along Baronne till he reached Common Street and turned right – it wasn't the most direct route home, but he had to make a stop on the way.

The previous afternoon Michael had interviewed the Creole who ran the detective agency, but nothing had come of it. The man had stuck to his story – claiming Schneider had come to him for a bodyguard and he had sent him away empty-handed. He was adamant that Schneider never gave a reason for wanting protection, and despite the fact that Michael knew the Creole wasn't to be trusted, he believed him in that regard. So he had sent him on his way, feeling sorry for him. If things came to a dead end, he'd bring him in again. Press him some more.

The results from the manhunt had also trickled in over the previous few days and, as Michael had expected, they too had yielded nothing of importance. Of the eighty suspects they had collated from the prison and asylum records, forty had alibis for at least one of the nights in question, a further score were not in good enough physical condition to be the killer, and the remainder could not be found. Michael had thought briefly about allocating more resources to tracking down these men, but he'd quickly come to the conclusion that it was all a fool's errand. He'd gone through the reports relating to the 1911 murders more thoroughly, and now he believed that Hatener was right all along – the 1911 killings had nothing to do with the Axeman. The killings had contained none of the savagery, nor the joy in violence, of the current crop. But protocol was protocol, and the lead had to be chased. Now if the press found out about the previous murders, at least he could say they had thoroughly looked into any possible connection. And so the only lead left was the one Rocco had given them, the name of the man who had paid Ermanno Lombardi to drop off a list containing the victims' names out in the bayou. The name of the man, and the bar he drank in.

Tito's was just a couple of blocks north of the church, on the inter-section with O'Keefe Avenue. From the outside it looked like it was closed, but Michael pushed on the door just to check, and to his surprise it opened. Inside was a narrow, sleepy saloon, filled by a long, dark wood bar and a row of stools, and a smell of stale beer and tobacco smoke. A blind had been pulled down over the solitary window, severing all connections with the world outside, encasing the place like a tomb. A clutch of silent barflies sat hunched over their drinks, and behind the bar was a barrel-chested Italian in a yellowing vest who seemed a little bored to be there.

Michael approached the bar and sat. A few of the customers looked his way disinterestedly, then turned their attention back to the drinks in front of them. Michael wondered why they had chosen to spend their Sunday in a deserted, gloomy bar in a deserted, gloomy business district. His mind drifted back to the Creole he had interviewed in the precinct the day before. A man with the same melancholic air as the patrons of the bar, alcohol-broken and watery-eyed.

The barman swung a cloth over his shoulder and nodded at Michael.

'What'll it be?' he asked in a deep, gravelly voice.

'You the owner?' asked Michael, flashing his badge.

'That's my name above the door,' said the bartender, jutting his chin out. Michael returned the badge to his inside pocket, took his hat off and placed it gently on the bar.

'I heard a guy called Pietro drinks here,' he said. 'I need to get hold of him.'

The bartender frowned and thought for a moment, rolling the toothpick he was chewing from one side of his mouth to the other.

'Lotta people drink here,' he said eventually, with a nod. Michael made a show of craning his neck to look around the half-empty bar.

'What's he look like?' the bartender asked.

'My age, Italian, greased-back hair, 'bout so high,' Michael said, holding up a hand to what he guessed was the right height.

The bartender nodded his head gently as if confirming something with himself.

'Yeah, I know him. Troublemaker,' he said. 'He don't drink here no more.'

From the corner of his eye Michael could see the barflies slowly edging away from them. He tapped his fingertips against the bar and smiled.

'You know where I can find him?' he asked.

'Sure,' the barman said with a smile. 'He works the doors at the Kitty-Kat Club over in the Tango Belt.' The bartender grinned at him and Michael got the feeling he was happy to be sending trouble Pietro's way. 'Tell 'im Tito sent you.'

Michael nodded and smiled.

'I'll be sure to do that,' he said. 'Thanks for your help, Tito.' He stood and put his hat on.

'So what did he do?' the barman asked as Michael was turning to leave. 'Molest another kid?'

Michael stopped and turned back around, suddenly afraid they had been talking about a different man.

'That's how come he don't drink here no more,' the bartender explained.

Michael stared at him for a moment, then took his hat back off.

'What happened?'

'One o' the other guys here, old-timer called Joe, he heard some rumors, called him out on it. The animal put him in the Charity Hospital, didn't care that Joe's going on sixty. I ain't having no one like that in my bar. I got kids o' my own,' he continued, tapping his chest with his index finger. The man's indignation seemed false, somehow, as if he was just playing the outraged man because he knew it was expected of him.

'Good for you,' Michael said, trying not to sound sarcastic.

He smiled, turned and left the bar, glad to get into the cold, wet air of the street. It was a forty-minute walk to his house, through roads that were empty and slick with reflections of an overcast sky.

As he walked he mulled over this latest turn of events. He was surprised at the barman's description of Pietro. He had expected the man to be a Mafioso, not a violent doorman for one of the city's nightclubs. And a child molestor to boot. Was Michael wrong about the killings being orchestrated by the Family? Were they actually related to some kind of prostitution ring or Tango Belt vendetta? The case kept on changing, squirming about in Michael's hand like a thrashing fish. But after so many weeks of disappointment, he could sense he was close to the end. Pietro had arranged for the delivery of the list of victims to the killer, and now that Michael knew where he worked, finding him would be easy. He was just a few steps away from solving the case.

36

Lewis sat in Ida's kitchen while Ida scurried around the house looking for a couple of umbrellas to take on their journey. The kitchen was bright and cleanly furnished, and on one of the walls was a series of photographs, each one framed in thin, burnished metal. Lewis killed time by studying the photographs and reminiscing, his eye caught by one in particular. It showed, in pale shades of black and white, fifteen Negro boys sitting in rows in a dusty yard, wearing peaked caps and ill-fitting tunics. Each of the boys held an instrument, and on the bass drum at the bottom of the picture were inscribed the words:

The Colored Waifs' Home Brass Band

None of the boys smiled, wearing instead looks of uncomfortable pride – a mixture of embarrassment, posturing and budding self-worth. At the bottom of the photograph the names of the boys had been stamped in copperplate print: Isaac 'Ikey' Smooth, Thomas 'Cricket' Walker, Gus Vanzan . . . The writing identified the boy fourth from left in the back row as 'Little' Lewis Armstrong. The boy in the picture was a slighter Lewis, thinner, with a look of uncertainty about him.

The whole wall was taken up with photos of the band, each from a different year. Lewis looked over the rest of the pictures, noting how the faces changed, how people flickered in and out – arriving in one frame, growing old in the next, disappearing in a third or fourth, to be replaced by a new face, a new personality to be molded. The only constant was the thin middle-aged man who sat in the middle of each group, growing a little more stooped in each photograph – Peter Davis, Ida's father and the music teacher at the Waifs' Home.

The home was located in a rural area outside New Orleans, an area of dairy farms, dirt-tracks and honeysuckle forests. Whenever Lewis happened to catch the fragrance of the blossom, he was instantly reminded of his time in the home. It was a time he looked back on fondly, although his arrival there was anything but pleasant. He had been sent to the home when he was twelve, in the second great wrenching of his life, arrested on New Year's Eve for shooting a gun into the air. It was the custom in Back o' Town to celebrate the festive season by letting off Roman Candles and guns of all descriptions. That particular New Year's Eve, Lewis had snuck into the cedar chest that Mayann kept at the foot of her bed, taken his uncle's .38 pistol from it, and filled it with blanks. He met up with the members of his street-corner quartet out on Rampart Street, and in the middle of the celebrations, he pointed the gun skywards and let off six shots, unaware that a grim-faced policeman was standing a few feet behind him. Eighteen hours later, after spending the night in a cell, Lewis was in the back of a police-wagon, heading out of town with a clutch of other doleful Negro boys. Without being present at his own trial, without having seen a lawyer, or even his own mother, Lewis had been convicted by the juvenile court and sentenced in his absence to an indefinite stay at the home.

Professor Davis didn't think much of Lewis when he first arrived – Lewis was from Liberty and Perdido, the worst two streets in New Orleans, and Professor Davis expected him to be nothing but trouble. So Lewis had to wait for six months before he was allowed to join the band for practice. And when Professor Davis did let him join, he started him out on the tambourine. Lewis took the snub in his stride, and eventually the professor showed him how to play a cornet. Lewis excelled and ended up becoming the bandleader, marching the boys out on the parades they performed in at Spanish Fort, Milneburg, the West End and Front o' Town. When they paraded through Lewis's old neighborhood, Mayann came onto the street to watch him and the locals showered them with coins.

Professor Davis tutored them to an exceptionally high level, teaching them a repertoire that included Liszt, Haydn, Rachmaninoff, Bach and Mahler, music Lewis still listened to on the windup Victrola. On Sunday nights Freddie Keppard and his jazz band would play at a concert hall not too far from the home, close enough for some of the boys to catch the music as they lay in their bunks, listening intently, the evening air thick with the scent of the honeysuckle trees.

The kitchen door opened and Ida came sauntering in, breaking Lewis's reminiscences. She smiled and handed him one of the two umbrellas she was holding.

'Ready?'

Lewis nodded, and Ida noticed what had caught his attention. She joined him in staring at the photographs for a moment, but for her they were just pictures she passed every day.

'Lewis?' she said after a while, turning to face him with a serious look. 'This ain't an art gallery.'

They walked to City Park Avenue and caught a series of streetcars that took them across town. As they journeyed, Ida cast a few furtive glances towards Lewis, who was unusually silent. She wondered if he was still mulling over the waifs' home photographs and the memories they had provoked, or if he was still shaken from the attack in the Irish Channel. At one point during one of the walks between tram stops, he turned to her and asked her how she was getting on since the attack. Ida shrugged and told him she'd had a few sleepless nights and maybe it would take a while for her to really get over it. She also told him about how she'd thought of giving up the investigation, but that something had pulled her through, had forced her not to quit, and now she was glad she hadn't.

She didn't, however, tell him about her biggest fear, that she might have fatally wounded the boys when she swung the rock at their heads, or given them some kind of permanent injury. Instead she thanked Lewis for all his help, for taking her back home and comforting her. Lewis had smiled, somewhat sadly, she thought, and she took the opportunity to ask him how he was doing.

'Just fine,' he had said, telling her he was used to getting into scrapes, but Ida knew he was lying. She guessed that, just like her, he didn't wanted to talk about it too much, choosing instead to process it all internally. The episode had reminded them both how much hatred there was in the city, and how much of it was directed at people like them. It was a dispiriting reminder, but they knew, from years of living within a system of organized malice, that there was no point dwelling on the venom of others.

They continued the journey in silence, trekking to and from the stops under the inadequate shelter of the moth-eaten old umbrellas Ida had fished from the back of a broom cupboard. By the time they arrived at the tumbledown building at the edge of Robertson Street, they were soaked through. Lewis checked again that they were at the address Lulu White had given him, then he knocked on the door and the two of them stepped back and inspected the building – the timbers were warped and rotting, the structure straining hard not to collapse under its own weight.

A slim octoroon girl opened the door. She was young and bare-footed, wearing a ragged skirt and a white cotton vest that squeezed against her breasts. She had a pretty face, but it was marred by an eye bruised purple.

'Carmelita Smith?' Lewis asked, and the girl frowned as she tried to figure out who they were.

'You the two detectives?' she said eventually, with a patronizing smirk that made Ida instantly dislike her.

Lewis nodded and tipped his hat.

'You can call me Leeta,' said the girl, before turning back into the building.

She led them up a staircase and through a corridor that was lined with doors, each one leading onto the crib of a sporting girl, and Ida thought of an animal market, poultry in cages, one stacked on top of the other.

Leeta led them into a dank, shadowy room, eight feet by ten, where the wallpaper peeled off the walls in wide fern-like arcs. The furniture was utilitarian – an iron-frame bed, a cabinet and a wash-stand – and it made Ida think of a workroom or a factory. She noticed the rat holes in the skirting boards, and the thick stench of mold in the air, and she curled her lip without thinking. Leeta caught the expression and glared at her. Then she lit a cigarette and propped herself up against the windowsill.

'Well, ain't we the bruised threesome,' she said sarcastically, nodding at Ida and Lewis's faces. 'Make yo'selves comfortable,' she added, gesturing towards the bed. Lewis and Ida smiled as best they could and sat.

'First things first,' said Leeta. 'I don't like strangers poking around my business. I only said I'd talk to you cuz Lulu said you was friends o' hers, and Lulu's offered me a job once my face clears up. So ask your questions quick-like.'

Lewis and Ida shared a look, both of them put off by the girl's practiced brusqueness.

'Did he do that to you?' Ida asked, motioning towards Leeta's face.

'Morval?' said Leeta, with a sideways smile. 'No. One o' his johns. You could call this the last straw. Hence my moving over to Lulu's employment. This and how I'm getting a little old for some of Morval's clientele.'

She spoke in a matter-of-fact way, with a world-weary demeanor and a resignation that said she had accepted the way things were. But Ida sensed there was something contrived to it all, that the defiance was just bluster, a way of hiding herself from the world.

'Lulu said Morval closed down his stable when the new ordinance came in,' Lewis said, frowning.

'Lulu got that wrong,' Leeta said, turning her acid glare in Lewis's direction. 'He never closed it down, just made himself a whole lot more discreet.'

She blew smoke into the room and the smell of tobacco mixed with the smell of mold, making the air even more unpleasant to breathe.

'We, uh, we're looking into the Axeman killings, and we think Morval might be involved,' Lewis said finally.

'Nothing Morval does is ever on the up-and-up,' Leeta said, raising her eyebrows. 'He was always more into knives than axes, though. What gave you the idea?'

'Morval's been sending someone called Johnson to search the crime scenes,' said Ida, and Leeta nodded.

'Johnson's Morval's flunky,' she said. 'Morval keeps him hooked on snow and Johnson does whatever he's told.'

Leeta took a long, heavy drag on her cigarette and Ida noticed the black dots and purple lines splayed out across her arms.

'I hear there's a reward,' Leeta said abruptly. 'Few grand, I hear. I know somethin' might help you. How about we talk numbers?'

'Sure,' said Lewis, shrugging.

'I want a grand.'

Lewis turned to look at Ida, who nodded.

'OK,' said Lewis, 'if we get the reward, we'll give you a grand.'

Leeta smiled like a child who had got her way. She took another long slow drag on her cigarette and began to tell her story.

'I dunno what you know about Morval's stable,' she said, 'but it's kids. He pays the parents off in the hick towns he goes to buying furs. Tells 'em he needs kids for sewing and factory work in the city. I guess some of the parents are stupid and some of 'em just plain greedy. He puts 'em in houses around town. Sends 'em out to parties or to people he knows.

'Well, one o' these girls stayed in the same house as me for a while. Morval done brought her in from some village up north o' town. Anna. Little slip of a thing not mo' than ten years old – blonde hair, green eyes. Thought she was in town to work in Morval's factory. Cried day and night till she got used to things.

'Anyway, one morning she came back and told me about a party she went to with a few of the other girls. Some mansion somewhere. On the way back, she overheard Morval talking to some dago 'bout *getting rid o' evidence* and *needing a stash spot*. Anna thought they were talkin' 'bout the girls, and she got nervous she was gonna get killed. Next day, Morval moved her in with some family on the other side o' town.

'I got to liking the girl while she was there. Felt sorry for her, you know. And the girl looked up to me like I was the moon or something. I ain't never had that before. So a few days later I paid her a visit. Wasn't really a family there, just a pa and his two daughters. The pa liked the girls a lil' too much and made extra dough having 'em work for Morval. Anna said she liked living there, what with the two daughters being the same age and all. I teased her a bit, 'bout how scared she'd been, and she said she'd seen Morval come to the house a heap, to the basement there, and that's what he meant when he said he had to stash the evidence somewhere new.

'I thought that was kinda odd, you know, why he was hiding things in this cat's house? So I asked her about it. She said him or Johnson would come round some nights and mess about in the basement. Woke her and the two daughters up. The two daughters said they knew what was going on, and that it had to do with the Axeman, cuz they'd heard their father argue with Morval about it. I asked her what she meant, and she said the daughters wouldn't tell her. Kept it a secret cuz if their father found out there'd be hell to pay.

'Day after that, Morval came round to see me, all red in the face and pop-eyed, threatening to beat the breath outta me. Asked me what in hell I was doing going over to the house and talking to

Anna. I told him we got close and I was being friendly. Nothing more.'

Leeta paused and Ida saw a sorrowful look pass over her face, the first slip of emotion she had failed to keep hidden since they had been in her presence.

'I heard from some of the other girls a couple of weeks ago that Anna had disappeared. That's kinda why I'm telling you. I'd like to see that devil pay. If you wanna find evidence linking Morval to the Axeman, it's plumb easy. All you gotta do is break into the basement o' that house. I got the address.'

A few minutes later they stepped out of the building and back into the rain. As they made their way to the tram stop they both stayed silent, lost in their thoughts, spirits depressed. Despite Leeta's barbed manner, Ida felt sorry for the girl, and she wondered how she'd tumbled into a life of violence and prostitution, living in an apartment that felt more like a prison cell than a home. Ida was not that much different to Leeta in age and looks and race, and it chilled her to think that it was only the slightest divergence in fate that had left her so much better off.

She looked over to Lewis as they trudged past the cemetery, and saw that he too was lost in thought, a frown playing across his brow. He had more experience of the sporting business than she did, but she could tell that even he was upset by the state of the girl. Ida guessed that if there was any hope for Leeta it was in her finding a better life in Lulu's employment.

As they waited for the tram, Ida thought about the little girl Leeta had talked of, the slip of a thing with blonde hair and green eyes, and she wondered what had become of her. Then she remembered the other girl she had seen recently – the dead girl dredged from the river when Ida had been searching the docks. She'd read in the newspaper a few days afterwards that no parents had come forward to claim the body, and Ida thought about what Leeta had said, about the parents in the hick towns selling their children to Morval.

The tram arrived, splashing its way up the street, and as Ida boarded it she realized that it was no longer a case of simply wanting to be involved in an investigation; now she felt an obligation to be involved, an obligation to stop Morval once and for all.

PART FOUR

PART FOUR

The Times–Picayune

Thursday 8th May, 1919

The Axeman Speaks!

Yesterday morning a man claiming to be the Axeman that has been terrorizing our fair city these past months sent *The Times–Picayune* a letter. We reprint the letter here in full for the benefit of all our citizens. Will the city bow to this madman's terrorizing and 'jazz it up' on the night in question? Only time will tell.

Hell, May 6th, 1919

Esteemed Mortal:

They have never caught me and they never will. They have never seen me, for I am invisible, even as the ether that surrounds your earth. I am not a human being, but a spirit and a demon from the hottest hell. I am what you Orleanians and your foolish police call the Axeman.

When I see fit, I shall come and claim other victims. I alone know whom they shall be. I shall leave no clue except my bloody axe, besmeared with blood and brains of he whom I have sent below to keep me company.

If you wish you may tell the police to be careful not to rile me. Of course, I am a reasonable spirit. I take no offense at the way they have conducted their investigations in the past. In fact, they have been so utterly stupid as to not only amuse me, but His Satanic Majesty, Francis Josef, etc. But tell them to beware. Let them not try to discover what I am, for it were better that they were never born than to incur the wrath of the Axeman. I don't think there is any need of such a warning, for I feel sure the police will always dodge me, as they have in the past. They are wise and know how to keep away from all harm.

Undoubtedly, you Orleanians think of me as a most horrible murderer, which I am, but I could be much worse if I wanted to. If I wished, I could pay a visit to your city every night. At will I could slay thousands of your best citizens, for I am in close relationship with the Angel of Death.

Now, to be exact, at 12:15 (earthly time) on next Tuesday night, I am going to pass over New Orleans. In my infinite mercy, I am going to make a little proposition to you people. Here it is:

I am very fond of jazz music, and I swear by all the devils in the nether regions that every person shall be spared in whose home a jazz band is in full swing at the time I have just mentioned. If everyone has a jazz band going, well, then, so much the better for you people. One thing is certain and that is that some of your people who do not jazz it on Tuesday night (if there be any) will get the axe.

Well, as I am cold and crave the warmth of my native Tartarus, and it is about time I leave your earthly home, I will cease my discourse. Hoping that thou wilt publish this, that it may go well with thee, I have been, am and will be the worst spirit that ever existed either in fact or realm of fancy.

The Axeman

37

Mayor Behrman held a press conference early the next morning outside City Hall to announce the administration's response to the letter. Underneath a tarpaulin canopy, on a squat podium, stood Captain McPherson, Michael, a cabal of mayoral employees and the mayor himself. Beyond them, on the lower steps and out on the street, a gaggle of reporters hunched unprotected in the rain, wet and irritated, writing in sodden notebooks.

McPherson had told Michael he wouldn't be required to speak, but his presence had been requested regardless, to 'show a unified front', in Mayor Behrman's words. Michael only half-listened to the mayor's booming voice as he read from a sheet of paper; his attention had been caught by the drooping canopy above him. Just after dawn, workers had hastily stretched the tarpaulin above the front steps of the building, and the groaning blue sheet had been collecting rain ever since. The weight of the water was dragging the tarpaulin's bloated center towards the ground, making Michael feel like he was standing beneath a giant creature, looking up at the underbelly of a watchful Cerberus.

He caught snippets of what he already knew – the administration thought the letter to be a hoax, but all police leave was cancelled regardless; a full presence on the streets for the night; plainclothes officers to mingle with the crowds; and a plea to all citizenry to be watchful and to stay indoors – the last causing an ironic, murmuring laugh from the reporters. Michael heard Behrman mention the possibility of deploying the National Guard. He frowned at McPherson when he heard this, and the captain shook his head almost imperceptibly. When Behrman finished his statement, he opened up the conference to the reporters, who launched forth a cavalcade of questions, shouted over the noise of the rain, which the mayor batted away with his usual sangfroid.

Michael gazed across the tangle of faces in the crowd and noticed Riley milling around at the back of the huddle. He made eye contact with him and the reporter nodded and smiled. He appeared even more haggard than he normally did, and even at such a distance, Michael could see Riley's hand shaking as he raised his cigarette to his mouth and took deep, heavy drags on it. Michael made a signal by moving his head sideways, and Riley seemed to get the gist of it. He nodded back at Michael and tapped the pocket watch in his palm.

The conference wound down and Behrman and his entourage retreated to the warmth of their offices, McPherson returned to the precinct, and the crowd of reporters rushed back to their newsrooms to change their wet clothes and type up their copy. Michael stepped down into the street and over to Riley, who had procured two cups of coffee. He handed one to Michael and they moved to the cover of a doorway on the opposite side of the road. They each lit a cigarette and stared at City Hall. The gray slate steps were empty, reflecting the bright blue of the tarpaulin above them.

'Be honest,' said Michael. 'You guys make it up?'

Riley shook his head. 'I picked the damn thing out the mailbox myself. Either the guy's a lunatic or a very enterprising jazz musician.'

Michael smiled and took a sip of his coffee.

'Or a vet,' added the reporter.

Michael thought for a moment. 'You mean the line about Franz Joseph?'

Riley nodded.

'Maybe,' said Michael. 'He spelt it in the German style.'

Since the beginning of the year, New Orleans had been filling up with veterans returning from the war in Europe, and Michael had noticed a rise in the number of crimes involving former troops, those men who had returned but couldn't readjust.

'Either way it's gonna upset the Italians,' said Riley, and Michael peered at him quizzically.

'The date in the letter,' he explained, 'it's St Joseph's day. The patron saint of dagos. The church parades are going to have to dodge around the jazz bands.'

They both laughed before taking sips of their coffees.

'You ain't exactly been keen to chase up your debt,' Michael said.

Riley shrugged and stared into the street and Michael noticed an edginess in him. Riley had always been a furtive, jittery type, but now he had a distracted air to him as well – his mind was on distant things.

'I've been busy,' he said. 'The Lombardi angle worked out then?'

'Sure,' Michael replied. 'How'd you find out about him?'

'Tell me your angle.' said Riley. 'I'll level with you.'

Michael sighed. 'We traced Lombardi to a low-level enforcer called Pietro. Pietro gave Lombardi a list of victims to deliver to a hit-man out in the bayou somewhere. Bayou suggests an out-of-towner. Pietro's looking to get made. My guess? This is all Black Hand stuff that got out of control.'

Riley took a drag on his cigarette, exhaled and nodded.

'Tallies with what I know,' he said.

'Good. Now you gonna tell me how you knew about Lombardi?' asked Michael.

'I meet a lot of people doing this job, Talbot,' he said. 'A few of them pretty high up. This Black Hand angle you've decided on – it might cause you trouble. After you speak to Pietro, I'm gonna call in my debt.'

The two men looked at each other and Michael nodded. Riley smiled and tipped his hat, then dashed his coffee onto the sidewalk and trudged out into the rain.

Michael watched him go, shook his head, and leaned against the cove of the doorway while he finished his coffee and cigarette. He heard a groaning noise and fearful shouts and swung his gaze to the City Hall steps to see the ropes holding the tarpaulin to the sides of the building snap and break free. The tarpaulin and the rainwater it held dropped onto the steps with a crash, and the single body of water shattered into a million drops, flying like shrapnel.

38

Luca's alarm clock drilled him awake at 4.30. He rose, felt his way through the darkness to the window, and moved the muslin in front of it back an inch. In the street below, a hundred yards down the block, a black sedan was parked in a spot that violated the local parking restrictions. If cops still conducted stakeouts the way they did when Luca was on the force, both the policemen in the car would be fast asleep, and they wouldn't wake up till the dayshift came to relieve them.

He moved from the window to the nightstand, removed his vest, and stared at himself in the mirror. The bruises and cuts had spread like a mold over his abdomen, a purple-and-ruby mildew. He pressed his hand against the skin where he thought the broken rib was and winced under the pain. Then he turned from the mirror to the jug on the nightstand, poured stale water into a basin and washed himself gently with a cloth and a bar of soap.

He wrapped new bandages around the wounds, dressed and snuck out of the hotel, slipping into the night through the kitchen exit. He padded along an empty Canal Street, silent except for the rain, and skirted along the edge of Storyville. He turned onto Basin Street and entered the New Orleans Terminal Train Station through the towering neoclassical arch. He stopped at a newsstand and bought an early edition of the *Picayune*, quickly scanning the bizarre letter on the front page. The station interior was empty and dim except for a twenty-four-hour diner that spilled harsh yellow light onto the concourse with a prickling electric buzz.

Luca took a booth, sliding into it slowly to save his injured body, and he laid the paper out flat on the table in front of him. The owner, a fat Greek in a white vest, with eyes puffy from years of nightshift work, ambled over with a jug of coffee.

'Crazy, huh?' he said, filling the cup on Luca's table.

Luca peered up at him blankly.

'The letter from the Axeman,' said the owner, shaking his head. 'Crazy sonofabitch. I'll tell you one thing, when that night does happen, every bar and club and restaurant gonna be full to bursting. Damn Axeman's done more for our business than those crooks up in City Hall ever did.'

Luca nodded, ordered eggs and toast, and watched the man saunter back to the kitchen half-asleep. He spent two hours in the diner, most of it whiled away with coffee and cigarettes.

A half-hour before his train was due to leave he took a walk around the station. Daylight had arrived and the walkways and shops were busy with travelers. In the rafters high above a rustle of pigeons swooped about, dropping to the concourse occasionally to pick up scraps. He found some street kids shooting dice for nickels and dimes in an alley behind the Krauss Department Store and paid one of them a quarter to go to the ticket office and buy him a return to Lafourche Parish. He reached the train just as it was leaving, casting a final look around the station to make sure no one had followed him, before swinging onto the car by the handrail.

He found a seat, sat himself down and spent the journey looking out of the window, still half-asleep despite the river of coffee he'd drunk.

It was only a short walk from the station to Thibodaux's main drag, a forlorn street of agricultural suppliers, grocers, saloons and a municipal building.

The lady in the records hall, a frail, smiling woman who was clearly pleased to be talking to someone, explained the filing system to him. He looked up the Belle Terre Estate and found the folder relating to it. It had most of what he needed to fill in the blanks. A claim drawn up by Edvard Schneider had been filed in 1888 on behalf of the Tenebre Company. The company's owner, Maria Tenebre, had died a few months later intestate. Care of the company was transferred to a board of trustees, who sold it a few months later at auction to the Thibodaux Venture Company. For half what Tenebre had paid for it. The company was still the owner of the estate. Luca wondered if the company had been registered in Thibodaux.

He checked with the smiling woman, and she led him to the register of companies, where he found the right file for the venture company. The names of its directors were the ones he expected to find. He put the file back in its place, and went out onto the street, deciding to double check something while he was still in town.

He got directions to the post office and used the payphone there to make a call to Jake Hatener. He waited a few minutes while the operator connected him, then Hatener's voice crackled down the line.

'Morning, Luca,' he said, sounding concerned.

'Jake, I need a favor. Can you call up Thibodaux and get them to run a check on a Maria Tenebre, deceased? Belle Terre Estate. Lafourche Parish.'

The line fuzzed for a few seconds and Luca wondered if they had been disconnected, then he heard Hatener's voice again.

'Sure. Why you want it?' the old man asked.

'Take a guess,' said Luca. 'She owned a company called Tenebre Holdings back in eighty-eight, based out in Thibodaux.'

'Tenebre? OK. Gimme an hour.'

Luca put the receiver down and headed to one of the saloons he had passed on his way from the station. He stepped inside and a group of locals at the bar turned his way and frowned. He tipped his hat at the men and took a seat at an empty table, and the locals turned back to their beers and conversations.

A stern-looking bartender approached and Luca ordered a steak, fried potato slices and green beans. When the food arrived the steak was tough and the green beans were boiled dry. For a moment he considered asking if they had any olive oil to pour over the greens, then thought better of it. He ate and then smoked a few cigarettes before he asked for the check, paid and headed back to the post office. He called Hatener back a few minutes early.

'One record for a Maria Tenebre,' said Hatener, his voice hushed. 'Died in August 1888. You want the details?'

'Sure.'

'Head injuries sustained after falling off a bridge. Seems she was drunk and on her way home at two in the morning. Took a tumble down a ditch.'

Luca nodded and drummed his fingers as he thought.

'No KAs,' continued Hatener, 'but a few raps. Sounds like she was the village lush. Three counts of public drunkenness between 1870 and 1888. All of them *nolle prosequied*. One charge stuck, though: she was caught in a saloon drinking liquor in 1885, twenty-dollar fine and three months' detention.'

Hatener's voice grew silent for a moment, then returned in a ruffle of static.

'You get what you wanted?' he asked.

'Pretty much. Thanks, Jake. 'Preciate it,' said Luca.

'No problem.'

The line went quiet again before Hatener spoke.

'I heard from Talbot's boys you caught a beating,' he said, his tone softer, concerned.

'Nothing too bad.'

'OK,' said Hatener, not sounding entirely convinced. 'You take care now.'

Luca hung up and headed back to the records room. He took the file for the venture company out again and reread it, staring at the names once more. A series of events formed in his mind: a group of people wanted to get hold of an estate, so they used Maria Tenebre, the local drunk, as a proxy. She bought the estate. They waited a few months, then threw her off a bridge. They let ownership slide to a board of trustees who, with some greased palms, most probably, sold on the estate to the people who really wanted it. Schneider, the group's lawyer, held all traces of the transactions, registering the Tenebre Company in New Orleans and the venture company down in Thibodaux, hiding the documents in a box under his floorboards.

The police hadn't found the link because the only piece of paper to prove it all was in Luca's hand, fetched from a dusty filing cabinet in a small town in the middle of nowhere. Luca stared at it again – the owners of the Belle Terre Estate were Mr Charles Cortimiglia, Mr Joseph Romano, Mr Steven Boca, Mr Michael Pepitone and Mr Joseph Maggio, all of Orleans Parish. The Axeman was killing the estate owners. One by one. Despite their doing everything in their power to hide the fact that they were the owners of the Estate. How and why did a group of greengrocers in New Orleans end up owning farmland in the middle of nowhere?

Luca looked again at the piece of paper in his hand. He wondered if he should take it with him. If he left the paper here in Thibodaux, somebody else might come looking, might find it and piece things together, and that somebody would probably be Michael. He thought for a moment longer, then he put the files back in their place for a second time.

39

Ida and Lewis had spent the morning sitting at the worm-eaten bar of a Back o' Town honky-tonk waiting for a friend of Lewis's to arrive. The honky-tonk was a broken-bottle joint, a raggedy place with sawdust floors and a drinks menu that consisted solely of bath-tub rye and high-strength lager. There was a smell of stale yeast to the place, of marijuana smoke, sweat and urine, and it was empty except for the bartender, Lewis and Ida, and three Negro men in their Sunday best who were sitting at a table loaded with empty glasses. The men must have been drinking all night and through past dawn, as they had been there when Ida and Lewis had arrived and they were all of them fast asleep. The bartender had set 'Jazz Baby' by Marion Harris to play on the bar's Victrola, and the three men, their heads nodding and swaying as they slept, reminded Ida of a trio of dancers, moving to the music as if in a trance.

Lewis had warned Ida his friend would probably be late, so she had brought along the newspaper to pass the time, and now she read aloud the Axeman's letter, while Lewis and the barman listened in. Lewis was propped up on a stool next to Ida, nursing a beer, and the barman was shaking his head ruefully at each bizarre statement Ida read out, as if listening to the reckoning of a man's sins.

'This just don't fit in with *you-know-who*,' said Ida after she'd finished, conscious of the barman's presence.

'Don't make a lick o' sense,' said Lewis. 'Newspaper probably just faked the whole thing to sell a few copies.'

'That's what I'd do if I owned the paper,' the barman said, peering at the two of them knowingly.

'If you owned the paper,' said Lewis with a grin, 'it woulda gone bust by now.'

The barman frowned at him and sauntered off down the length of the bar.

'He spelled Franz Joseph wrong,' Ida said.

'It's probably nothing,' Lewis replied, rubbing his eyes.

There is nothing so important as trifles, Ida thought to herself. 'It might be someone's trying to cover their tracks,' she said.

The front door swung open and a gangly Negro a little older than them strutted in. He scanned the room and smiled when he saw Lewis, who signaled him over with a wave.

'How you coming?' the man said with a grin, and Ida watched as they hugged each other and shook hands in a complicated series of choreographed moves. The man had a hustler's swagger and clothes to match – a brown felt Stetson, Burtenard and Wager trousers, wingtip shoes and a gold watch-chain that swung from a velvet waistcoat. Lewis and the man took a moment to look each other up and down, then the man grinned and shook his head.

'Shit, blacker'n me, you getting so fat, when I came in I thought there was an eight-ball sitting at the bar,' he said, and they burst out into raucous laughter that woke up the men at the table, who glanced about them for a few seconds, then closed their eyes and drifted off once more.

'Ida, this is Cocaine Buddy,' said Lewis. 'Buddy, Ida Davis.'

Buddy smiled and tipped his Stetson at Ida before taking it off with a flourish. They ordered another beer for Buddy and moved to one of the tables out of the barman's earshot. After their order had been served and they were alone, they clinked bottles and smiled.

'So what's new?' asked Lewis.

'Nothing,' said Buddy, 'white man still on top. What you wanna see me 'bout?'

Lewis filled Buddy in on their investigations and Buddy

listened with a smile on his face, and when Lewis had finished he laughed and shook his head.

'Well, I'll be. You still crazy, Lil' Louey,' he said. 'You want hell on your hands? Ain't you ever heard o' Morval?'

'Sure I heard,' said Lewis. 'I spoke to Lulu about it.'

'Lulu White?' asked Buddy, lighting a cigarette. 'That ol' dyke? I didn't even know she was still alive.'

Ida grimaced, annoyed by the curse word and Buddy's offhand tone. The man grated on her, the swagger, the arrogance, the wisecracks. Back o' Town was full of men like him, and as far as Ida was concerned it was men like him who made Back o' Town the slum it was.

After they'd received the address from Leeta, Ida had discussed with Lewis how best to go about breaking into the basement of the house, and Lewis had suggested he ask Buddy to help them out. He was one of Lewis's oldest friends and an expert housebreaker. Ida wasn't sure about bringing in someone she didn't know, but as Lewis had explained, it would be stupid of them to attempt to break into a house when neither of them knew what they were doing. Especially when the house was a stash-spot for Morval. They needed help, and Buddy was it.

'OK. Here's the deal,' he said. 'I'll ask around, case the joint, see if it's worth my while. Purely as a favor to my old pal. When you want this done by?'

Lewis shrugged and turned to look at Ida, and Ida cleared her throat. 'There ain't a deadline,' she said, 'but we'd like to get it done as soon as possible.'

Buddy smiled. 'What a sheba,' he said to Lewis while gesturing in Ida's direction, further riling her. 'Gimme a couple o' days,' Buddy said, after taking a sip of his beer. 'I'll see what I can do.'

He smiled at them both again, returned the Stetson to his head and sauntered out of the bar. Ida watched the man go, wondering how long it would be before they could break into the house and find the evidence Leeta claimed was in there. They stayed a while longer, finishing their drinks to the sound of Marion Harris looping over and over again on the Victrola. The honky-tonk was the sorrowful kind of place where people came to lose themselves, and Ida was glad when they finally stood up to leave, passing by the three sleeping men in their church clothes, still lost in their drunken haze.

40

After the press conference Michael returned to the precinct and wandered around the bureau asking the various teams if they had any information on a man named Pietro, a tough guy and possible pederast who worked the doors of a nightclub in the Tango Belt. A detective in Vice, a slack-eyed young man with an easy smile, said he remembered arresting someone on a molestation charge named Pietro a few months previously. The detective couldn't remember his second name, but the descriptions matched, so Michael went through the detective's arrest reports and eventually found the right one.

Pietro Amanzo – arrested most recently on Christmas Eve. Found by the vice officer in a car in Storyville with an underage girl at four in the morning. Amanzo claimed he was a friend of the girl's father and he was driving her back home from a stay out of town. For some reason the girl's father corroborated the story and the charges were dropped.

Michael went on to check Amanzo's personal file which was thick with arrest reports and court records. He had been in trouble with the police since his teens, for infractions that oscillated between severely violent assaults and child abuse. Amanzo had been sent to juvenile detention at fourteen for attacking his younger sister, and was released at eighteen, when he started working for known mob figures. His file was peppered with arrests from then on; every few months he was picked up either for violent behavior and unprovoked attacks, or for being caught in compromising situations with underage girls. He'd served two six-month sentences, and one eighteen-month sentence in Angola. His known associates included low-level Family members and an informer for Vice. The file still contained a home address, an apartment above a shop in the Tango Belt.

Michael signed out a paddy-wagon and drove over to the address, with Kerry and three blue-coats, just to be on the safe side. They parked a block away and made their way to the building on foot. They found the street-door open, so stepped inside, went up the stairs and knocked on Amanzo's door. A short man of swarthy *paesano* stock opened it.

'Pietro Amanzo?' said Michael.

'Yeah. Who's asking?' Michael turned to stare at the men in police uniforms next to him, and Amanzo grinned broadly at his own joke.

'The tooth fairy,' said Michael, holding up his badge. 'We want to talk to you about the murder of Ermanno Lombardi.'

'That faggot?' said Amanzo, and he laughed in an obnoxious, dismissive way.

'I can arrest you if you want,' Michael said, keeping his temper.

Amanzo glared at him then nodded. 'Let's go,' he said, and he grabbed a coat from a rack by the door and pushed past Michael towards the stairs.

When they returned to the precinct, Michael sat Amanzo down in one of the smaller interview rooms and uncuffed him. Amanzo curled his lip and stared at the far wall in a surly, adolescent way. Michael ignored him and placed his paperwork on the table, not because he needed it, but because he wanted to scare Amanzo into thinking there was already a weight of evidence against him. Next Michael took his silver cigarette case and his matches from his pocket and placed them by the paperwork, and moved the ashtray to the center of the table for the both of them to share.

Kerry arrived with coffees, put them on the table and sat to one side with a notebook.

'Let's get started, shall we?' Michael said when Kerry was

settled. 'Were you acquainted with a man called Ermanno Lombardi?'

'Sure,' Amanzo replied, glaring at Michael across the wooden table that separated them.

'What was the nature of your acquaintance?'

'He's Sicilian, I'm Sicilian. I saw him around.' Amanzo shrugged, keeping his eyes fixed on Michael. Michael opened his cigarette case, took a Virginia Bright from it and lit up. He offered one to Amanzo, who grimaced and shook his head. Michael shrugged, took a drag and smiled.

'You ever work with Lombardi?'

'With a fruit? Never.'

'Word is you palmed jobs off to him,' Michael pressed.

Amanzo said nothing and continued staring at him. The constant glare was supposed to be disconcerting, a gangster's trick that had lost its effect on Michael years before.

'Are you aware that Lombardi was killed last week?'

'Sure.'

'How did you hear?'

'Word gets around,' Amanzo replied, and a broad grin spread across his thin, bloodless lips. Michael heard the sound of Amanzo's feet tapping against the black-and-white checks of the linoleum floor. The room was bare except for the table and chairs, and the sound reverberated with a shrill hollowness.

'Where were you the night Lombardi was killed?' asked Michael, pressing on with the list of questions he wanted to get out of the way.

'At work. The Kitty-Kat Club.'

'Oh yeah? That's funny.'

'Why?' asked Amanzo.

'Because I never told you what night he was killed.'

Amanzo stared at him for a moment, then grimaced. 'I'm at the club every night.'

'Yeah?' said Michael. 'You got any witnesses for last Monday?'

'No. But I can get 'em,' said Amanzo, smirking.

Michael smiled, leaned back in his chair and folded his arms.

'I heard you had Lombardi cheese-wired because he started shooting his mouth off about the Axeman.'

Amanzo flinched, a blink of movement, but Michael noticed it.

'You heard wrong,' said Amanzo, a little too quickly.

'Yeah? I heard you gave Lombardi a job to do cuz you heard he was leaving town, and when it turned out he was sticking around, you clipped him to cover your tracks.'

Amanzo stared at Michael, the menace in his eyes replaced momentarily by a realization that Michael knew more than he should.

'I heard you asked Lombardi to drop off a list of Axeman victims out in the bayou.'

Michael could see the doubt spreading across Amanzo's face and the attempts the man was making to keep it from showing. Michael took the opportunity to make an offer.

'Come clean, Amanzo. We got witnesses to prove you gave the job to Lombardi. Enough evidence to have you electrocuted.'

Amanzo leaned back in his chair, took a slow sip from his cup and stared at Michael over the rim, dark eyes shining through the curling steam.

'This is the death penalty,' Michael said, pressing on. 'It isn't a drunken assault. Tell us what you know and we'll drop your involvement. You can carry on just as you were. Running doors, touching up kids, beating up anyone who says you're not a man because you like fucking little girls.'

Amanzo jumped at Michael in a flash. Michael dodged and kicked the table so it caught Amanzo in the gut. Amanzo bent over, winded, and Kerry rushed behind him and pushed his head onto the table. He squirmed and tried to lash out, but Michael held him down and Kerry returned the cuffs to his hands. They lifted him up and dropped him back into his seat.

'You OK, son?' asked Michael, and Kerry nodded, breathing

heavily. They looked over to Amanzo, who was panting, and glaring at them with wild eyes, greasy hair astray.

'Fucking pigs,' he muttered. 'I ain't even under arrest.'

Michael peered at him and shrugged.

'You're under arrest now. For assaulting a police officer,' Michael spat, and Amanzo laughed and shook his head.

'I wanna see a lawyer,' he said in a stony, clamped voice.

'You wanna a lawyer? Fine. I'll press charges on the assault. Answer my questions and you can walk out of here in fifteen minutes.'

Amanzo paused and thought for a moment. He stared at the scratches on the table in front of him and suddenly looked shaky, conflicted.

'If I tell you, I die.'

Michael sighed and sat back down in his chair.

'Amanzo, I'm gonna check your alibis for the night, I'm gonna search your house, I'm gonna talk to your friends, to your enemies. I'm gonna find something. We both know I'm gonna find something, so save us the trouble and you can walk out of here a free man.'

'You just gonna forget about the faggot?' he said. 'I'm already dead.'

Amanzo sat back and scowled at Michael, and Michael realized from the man's expression that he wouldn't talk. His only option was to keep pushing him in the hope that he would let something slip. He booked him for the assault and sent him back to his cell to await a lawyer.

Michael knew how it would pan out. In a few hours the lawyer would arrive and the next day Amanzo would be up in front of a judge, where he'd either make bail or be sent to jail. Either outcome left Amanzo liable to being killed by someone who wanted him out of the way, and when word of his arrest got out, someone would definitely want him out of the way. By bringing in Amanzo, Michael had set a clock ticking, and it was only a matter of time before someone made a move, either against Amanzo or against Michael, and Michael needed to be prepared for it. He was reaching the endgame, but he didn't have a clue what his next move should be.

REPORT OF HOMICIDE
Department of Police

Fourth Precinct, New Orleans   Thurs. May 8th 1919

Name of Person Killed: Carmelita Smith, colored

Residence: 1503 Robertson Street

Business: Prostitute

Name of accused: Unknown

Residence: Unknown

Business: Unknown

Location of homicide: 1503 Robertson Street

Day, date, hour committed: 6 P.M., Thurs. May 8th

By whom reported: Sergeant William Kingman

To whom reported: Sergeant Joseph J. Carter

Time reported: 6 P.M., Thurs. May 8th

If arrested, by whom: Still At Large

Where arrested: N/A

If escaped, in what manner: Left the scene prior to our arrival

Witnesses: Martha Cheri,
Henrietta Russell,
Corinne Edwards,
1503 Robertson Street,
all colored

Detailed Report

Sergeant William Kingman reports that at 6.00 o'clock this P.M. Thurs. May 8th a telephone message was sent to this station that noises of a disturbance had been heard at 1503 Roberston Street. I immediately, in the company of Sergeant Wlm. Kingman and Patrolman John Mayer, proceeded to the address and on reaching it discovered Carmelita Smith, a Negress prostitute, aged 17, dead in the single room of her crib. Furniture was disturbed and bloodstains were found on the pillow, mattress, sheets and floorboards. Blood spots were also visible on the victim's drawers, which had been removed.

The victim was found naked except for a white vest. Knife wounds could be seen on the upper thighs of both legs, groin, and all about the abdomen and face. Also, a large gash across the neck, from the left jaw to right clavicle. No weapon was found at the scene.

Money totaling three dollars and forty cents was found in a bedside cabinet, and underneath the mattress a gold crucifix.

Your office was notified at 6.35 P.M.; Dist. Attorney St Clair Adams and Coroner Joseph O'Hara at 6.45 and 6.50 P.M. Chief Detective Daniel Mourney and Patrolman Joseph Reggio came immediately on the scene and assisted in the case.

By order of the Coroner the Body was removed to the Morgue in the Fourth Precinct Patrol Wagon, in charge Driver George Brandt and Patrolman Francis D. Peyronnin. One lot of bed clothing, consisting of: sheet; pillows; and mattress; two towels; one pair of drawers; and one vest were turned over to the Coroner by order of the Dist. Attorney to be used as evidence.

Statement of the above mentioned witnesses, all Negress prostitutes with cribs in the building, are hereto attached.

> Very respectfully,
> Joseph J. Carter
> Captain Comd'g Prec't
> A. J. Escude, Clerk

41

'The Axeman's gonna get us all paid, boy!' shrieked Baby Dodds. It was just past eight and the band was taking a break in the Dixie Bell's storage room. Baby chugged on a beer and smiled, and Lewis mumbled something in return. He was resting his head against a wall, trying to get some sleep, and his eyes were only half-open, not that Baby noticed any of this. Lewis never felt comfortable around Baby when he was drinking, not since an episode on the steamboat when Baby had gotten drunk on the job and started shouting and swearing in front of all the customers, and the whole band had nearly been thrown overboard by a posse of enraged whites. Baby was an excellent drummer, he had a trick of standing up and dancing whilst drumming, moving about the drum kit in a bewildering shimmy whilst keeping the beat going. The trick always brought cheers from the crowds and a rain of tips, but when it came to alcohol, Baby was an angry, impossible drunk.

'Didn't Pops tell you?' said Baby. 'Axeman night. Twenty-five bucks a piece. Plus tips.'

Lewis woke up a little and frowned at Baby.

'No fooling?' he asked.

'No fooling, Lil' Louey. Cats are worried 'bout not getting a jazz band in. Ain't that truth, Fate?' Baby shouted at Fate Marable, who was on the other side of the room, in deep conversation with Pops Foster, the band's bassist. Fate and Pops swung their gazes across the room at Baby.

'Axeman night,' repeated Baby. 'Twenty-five bucks a piece.'

'Yeah, that's the truth,' said Marable in his honey-soaked voice.

'Gonna have to learn the new score, too. Damn manuscript cost me two dollars.'

Lewis peered at Marable blankly and the band leader shuffled over to a canvas satchel resting on top of a broken bass drum. He opened the buckles, took a manuscript from it and passed it over to Lewis. Lewis examined the front cover. 'The Mysterious Axeman's Jazz (Don't Scare me Papa)' was written in large copperplate print across the top, and underneath it, in smaller point, 'by Joe Davilla, author of the noted Coon Novelty Song "Give Me Back My Husband, You've Had Him Long Enough"'.

Below the title was a cartoon that Lewis recognized from the *Picayune* – an ink drawing of a white family trying to play a jazz song on the home piano. Clouds of wavy black lines rose up from their hands, implying, Lewis guessed, that they were shaking with fright. In the background another member of the family stood watch at the front door with a shotgun. Lewis turned over the front cover and looked at the musical notations inside – lines and dots dancing across the pages like worms on a grill.

Lewis had begun learning to read music with Kid Ory, and his lessons were continuing with Marable, but he hadn't reached the point yet where he could sight-read a manuscript. Marable knew as much when he hired Lewis – reading music was a Creole skill that the Negro musicians from uptown rarely shared. Lewis was halfway between the two worlds – although he could read a little, he found it easier to listen to an arrangement a couple of times, memorize the piece, then play it by ear. Lewis's memory and his talent for picking up new pieces at speed led many of the musicians he played with to think he could sight-read, a misconception he did nothing to correct.

'We'll practice a little tomorrow,' said Marable, staring at Lewis with a smile that said he understood his concern. Lewis smiled back at Marable and returned the manuscript to him.

'I need to talk to you after we finished tonight,' said Marable in a hushed tone. 'Meet me in here after we've packed up.' Marable stuffed the manuscript back into the satchel, and Lewis felt like he'd been summoned to the principal's office.

When the *Dixie Belle* had returned to its mooring off Canal Street, and the few customers they had that night had left, Lewis made his way to the storage room, where Marable and Pops Foster were waiting for him. Lewis guessed he must have had an apprehensive look on his face, because when he walked in Marable and Pops peered at him and burst out laughing.

'Ain't nothin' to worry about, Lewis,' said Pops, chuckling along with Marable, and Lewis smiled back at him, still a little unsure. Pops motioned towards one of the half-broken chairs opposite them and Lewis sat. Then Marable approached and grinned at him, and Lewis saw the sparkle in his eye.

'We want to offer you a job on the *Sidney* this summer,' said Marable, 'running the cruises outside New Orleans.'

Lewis smiled at them and breathed a sigh of relief; he was being promoted.

'You'll be away for four months,' Pops explained. 'Boat goes all the way up the Mississippi – St Louis right up to Minnesota.'

'The pay's real good,' said Marable. 'Thirty-seven fifty a week, room and board, and a weekly bonus of five dollars paid at the end of the trip.'

The money was twice what Lewis was making with Ory's band, and that was before the bonus.

'And as an extra piece o' sugar,' continued Marable, 'Captain Joe said he'd buy you your own cornet, so you can give that one you're playing now back to Ory.'

Lewis grinned at them and nodded.

'That's a mighty fine offer, Mr Marable,' he said. 'I greatly appreciate it.'

'You're a good player, boy,' said Marable. 'You still need a little bit o' work, need to fix your embouchure, need to learn sight-reading, work on your divisions and your phrases. But we'll teach you all that. It'll be like going to university.'

Marable turned to look at Pops and Pops nodded.

'I couldn't read for shit till I started working with Marable,' said Pops, nodding at the band leader. 'Neither could St Cyr or Dots. We'll help you, kid. Get you to that next level.' Pops spoke in a slow, drawn-out way, his voice deep and warm.

Lewis looked at the two of them with a smile, but slowly a change came over him that Marable and Pops both noticed.

'It's a great offer, thank you both,' said Lewis. 'Can I have a bit o' time to think about it?'

Marable and Pops exchanged looks again, surprised that the boy even had to consider the offer, then Pops turned to Lewis and spoke.

'I remember the first time I heard you play, Lil' Louey. You was playing the clarinet solo on "High Society". Those arpeggios are hard enough to play on a clarinet, how the hell you played 'em on a cornet I got no idea. At seventeen years old, too.' Pops looked to Marable as he said the last, and Marable nodded in agreement. Then Pops returned his gaze to Lewis and spoke in a soft, fatherly tone. 'What I'm saying is, it'd be a shame to waste all that talent, just cause you a lil' worried 'bout leaving town. If you wanna be everything you can be, you gotta leave New Orleans.'

The gang-plank onto the quayside was slick with rainwater, and as Lewis padded down it he thought about Marable's offer and everything it entailed. The money was far beyond anything he could earn in the city. Over forty dollars a week for four months, when the average New Orleans carpenter, a skilled profession for a Negro, never made more than about fifteen. But leaving New Orleans was a scary prospect.

He'd heard the stories of musicians being promised big money outside the city, then being left stranded by unscrupulous promoters or shady record producers in the middle of nowhere, with no way of getting back home. He saw the musicians returning to New Orleans broken and in rags, swearing never to leave the city again. Even when record-company men came calling, ready to hand out big-money contracts, all the best players turned them down, and not just because putting your solos on record meant other people could steal them. Freddie Keppard even played with a handkerchief over his hand at gigs, so people couldn't see his fingering and steal his solos. Such was the level of distrust. And all these people were older than Lewis, and wiser, so they must have a reason for being so suspicious.

But then he thought of his old mentor, King Oliver, who was making it big in Chicago, and of the Original Dixieland Jazz Band, who'd gone to New York and cut the first ever jazz record. And Jelly Roll Morton and Bill Johnson who'd moved out to Hollywood.

But the riverboat wouldn't be going to New York or Chicago or LA, it'd be going up through the Midwestern states, playing to white folks mostly. People who still thought jazz was some kind of devil music. New Orleans might have been segregated and prejudiced, but Negroes had a good deal of personal safety there. And in that respect, it was an oasis compared to the rest of Louisiana, and the hell-hole of a state next door that was Mississippi.

Wasn't that why thousands of Negroes from all over the South kept pouring into New Orleans? Because it was a damn sight better than anywhere else? Could a handful of black men on a boat in the middle of the wilderness really be safe? Then he thought about Mayann and Clarence, and it was only after all this that he wondered what his estranged wife's reaction would be.

He descended onto the quayside and was about to head towards the tram stop when he noticed someone waiting for him at the end of the quay – a half-soaked, frozen-looking Ida, pale and distraught. Lewis ran over to her and grabbed her by the elbows.

'They killed her, Lewis,' she said between sobs, holding out a newspaper the rain had turned into a pulpy mess.

'Morval killed Leeta. It's in the paper,' she said, her voice breaking. 'What if he killed her because of us?'

Ten minutes later they were sitting in an empty harbor-side diner nursing hot coffees. It was a diner in the loosest sense of the word, more a shack with a gas stove and a few scavenged tables. The place had been set up to service the Negroes who worked on the docks, who weren't allowed into the other diners dotted along the quayside. The owner, an old, silent man, emaciated and stooped, brought them over a complimentary plate of biscuits and molasses to have with their *café brûlots*.

Lewis thanked the man, who with a quick glance at the ragged-looking Ida, made his way back to the counter. Ida was feeling a little better now she had met Lewis and was sitting warm in the diner. Calmer for having someone to share the news with, but still looking a mess, hair matted, dress soaked, make-up smudged.

'What if he killed her because she spoke to us?' Ida repeated, cupping her hands around the coffee to warm them.

'He didn't kill her for that,' said Lewis, shaking his head. 'Anyway, how you so sure it was Morval?'

Ida nodded to the newspaper on the table.

'She said he liked knives. You read what he did to her. What if he had someone watching her and they saw her talk to us?'

'That's a big *if*,' said Lewis, his voice a little sharper than he meant it to be. 'Even if it was him that killed her, don't mean it had anything to do with us. She'd just left his stable, right? Pimps don't like that. And she said she got hit by one of his johns recently. Might've been she was running his customers on her own and he found out.'

Ida sighed and looked down at her coffee, not entirely convinced. She took another sip of the *brûlot*, the mix of caffeine and brandy beginning to take the edge off her shock.

'We gotta wait and see what Buddy comes up with,' said Lewis. 'Ain't no point speculating.'

'Sure,' said Ida, deflated and weary, her voice still quavering. She turned her head to the front door, hanging off its hinges at an angle, and stared at the quayside. Despite the weather and the hour, a couple of ships had arrived at the docks and passengers and freight were being offloaded by a skeleton crew of officials and longshoremen. She couldn't tell Lewis that it wasn't just the guilt that was making her upset. She felt like a fool yet again. She had been playing at being a detective and now someone might be dead because of it. Her dream had become painfully real and had made her feel stupid, ashamed and disenchanted.

She took another sip of the *brûlot* and peered at Lewis. 'What you doing for Axeman night?' she asked, and Lewis frowned at her, surprised at the change in subject.

'Playing at a cabaret,' he said. 'Why? You wanna tag along?'

She smiled and Lewis smiled back and they sat in silence for a little while. Then out of nowhere, she put her hand on his.

'Thanks, Lewis,' she said. Lewis frowned at her, not quite sure what to make of the gesture, then he shrugged.

They stayed a little longer and finished their coffees, then they went their separate ways. Lewis caught the streetcar to Back o' Town, and Ida walked to a taxi stop to catch a cab back to her house. As she approached the stop, she noticed light spilling out of a building on the corner of the road in front of her, a hubbub of movement and the sound of cutlery tapping against plates. She thought it strange that a diner was open in this part of town so late at night, and that it appeared to be doing such a lively trade.

She approached the building and saw that it had no sign on it, nor anything else to identify its purpose. Its frontage was taken up wholly by two steamed-up sheet-glass windows and a wooden door in the center with an 'open' sign hanging from it. Ida padded towards the nearest window and peered through it. Inside was a cramped, shabby space occupied by rows of long tables and benches, at which a few dozen bedraggled men sat, eating bread and soup. At the rear of the space, a handful of workers in aprons tended to some vats that steamed away on a stove, or else they ladled out soup into bowls lined up on trays.

A silence seemed to pervade the place, no one spoke to their neighbors on the benches, and there was an air of despair to it all. Ida guessed it was a hostel, some kind of breadline eatery, set up by do-gooders to feed vagrants. But she noticed that all the people sitting on the benches were young-looking men, and they had a certain hollowness about their eyes. And then she realized they were destitute veterans, back from the Great War and traumatized by what they had been through, falling on the charity of the people who ran shelters like this one.

She was about to step away from the steamy window and the yellow electric light that spilled from it when she noticed the sign on the far wall. It took her a few seconds to understand its importance. *The Veterans Association of New Orleans, Shelter for Soldiers of the Great War, supported by the kind donations of Samuel Kline Junior.* The eatery was being paid for by the Brigadier General who Lefebvre had gone to see in the Louisiana Retreat. And then it clicked in her mind, and she realized why it was that her boss had visited the war hero in the sanatorium.

The Times–Picayune

Tuesday 13th May, 1919

Features Section – Comments by Muzz

The Axeman Cometh!

Since this newspaper exclusively published the Axeman's ghoulish letter to New Orleans last week, the city has been plunged into feverish preparation for tonight and everything it may bring. Despite all but proclaiming the letter a hoax, Mayor Behrman has been making sure his administration will not be left with egg on its face – all police leave has been cancelled, supernumeraries have been brought in, back-up forces from surrounding parishes (one shudders to think) have been called up and all New Orleans's finest are working overtime (at double rate, our friends in the force inform us). And just think, it was the mayor that insinuated that the *Picayune* had a penchant for profiteering from the macabre!

But perhaps of more interest to our readers are the plans the citizenry are making. The entrepreneurial spirit shown by our night-spot owners in turning the situation to their advantage has led to rumors that every cabaret, bar and restaurant in the Tango Belt is fully booked for the night. Will Axeman Night be the biggest party in the history of the Crescent? Quite possibly, by all accounts.

Exactly what has fuelled the excitement surrounding this grisly situation, apart from entrepreneurship of course, is a matter of debate. I'd like to think it's the Big Easy's natural inclination for a good time. Generally this spirit finds its outlet in Mardi Gras every Spring, but since our world-famous parade has been cancelled these last two years thanks to the Hun over in Europe, there might be a little extra *joie de vivre* in reserve, suppressed and bursting to see the light of day.

Of course, it's not just night-spot owners cashing in. The chosen anthem for the night (apart from 'Nearer My God to Thee') is local composer Joseph John Davilla's 'The Axeman's Jazz'. The manuscript hit the shops a few days ago and has been so popular the publishers had to hastily organize a second printing. Your ever selfless correspondent caught up with the melody-smith over drinks at the Ringside Café and was surprised to learn that the ditty was inspired by a cartoon the composer saw in the *Picayune*.

Davilla, a native Orleanais and resident of Elysian Fields Avenue, said: 'This is my tenth musical composition in the last three years, all coon songs. And while I've had some successes in the past, this has eclipsed them all. I'd like to dedicate the song to the New Orleans Police Band.'

Despite the wealth of choice out there for entertainment-lovers tonight, I will be having a little soiree of my own. And I'd like to cordially invite the Axeman to come along. It will be a small, select affair and I'm sincerely hoping the self-proclaimed *worst spirit that ever existed* does not have his social secretary send sad regrets. The stag do will be at 552 Lowerline Street, and all doors will be left open.

Axeman, you are as welcome as the flowers in May.

Yours, as always, Muzz

42

Luca got out of bed late the next morning. He'd bought an envelope and paper the previous night, and after waking had propped himself up in bed and tried to compose a letter to the manager of the Belle Terre estate. But he wasn't a writer, and the intricacies of tone and information he had to weave into the letter resulted in half the pad being used, ripped out and thrown onto the floor in a crumple before he finally arrived at something he was happy with.

He rose, threw the discarded sheets into the wastebasket, washed in the cold water of the basin and changed. He took the letter and the trash bag with him and descended the stairs to the hotel lobby. The concierge was in his usual place behind the counter, filling in an order book. He looked up when he heard Luca's steps echoing towards him and smiled.

'Morning, *signore*,' he said.

'Good morning, Paolo. I was wondering if I could ask you a favor. I'd like to post this letter but I don't want the policemen outside to see.'

'Ah,' said the concierge, nodding like a doctor who had just heard a patient tell him of some intimate affliction. He stroked his chin and thought for a moment, and then his face lit up.

'I have to go out to buy some things,' he said, smiling. 'If you look after the counter while I am gone?'

'Certainly,' said Luca.

'Good, good. Give me . . .' the old man checked his pocket-watch, 'five minutes?'

Luca bowed his head, and the old man nodded and returned his attention to the order book in front of him, writing something in a slow, confused hand.

'Paolo, how do I get to the boiler?' asked Luca.

'Eh?' said the old man, peering at him.

Luca held up the bag of wastepaper, and the concierge smiled and pointed to a staircase on the far side of the room. Luca turned and headed down the stairs. He made his way along a dark corridor, saw the boiler room halfway down and stepped inside. In the center of the room was the boiler, twisting brass tubes disappearing into the darkness above.

Luca opened the grating with a dusty, warped poker, and threw the paper bag into the fire within, watching it for a moment as the pages curled and writhed, the heat drying out his eyes.

He returned to the lobby, saw the concierge off, settled himself behind the counter and smoked a cigarette while he waited. He browsed through the guest-book and saw that, as far as he could tell, he was the hotel's only current guest. Behind the counter was a corkboard to which the concierge had pinned photographs – gray images of family and friends, baby pictures, a snapshot of an ocean liner, and a postcard printed with a photograph taken from the hills outside Naples. Luca pulled the postcard from the corkboard and stared at it – it showed the city from above, stretching out to meet the wide curve of the bay. Tiny boats clustered around the wharves like schools of feeding fish, and in the far distance, sloping gracefully into the sky, the pale shadow of Vesuvius. All he could really see of the city itself was the rooftops of the buildings, tiny squares of red tiles mosaicking haphazardly, sliced by streets and pinned with a hundred campaniles.

Luca had once spent a day in Naples, years before, when he and his parents had caught the ship that brought him to America. It was the first time he'd been in a city; he remembered being bewildered by the narrow streets, the tall buildings one on top of the other, the noisy market squares, the beggars, the drunks lying in the gutters. He remembered staring at his father as they wandered through the docks, searching for their connecting ship with a faint, tourists' disquiet, realizing that the city was as perturbing for his father as it was for him.

The memories didn't make Luca nostalgic, didn't make him yearn to return, like they had when he thought about his childhood in Monreale during the nights he spent lying awake in Angola. The city in the postcard looked alien and unsettlingly real. The buildings looked too small, the volcano in the background like a foreign god he didn't know how to worship. The land in the picture meant as much to him as St Petersburg, Manila or Athens and he realized with a flush of anxiety that even if he did go back to Italy, he'd still be in exile, a man with no home, because a home wasn't just somewhere you lived, it was somewhere you were happy to die.

He put the postcard back on the corkboard, pinning it carefully into position like a butterfly, and smoked another cigarette while he waited. The concierge returned a few minutes later, shaking water from his umbrella with a smile. He nodded at Luca to signal his mission had been accomplished.

Luca left the hotel directly. He strode down the wet streets, shoulders hunched, staring out at the world from under the brim of his hat, walking with no end destination in mind. He had realized with a stab of panic that he was starting to have doubts about moving back to Monreale. He wondered if the idea was just the foolish dream of an old man lying in a prison bunk, and he thought of Carlo's laugh when he had told him his plans. Luca stalked the banquettes and brooded, running things over in his mind. Every now and again he'd look over his shoulder to see the two policemen following him, red-faced, annoyed that he was forcing them to travel through the rain.

After pacing about for a quarter of an hour he realized he was in the Tango Belt. On the banquettes, the paperboys were hollering 'Axeman Night Special!' and the boards and posters outside the cabarets, restaurants and saloons were proclaiming the names of the jazz bands they had secured for the night:

THE OASIS CABARET PRESENTS ITS
AXEMAN SPECIAL:
The Onward Brass Band here tonight!
No Axe killings or your money back!

THE TUXEDO BRASS BAND!
TONIGHT AT THE HAYMARKET!
Playing Jazz all night long!
Leave your axes at home, now!

The morbid humor of the signs and the excitement in the streets only increased his restlessness. He realized he hadn't eaten yet, so he decided to make his way to the Grocery, an Italian-owned eatery on Decatur Street.

He walked with his head down and his hands shoved firmly into his pockets, no closer to finding an angle through the thoughts in his head. When he arrived he found the place almost empty. He ordered a muffuletta and a coffee and took a seat at an empty table.

He lit a cigarette and scanned the interior while he waited, and it was only then that he noticed the altar in the corner and remembered that it was St Joseph's day. People all over the city set up altars dedicated to the saint, laden with braided loaves, cakes, fruits, pastries and bottles of wine, all scattered among flickering red vigil lights and overseen by statues of the holy family. The altars overflowed as each individual, household, business and church tried to outdo the next.

Bartolomeo, the owner of the Grocery, brought him over his coffee and muffuletta – a flatbread sandwich of mortadella, chopped olives and provolone. As he ate, Luca looked at the altar, at the food and the candles and statuettes of St Joseph and he wondered if the Axeman had planned his night deliberately to coincide with the saint's day. He overheard the other customers talking to the staff about their plans for the evening, which cabaret they had booked tickets to, and the merits or not of 'jazzing it up'.

He listened to them and ate and as the food seared through his stomach he made his own plans. For Luca, St Joseph's Day normally meant going to the church parades around the French Quarter, watching the faithful carry the statue of the saint on their shoulders, and then going back to Carlo's house for a banquet, all the members of the extended family eating and drinking together. Carlo would consider it a snub if Luca didn't make an appearance, and yet he didn't feel he could go. The false sincerity and warmth of the men there, sharing jokes with each other as intrigues were plotted – he would much rather spend the day in someone else's company. He could maybe use the case as an excuse for not turning up, but now the letter was sent he had nothing to do but wait. He decided to visit Simone, realizing she was the anchor keeping him in New Orleans, and he wondered if there was any point trying to shake off the two policemen who would undoubtedly follow him there.

He finished his drink and sauntered over to the counter with his ticket. At the counter, Bartolomeo was showing off his shotgun to two women in fine coats, with moneyed, pale faces. Bartolomeo was boasting about how the Grocery would be open all night, and he wouldn't be playing no coon music, Axeman or not. The customers laughed at the funny old Italian, gloved hands in front of their mouths.

Luca handed over his ticket and paid, then stepped out into the street. He lit a cigarette with his hands cupped against the rain, and began the long walk to Simone's.

A few hours later he was sitting on her porch and watching the rain beat down on the surface of the bayou. The two plainclothesmen had followed him all the way there and had hidden behind a shack on the opposite side of the path. They had stayed for at least the first hour, occasionally peeking around the corner, rain-drenched, cold and annoyed. But he guessed they must have shirked off their duties and headed back to the precinct, or more likely to the closest bar.

The door behind him squeaked and Luca turned around to see two Cajuns exit the cabin. The husband had his hand over his gut, and he smiled at Luca warmly and said something in French that Luca didn't catch. The wife followed him out, adjusted a shawl so that it covered her head, and the couple stepped out into the rain.

They had arrived an hour before, when Luca was in the shack with Simone and he was trying to explain to her why the policemen were following him. The Cajuns had knocked and greeted Simone with familiarity. The man was tall and broad-shouldered with wispy black hair and a bushy mustache. He wore a white shirt and a hat with a wide brim and Luca recognized him instantly as a Cajun fisherman. The wife was equally tall and dark-haired, but for someone who worked in the sun she was surprisingly pale to Luca's eye. Simone had asked Luca to step outside while she consulted with them, so Luca had sat on the porch, smoking cigarettes and watching the rain, feeling like both an intruder and an exile.

He eyed the couple as they walked along the path, heading back to whatever corner of the local backwaters they had come from. Then he stood, flicked his cigarette into the yard and re-entered the cabin. Simone was busying herself by the stove, setting some kind of broth to cook. He could tell from the way she concerned herself with the cooking that she wasn't in the mood to talk. He sat at the table and watched her as she chopped vegetables on a board and threw them into the pot.

'Are those two idiots still outside?' she said without looking up.

'The Cajuns?'

'No, the police,' she replied curtly, unwilling to acknowledge the joke.

'I didn't see them,' he said. 'I think they've gone home.'

She nodded and continued her work. She had been distant since he had arrived, so much so that when the Cajuns came knocking, he was glad of the distraction.

'How did it go with the patients?' he asked, settling on a neutral topic.

'Stomach ulcer. Same as what you've got,' she answered curtly. 'I gave him some herbs.'

She picked up a pan from the stove absentmindedly, without first wrapping a cloth around the handle. She shrieked and the pan clanged to the floor. Luca jumped up and ran over to her.

'*Merde*,' she hissed, holding her hand in pain.

'You OK?'

She nodded, shrugged him off, and dipped her hand in the pail of cold water at the foot of the stove.

Luca grabbed a rag and cleaned up the contents of the pan from the floor – some kind of sticky brown goo that reminded him of the fig jam his grandmother used to make every September back in Sicily. Simone watched him as she knelt, her hand plunged in the cold water, something angry in her eye, as if she blamed him for her accident.

She stood, dried her hand and walked over to the rows of jars. She opened one, took out some papery yellow arnica leaves and pressed them against the burn mark on her palm, wrapping a bandage loosely around it. She returned to the stove and held her hand out to Luca, who took it and tied the bandages tight.

'Thank you,' she said.

He smiled, finished off the bandage with a bow-knot and stood. They peered at each other, their faces close for the first time since he arrived. He leaned forwards and kissed her, and to his surprise she kissed him back. Then she turned, picked up a cloth and stooped to finish off wiping the mess from the floorboards.

Luca sat at the table again and watched her work. He noticed that his nose was running a little, and guessed he was coming down with something after walking through the rain all morning.

'You got anything in there for a cold,' he said, motioning towards the shelves.

'Lots of 'em are good for colds. Pimento tea, pepper-grass, cirier-batard leaves, honeysuckle. I'll make you a *tisane* after I clear this up.'

'A *tisane*?' asked Luca.

'Medicine tea.'

A half-hour later they were sitting on the porch drinking the *tisane*, a yellow tea of ironwort that tasted faintly of chamomile. They sat without speaking and watched the rain as it danced in the mud track, drumming a cacophony against the sheet-metal roofs of the shacks opposite. Simone seemed calmer now, less annoyed.

'*And the windows of heaven were opened,*' she said. '*And the rain was upon the earth for forty days and forty nights.*'

Luca frowned and turned to stare at her.

'Two weeks of solid rain,' she said. 'Haven't seen anything like it since the hurricane in 1915. Remember?'

Luca shook his head. 'I was in Angola that year,' he replied, matter-of-fact. Simone peered at him and nodded, then turned back to stare at the downpour sheeting onto the lake.

'It rained for a week before the storm came, and when it did . . .' She made a waving gesture with her hand, to indicate that whatever was being described was too great for words. 'I remember the noise when the dams broke – like thunder. And then the next day all the bodies floating down the street. People, cows, dogs, all of 'em dead and white and bloated and rolling on the water, floating down the street.'

She shook her head and gazed at the cup of tea in her hand before taking a sip.

'You think it's brewing for another hurricane?' asked Luca.

'Two weeks of rain,' she said flatly, as if that explained it all.

'A hurricane in May?' he said.

She shrugged. 'It's happened before.'

She stared out across the track, looking with concern at the bayou in the distance and the tender gray storm clouds gathering above it.

They continued to stare out over the desolate view – the rickety shacks, the swaying trees, the lake, the rain smashing itself stupidly into the earth. Luca should have recoiled from the scene, it had an oppressive bleakness to it. It was the kind of view only afforded to people on the very edge of things, one step away from the chaos beyond. But he found some kind of beauty in it, an unexplainable reassurance, a sense that, despite the bayou's forsaken form, this half-world was where life began.

At some point, the neighbor with the mandolin struck up a tune, this time joined by someone else on a fiddle, the duet broken by the rain into a jaunty staccato. Luca wondered if the performance was prompted by the Axeman's letter, if the two musicians were trying to buy their safety with the tune. The music was less mournful than the previous time Luca had heard the neighbor play, as if now that the mandolin had found its partner, its song was less lonely.

He looked over to Simone and she smiled at him warmly, her bad mood from earlier completely gone. He held out his hand and she took it in hers and they watched the storm. The anxiety that had been in Luca's heart all day slowly dissolved, became so meaningless as to lose all threat, something he could forget ever existed. When it grew dark they would light a fire and eat a stew of vegetables and chicken, and then they would spend the night wrapped around each other, as the music played and the fire flicked an orange glow around the room, and neither of them would care anymore about the storm circling over the cabin's tin roof.

43

Lewis had never seen anything like it. The city was awash with jazz. From the honky-tonks in Back o' Town to the night-spots in the Tango Belt to the normally quiet houses and cafes, a thousand and one songs were spilling out onto the streets. It seemed to Lewis, as he made his way from Mayann's to the cabaret, that every possible means of creating music had been pressed into service – in places where there wasn't a band, Victrolas, phonographs and inner-player pianos supplied the songs, while elsewhere hobbyist musicians had dusted down long-idle instruments and banded together with anyone that could strum a few drunken notes. It was as if a spirit had seized control of all the instruments in the city and spellbound they had burst into song. The sound came together in the streets, where despite the fact that it was still early in the evening, Lewis had to dodge past crowds already drunk and stumbling between bars and clubs.

When he got to the cabaret he noticed an electric, expectant mood. The place had been decked out in a tropical theme for the night, with spools of crêpe paper strung from the ceiling, and multicolored lanterns casting rainbow lights, and the bar and stage decorated with palm leaves, coconuts, and fake Hawaiian reeds. He overheard the owners arguing about whether to set extra tables on the dance floor, or to make the dance floor bigger by moving tables out.

The band rehearsed the new song a few times, and then the doors were flung open and within half an hour the place was jammed, and everyone was dancing, stamping the boards and clapping their hands in a sweaty, liquor-fuelled frenzy. Strings of pearls broke, shirtsleeves ripped, suits and gowns were drenched in champagne and perspiration. Even the big-timers who normally sat at the back and never looked excited were dancing away with everyone else. The crowd become so fevered the band veered from their standard Tango Belt repertoire and started playing the bluesy, growling songs that were never normally heard outside of Back o' Town – 'Kiss My Funky Ass' and 'Brown Skin Who You For?'.

Lewis remembered his grandmother telling him about the days before emancipation, when the slaves in New Orleans spoke French and they would gather every Sunday afternoon in Place Congo to dance the Bamboula or the Conjaie to African music rattled out of drums and slides and cow-horns and bells – anything people could get ahold of to make a noise. She had told him about the fervor with which the people there danced, and for the first time in his life, Lewis thought he was witnessing a scene that resembled those of his grandmother's stories.

They were a couple of minutes into 'Tiger Rag' when Lewis heard a cue from Baby as they came to the end of a chorus, a half-bar drum fill, a double hit on the snare. He closed his eyes and launched into a solo, but not one of his usual solos because none of those felt quite right. Tonight he made it up as he went along, feeding off the crowd and their frenzy. His mind drifted as he played, away from the music, and he thought about the day when he was a child by the river, about the blues he heard the wild-man play on his old dented Kress horn. Lewis had never been able to recapture that sound, it was always just at the back of his mind. But now he managed to remember it clearly, and used it in his solo, picking out tones he would never normally pick, letting the memory guide him in his choice of notes.

Other memories flooded into his head – the sound of church when he was a child; singing for dimes with his street-corner quartet; sneaking out at night with his friends to peek through the cracks at Pete Lala's and the Funky Butt Hall so they could watch their heroes on stage, Buddy Bolden, Sidney Bechet, Jelly Roll

Morton. He remembered Joe Oliver showing him how to use a mute and performing in parades with the Waifs' Home brass band, even playing the blues for whores at four in the morning in long-gone bordellos. The memories found their way into the music he was making now, all of them aligning. And a beautiful peace passed over him that seemed to last an eternity.

But just as quickly as it came, it was gone. And he suddenly felt fearful. He'd forgotten where he was. What had he been playing? He heard Baby roll out another half-bar fill, signaling the end of his solo and a crash into another chorus. He felt it was too early for sixteen bars to be up, and a sinking, dreadful feeling came over him. He opened his eyes to see what was happening.

The sound of the cabaret came flooding back first – people were screaming, grins on their faces, others were staring at him open-mouthed. He turned to look at Fate and Fate gazed back at him with something he guessed was pride. The noise of the crowd morphed into shouts for an encore and Lewis felt warm relief run through him and then a boundless joy. They wanted to hear it again, but he couldn't remember what he'd played. He looked over to Ida, who was beaming at him from the edge of the dance floor. Fate gave Baby a nod and at the next spot Baby hit another roll. Lewis closed his eyes again and dived back into the dark and beautiful light.

The second solo was played to a stop-time chorus, with long gaps between the band's thumping chords, gaps that allowed Lewis to show his dexterity, leaping over the silences gleefully, with mer-curial, acrobatic vaults. His phrases became ever longer, rising upwards through a spiral of arpeggios, before holding a long high B for four whole bars, his tone perfect, clear and pure. And then he descended from it, like a dove from heaven.

A roar went up and Ida turned to look at the crowd – Lewis had them spellbound. An eighteen-year-old who didn't even own his own instrument, speaking a language so elegant and natural that some unconscious part of them understood it and responded with an equally beautiful joy. Ida grinned and made her way to the bar for another drink. She squeezed through the crowds, feeling none of the nervousness she normally felt in these situations. No men were approaching her or staring at her in the clawing way they normally did. There was no sexual element to the party, all anyone was concerned with was drinking and dancing and getting high. The pursuit of a liaison would have drawn them away from the fun they were having, from the beautiful now.

The crowd at the bar was five deep, and as she waited Ida checked the state of her dress, a pink muslin one-shoulder trimmed with gold beads. She brushed some lint from it and as she moved closer to the front she looked up and noticed two women on the far side of the room, a few years older than her, with bob haircuts, clingy dresses and waifish, porcelain looks. One of the women whispered to the other and the two of them laughed, and for an instant Ida felt lonely and wished she had a friend to share the evening with. The man in front of her moved away with his drinks and Ida approached the bar and ordered a whiskey and ice. She turned again to look at the two women, but could no longer see them; standing there now was a tall man in a black pinstripe suit. The man had a stillness to him, a blank expression and upright posture that didn't fit with the atmosphere of the place, and he was staring at Ida in a fixed, displaced sort of way that left her feeling unsettled. She turned her gaze back to the bar, wondering if she knew him from somewhere.

The barman placed her drink on the bar and Ida paid and squeezed back out through the crowd to her spot at the edge of the dance floor. When she turned back around to watch the band, she noticed the man had begun to move through the throng towards her. Ida felt a stab of panic, and with Leeta's murder fresh in her mind, she wondered if the man posed a threat or if it was just her agitation sparking paranoia.

As she watched him make his way across the room, he brushed

past a dancing couple and his jacket was briefly pushed back by the contact, allowing Ida to see something glinting in the darkness by his shirt. A knife? A gun? She felt another stab of panic and wondered what she should do. The man was getting closer. The people were packed so close he could slip a knife through her ribs and no one would even notice. She could run to the washrooms and hide in the stalls, but maybe he would come in and find her and then she'd be trapped. She'd be safer on the street, where she could run, and people could hear her scream and cops were more likely to be milling about. She made her way to the exit, pushing past people as quickly as she could, causing some of the dancers to turn her way and scowl. She looked behind her. The man had changed direction and was heading her way.

She sped up and reached the edge of the throng, the space by the cloakroom and the front door, and just as she was stepping out, a hand grabbed her elbow and a chill ran down her spine.

'Leaving so soon?'

She turned to see the waifish woman she had seen at the bar with their friend. Ida breathed a sigh of relief before looking over her shoulder at the man in the black suit. He saw Ida was engaged in a conversation and he stopped abruptly, turning sideways as if he were inspecting something on the opposite side of the room. Ida turned back to the woman, who was still smiling at her, her face delicate, her eyes reflecting the glow of the rainbow-colored lights above them.

'I'm sorry, I have to go,' Ida said, after staring at the woman for a moment. Then she turned and darted out of the cabaret. When she burst onto the packed street she saw that it was just as busy as the cabaret, cloying with drunk stumblers, people dancing and couples hanging onto each other for support. She made her way up the road, pushing past the hordes, and she turned to see the man run through the cabaret doors and try and find her in the crowd. He saw her and they locked eyes.

Ida dashed down the street, bumping into people, looking

behind her every few seconds to see the man getting closer, slamming people out of his way. She jumped off the banquette and onto the road where there were fewer people to impede her flight. The man caught up with her and grabbed at her just as she was turning a corner. She pulled away and a car swung into the road, blaring its horn, and she leapt onto the other side of the road. The man stopped in his tracks, the car between them, and for an instant they stared at each other. Then, quick on the car's tail, a group of policemen ran down the street.

'Officer!' shouted Ida, and one of the cops peeled off from the pack to stop in front of her, breathing heavily from whatever chase he had been involved in. Ida smiled at the policeman and turned to look at the man in the black suit. He had turned away from her and was striding down the street in the opposite direction. Ida returned her gaze to the policeman.

'I'm sorry, sir. I mistook you for somebody else.'

The policeman scowled at her and ran off up the street to rejoin his colleagues, and Ida, her heart still pumping, ran to the nearest taxi stand. She caught a cab home, checking behind her constantly to make sure no one had followed her, but even when she got inside her house she didn't feel entirely safe. Despite double-locking the doors and checking the windows a hundred times, she was unable to sleep until the early hours, lying in her bed anxious and awake. In the darkness she could hear jazz music sounding faintly from somewhere nearby, jumpy and taut, shadowing her thoughts as she wondered who it was that had sent the man to kill her.

44

Riley had spent the evening bar-hopping with his old university friends – men who had become rich and influential over the years Riley had been stagnating at the *Picayune*. They had gone from cabaret to cabaret in their convoy of chauffeur-driven carriages, had sat at the best tables, drinking champagne, smoking cigars, laughing boisterously, full of joy for lives that had done them so well. They all agreed it was the best night in the history of the city, and as for the jazz they were being exposed to, well, there might just be something in this jig music after all. So they raised their glasses numerous times and toasted the Axeman for laying on such a fine spread.

It had reached the point in the evening, at their fourth cabaret, when Riley could no longer keep up with their spending. They noticed his awkwardness, and aware of his situation, had started buying him drinks, and telling him in slurry, patronizing voices, not to worry about it. But their camaraderie only made him feel worse, and as the evening progressed he increasingly withdrew into himself.

One of the men suggested that, as they were free from their wives for the night, they should move on to a bordello and really live it up. The others agreed with raucous cheers, and they asked for the bill, tossed money onto the table like confetti, and stumbled through the crowds towards the cabaret's exit. Riley's heart was sinking – a night in the type of bordellos they frequented would set him back a week's wages. On top of that he was feeling his nightly nausea. He could have stayed with them – he had his little brass pipe in his pocket, along with his emergency supply of resin in a tiny lacquer box. But somehow he craved the peace of the laundry, the anonymity.

They stumbled out onto the street, five middle-aged men in tuxedos, their faces red from liquor. The scene outside was chaotic; bodies packed the streets, swaying through the rain, the atmosphere heavy with alcohol and abandon.

The fresh air hit Riley's wine-warmed head and he suddenly felt woozy and ill. His friends were stumbling about, waving at their chauffeurs, shouting at them through the crowds. He approached them and told them he was going to call it a night, and his friends' boisterousness dimmed. They grew quiet and frowned at him, and then they asked him questions and he made weak excuses, explaining he wasn't really feeling up to it. With sad regrets they said their goodbyes and Riley made his way up the street in a mood of self-loathing. He had turned his back on his friends, he had turned his back on the greatest party the city had ever known, to go and sit alone on the floor of a joyless laundry on Elysian Fields Avenue.

As he made his way out of the Tango Belt, along the roads that led north, the crowds and noise thinned out, until Riley was left completely on his own. He could no longer see any bright lights and revelers, but he could still hear the music, faint and thin, seeping through the streets. There weren't any cabarets nearby, and Riley wondered from where the city conjured its music.

Lost in the traffic of his thoughts he didn't notice the two men in flat-caps stalking along in the shadows behind him. As he reached the river, one of the two men dropped a club from the sleeve of his coat into his hand, and the other checked again the rope that was coiled in the bag slung over his shoulder. Riley had reached the bend on North Peters Street, halfway between Elysian Fields and the dark, nourishing water of the Mississippi, when the two men approached, and asked him the time.

45

Carnival sounds drifted in from the street, through the precinct's open windows and up to the detective bureau, where Michael lay slumped over his paperwork, sleeping fitfully. The street noises seeped into his dreams, mingling into an eye-fluttering nightmare – a walk through a hellish recreation of New Orleans. It was night and the streets were packed as if for Mardi Gras, but the faces of the people were distorted and grotesque, fixed in sneers or narrow-eyed smiles. He saw angels and devils roaming among the crowds, voodou doctors in top hats, Negroes with faces painted white, and whites in minstrel clothes. A skeletal Creole stirred a cauldron over a street-corner fire and Michael stopped to look inside it; a stew of severed limbs and the faces of people from his childhood who had long since died.

He stumbled on, passing buildings that were on fire, their wrought-iron balconies glowing white-hot, floating like arabesques in the night sky. In other places, hurricanes blew down streets and swept grinning couples up into the air. All through the chaos, people laughed and drank moonshine, or stumbled into embraces, their clothes tearing as they fell, their eyes flaming red. Others linked arms with the demons and danced to the sounds of brass bands playing outlandish nocturnes in a dark land beyond the city limits. The music got louder and louder, began to ring insistently, unstoppingly, in a pain-making dull tattoo.

Michael woke and rubbed his eyes. The bureau floor blurred into his vision, the overhead lights burning. He lifted the phone off its cradle, more to stop the ringing than anything else. Two o'clock and all was clear in the 7th Precinct – no sightings, no attacks, just arrests for drunk-and-disorderly and other misdemeanors. A minute later another call came through – the 4th Precinct, also reporting the two o'clock all-clear. Within ten minutes all twelve precincts had called. Nothing. If the Axeman had struck at 12.15 like he'd said, either they would have found out by now, or it wouldn't be discovered till morning.

Michael rubbed his eyes again and scanned the floor. Kerry lay asleep in his chair on the other side of the desk. Michael decided to stay another couple of hours then call it a night. He was getting cabin fever from being cooped up in the building so long. That morning, as the rest of the men were being assigned their duties, Captain McPherson had informed him that he would be staying in the precinct that night. 'We want you in the HQ, to coordinate things,' he had said, matter-of-fact. 'Central, so you can get any-where quick if the Axeman does strike.'

In his attempt to assure Michael that the decision wasn't a snub, he confirmed the opposite – that Michael was being taken off the streets on the most important day in the history of the department. Dismissed from his own case for the night, for God knew what reason. Michael had stared at the old man incredulously, but he hadn't gotten angry, he had nodded and gone on his way. He was coming to the end of things, and the knowledge of that made him calmer than he would have been otherwise.

Earlier that day Amanzo had been up in front of a judge and had made bail. Michael had assigned two men to trail him, and had brought in his alibis for the night of Lombardi's murder: a fellow bouncer, the manager of the club, and two girls from the chorus line. All of them had backed up his story. The men had searched Amanzo's apartment and found nothing. Michael's only hope now lay in Amanzo slipping up, and the two men on his tail catching him out. Either that or someone above Amanzo bungling an attempt on his life. What was more likely, however, was that Amanzo would skip town, Michael's only remaining lead disappearing into the unknowable vast interior of the country.

Michael trudged over to the window and gazed down into the street below. It was still engulfed by the festivities, packed with people, drunk, stumbling, their evening dress drenched in rain. The precinct wasn't even on the main drag – it must have been even worse up in the center of the Tango Belt. He wondered how Annette and the kids were doing, then he went over to the water-cooler and filled a couple of paper cups. He went back to Kerry and nudged him awake. The boy peered at him with bleary eyes, his hair flattened on one side.

'Some water, son,' said Michael. 'I'm just gonna go outside for some fresh air.'

'I'll come, too,' said Kerry, his voice groggy.

They drank the water and headed outside, trotting through the lobby and out onto the precinct steps. Michael lit a cigarette and yawned, the iron-clad humidity of the night sapping his energy. He put his hands on his hips and stared out at the revelers swaying their way down the streets. It wasn't dissimilar to the abandon and debauchery of his dream. He even noticed some 'baby dolls' in among the crowd, uptown Negro prostitutes who dressed for parades in revealing lace baby costumes. A well-dressed drunk couple stumbled their way up the street and bumped into the baby dolls, who tutted and scowled until the man smiled and offered the girls a drink from the champagne bottle he had in his hand.

Further up the block, a blue Paterson touring car started up and made its way slowly down the street, the revelers parting around it like a stream. The car passed the precinct and stopped a few yards further down, the mass of people blocking it from view. Kerry yawned, then Michael noticed men jumping out of the car, something flashing in their hands. They pulled dark tubes from their jackets and swung them towards the precinct.

Michael shouted at Kerry and gunshots exploded with ear-piercing snaps. The steps around them began cracking as the bullets hit, fragments of stone flying upwards as if drawn to the sky. Michael grabbed Kerry by the collar and they dashed for the cover of the squat stone wall that ran along the side of the building. They fell to the ground behind the wall as volley after volley rained down around them. The stone came alive as it splintered under the hail of bullets. The noise of the metal slugs smacking into the granite sent shrill, deafening noises ringing into Michael's ears, and the world became silent. He watched as puffs of stone dust bloomed noiselessly in the air after each bullet hit the scorch-marked steps. And then a sound filled the silent void in his head, the music from his dream, the deathly serenade of the brass bands.

He looked up – the car was surrounded by faceless men, each one with a shotgun, orange blooms flickering through the rain, gun-flashes tracing a silhouette around the dark mass of the car. He saw bystanders screaming and running for safety, the well-dressed couple cowering in the doorway of a store.

He wasn't sure how long it lasted or when the flashes stopped, but he remembered hearing ringing in his ears, then shouting. Then the sound of car wheels screeching. He opened his eyes and scanned the road in front of him – the car was heading off down the street, blaring its horn. He stood to chase after it but nearly fell to the ground, the steps below him rolling and pitching. He put his hand against the wall to steady himself and that's when he saw Kerry, lying in a pool of blood, limbs twisted at unnatural angles like a ragdoll tossed aside.

Michael stared at him, then knelt and tried to lift him up, but as he did so, blood gushed from the boy's mouth. Kerry tried to breathe but his windpipe was clogged, scraps of metal burning into his lungs. He stared at Michael with a pathetic look of fear and shock, and then his eyes turned milky and blank and Michael felt the breath leave the boy's body in a spasm that shook them both.

Michael felt dizzy and sick, and Kerry's body suddenly became heavy in his hands. He had the sense of a pain in his arms, both immediate and distant, and he laid the body down and breathed deeply for a few seconds. He noticed some of the old-timers from the precinct busy about him, some putting hands on his shoulders, others rushing off down the street. He stared at Kerry's face again – at the scared, pale expression and the rainwater collecting in his forest-green eyes. He reached over and closed the boy's eyelids, and as he did so a wild, violent anger filled him, making the dizziness, confusion and pain disappear. He stood up shakily, glared at the crowd that was gathering around them, and tore off down the street.

He waved his gun in the air and screamed at people to get out of the way and joined the old-timers in their pursuit. Revelers shrieked and watched in shock as the gang of police pushed them out of the way. They made it to the corner and saw the car at the end of the street – its path blocked by something, the driver honking the horn wildly. The men in the backseat looked behind them. Michael fired shots in the air and bystanders ran for cover. The men in the car leaned out of the windows and fired back but Michael carried on running at them. He shot at the car, releasing every bullet in the gun, praying each one would find its mark. But the bullets clanged into metal, and then the obstacle in front of the car cleared, and it swerved around the corner and sped off into the night.

Michael carried on chasing it, even though he knew there was no chance of catching up. He continued to run until he suddenly felt jelly-legged and sick. He fell to the ground, his revolver bouncing along the street, and after a moment, he vomited.

Eventually the old-timers caught up with him and he heard them discussing gunshots, arteries and blood, and in his dazed state he couldn't catch what they were talking about. But then he looked to his shoulder and saw blood streaming from it and he realized he had been shot. The old-timers lifted him up and walked him back, stumbling past the crowds as they went. They reached the precinct and Michael caught a glimpse of Kerry's body, still splayed out on the steps. A few of the bluecoats had formed a cordon to hold back the onlookers, and another was laying a blanket over it. He noticed Kerry's blood dripping down the steps, swept by the rainwater towards a mud-caked gutter.

PART FIVE

PART FIVE

The Times-Picayune

Weather

United States Department of Agriculture, New Orleans, La, 14th May
Weather Conditions: New Orleans, La, 13th May, 1919, 9 p.m.

Unusual weather patterns set to continue
Possible storm warnings in place

Pressure and wind conditions over Santo Domingo and the Bahamas indicate the possible presence of a disturbance over the eastern Bahamas. National Weather Bureau Officers have received an evening report from Nassau suggesting any possible storm will landfall in the Florida region. If the direction changes hurricane flags will be raised.

Forecast

Louisiana: Wednesday, rain and wind set to continue in the north, possible storm in the south portion: no change in temperature. Thursday, lighter winds, chance of rain in south portion.

46

The next morning Ida woke heavy-eyed and hung-over and her mind flashed back to the man who had pursued her, to his stony face, to the look of cold menace in his eyes and the glinting of the weapon concealed beneath his jacket. A spike of agitation ran through her chest, and in its wake, a sickly feeling in the pit of her stomach. It took her a while to get out of bed and summon up the will to try to make something of the day. She had time to kill before she met up with Lewis and Buddy, so she washed and dressed and made her way to the tram stop, looking over her shoulder the whole time.

She had spoken to Lewis the previous night and he had told her that Buddy had completed his reconnaissance of the house and they had arranged to break into it tonight. But with the events at the cabaret she wondered if it was still a smart move to make, if someone wouldn't be watching them all the way. That she was no longer conducting her investigation in secret changed so many things, and she wondered how it was that she had been found out. They must have told someone who had told someone else. Leeta? Buddy? Lulu White? Lefebvre?

It was only when she sat down at the back of the tram, knowing she was on her way without anyone in tow, that she relaxed a little. She noticed someone had left a newspaper on the seat next to her, so she picked it up to keep her mind from brooding. The front page was mainly taken up with an article about the preparations for the previous evening, the newspapers having gone to press long before Axeman Night itself unfolded. There were quotes from the mayor and a police captain on how the city would protect its citizens, and mention was made of the detective in charge of the case, Michael Talbot.

Ida had never seen the detective, but she had heard Lefebvre talk about him on a few occasions, most recently just a few days before, when he cursed the man's name after two policemen visited the office, asking Lefebvre to accompany them to the precinct to answer their questions. There were many rumors, most of them concerning a colored woman the detective supposedly kept hidden in his house.

Eventually the tram reached her stop and she rang the bell, descended and walked to the Louisiana Retreat for the Feeble-Minded, entering the building from the front this time. When she had seen the soup kitchen for veterans two nights previously and understood its connection to the case, she wasn't sure what she should do with the information. But now that her cover was blown, she had nothing to lose by going straight to the source of the mystery. She made her way up the path to the porch of the main wing and stepped into the reception area.

She shook the water off her umbrella and approached a desk, where a middle-aged nun sat staring at Ida with a faint smile on her lips.

'Hello, miss,' said the nun, nodding at Ida's umbrella. 'Terrible weather out.'

'It sure is,' Ida replied with a smile. 'I'm here to visit Brigadier Kline.'

The nun eyed her for a moment. 'What's the nature of your call, miss?' she asked, her tone sweet but suspicious.

'I work for John Lefebvre. He'll understand.'

The nun peered at her for a moment, her smile strained.

'I'll see if he's free,' she said finally, rising and striding out of the reception area through a swing-door that shuttered loudly after her. Ida peered about her while she waited. It was a simply decorated place, black-and-white tiles checkered the floor, and ferns in bulblike terracotta pots had been placed in the corners. Behind the desk was a portrait of a medieval monk, and underneath it a name plaque, 'St Vincent de Paul', the patron saint of the order that ran the sanatorium. Ida stared at the portrait for a moment, at the kindly old Frenchman in a black cassock. She heard a noise and looked up to see the nun returning with a smile on her face. 'Please fill out the visitors' register,' she said, gesturing to a ledger on the desk, 'and I'll take you to see the brigadier.'

Under the curious gaze of the nun, Ida filled out the register in the name of Carmelita Smith. Then she was ushered out of the reception area and down a long, carpeted corridor. They approached a numbered door and the nun rapped her knuckles against it gently.

'Come in,' called a voice from inside.

The nun opened the door and gestured for Ida to step in. Ida smiled and entered. The room looked more like a presidential suite than a cell in a psychiatric hospital – spacious and clean, and well-appointed with French-era furniture. A mahogany desk and bookcase stood in one corner, and in another a reception area with a coffee table and button-back armchairs. A great window looked out onto the rain-swept gardens at the rear of the building where Ida had bribed the maid on her previous visit. In front of the window, sitting in a baize chair, with his hands pressed together in front of his chin, was an ancient-looking white man dressed elegantly in a navy-blue lounge suit and burgundy cravat.

He smiled at Ida with a slight look of puzzlement, and opened an unsteady hand to the chair opposite him. Ida smiled and sat primly where she'd been bidden.

'Brigadier,' she said.

'Samuel,' he replied warmly.

He had the air of a patrician about him, friendly, urbane and statesmanlike – no hint of madness, no glint of evil.

'I'm here to talk about John Morval,' Ida said flatly, and Kline raised his wispy eyebrows.

*

An hour later Ida left the sanatorium, the mystery of the Axeman solved as well as she could have hoped, but she didn't feel any elation, or a sense of achievement, just a heavy, clawing dread. She caught the tram to the city center and stopped by the Hibernian Bank and Trust Co, where she kept her meager savings, and withdrew almost all of them. Then she walked along Lafayette Street in the rain, looking for a lawyer.

47

Luca trudged through the outskirts of the city in the pre-dawn twilight, heading towards the river. An army of stevedores were making their way to work, and he fell in line with them, following the Mississippi as it arced its way south. Even before dawn and with the rain pelting down, the river smelled of heavy industry, of gasoline, turpentine, sewage and smoke. Luca turned westwards as they reached the city center and headed towards the French Market. The traders were already out, setting up their pitches, and he stopped to buy a coffee and a pastry from a cart. He headed to the post office opposite the market's entrance and used the payphone there to call the hotel. The concierge told him a letter had been left for him that morning and Luca asked him if the police were still outside the hotel. When he was told they were, Luca asked the concierge to open the envelope and read him the letter. He noted down the details then told the concierge to burn it. The message was from a former steward of the Belle Terre estate in reply to Luca's own letter. The man was willing to talk, but he wanted money.

Luca hung up and walked to Sandoval's office, a well-appointed three-room suite in the business district. Sandoval seemed a little preoccupied when Luca arrived, and handed over the money without too many questions. Luca gave him his thanks and headed back out into the streets.

He stopped by Krauss's and bought a new set of clothes, asking the shop assistant to throw away the ones he had worn to the store, and five minutes later he was in the Terminal. He lapped the concourse twice over and failed to notice anyone following him, so he went to the ticket counter and bought a return to Lafourche, then made his way through the crowds and boarded the train.

After a brief wait, the train pulled out and Luca watched the buildings and houses spin past crookedly through the raindrops racing across the windowpane. The train rattled over the river bridge and passed through the outskirts. Just as it was crossing the second bend in the river, he noticed something: workmen on the banks, frantically moving soil and laying down sandbags. The river was overflowing. Not a great deal of spillage, he thought, but if the rain didn't stop soon it could escalate into a flood. It was the same story when the train reached open country; all along the levees gangs of workmen and farmers were at work, barking orders to each other, fear and anxiety on their faces.

Luca got off the train at a stop that was nothing more than a rundown station-agent's hut and a pair of wooden walkways on either side of the tracks. Beyond the stop he saw a clump of buildings and, further on, empty fields all the way to the horizon.

He reached the plantation after a half-hour's walk and began to explore, trying to trace a path along the estate's boundary lines. The estate fields were set aside for sugarcane, field after field sprawled out over lightly undulating hills, and as the sugarcane was on a new ratoon it was low enough for him to get a decent view of everything. After an hour he had circled what he thought was the estate's perimeter and he had seen nothing unusual. No dope plants, no whiskey stills, no copses or woods or other places where the owners could hide illegal cargo or crops.

He found a signpost for the estate at the head of a muddy path, and trudged along it. After a few minutes an abandoned antebellum plantation house came into view, a sprawling building at the end of a long avenue of oaks, magnolias and pecan trees. Luca guessed that at some point the gardens surrounding the house had been well-maintained, brimming with camellias and azaleas and other delicate plants that needed an army of workers to tend to them. But any order imposed on the grounds by its keepers had long since broken down under the strain of neglect, and now the gardens looked more like fallow fields, puffed up with wild grasses, bushes and saplings.

He reached the end of the avenue and stopped to stare up at the house, scanning its broken facade with a rising disquiet. It was three stories high, with a row of white Doric columns across its front, a veranda, balconies on each floor and gabled dormer windows dotted along the roof.

But it had been left to rot. The windows had been boarded up, and the wooden planks that coated the house had been twisted, broken and battered by storms. Birds had made nests in the eaves and had fouled the walls, and the white paint that had once coated the house was cracked and scarred. In its emptiness and dilapidation, the house gave off a brooding, haunted air.

Luca stepped through the tangle of bushes, shrubs and vines that grasped at the building, and hopped onto the veranda. As he approached the front door he noticed there was a smell of death about the place, of rotting flesh. He wondered if animals had not entered the ruin somehow, and had found themselves trapped, or if bears brought their kills there to eat them undisturbed. He felt a malevolence emanating from the building as it stood amidst its own decay.

He peeked through the cracks in the boards that covered one of the windows to the side of the main door. Slivers of a view – an empty, dusty space – and the same scent of putrefying flesh wafting outwards. Two rats scurried about what he assumed to have been a ballroom, sending waves gliding across the pools of rainwater that blanketed the great carpets and the parquet floors. Towering blooms of mold had flowered across the walls, and the gilded friezes that once ran along the upper sections had fallen to the floor, lying at broken angles, glinting in the dirt. At the far end, he could see a grand staircase with its carpet and oak balustrades still intact, spiraling into the darkness above.

He stepped back from the window, disconcerted by the house and its rotting scent, and the malignancy that seemed to emanate from it. He turned and made his way back across the veranda, returning through the bushes to the avenue. He checked his directions once more, glad to be away from the house, and took a path that veered off to the right.

After a few minutes' walk over a small hill and past a dilapidated sugar mill, he reached a large cordwood cabin, set alongside a stream. He approached and saw an old man sitting on the porch, staring out over the rain-swept fields, smoking a cheroot, gently rocking back and forth in a rocking chair. As Luca got closer he saw, next to the man, a side-table piled high with books, an ashtray and a porcelain cup.

'Good morning, sir,' said Luca, taking off his hat. 'I'm the one who sent you the letter.'

The old man peered at him and nodded.

'I know,' he said. 'Don't get so many visitors so as not to know who's who.' He spoke slowly, taking his time with the words, his voice rich and drawling. 'You better get in outta that rain, boy,' he continued. 'Rosie'll fix you up with a towel and a change o' clothes.'

A woman as old and frail as the man appeared from the door that led into the cabin and smiled warmly.

'Well, look at you. Get inside and we'll dry you up,' she said.

'Thank you, ma'am.'

She led him into a bathroom and fetched him a basin of hot water, a towel and a rough cotton shirt and trousers. He washed in the basin, dried himself and changed into the clothes. He hung his old clothes up to dry and transferred Sandoval's money to the new shirt.

When he returned to the porch the old man was still rocking back and forth, staring out across the fields.

'Take a seat,' he said. 'Rosie's left you a cup of tea on the table there.'

Luca thanked the man, sat and took a sip of the tea – mint with plenty of molasses. The two men stared out over the fields, watching the rain batter the plants. On the far ridge Luca could see the house he had passed on his way, standing out above the horizon line, silhouetted against the storm clouds.

'Crop's pretty near ruined,' said the old man flatly, no hint of pity in his voice. 'Sugar-cane don't like waterlogged soils. You farm?'

Luca shook his head and the old man nodded.

'Too bad,' he said. 'Nothing to do now 'cept wait for the rain to stop. I'm Jacob.' He turned his head to look Luca in the eye.

'Luca. Glad to meet you,' Luca said, holding out his hand for the old man to shake.

'Italian?' The old man made no movement to take Luca's hand.

Luca nodded and the old man eyed him suspiciously.

'Yeah. I thought as much when I saw you walk up the path,' he said. 'Don't worry, I won't hold it against ya.'

The old man finally reached out and shook Luca's hand.

'First things first, I guess,' he said. 'No matter how old you get, things like this don't get any less awkward.'

Luca smiled and pulled the packet from his shirt pocket. The old man took it, counted the bills and put the envelope in an inside pocket.

'Greatly appreciated,' he said. He leaned back in the rocking chair and set it off rocking once again. 'So, what do ya already know?' he said. 'And what do ya wanna know?'

Luca thought for a moment before speaking.

'I know this estate is owned by a holding company, and the owners of that company have been killed off one by one by the Axeman. I know the company got hold of this place back in 1888 by duping a local drunk called Maria Tenebre to act as intermediary and that a few months later they killed her off. I also know the lawyer who arranged it all tried his hardest to keep it a secret, and that you were registered as the estate manager here from 1902 till you retired.'

Luca stared at the old man, who stared back at him hawkishly for a moment before replying.

'If that's all you know, son,' he said, 'then you don't know the half of it.'

The old man smiled, stopped the rocking chair and leaned over to the table. He took a cheroot from a tin tobacco box and put it in his mouth, running it around his lips for a moment. He offered one to Luca, who accepted, then they lit up and the old man settled back into his rocking chair.

'Tell me, boy,' he said. 'You like ghost stories?'

48

'Kids'll be getting up soon,' said Annette, keeping her tone free of implications. She peered at Michael, rose from the kitchen table and padded over to the counter, her bare feet gentle and soundless on the night-chilled floor. Michael stared at the marks her feet were leaving on the tiles – fleeting islands and atolls of warm condensation. He guessed she wanted him to get cleaned up before the kids saw him, to take a shower and change his clothes, or at least go and lie down in the bedroom till Thomas and Mae were out of the house. The thought of his children seeing him bloodied and sleep-deprived induced a limp sort of panic in him, and the bile and rye in his stomach folded over themselves once again in a nauseous churning motion that was becoming alarmingly familiar.

Annette lifted the kettle from the stove, placed it under the tap and turned the water on. As she waited for it to fill, she moved the voile a touch from the window and peeked into the backyard. Daylight was creeping over the fences, slanted and pale, silhouetting the two policemen who were standing by the backdoor, sheltering themselves from the rain. She stared at the outline of the rifles slung over their shoulders, at the barrels pointing towards the dawn, at the bulky wooden stocks, and she wondered if the children would see the two men from the bathroom window when they were getting ready for school.

Michael's colleagues had woken her at just past four. They had let themselves in with Michael's keys, dragged her husband into the living room and laid him down in the armchair by the hearth. She had walked in on them, roused by the noise and the emptiness in the bed beside her. She introduced herself as *Detective Talbot's maid*, feeling foolish even as she said it, and after an awkward moment of realization, the man who seemed to be in charge recounted to her what had happened to Michael. She listened to him intently, feeling cold and vulnerable in her nightgown, her arms folded over her chest. The man spoke to her with a chilly authority, his eyes flicking every now and then to her exposed shoulders. He told her they would be posting four men to the house for the family's safety – two in a car out front, and two on the back step. When she asked about the bullet wound in Michael's shoulder, she was told it was just a flesh wound, that the wound had been cleaned and that Michael had refused to go to the hospital. The men left the house soon after that, traipsing mud across the rugs with their heavy police-issue boots. As Annette walked back from seeing them out, she had a feeling of disruption, of her house having been tainted; of violation.

When she returned, Michael had propped himself up in a chair at the kitchen table, a bottle of rye and a glass in front of him. He hadn't switched the kitchen light on and was sitting half in darkness, half in the burning, naked rays slanting in from the lounge. The angle of the light cast the scars on his face into high-relief, making him look unfamiliar, ghoulish.

She stared at him, strode into the kitchen, took a second glass from the cupboard and sat at the table. He poured them both large measures and for the first time since he had arrived, he spoke to her.

'After this is finished, you wanna leave New Orleans?' he asked, sliding her glass across the table. He said it as if he was confessing to something, unburdening himself of some great secret. She bit her lip when she looked at him, at the blood on his rumpled, torn suit, at his ashen face.

'When's it gonna be finished?' she asked, not quite sure what *it* was.

He shrugged and took a sip of the rye. 'Soon, I guess.'

She had the good sense not to ask him how much danger they

were in, nor who it was that had tried to kill him, nor what it meant that there were policemen guarding the house. She sat with him and listened, watching him drink, keeping a motherly eye on him. Michael worked through the rye steadily and talked about the look on the boy's face when he died, how pathetic and unfair the whole thing was. He had spoken to her about the boy before, and she realized now how much it had meant to him to have someone to mentor. He spoke about it all with a resigned, glassy-eyed distance that only increased the more he drank.

By the time Annette was standing at the counter watching the dawn rise over the backyard, he had finished the first bottle of rye and had started on a second. As she stared out of the window one of the policemen happened to turn around and catch her eye. Startled, she turned her head and let the voile spring back over the window. Then she cursed herself for letting them make her feel embarrassed in her own house.

She turned off the tap and heaved the kettle from the sink. Through the voile she saw the policeman turn back around and say something to his colleague, and the silhouetted gun barrels swayed as the two men chuckled. She clanged the kettle onto the cooker, lit the range with a splint and went about getting coffee and toast ready for Michael. She checked the clock on the wall and guessed she had enough time to make breakfast and put him to bed before the children got up and started asking questions. She opened a cupboard and pulled down a jar of ground coffee.

'I'm gonna make breakfast and you're gonna eat,' she said, sounding sterner than she meant to.

When Michael didn't answer she turned around and was surprised to see the room behind her empty. She frowned a moment, then she heard the front door slamming. She sighed and strode through the kitchen to the living room windows, noticing the dried mud on the carpet as she went. On the street in front of the house, Michael was leaning into the police car, talking to someone through the passenger-side window. Annette noticed the rain pelting onto his back and hoped it might wash off some of the blood.

Michael banged his fist against the roof of the car. The two policemen looked at each other, then one of them got out and Michael took his place in the passenger seat. The policeman in the driver's seat started the engine and the ousted man trotted up the front steps of the house and took up a sentry's position by the porch. The driver put the car into gear and drove off through the rain-washed, empty street. Annette watched the car disappear around the corner before she moved back from the window. She returned to the kitchen, feeling alone, with an overwhelming sense that things had changed for the worse.

Twenty minutes later Michael was stumbling up the precinct steps. He felt guilty for leaving without saying anything, but he knew Annette would have tried to stop him, that her good sense would have prevailed if it came to an argument. He knew who had tried to kill him, and he knew he had to act before it was too late.

He passed the spot where Kerry's body had fallen the previous night and noticed that someone had already scrubbed away the blood. He wondered where the body was now, before realizing it was probably at the morgue, naked and cold on a slide-out tray. He felt a bitterness in his stomach as he looked at the paving stones, cracked from the bullets, as pockmarked and scarred as his own skin. To one side people had placed bouquets and wreaths. Someone had left a candle enclosed in a glass jar in front of a dime-store postcard of the Archangel Michael, patron saint of policemen. The candle had gone out, the jar already filled with brown, sludgy rainwater.

Michael stepped out of the downpour and into the half-empty lobby. The atmosphere was hushed and he wondered if it was on account of Kerry's death, but then he realized that most of the regulars were probably at home, sleeping off the nightshift, and those remaining were reaching the end of a twenty-four-hour stretch on the job. He walked past the booking hall and noticed that the officers manning it looked burnt out and grumpy, having spent the whole night booking in scores of arrests during the previous night's party. The men noticed him walking past, looked up, and nodded to him somberly. He nodded back and made his way to the staircase.

The bureau was a lot busier than the lobby. Half the shift was already at work, and the place was noisy with activity. When Michael entered, the floor went silent, his colleagues staring at him with puzzled, almost shocked expressions. Then one by one they approached him and offered their condolences. They patted him on the back and shook his hand, and told him how much they had liked the boy and how sorry they were. Michael mumbled his thanks in return, angry that they were acting like his friends after all the years of making his life a misery. He suppressed an urge to rant at them, and kept his mind on his goal. He shook their hands, while scanning the floor for Detective Jake Hatener.

Before he could locate him, however, McPherson bustled through the crowd, put a hand on Michael's shoulder and ushered him into his office. The men quieted down and returned to their work, and McPherson closed the door on the bureau with a gentle hand.

Michael sat across the desk from him, and the two men stared at each other. McPherson's look was inquisitive and probing; he was studying Michael for signs of something, but Michael wasn't sure what.

'You stink of liquor,' he said, 'and is that the dead boy's blood on your jacket?'

Michael peered at the stains on his clothes, as if seeing them for the first time, and then he looked back up at McPherson and frowned. There was something false in the captain's tone and he realized what it was – it was McPherson who had ordered him to stay at the precinct the night before, who had made him a sitting duck for the shooters.

'It's always tough to lose a fellow officer,' McPherson sighed. 'I know. I was on duty back in 1890.'

He nodded at Michael, and Michael nodded back, unsure of what McPherson had just said. He was losing focus on the conversation. The alcohol and the lack of food and sleep was making his mind blurry. McPherson's form shimmered in and out of his vision.

'I think you should take some leave.'

'Sir?' Michael was startled.

'Take some time off, lad,' said McPherson.

Michael frowned at him. The old man seemed different all of a sudden, shorn of his usual authority. Michael stared at the long bony face and the piercing eyes that had in the past caused him to fear McPherson. But now the man inspired no feelings in him at all, his was just another worn-out, old policeman's face.

'I'd rather not,' he said.

McPherson stared at him for a moment as he chose his next words.

'If you want to stay on working you have to show that you're fit to do so. Turning up here looking like that won't help your cause. Take today off at least. We'll talk properly tomorrow.'

'Yes, sir.' But Michael had no intention whatsoever of following McPherson's advice. He nodded, rose wearily, and headed for the door. He stumbled into the main floor of the bureau and made his way over to the homicide division, keeping an eye out for Hatener. Eventually he saw him filling a cup from the coffee pot at the far end of the rec area, looking unkempt and faintly grumpy.

The Gyor Diner was run by a family of Hungarian Jews and was located on a corner just across from the precinct. The food had a reputation for being stodgy and badly cooked, but because of its location, and the friendliness of its owners, it was popular with the men from the precinct, although it was near-empty when Hatener and Michael entered. They sat at a booth and Hatener ordered coffee, fried eggs and toast for the two of them. When the food arrived the smell of the eggs made Michael feel sick.

'Have you slept? You don't look too good.' Hatener shoveled some egg yolk onto a piece of toast and ripped a bite from it.

'I need your help getting some info out of someone,' said Michael.

Hatener paused, then nodded, understanding what it was that Michael wanted him to do.

'The good cop turns bad,' he said flatly, staring at Michael, who didn't meet his gaze and peered instead at the untouched plate of food in front of him, at the reflection of the electric lights in the glossy domes of the egg yolks.

'Amanzo?' Hatener asked.

Michael nodded.

'He's the key to the whole thing,' he said, 'and he's lock-jawed.'

Hatener thought for a moment, a look of concentration crossing his hangdog features. Then he stared at his plate and shoveled a forkful of food into his mouth.

'How do you know he hasn't skipped town already? If I was Amanzo, and I'd arranged that hit last night, I'd be getting on a train as fast as I could.'

'There's been two men on his tail since I arrested him. He's still in town.'

'Well, he probably won't be for much longer,' replied Hatener. 'We'll have to do it tonight.'

Michael glanced up at him. 'That means you'll do it?'

Hatener nodded, a somber, urgent look in his eye.

'I'll do it for the kid,' he said. 'Not for you.'

'Thanks,' said Michael. He eyed his coffee and decided to take a sip. It hit his stomach like a slab of lead. He winced and noticed Hatener was staring at him with an expression that mingled pity and curiosity.

'Blood-lust ain't good, Talbot,' he said. 'You sure you wanna do this?'

Michael nodded.

'I wanna do it while my blood's still up. Maybe if I don't do it now, I'll never do it.'

Hatener continued to stare at him with the same expression and Michael sensed he wasn't entirely convinced. Eventually Hatener nodded and mopped up the last of his food with a piece of toast.

'You want him dead? Or you just want the info?' he asked, chewing away, his great jowls rotating. Michael hadn't thought about it in those terms before. He knew he wanted to hurt Amanzo, to avenge Kerry, and to get to the bottom of the case. But did he really wish the man dead?

'I dunno,' he said eventually. 'Kerry was an orphan, you know that? Didn't have a soul in the world to look after him, and he picked me for the father he never had.'

'You didn't kill the boy, Talbot. Amanzo did,' Hatener replied, and Michael was surprised to hear the compassion in his voice. But then he remembered Hatener's own son had been killed not too long before, and he guessed the man sensed something of his own pain in Michael.

'So how's it all work?' asked Michael, who had only been vaguely aware of Hatener's techniques during his time with Luca.

'We pick up the mark, take him somewhere private, little place me and the boys know about, and we get to work. It's not sophisticated but . . . they always talk in the end.' Michael noted that there was nothing sinister in Hatener's tone, he was simply stating a fact. He lit a cigarette to get the smell of grease and eggs out of his nose – the hangover was taking a hold and his head was beginning to throb.

'Listen buddy,' said Hatener, 'are ya sure ya wanna be a part of it? It takes a certain kinda character, and if ya get found out, it's ya career down the drain.'

Michael took a long drag on his cigarette and his head swooned.

'My career's already over,' he said. 'And I owe the boy.'

REPORT OF HOMICIDE
Thibodaux Police Department

Thibodaux, Lafourche Parish	Wed. May 14th 1919
Name of Person Killed:	Joseph Fisher
Residence:	336 Plantation Road
Business:	Accountant
Name of accused:	Unknown
Residence:	Unknown
Business:	Unknown
Location of homicide:	336 Plantation Road
Day, date, hour committed:	12.00 – 12.30 A.M., May 13th
By whom reported:	Sergeant David Pettersson
To whom reported:	Sergeant Martin Schluepp
Time reported:	6.00 A.M., May 14th
If arrested, by whom:	Still At Large
Where arrested:	N/A
If escaped, in what manner:	Left the scene prior to our arrival.
Witnesses:	N/A
Witness report:	Neville Clark, no fixed address (colored)

Detailed Report

Sergeant David Pettersson reports that at 6.00 o'clock this A.M. Wed. May 14th 1919 Neville Clark (13 years), an employee of the Du Pont Coal Co, arrived at the precinct reception and informed the night duty booking clerk, Sergeant Wllm. Jones, that he had discovered a body at 336 Plantation Road during his daily coal-delivery rounds. (See witness statement attached – Clark, N. #2373-1919).

I hastened to the address along with Sergeant Martin Schluepp, and on reaching it discovered Fisher dead at the scene. Fisher's body was lying in the hallway of the building, and had been severely bludgeoned about the head with a blunt instrument – extensive bleeding and bruising all across the face and cranium. A trail of blood from the kitchen to the hallway suggested the victim had been initially attacked in the kitchen and was attempting to flee the premises when he was overcome by his substantial wounds. A fountain pen was found embedded in his right eye. Bloodstained pages from accounting ledgers were found ripped and strewn across the hallway and a home office in the front of the house.

A cursory search of the premises was conducted. Pools of blood were discovered on the floor of the kitchen, and a bloody metal pole, some 15 inches long. Also, upset kitchen furniture, suggestive of a struggle. No means of forced entry were discernible.

Your office was notified at circa 6.55 A.M., Patrolmen Reginald Hurst & David Fornes, and also County Medical Examiner Dr. Sam. Connolly.

By order of the Medical Examiner the Body was removed to the Morgue at the Thibodaux Regional Hospital. Victim's clothes, the pole, the pen, and various other blooded objects from the kitchen (one carpet; 3 instances of cutlery; a whiskey tumbler), and blooded accounting ledgers from the hallway and office were turned over to the Medical Examiner by order of the Dist. Attorney to be used as evidence.

This report and all attached reports, statements, evidence

summaries etc. have been forwarded to the Lafourche County Sheriff's office, Detective Department, Lockport, with a request for assistance (c.c. attached for your records).

Respectfully yours,
L. Donald Greer,
Captain, Comd'g Prec't

49

The old man told his story with a glazed look in his eye, staring out across the rain-swept fields. Only occasionally did he swing his glance towards Luca, as if to make sure he was still there, bearing witness to his tale.

'Back then this estate was owned by a Creole family – Negro Creoles, I mean, by the name of Baudet. A husband and a wife and two children, they had. That sounds kinda odd to hear these days – Negro landowners, I mean. But back then things were different – French influence was still pretty strong round here. I guess these out o' the way places take longer to catch up with the rest o' the world. See, the French had a different approach. Some places you even had some Negroes owning their own slaves. Sounds kinda upside down, don't it?'

The old man peered at Luca and raised an eyebrow. Then he took a short drag on his cheroot and turned back to look out over the fields.

'Everything changes eventually, I guess,' he said. 'People say the world moves forward. Sometimes I ain't so sure. Old Man Baudet gave me a job as a farmhand when I was twelve years old, and I been here ever since. The old estate house was beautiful back then, not the mess it is today. Monsieur Baudet, the father of the family, he was about your age back then, chubby man, spoke French. Had airs and graces about him, you know, but in a good way. Made him pleasant to be around, not like those dicty Creoles you get these days. And the mother of the family, well, she was the most beautiful creature I ever saw. You ever hear the saying *nature's aristocrat*? Thomas Jefferson said it first, I think. Means someone who's royal and elegant, not cuz they're a prince or princess or whatever, but cuz nature just made 'em that way – a cut above. Well, that was her.'

A hint of a smile crossed the old man's face, and he paused for a moment. Then the smile was replaced by a look of sadness, of mourning for beauty that had faded from the world.

'She used to take care of the local coloreds. Studied medicine at some French school, but she mixed it up with all that African stuff. They call it voodou these days, but it ain't no different to old wives' remedies. Potions and ointments and compresses, that kinda thing. Had a line forming outside the house some mornings – locals looking to get fixed up. I remember 'em – all raggedy blacks, standing in line, their breath frosting up in the cold. And she did a good job of it too, and never charged anyone a cent.

'Few years before was about the time the newcomers started arriving – foreigners looking to start up their own little farms. Germans, Spanish, Swedes, you name it. Mainly Italians, though. You can understand how they felt about things, coming here and having to farm tiny pieces o' land with godawful soil, watching their kids go hungry and all the while looking over to see a family o' Negroes doing so much better. That didn't sit right with how they thought things should be. Caused tensions. Didn't start right away, took a few years to ferment, but eventually it became so's you'd notice it. And then it became so's it was impossible not to notice it.

'They even started hassling me, for working on *the coon farm*. Like I should feel ashamed. Got to so's I couldn't go to the bar Saturday nights for fear o' things turning ugly. Atmosphere in the town changed. When we went in to get supplies, there was a whole lot more silence around the place. I think that's how these things always start, people not talking to each other.

'Situation weren't helped by the mother being a doctor for the whole damn parish, neither – that made her a *strega* in the Italians' eyes – a witch. Over time, more and more newcomers moved in, and people felt threatened. The other Creoles started moving to the city. One by one. The newcomers buying up their land for nothing. Got till Baudet was the only one left. He wouldn't leave for nothing.

'Well, it all came to a head in eighty-eight. See, Baudet used to get these chemicals delivered from up north somewhere, Connecticut I think. They stopped the crops getting ill and dying. And in eighty-eight there was a blight o' some sort or 'nother and everyone's crops failed. Everyone except the Baudets', cuz he'd had 'em sprayed.

'Newcomers didn't see it that way. They saw witchcraft. 'Course, they might have been using the whole thing as an excuse for what happened next. A rumor got spread around town that Madame Baudet had put a curse on their lands, and that's why their crops had failed and the Baudets' hadn't. And that was just the excuse they'd been waiting for.

'There used to be a long shack just near the estate house where the seasonal workers'd stay, people that came in to town looking for work for a few months every summer. I used to stay there too sometimes cuz my family's house was a six-miles walk away. It was an old wooden building, bunk beds, drafts, that kinda thing. When it happened, we all got woke up in the middle o' the night – screams and shouts and running o' feet. I got up to see what all the fuss was about but I could tell before I even got outside – an orange glow coming in from the underside o' the door. Remember how strange it felt seeing that glow at gone two in the mornin'.

'Outside it was like a firestorm. As far as my eye could see fields were burning, lighting up the sky. Looked like damnation. People were running around trying to organize a water chain for all the good it'd do. Baudet and a few o' the workers were getting a posse together to go find whoever did it. They come back holding an Italian boy by the elbow. I knew who he was, seen him about town. Scared as a rabbit, he looked, dazed too, probably out o' his mind on julep. There's no way one kid coulda started all them fires, so they start questioning him, out in front o' the house – Who was with him? What names he could give? I dunno if it was the julep, or they beat him on the way back, but the kid wasn't making a lick o' sense.

'Well, I guess the boy's partners figured he'd gone missing and went looking for him. A clutch o' them rolled up the path, shotguns in tow. Now Baudet and his boys only had a few guns between 'em, and, well, they look up to see they're outnumbered.

'To this day I ain't sure how it happened . . . The Italians took their guns off 'em. They were drunk, too, raving 'bout this and that. Then I jus' remember a scuffle and one o' them caught Baudet in a headlock and pushed him to the ground. Next thing I know there's an axe up high. And then a thumping sound. I'll always remember that sound. Baudet screamed, but it's that thump I remember. Can still feel it now.

'Madame Baudet sees what's happened cuz she was on the steps o' the house. Standing there with the two children. A couple o' the hands were holding her back, but she broke free when she saw that. Ran over to where her husband was and dropped to the floor next to him. Starts crying and wailing and holding his head while he bleeds to death right there in front o' his own goddamn house. And the others are laughing. Then they start calling her a witch. Start talking about showing her what's right. The other farm hands have scattered by now – so it's just the Baudets and them.

'They get her down on the dirt and pull her skirts up. They took turns, and all the while the husband's laying there next to her bleeding to death and all around the earth's on fire, and she's screaming and wailing and kicking up a fight. And after it's over, I guess some kinda shock kicks in and they realize they gotta cover their tracks. So they bring the axe down on her too. And that's when they hear the screams. Coming from the steps o' the house. They'd forgotten about the children. The boy and the girl. Not even teenagers yet and they just saw all that happen to their parents.

'The newcomers run up towards the house, try and grab a hold o' the kids before they can flee, but the little 'uns run back through the house and out into the fields. Got clean away. So they pick up the bodies and dump 'em in one o' the fields and let the fire do its work. The sad thing is, I watched the whole thing happen. From the corner of the worker's house. There weren't nothing I coulda done to stop it all, but . . . well, I'll carry the guilt to my grave.'

He stopped and sighed, and for the first time Luca saw the shame in his face. Then the old man flicked the end of his cheroot out into the field – the glow of its tip a firefly through the rain-drops.

'If you looking for an Axeman,' said the old man, 'I'd say Baudet's son would be about the right age. And what with him killing all the people that killed his parents, whole thing seems like justice to me.'

The old man stared out across the fields and Luca followed his gaze to the dilapidated house perched on the horizon line, and the two men sat in silence for a moment.

'*O Louisiana, fair paradise of the south, if still so lovely in thy ruin, what were you in the day of thy glory?*' Luca peered at the old man as he spoke the words. The man smiled and patted the stack of books on the table behind him.

'Lafcadio Hearne,' he said, by way of explanation.

Luca nodded. 'I don't read much,' he said.

'Plenty don't,' replied the old man. 'Baudet sent a bunch o' us farmhands to the local school after we got back from the War Between the States. One night a week. That's where I learned my letters. I'm mighty grateful too, cuz when you get to be as old as me, there ain't a lot else ya can do 'part from reading.'

Silence descended on them again and Luca leaned over and picked up his cup from the table. He took a sip of the sweet tea and the porcelain warmed his chilled fingers. He was thinking about smoking a cigarette when the old man reached over to his tobacco box and offered him another cheroot. Luca accepted and the old man leaned over and lit it for him.

'What happened next?' Luca asked.

'Nothing,' said the old man. 'That's the sad truth. We all knew who it was that did it, but they outnumbered us.' He shrugged, an exasperated, world-weary shrug. 'They greased the palms o' the police, and then the estate came up for auction. I dunno if they planned it all along, or it was just a coincidence, but the ones that did the killings got together and bought the estate. Bought it fo' a nickel too, on account o' the auctioneer the parish commissioned fo' the sale being a crook. 'Course, they weren't so stupid as to buy it outright, so they did what you already know, got the Tenebre woman to buy it on their behalf, and when enough time had passed, they got rid of her.

'Didn't seem quite right fo' 'em to carry on living hereabouts what with everyone knowing what happened, so they moved on out to New Orleans. Left the estate in the charge of a steward. Set it up so they could get the profits without ever showing their faces round here again. When the old steward retired, I took over the running o' the place. Never was quite sure if I did the right thing, but I guessed if the Baudets were anywhere they could see they mighta been happy one o' their own was looking after the place.' The old man paused and took a drag on his cheroot, then he turned to look at Luca and a peculiar smile broke out on his lips. 'So, you find what you was looking for, son?' he asked.

'Yes, sir. Thank you,' Luca said, nodding.

'Yeah,' the old man said ruefully, 'people always find what they looking for. That's why Baudet's boy's doing what he's doing.'

Luca frowned at him. 'Sir?' he asked, and the old man shrugged.

'Just my idea on how the world works,' he said. 'The Axeman's a mystery, an empty thing that can't be explained. And our minds don't like empty things. So whenever we see one, we start filling it up. And what it gets filled with is what's in the back o' our minds – the dark things we're scared of. Those Italians that killed the Baudets, they saw something they didn't understand and their minds filled with what they was scared of – witchcraft. It's the same with the Axeman, I reckon. Italians see the Axeman and figure it's a Negro. Police see the Axeman and figure it's the Black Hand. I reckon the Negroes probably think the Axeman's some big, powerful devil of a white man. They all looking at the same thing – a whole lot o' nothing – but they all seeing it in their own different way, depending on what fears they got buzzin' about the back o' they heads. They just finding what they've already decided was real, their own fears made fancy.'

The old man settled back in the rocking chair, and for a while they both sat in silence, smoking their cheroots, taking sips of the tea, watching the rain.

'There's one other thing I think ya should know,' the old man eventually said. 'That list o' victims I read 'bout in the paper don't tally up with the people who killed the Baudets. There's a couple missing.'

Luca frowned. 'Who?'

'There was an accountant who helped set it all up for them. Lived out Thibodaux way. Heard he got bumped off too, the other day. Same evening that Axeman Night hullabaloo was going off in New Orleans. I fancy that was Baudet's boy, too. He's going after everyone that had a hand in the thing, so I reckon maybe he'd go after the steward too. He wouldn't be on no list of estate owners, but sure as hell he was involved in the thing.'

'What's his name?' Luca asked.

'Rodrigo Bianchi,' said the old man, pronouncing the name slowly. 'He's retired now. Moved to New Orleans when he gave up working, so's he could be with his son. If he hasn't been killed yet, I reckon he'd be on the list.'

'Do you have an address for him?' asked Luca, and the old man shook his head.

'Can't say as I do.'

Luca nodded and thought for a moment.

'What happened to Baudet's children?' he asked, and the old man made a face, wearying of the painful questions.

'That's a whole 'nother mess,' he said. 'For the first few weeks after it happened they stayed close by. Hiding in the fields. I done see 'em a few times. Took 'em food to eat when I could. Tried to tell 'em to come back into town, but they was too scared. Lost contact with 'em after that. Rumor was they disappeared into the backwaters. Ain't sure exactly how they lived. I guess some o' the folks lived out that way took pity on 'em. There's been stories about a wild-man living in the swamps for years now. I always figured it was him. About the girl, I couldn't say.'

The old man reached over to the table and with a shaky hand opened a drawer set underneath its top. He rummaged about for a moment then pulled out an old photograph and handed it to Luca. Luca inspected it and saw it was of the Baudet family, taken sometime in the 1880s, he guessed. The family wore formal clothes, stiff suits and stiff old-time poses, and they stood outside the estate house, which gleamed white in the sunshine.

'That's Monsieur and Madame Baudet,' said the old man, pointing to the two figures. Luca stared at the faces. There was something familiar about Madame Baudet.

'And that's the children, Davide and Simone,' he said. Luca peered at the children standing in front of their parents, at their somber, almost downcast faces, and it was only then that Luca realized who the girl in the photograph was – Simone, standing next to her brother, thirty years younger.

50

They had been parked in Little Italy for over an hour, a half-block from the address they had on file for Pietro Amanzo. The cream-colored Chevrolet Detective Jones had procured for the night was fast, but incredibly cramped, especially for a man of Hatener's size. He was in his usual position in the backseat, along with Detective Gregson, and Michael was sitting up front with Jones. Hatener was pleased Michael had gone home while his wife was at work and changed his clothes, but he could tell from the man's glazed eyes that he hadn't slept.

After Michael had left him in the diner, Hatener had called the hotel he knew Luca was staying at and spoken to the concierge. The old Sicilian had sounded guarded on the phone, and claimed not to know who Luca was. Hatener had hung up and dialed about, until he reached Sandoval in his office. Sandoval sounded surprised to hear from him and when Hatener explained the situation, Sandoval told him Luca had gone out of town for the day. Hatener had thought about whether he should come clean or not. From what he could tell, Amanzo wasn't a made man yet, just an associate of the Family. He decided to err on the side of caution and explain to Sandoval what Michael wanted him to do. There was silence at the other end of the line, then Sandoval gave him the all clear — if Amanzo was killing policemen without the Family's authorization, they needed to know.

So Hatener had returned to the precinct and organized things for the night, calling in Jones and Gregson, arranging the car, gathering up the tools they needed. Then when evening swung around, they drove over to Michael's and picked him up. Hatener had to speak to the men guarding his house, explaining to them that if anyone asked they had never been there and Michael had spent the evening at home. The men had agreed readily enough and Hatener and the others had then driven over to Little Italy. When they reached Amanzo's street, they had to speak to the two men tailing him and explain to them in similar terms that, should anyone ask, they hadn't seen Amanzo emerge from his apartment all night. After that, they had settled back and waited in the cramped interior of the Chevrolet, not wanting to break into Amanzo's apartment unless they had to.

Hatener had grown steadily more annoyed by the wait – the canvas roof of the car was leaking rain onto the seats, and the cigarettes Talbot and Jones were chain-smoking were making his throat burn. He remembered himself as a young man, when he had first started taking on these kinds of jobs. He remembered the edge, the anticipation, the bolt-like rush of energy. These days he just felt grumpy at the disruption to his routine and faintly anxious that something might go wrong. He stared at Jones and Gregson, his two protégés, their faces sinister in the shadows of the car, and he wondered if he had done the best by them. Then he thought of his son, lying in a muddy field somewhere in France. He looked out of the window and watched the raindrops crawling down the window, distorting the world beyond.

Time passed and at one point Jones perked up.

'Hey-ho. I think we got our bird,' he said, nudging Michael.

They sat up and peered through the windows. On the opposite side of the street, a few houses down, a front door had opened and a short Italian man stepped out into the rain with a travel case in one hand.

'That's him,' Michael said.

Jones started up the car, put it into gear and kept it on the biting point. When Amanzo was a few feet away from them, Jones put his foot down. The car lurched forward, bumped over the curb and screeched to a halt in front of Amanzo. Hatener swung open his door and caught Amanzo by his coat. Amanzo flailed his arms about, swinging the edge of the travel case into Hatener's stomach. Gregson ran around from the other side of the car, kneed Amanzo in the groin, and together with Hatener, one pulling, one pushing, they bundled Amanzo into the car. Gregson jumped in on top of him and Jones reversed into the road and tore off down the street, the back door flapping in the wind. Amanzo struggled on the seat, twisting his body around, trying to land punches and kicks on whoever he could. Hatener took out his gun from his coat, and cracked it against Amanzo's skull with a noise like a snapping branch, and he kept on doing it till Amanzo lost consciousness. Then Gregson leaned over and pulled the flailing door shut, and the sounds of the storm became instantly dull.

51

Luca got back to the train station with less than a quarter of an hour to spare before his train arrived. He used the telephone in the station agent's hut to place a call to Sandoval and waited anxiously for the few minutes it took the operator to connect him.

'Alessandro? It's Luca,' he said when he finally got through.

Sandoval's voice crackled over the line. 'Luca? The line's bad. Where are you?'

'Out of town,' said Luca, switching into Italian to guard his words from the ear of the station agent, who was sitting at his desk staring at him. 'Tell Carlo I found out who he is. It's a Creole by the name of Davide Baudet.'

Luca glanced at the station agent who made a show of checking his pocket watch, standing, and stalking out onto the platform.

'I need you to check up on a man called Rodrigo Bianchi,' Luca said. 'If he's still around, he's next on the list.'

'You got an address?' asked Sandoval.

As Sandoval spoke, Luca heard his train approaching, its engine clattering, its wheels screeching as the driver applied the brake.

'I don't have an address,' Luca shouted over the noise of the train. 'Sandro, you need to find him.'

The train came to a halt and its engines hissed. Luca peered out onto the platform and saw people bustling about the train, loading and unloading.

'OK, I'll get things moving,' said Sandoval quickly. 'When are you back?'

'Tonight. Leave an address at the hotel.'

Luca put the phone down and stepped out of the hut. He jostled his way along the platform and hopped onto the train just as the station agent blew the whistle for it to leave.

He spent the return journey staring out of the window, thinking about what he had learned. Bechet had known all along. Luca had asked him for someone who could help him find the Axeman, and Bechet had sent him straight to the Axeman's sister. *She can help you out. In more ways than one*, he had said, and Luca had misunderstood his meaning. All Bechet's comments started to make sense as Luca reran their conversation through his mind. *Conspiracy is greater than witchcraft*. Luca realized he hadn't really been listening at all. He thought about Simone, and her behavior began to make sense, too – why she was so eager to keep him around, why she had been out of sorts when the two policemen followed Luca to her house, why she was worried about a storm coming, a storm that might drown her brother who lived out in the backwaters.

And the intricacies of the case began to make sense, too. The letter the Axeman had sent to the newspaper, for all its talk of demons and jazz, had directed the police into New Orleans on the night Baudet had left the city to kill the accountant. Luca guessed there was a high chance of Baudet being caught under normal circumstances – a lone colored man travelling into a secluded, rural district to carry out a hit. But the letter had drained all the surrounding parishes of their law-enforcement, funneling them into New Orleans. But why had he killed the accountant in a different manner to the other victims? And why had he left no tarot card?

Maybe there was no need. Baudet had killed his parents' murderers with an axe, playing out his revenge with the exact same weapon they had used to commit their crimes. And the tarot cards added to that revenge. The tarot cards, and the doors and windows locked shut at every crime scene. Baudet was making himself seem like a demon because the Italians had thought his mother a witch, and so he had couched his attacks in occult imagery and conceits. Luca imagined what it must have been like for the victims, wondering if there was not some unearthly form of justice at work. Then he thought of what the old farmhand had told him about fear, about the demons lurking in the back of people's minds. Baudet had taken their fear and made it real.

It took Luca two hours to get from the New Orleans Terminal Station up to Simone's. The storm had unleashed torrents of rain and wind onto the city, making the paths through the bayou treacherous and waterlogged. By the time he reached Simone's he was tired and soaked to the skin.

She was at the table mending a piece of clothing when he entered. She peered at him, at the glare on his face, and Luca could tell from the way her expression became solemn that she had realized he had discovered the truth. He pushed the door back against the wind and approached the table.

'Your brother,' he said coldly.

She said nothing. She put down the cloth and peered at him with a blank expression, and they stayed like that, staring at each other wordlessly, for a long, leaden moment. He had expected an argument, recriminations, tears, but now he felt sapped of energy, despondent and strangely calm, and he got the feeling Simone felt the same. Neither of them had the desire to fight. They were too old to claw at each other, and too wise to blame their situation on anything other than the callow whims of fate.

He sat at the table opposite her and put a hand to his head.

'You should have told me,' he said eventually, rubbing his temples.

'I know. But how could I have told you? I didn't know who you were.' She paused and looked down at the table in front of her. 'He's sick, Luca. He has been ever since my parents died.'

Luca studied her. She didn't shake, or make any noises, and her voice didn't waver, but tears began to well up in her eyes and Luca remembered what the old man had said about her mother's elegance and poise.

'I have to look after him,' she said. 'What would you have done?'

Luca put his hand on hers.

'How did you find out?' she asked.

'I went down to Belle Terre today. Spoke to the old farmhand. He told me what happened to your family. I'm sorry.'

'It was a long time ago,' she said flatly, and the tears began to roll down her cheeks.

'I'll protect him if I can,' he said, and she smiled and wiped the tears from her face with the back of her hand.

'He said he would stop,' she said. 'After the next one. He said there's one more.'

Luca nodded. 'I know.'

'Just let him do it and you'll never hear from him again. I swear.' She sniffed back her tears, then shook her head. She put her hand to her face and Luca stood and moved across to her, stooped down and they hugged. It was only when he couldn't see her face that she started to sob.

After a while she moved away from him, stood and walked over to the stove. She took a bottle of rum and two glasses from a shelf and came back to the table. She poured them both shots and they drank. The rum was dark and sweet and it warmed Luca with a sharp burn.

'Where is he?' he asked.

'I don't know. He lives out in the swamps northeast of here. He comes sometimes, for food.' She sniffed back more tears and looked Luca in the eye. 'He doesn't know what he's doing.'

Luca wasn't so sure about that. He reached into his pocket and pulled out a pack of damp, unsmokeable cigarettes.

'You got anything to smoke?' he asked.

She nodded to the shelves behind him, where he found a pouch of tobacco and some cigarette papers. He brought them back to the table and started to roll them a cigarette.

'What happened after you ran away?' he asked.

Simone poured herself another shot of rum.

'We stayed in swamps for a while,' she said with a shrug. 'We had to look after ourselves. Davide had to trap animals. One of the old farmhands used to give us food. Eventually we got taken in by a Cajun family that lived in a fishing village up by the lake. We stayed there till we were older. I moved to New Orleans, and then on to here. Davide joined the army, the Buffalo Soldiers. He travelled around, Cuba, the Philippines. Fighting and killing, winning medals.'

She stood and went to one of the bookshelves that ran across the walls of the cabin. She opened up a tin box, took a photograph from it and returned to the table. She held it out and Luca took it. The photograph was a portrait snap of her brother during his army days. The man in the photo was young and somber-looking, and his jacket was heavily laden with medals. Luca recognized something of Simone in her brother's face – the same high cheekbones and deep-set eyes, the same natural elegance in his bearing.

'They started sending him on special missions,' she went on. 'He'd never say what. But when he was discharged and he moved back here . . . he was never the same.'

Luca nodded. A military past made sense. If the army had sent him on special missions, he must have been trained in stealth, which explained how he could plan his attacks so well, how he could get in and out of buildings undetected. Whatever had happened to Baudet during his years of active service, it had unhinged an already unstable mind.

'A while ago he came to see me,' she said. 'He told me he'd found out from someone in New Orleans where all the people were that killed our folks. Said he was gonna set things right. I told him it wasn't worth it, but he wouldn't listen.'

She stopped talking and they stared at each other. Then Luca passed her the cigarette he had rolled. She lit it and they shared it, passing it back and forth, inhaling deep mouthfuls of the heavy, dry smoke.

'The man your brother wants to kill. The last man,' said Luca. 'He's being guarded.'

Simone frowned and stared at him with a pleading look.

'Luca, he's the only thing I've got left,' she said, shaking her head, and Luca's heart sank. He realized what he had done, and that he had no choice now but to go. He had to cross back into the city and see to its conclusion the train of events he'd set in motion.

'I'll try and help him if I can,' he repeated, his voice low and somber.

He rose and kissed her, and they stared at each other despondently. Then he crossed the room to the cabin door, and stepped out into the howling storm beyond.

52

Just after eight o'clock, when they'd heard the car start up and the sound of its engine gently recede into the distance, Buddy had turned to Ida and Lewis and nodded at them that it was time to move. Buddy's reconnaissance of the house over the previous few days had established that the father took the two girls of the house out at eight o'clock most nights, and didn't bring them back till after midnight. So when he met up with Lewis and Ida earlier that day, Buddy had suggesting waiting in the alleyway behind the house until they heard the car depart. The plan made sense to Ida, but it meant they had to stand in the open during the rainstorm, and now the three of them were thoroughly drenched.

Without a word, Buddy jumped the back fence of the house and opened up the gate for them from the inside. They stalked through a shadowy yard until they reached the rear entrance, a kitchen door covered by a porch. Buddy knelt down, took a flashlight from his pocket, quickly switched it on and shone it at the lock. He peered at the lock for a couple of seconds before hastily switching off the light again. Then he took a greasy canvas roll about the size of a large cigar from the inside pocket of his coat and unrolled it onto the porch. The canvas had strips of cloth sewn into it that formed a series of loops, each of which held some kind of pick – slim instruments of dull metal. He took two from their loops, prized them into the keyhole and got to work. Blowing on his hands and rubbing them together to keep them warm, it took Buddy just over five minutes to pick the lock, the tumblers eventually falling into place with a noise like someone clicking their tongue. He smiled and turned the door handle, sliding the door open slowly.

They crept inside and found themselves in the kitchen. It was dark, but they could make out the shape of a door at the other end of the room. They tiptoed towards it and into a corridor, where they found a door under the stairs, which they guessed was the entrance to the cellar. Lewis tried the door but it was locked. He looked at Buddy and Buddy rolled his eyes playfully, then knelt and got to work once more, repeating his actions with the flashlight, the canvas roll and the picks. After a few minutes the cellar door was open and Buddy smiled to himself, stood, and rubbed his knees.

He took two candles from the inside of his coat and handed them to Ida and Lewis.

'Don't light them till you down in the cellar,' he said. 'I'm gonna have a mosey round the house.'

Buddy winked at Ida and sauntered off down the corridor. Ida grimaced at his retreating figure. Buddy had been flirting with her all evening, showering the conversation with innuendos, sly looks and smiles, and she had grown evermore annoyed at him. Even though she knew it wasn't just Buddy that was responsible for her bad mood – she had a horrible feeling there would be no evidence, that she had led them all into danger for no good reason at all. Her visit to the Retreat earlier that day had made her understand just how high the conspiracy went, and that it would require incontrovertible proof to make a solid case against Morval. She had realized with a growing sickness in her stomach that there was only the most minuscule chance of finding just the right piece of evidence, and most likely, just the right piece of evidence didn't even exist. But Buddy and Lewis had already arranged everything, and Ida felt a duty to Leeta to see it all through. She wanted to prove Leeta right against all the odds, and find the smoking gun in the place she'd said it would be. And on top of that, this was the only lead Ida had left.

They descended the stairs, and at the halfway point they lit the candles. The orange glow threw the space below them into long shadows. The cellar was big, covering the whole floor-space of the building, and all across it was a pool of water almost a foot deep, which reflected the light from their candles. They looked at each other and grimaced – the rain was flooding the basement, and they'd have to wade through the water. They swung their candles about and illuminated the hulking, half-soaked shapes below them – old furniture covered in dust sheets, and in one corner a stack of cardboard boxes which was leaning over to one side, the bottom boxes having been drenched by the water.

They stepped down into the cold, dank water and made their way over to the boxes. Ida handed her candle to Lewis and began to go through them. Each one contained dossiers and files – mainly business reports, accounting ledgers, lists of expenses and contracts, and a folder containing property deeds.

The fourth box Ida opened had the evidence – files relating to the accounts of cribs in the District, lists of employees, license fees, revenue streams, and a small book containing a list of initials, addresses, dates and dollar amounts. Ida took the book and sat on the stairs with it, flicking through its pages intently. If she could find the name of the person Morval had hired to carry out the killings, maybe that person could implicate Morval. Maybe one of the names in the book was the right one, maybe a set of initials was the clue, or one of the addresses.

'What you found?' Lewis asked her after a while.

'I dunno.'

She thought for a moment, and realized with a sense of despondency that this little book was the closest she was going to come to any real evidence. She'd need to sit down and study it more closely and see if it contained any clues to the whereabouts of the man Brigadier Kline had told her about, the man who had served in the army with the brigadier, the man Morval had hired. But there was no sense in studying the book here, where they were exposed and vulnerable.

'Let's get outta here,' she said, stuffing the book into her coat pocket.

'What's going on?' Lewis asked as they climbed the stairs.

'I'm thinking maybe that book's got the name of the killer Morval hired in it,' she said.

'You ain't taking no stuff about Morval's stable?' asked Lewis.

'Morval's stable ain't got nothing to do with it,' Ida replied. 'It's all about how the mayor fell out with the Matrangas. Morval had those people killed because the mayor asked him to kill them.'

'The mayor?'

They reached the top of the stairs and blew out the candles.

'In return, Morval got to run all the brothels outside of Storyville.'

Lewis stared at her and frowned.

'Ida, there ain't no brothels outside of Storyville,' he said.

'Not yet there ain't.'

They stepped into the corridor and out into the lounge. Buddy was sitting on the sofa on the far side of the room, a silent smile playing on his lips, his head tilted back. Lewis noticed something wild in his eyes, something strange about his smile, and then he saw the red line drawn across his throat.

'Buddy?' said Lewis, before something swung towards him and the world turned black.

53

The Hospital for Incurables was a sprawling collection of abandoned buildings set behind a razor-wire fence in scrubland to the southwest of the city. It had been closed down by the mayor's administration a few years before and the police had been left in charge of its security until its fate was decided. Somehow Hatener had managed to procure the keys. The hospital grounds were large enough to muffle the noise of what went on inside, and as they dragged Amanzo's body from the car, Jones had informed Michael, with a sinister smile, that the hospital's incinerator was still in working order.

They entered the main building and lit a pair of gas-lamps which provided a weak, flickering light. Hatener led them down a long, dingy corridor and into a windowless white-tiled room that Michael guessed used to be an operating theater. In the center of it was a medical contraption that reminded him of an electric chair, a shadowy nightmare of wood, leather and metal. Gregson and Jones placed the pair of gas-lamps on the floor, and then they buckled the still-unconscious Amanzo into the seat by his ankles and wrists. They told Michael to keep a watch, so he stayed in the corner of the room, smoking a cigarette, trying not to look at the scuff-marks and bloodstains around the foot of the chair, or the chair's occupant, who loomed through the gaslight in an eerie chiaroscuro. Michael occasionally glanced at the others as they set about getting their tools ready – medical instruments, a length of rope, a bucket.

When they had finished, Hatener nodded at Gregson, who picked up the bucket and threw the contents over Amanzo. Cold water smashed onto his face and he jolted upwards, inhaling sharply, eyes fluttering open.

He gazed drunkenly around the room, his mind slowly coming to.

'What's this?' he asked in a drowsy voice.

'The Hospital for Incurables.' Hatener spoke with a gleam in his eye. 'You've come down with a case.'

Hatener sidled over to the table where they had laid out the medical instruments. He ran his hand over the ageing, rusted tools – amputation saws, scalpels, forceps, a Hirtz compass, a scarificator. He went through them one by one as he spoke, picking up each in turn and inspecting it, making sure Amanzo caught a glimpse of things to come.

'My colleague Michael here says you've got some useful information relating to the Axeman,' Hatener said with practiced matter-of-factness, 'but you're not forthcoming with the information.'

Hatener picked up a scalpel and examined its rust-coated blade under the muddy light of the gas-lamp.

'The rusty ones are the worst,' chimed in Jones. 'They don't cut. They rip.'

Hatener grinned and, scalpel in hand, approached Amanzo.

'Now that you're here, the only choice you got is, tell us now, or tell us later.'

Amanzo peered up at Hatener and for a moment he looked apprehensive, frightened, and Michael felt a stab of sympathy. Then his teeth gleamed in the gaslight and he sneered.

'*Vaffanculo.*'

Hatener shrugged and brought the scalpel down onto Amanzo's face, not in a slicing action, but with a turn of the wrist, like a man gouging out a hole. Amanzo screamed, a throaty, full-bodied scream that bounced off the walls and reverberated endlessly. He was hyperventilating from the pain and shock, gasping for breath. He had a wild look about him, bewildered, feral and angry.

'Is that it?' he sneered between gasps.

Hatener brought the scalpel down again, this time on the other side of his face. Amanzo screamed and Michael caught a glimpse of exposed white cheekbone, like an iceberg in a bright-red sea. He turned to the wall and retched, hacking up bile that stung his throat and spilled onto the floor with a splatter. He heard Gregson and Jones laughing and he fumbled against the wall, scrabbling, reaching for the door handle. He stumbled into the corridor and slammed the door shut behind him. The corridor was black except for a faint orange glow coming from the gas-lamps in the other room. He wiped the bile from his mouth and slid down the corridor wall. He put his head in his hands and breathed deeply, the smell of vomit in his nose. He stared at the sliver of orange light creeping into the corridor from underneath the door, making a section of the floor tiles glow with a pale luminescence.

He heard Amanzo scream again, even more blood-curdling now he was in darkness. He took a cigarette from his pack, put it in his mouth, and shakily struck a lucifer. The phosphorous flared momentarily, and the corridor flooded into his vision, dust-covered and dirty, receding on either side of him into blackness. He lit the cigarette and shook the lucifer out, plunging himself back into the dark.

The screams became more frequent after that, accompanied by shouts from Hatener, goading and angry. Then he heard whispers and sobbing. He wasn't sure how long it lasted, but at some point someone inside the room, Gregson or Jones, shouted his name. The tone was matter-of-fact, like someone asking for help with a household chore.

He took a deep breath, stood and reentered the room. Amanzo's face was covered in blood, and its contours didn't look right. His eyes glistened and flickered in the gaslight and his head rolled around on his neck. Blood had doused his shirt and splattered across the floor tiles. Michael could see his chest pumping; he was hyperventilating, delirious from shock and blood-loss. They'd brought him to the very edge, to the point just before death, where he no longer had the energy left to lie, but just enough to answer questions. Michael wondered how fine the line was between the two states, and how many men had died in order for Hatener to perfect the skill of taking them there.

Hatener nodded at Amanzo and slowly, unnoticeably at first, Amanzo nodded back. Jones approached and took a hip-flask from his pocket. He undid the leather strap on one of Amanzo's wrists and pressed the hip-flask into his hand. Amanzo clenched his fingers around it, lifted it to his mouth and took a sip, his hand shaking, spilling the liquor onto the exposed flesh of his chin.

'You . . . you got a cigarette?' he asked.

Michael stepped over to him and lit a cigarette. He took the hip-flask from his hand and slid the cigarette in between his fingers. It was only when he was up close that he noticed the five clay-like slugs at the foot of the chair. He looked up at Amanzo's hand, the one that was still buckled down, and saw it was just a stump, dripping blood onto the floor.

'Gimme a minute,' said Amanzo.

Amanzo put the cigarette between his lips and put his hand up to his face – feeling the wounds from the scalpel. He took another drag on the cigarette and removed it from his lips.

'Ask,' he said, his voice quavering, and Michael realized he was looking at a dead man.

'Who's the Axeman?'

'Some . . . some French coon out in the swamps,' said Amanzo, gasping. 'Never met him. No one did.'

'Who gave you the job to deliver the list to him?'

'Sam Carolla,' Amanzo hissed, almost whispering.

Michael thought back to his meeting with Carolla in the barber's shop. He remembered the joke Carolla had made about Annette, and he remembered his parting words, that the Axeman was a ghost. Pieces of evidence started to link together, one after the other, and a sequence of events that fitted the evidence formed perfectly in Michael's mind, like an anchor-chain dredged link by link from ocean mud.

'Tell me what you know,' he said.

Amanzo took a moment to inhale, deeply, raspily, and Michael thought of the blood that must be flooding into the man's lungs.

'Axeman had some kind o' vendetta. Carolla had a list. He asked me to deliver it.'

'And he swore to you if you did it, and you told no one, he'd get you made,' Michael said, 'because you were still an empty suit after all these years.'

Amanzo nodded.

'But you palmed the job off to Lombardi because it didn't feel right, and you were worried about getting whacked, and you'd heard Lombardi was leaving town anyway. Except afterwards it turned out he wasn't.'

Amanzo nodded. Hatener and the others looked between the two of them, and then Hatener frowned and turned to Amanzo.

'Why did Matranga want 'em dead?' he asked.

'It wasn't Matranga,' said Michael, interjecting. 'Carolla was behind the whole thing. Isn't that right?'

Amanzo nodded again. 'Carolla wants rid of the Don,' he said. 'Been the number two for years. But . . .' Amanzo struggled for breath. 'But he didn't wanna war.'

Michael should have realized earlier on, and he cursed himself for not seeing it. Carolla had used the Axeman to destabilize Carlo Matranga. He'd found a hit-man from out of town to do the killing, someone with no links to the Family. A ghost. And he used the killings to spread fear throughout the city, to make the police crack down on the Family's operations. Carlo Matranga's position would be weakened to the point where eventually he'd be forced to step down. Then Carolla would take over in a bloodless coup, and the whole thing would look like nothing but pure bad luck for the Don.

It explained why no one in New Orleans knew who the killer was, and it proved Luca was telling the truth when he had told

Michael that Carlo had asked him to investigate. Why hadn't Michael seen it before? Especially as Carolla had acted so cocksure in the barber's shop – covering up his worry at having the investigation brought right to him. Michael thought of the tarot cards left at the scenes to make the murders look like the work of a Creole, or a Negro, designed to throw everyone off the scent. He thought of the crazed letter sent to the press, with its talk of hell and jazz and demons – racial fears that further misdirected and confused the city.

Amanzo coughed and a mouthful of blood spilt from his lips and landed on the floor with a slopping noise. Michael stared at the man and noticed a dazed, half-dead look in his eyes. His chest heaved as he struggled for breath, and again Michael had the sense he was looking at a man already over the river. 'They tried to kill you outside the precinct, they're gonna try again. Tonight,' he said, rasping desperately for breath. 'At your house.'

Michael stared at Amanzo, the full chill of panic and fear bearing down on him as he realized the danger Annette and the children were in. He balled his fists and swung a punch at Amanzo. The punch connected and Amanzo's head rolled back with a sickening crack. Michael turned and raced out of the room.

'You get in contact with the precinct,' Hatener said to Gregson. 'Tell 'em what's happening, and to meet us at Talbot's. Jones, you get rid o' Amanzo, then follow us.'

'Sure thing, boss,' said Jones. 'I'll get the incinerator fired up.'

54

Shin-high water rippled around Luca's legs before sluicing off down the hill in front of him. He stood at the top of an incline, surveying the path ahead – a road leading up into Marigny, houses on both sides, and in the middle, like white-water rapids, flood-water avalanching down the road, cascading into a pool at the bottom.

He had stopped by the hotel. Sandoval had found Bianchi and left him an address – an apartment to the north of the French Quarter, somewhere on the far side of the floodwater that was turning the city into a lake. Luca felt nauseous, his hands shook and his breathing was hard; spending all day in wet clothes had given him a fever.

He heard voices, and lights glimmered over the surface of the water, a bustle of people approaching from the side. They looked like refugees – hastily dressed and weary, led by three policemen in waterproofs who held all-weather electric lamps in their hands. They stopped when they saw Luca and exchanged puzzled glances.

'What you doing, bud?' asked one of the policemen, shouting over the noise of the storm.

'Going to a friend's house,' Luca replied.

The policeman frowned and pointed down the incline. 'Down there?' he asked.

Luca nodded.

'Ain't ya heard?' shouted the policeman over the sound of the wind and rain. 'River's burst, broke the levees. We're evacuating.'

'Thanks for the warning, officer,' Luca shouted. 'But I have to find my friend.'

The policeman eyed Luca suspiciously, guessing he must have been planning on robbing houses, or looting shops.

'Can't let you do that, bud,' he said.

'What you gonna do? Arrest me? You can't arrest me and evacuate all them people at the same time.' He nodded at the evacuees flocking behind the policemen. 'I'll be fine, officer. Thanks for your concern.'

The policeman stared at him then exchanged a few words with his colleagues.

'OK,' he said. 'Your funeral, bud.'

He waved his hand at the others and the group moved on down the road, the evacuees frowning at Luca as they stumbled past.

Luca watched them go, then took tentative steps down the road, the water pushing at his calves, threatening to take his legs from under him. He was about halfway down the incline when something crashed into him, some piece of debris picked up by the water. It was heavy and jagged and it knocked him off balance. He dropped into the torrent, felt himself spinning, moving downwards. With each roll he smacked into the road and his fractured rib burst with pain.

After a few seconds his body smashed into something hard. He grabbed onto whatever it was and pulled himself up, the pain in his torso excruciating. He opened his eyes and looked around. He was holding onto a lamppost in the middle of the lake that had formed at the bottom of the street. He stared back up the incline – the waterfall had pushed him at least a hundred yards – then he waded to the far side of the pool.

He made slow progress, holding onto the sides of buildings anywhere he could, and eventually he got out of the water, onto a road leading up the other side of the incline. The water was rushing towards him this time. He moved up the road like a mountaineer, making sure his grip was secure before he placed his feet. When he reached the top, the going was easier, perpendicular to the flow of the water. He crossed three streets and finally arrived at the tenement. Bianchi's apartment was on the second floor. He tramped up the stairs, knocked on the door, and after a few seconds it was opened by a heavy-set Sicilian in a gray cotton suit.

'Luca,' said the Sicilian with a grin. 'You look like a fish.'

Luca stumbled into the apartment and collapsed into an armchair, putting his hand to his face and breathing as deeply as he could, trying to force down the nausea coming up from his stomach. He heard voices around him, shimmering in and out of his mind, and felt someone shaking him. He glanced up. Sandoval was standing over him, looking concerned.

'Luca, you OK?'

Luca nodded. Sandoval stared at him, unconvinced.

'Get to the bathroom and dry yourself off.'

Luca rose unsteadily and looked around him. He was in a living room, dimly lit, along with a handful of *picciotti* – foot soldiers with heavy jaws and gun-bulges in their jackets. And sitting in an armchair further away was the man he guessed to be Bianchi, a gaunt figure, in his early seventies, wild-eyed and angry.

Luca found the bathroom off the corridor and stepped inside. Harsh electric light bounced off the white tiles, stinging his eyes. He turned the hot water on and splashed his face, then he took his clothes off, and for the second time that day dried himself off with a towel. He called for one of the men to bring him some of Bianchi's clothes.

He changed and returned to the living room.

'You wanna drink?' asked Sandoval.

Luca nodded. 'Something strong.'

Sandoval crossed to the drinks cabinet and took out a bottle of rye.

'Help yourself,' Bianchi said sarcastically.

Sandoval ignored him, poured two glasses and returned to Luca. He took a cigarette case from his inside pocket, offered one to Luca and they both lit up.

Luca leaned his head back in the chair and sighed.

'Where've you been?' asked Sandoval.

'Getting back from out of town,' Luca said, his tone making it clear he wasn't really in the mood to talk.

Sandoval nodded. 'He told us everything. I've spoken to Carlo. Good work, Luca.'

Luca nodded and took a gulp of the rye, finishing it in one. He passed the glass to Sandoval who refilled it for him.

'This guy definitely the last?' asked Sandoval.

'I think so,' said Luca.

Sandoval handed him the refill, and Luca took a sip. He eyeballed Bianchi, who was still sitting in his chair with his hands folded in front of his stomach. He was a thin, gray-haired man with defiant, birdlike eyes and leathery farmer's skin. Bianchi noticed him staring and the two locked eyes.

'Why didn't you run?' asked Luca. 'You saw all your partners getting killed and you stayed.'

'Why should I run?' He spoke vehemently. 'If I die, I die in my own house.'

The old man had a venom to him, a puffed-up righteousness that was jarring and somehow false. Luca stared at Bianchi for a few moments longer then he stood and walked over to the window, moving the blind aside to peer into the street below. The water had risen, making Luca feel like he was standing at the top of a ravine, surveying an angry river below. The storm had knocked out the streetlamps – he couldn't see much but the galloping flood and the lights of the surrounding apartments, murky in the darkness.

He turned back around and scanned the room. Bianchi was still in his chair, Sandoval was standing by the door to the kitchen, nursing his drink, and the foot soldiers were leaning over the coffee table, playing a game of *briscola* with a set of Neapolitan playing cards.

Luca realized that the smoke from the cigarette was making his breathing worse. He stubbed it out in an ashtray, poured himself more of the rye and went to sit down. He closed his eyes for a moment and before he knew it he had drifted off and was in the midst of a feverish dream. He dreamt of a field in Sicily, the field he used to farm with his father when he was a child. He saw his father standing some way off, and as he approached he saw that his father was crying because the field was barren, covered in rocks and the burnt stubs of trees. His father looked up at him, tears in his eyes, and Luca realized with a pang of panic that the man wasn't his father.

He awoke to shouts and a bustle of activity.

'Fucking storm,' he heard one of the *piccioti* say.

'Where's the fuse box, old man?'

Luca could see the room had been thrown into darkness – a power cut. He got to his feet, felt his way across to the window and peered out. The lights of the surrounding apartments were still working.

'It's not the storm!' he shouted, but he was too late.

One of the front windows smashed open and drops of glass and rain sprayed into the room. The blind flapped madly in the roaring wind and Luca saw a shadow in the confusion as the men began shouting. He backed up against the wall, squinting against the darkness, trying to get a picture of what was going on. He heard furniture thumping onto the floor and then a scream.

'He's in here!' someone shouted and the room flashed bright. The men began letting off shots, panicked in the darkness.

'Don't shoot!' Luca screamed over the roar, worried the men were going to kill each other. He slid down the wall onto the floor, hoping to be out of the way of stray bullets. Flashes of gunshots popped about him and the smell of burnt gunpowder mixed with the smell of floodwater coming in through the smashed window. Luca heard another scream and saw a silhouette of a man turning, heavy-shouldered in a long coat. The shooting stopped and something fluttered at the window, then the room became still except for the wind and the blind flapping against the smashed pane.

Luca rose and felt his way to the cabinet. He'd seen a lamp

there. Matches. A few seconds later the lamp flickered into life and he swung it round to survey the damage. The *picciotti* were dead on the floor, slumped over the furniture, some of them hacked by an axe, most of them shot by their colleagues' bullets. Sandoval was lying face-down on the carpet. Luca rolled him over – a bullet had caught him in the side of the face. Luca stared at him for a moment, then he sighed, shook his head and crossed himself. He looked over to where Bianchi had been sitting. He was still in the armchair, but a slice of his head was gone. In his lap was a tarot card. In the flicker of the lamplight Luca caught a glimpse of the figure on the card, a winged being with a horned head, gripping a thick, flaming torch.

Luca ran to the window and scanned the street below. He saw a figure at the bottom of the fire escape, squirming, his coat caught on something, struggling to get free. Luca grabbed a gun from one of the dead men, checked it for bullets, and jumped out onto the fire escape. The clang of his feet made the killer look up. Luca ran down the stairs, his head swooning, his ribs hurting with every heavy step. The killer yanked his coat away and broke free, jumping into the water below and running up the street.

By the time Luca reached the bottom of the fire escape, he was already halfway to the corner. Luca jumped off, stumbled, and ran after Baudet through the dark, flooding city.

55

Ida awoke punch-drunk and nauseous, a cement floor pressing coldly against her cheek. She sat up and rubbed her face, and noticed dried blood flaking onto her fingers. She saw Lewis lying next to her, passed out, a bruise rising up on his brow. She shook him awake and looked around her. It was a working room, huge and factory-like, and one she had seen before. Rows of coats hung along rails that receded into the distance like an army on parade. Boxes and pelts littered the floor in the center of the room, and a harsh bare light-bulb cast everything into bleak illumination.

'What happened?' Lewis asked, his voice weak.

'I dunno,' said Ida. 'Let's get the hell outta here.'

They stood and looked about the room. On a work-table by a mound of pelts Ida saw a trapping knife. She hesitated a moment then picked it up. It felt heavier than she expected it to, alien somehow. She slid it into her pocket, just to be on the safe side. Lewis turned to her and was about to say something when his eyes rolled upwards and he dropped to the floor with a thump.

'Lewis!' Ida shouted, running to his side.

'Feel sick,' said Lewis, clutching his forehead, his breathing shallow.

'You reckon you can walk?'

But before Lewis could answer, the door on the far side of the room opened and two roughnecks stamped in, gray-suited and surly, one a good foot taller than the other. They stared at Lewis and Ida for a moment, then the taller one turned to the other.

'Tell the boss they're awake,' he said, in a nasal pinch of a voice.

The shorter one nodded and left, and the taller one eyed them with a guard-dog glare. A few seconds later Morval stepped into the room. Despite his age, Ida could see he was well-maintained, broad-shouldered and straight-backed, his hair glossy in the harsh electric light. He stared at them blankly, a slight inquisitiveness to the tilt of his head, the way a dog might look at its master. He took off his jacket and hung it on one of the rails, and Ida noticed the muscles in his arms bulging underneath the silk of his shirt. He straightened his waistcoat, turned to face them, and nodded at the two men.

'Bring 'em over to the table,' he said.

In the corner of the room was a round table with a green baize covering, playing cards and ashtrays scattered across it. The men hauled Ida and Lewis up by their elbows, marched them across to the table, and pushed them onto a pair of chairs. Morval approached and picked up a whiskey bottle from the table. He poured out a glass and handed it to Lewis.

'Looks like you could use it, son,' he said, his voice fatherly and warm.

'Thank you, sir,' said Lewis, taking a sip. Morval poured a glass for himself, sat down at the table, and lit a cigar, staring at them both. There was something dead about his small brown eyes, a detachment, a lack of humanity, that unsettled Ida. When the cigar was fully lit, he drew some smoke into his mouth and smiled at them.

'What were you doing in my house?' he asked, no hint of threat whatsoever in his tone.

'Nothing, sir,' said Ida, her voice sweet. 'We broke in to stay the night. We live on the street and wanted to get away from the flood. We didn't mean any wrong.'

'Well, ain't you the best dressed street-girl I ever saw,' Morval said sarcastically. 'If you were getting out of the storm, why was you in the basement going through my papers?'

He spoke in a casual way, as if his questions were part of some inconsequential game.

'We was looking for kindling to start a fire with. It was getting cold,' Ida said in desperation, smiling as best she could.

Morval grinned and shook his head slowly. He took something from his pocket and threw it onto the table – the black book Ida had stashed in her coat.

'Were you going to start the fire in your pocket?' He puffed on the cigar, rolling the smoke around his mouth. 'If we thought you were housebreakers, you'd be dead by now. Like your friend in the expensive suit,' he said, and with a shock of fear and guilt, the image of Buddy sitting on the sofa flashed into Ida's mind.

'The only thing keeping you alive,' Morval continued, 'is the fact I wanna know exactly what your interest in my affairs is. You gonna tell me who you work for?'

'We don't work for nobody, sir,' said Ida.

Morval sighed and shook his head. He stood and stretched his back out, the fabric of his waistcoat straining against his chest. He strode over to the nearest clothing rail and unwound a length of rope from a pulley hook hanging from the ceiling.

'Tie her up,' he ordered, tossing the rope at the shorter of the two roughnecks. The man grabbed the rope and moved behind Ida. She suddenly felt claustrophobic, panic stabbing at her heart as the man grabbed her hands and tied them up. She thought of Leeta and all the warnings they had had about Morval, and she felt a wave of fear and shame at her own foolishness wash over her. She wondered if she should struggle against the ropes, or if that would only make things worse. Then a nightmarish paralysis came over her, a freezing of her muscles, and she found herself sitting still, acquiescing, as the rough twine of the rope tightened against her wrists. Morval watched the man tie her up with a slight grin on his lips, and when the man had finished, he nodded.

'Take the coon outside and let some daylight through him,' he said. 'I'll take care of the girl.'

Ida screamed and Lewis stared at her in desperate panic. The smaller thug took a cosh from his jacket and cracked it over Lewis's head.

He came to with a feeling of weight in his shoulders – the men were dragging him somewhere, their hands locked under his armpits. He looked about him and saw he was in a dank corridor, headed towards a set of dead-bolt doors. One of the men kicked the bolt and the doors flew open. The storm roared into the corridor and spits of rain sprayed onto Lewis before the door slammed shut again under the pressure of the wind.

'Goddamn it!' One of the men pushed the door open again with his shoulder and the wind roared into their ears once more. They dragged Lewis out into the storm, onto a jetty that overhung the river. The wind was whipping up the water below them, sending waves crashing onto the jetty, causing it to rock in stomach-churning arcs. The men dumped Lewis onto the wooden planks and the shorter thug then pulled a gun from his pocket and aimed it at him.

'What are you doing?' shouted the tall one over the roar of the storm.

'Whadda ya' think?'

'Move him to the end for Chrissakes.'

Lewis felt himself being picked up again and dragged along the wooden planks. He saw the angry river underneath him, and to his right, something moving towards him, a wall of foam, white and roiling, and growing larger. The men screamed as it hit, fifteen feet of Mississippi water crashing into the side of the jetty. There was a sound like an explosion and the wood all around them seemed to split and fly skywards, and the next thing Lewis knew, he was underwater.

The currents pulled him about like a ragdoll, swirling him through the silent darkness until he felt himself smack against something hard and upright and he burst back above the surface.

He grabbed hold of whatever it was he'd hit and looked about him. Where the jetty had once stood there was now only a row of stumps sticking out of the water, and all about him were the remains of wooden planks, rendered into a thousand shards that floated on the surface like a blanket of jagged, angry seaweed.

Lewis realized he was holding onto one of the stumps, and by reaching from one stump to the next he made his way back to the dockside. He found footholds embedded in the brickwork of the embankment wall and hauled himself out of the river. He lay on the deck a moment getting his breath back and then he stood. He looked around for any signs of the two men, and seeing none, he guessed they'd been pulled under by the waves. He took another breath and stumbled back towards the factory, praying he wasn't too late.

56

Michael was already starting up the Chevrolet when he saw Hatener running out of the hospital. The old man waved him down and opened the passenger-side door.

'You're gonna need help,' Hatener said, as he slid inside. Michael stared at him for a moment then turned his attention to the car's controls; he wasn't certain he could get the thing going. He pulled up the brake and churned the car into gear and they jerked forward and off down the path towards the hospital exit.

They drove in silence, Michael fixing on the road, Hatener staring out of the side window. As they approached the city, the roads got wetter, making the engine strain and the tires slide, but Michael kept the car's speed up as best he could. He prayed the four policemen who were guarding his house had not been caught unawares, or worse yet, were in the pay of Carolla.

A few blocks from his house they came upon a police cordon. Michael stopped the car and a patrolman in waterproofs approached and signaled for them to wind down the window. He peered into the car and recognized the two detectives.

'These roads are closed, sir,' he said to Michael. 'Storm's caused flooding right through. We're evacuating—'

But before he could finish, Michael put the car into reverse and sped backwards. He swung around and took a turn off a side road. Hatener stared at him.

'This road leads to high ground,' Michael said.

Five minutes later they were on a ridge that overlooked Michael's street. They got out of the car and Hatener beckoned for Michael to unlock the trunk. Inside were three Chesterfield shotguns and a few boxes of cartridges that had spilled loose during the ride over.

They took one each, checked the barrels, and crammed fistfuls of spare rounds into their pockets. Then they set off down the street, Michael making double time on Hatener, who stumbled along after him. They ran as best they could, trying not to slip up on the slick dark current cascading down the sidewalk. When they were nearly at Michael's house, Hatener motioned towards a car on the opposite side of the road – the unmarked black landaulet occupied by two of the four policemen. They approached and peered into the car – the men were slumped in their seats, garrote wires around their necks, their faces turning a mottled green.

'No gunshots,' Hatener whispered, and Michael nodded, understanding his meaning – if there hadn't been a gunfight, chances were the two men at the back of the house had also been caught unawares.

'You gonna wait for my boys to arrive?' Hatener asked.

Michael stared at him, turned around, and ran towards the house. Hatener watched him for a moment, then he double-checked his shotgun and followed. They crossed the rain-slicked street and passed in front of the house. As they reached the front steps, shots rang out behind them. They dashed up the porch and dropped behind the waist-high brick wall that ran along the front of the building. Bullets burst into the brickwork and into the wooden wall behind them, which splintered and cracked. As the volley continued, Michael and Hatener looked at each other to check they were both OK, then they glanced over the top of the wall – orange blooms of muzzle-fire spat at them from a car across the street.

'I'll stay here,' Hatener said.

Michael nodded at him, and Hatener pumped his shotgun and started shooting back over the wall. Michael turned around, pushed the front door open with the butt of his gun and crawled into the house. He continued along the corridor until he was out of range of the bullets thundering into the front wall, then he stood and padded quickly towards the living room. When he reached the connecting door, he stood by it, listening for noises. Nothing. He took a deep breath, and gently pushed the door open. The lights were still on, but the living room was empty. He stepped into the kitchen, scanning his surroundings as he went. Annette had left something cooking on the stove, the pot bubbling, releasing plumes of steam into the deserted room. When he reached the stove he turned it off and peered into the backyard. The bodies of the second pair of policemen lay slumped over each other on the back step.

He moved away from the window and tried to clear his head. Everything was silent in the house, the only noises were coming from outside – the rain and the wind and the gunshots in the street. Then he heard a noise behind him and swung round, his gun frantically fanning the room.

Everything was silent and still. But he knew he had heard a creak – a foot on a floorboard, maybe, or a cupboard door opening. He scanned the room once more, trying to gauge where someone might be hiding, and then he heard the noise again. At the far end of the kitchen was a cupboard space inset in the wall. The door to the space slowly swung open, and Michael saw Thomas and Mae hidden underneath the sacking at the bottom, their faces tearstained and numb with horror. Michael lifted his finger to his lips and they responded in kind, and he stepped over to the cupboard.

'You OK?' he whispered, kneeling down next to them.

They both nodded and he noticed Thomas had his arm around Mae, protecting his little sister. The gesture made Michael proud, and he rubbed his son's head.

'You're going to be alright,' he said. 'What happened?'

'Momma heard the noise in the street and hid us in here. Then there was another noise and we heard Momma crying. But . . . but she told us not to come out.'

Thomas began to sob, which set off Mae as well. Michael hugged them both.

'Listen. You two are safe here, OK?' he said. 'But you gotta be quiet. I'm gonna go find Momma, OK?'

The children nodded.

'But you gotta be quiet,' he repeated urgently, 'and you don't come out of there until I tell you to. You got it?'

They nodded again and Michael smiled. He stood and Thomas closed the cupboard door from the inside. Michael tried to imagine what had happened. Carolla and his men must have arrived and taken out the policemen, then they had come inside for him. But where had they taken Annette? It didn't make sense for them to go to all this trouble just to leave when they found he wasn't home. They must still be in the house – waiting to ambush him.

Michael crept back over to the kitchen counter and slowly eased up the window frame. Rain began smattering into the room and onto his hands. He got the window halfway up and levered himself through it, careful not to make any sounds. He dropped down onto the paving stones of the backyard. The rain and cold hit him, and he noticed that he couldn't hear Hatener and the others shooting in the road in front anymore. He scanned the side of the house and saw a light spilling from the window of his bedroom.

He crept along the back wall and reached the bodies of the two dead policemen. One of them had his hands around his neck, as if still trying to pull off the garrote. He reached down and closed their eyes, crossed himself, then carried on edging along the wall until he reached the bedroom window.

He turned and peered into the bedroom. He couldn't see Annette, but he could see Carolla and another man – a small, young-looking man in a cloth-cap and peacoat. Both of them were standing by the closed door, nickel-plated Colts in their hands. He guessed they had heard the shooting out front and were debating what to do.

Then he noticed Annette. They had tied her hands and laid her down on the floor at the foot of the bed. He turned away from the window and breathed a sigh of relief, and then he tried to formulate a plan. He looked about him and saw the rusting metal garden table that had been in their backyard since before they moved in, and he made a quick calculation of its weight and exactly how much strength he had left in his arms.

Thirty seconds later, rain, wind and noise rushed into the room as the table smashed its way through the window, arced through the interior and landed on the bed, before bouncing into the air again and crashing against the far wall. The younger man swung his Colt towards the backyard and began letting off shots. As he fired he approached the window, and when he was almost level with it, a shot from the darkness outside exploded into the side of his face. He stumbled, tried to right himself, then fell forwards, collapsing onto the shards of glass pointing upwards from the bottom of the broken pane, skewering himself through his gut.

As the man lay dying, Carolla turned and scrabbled to get the bedroom door open. Michael stepped in front of the window.

'Freeze!' he shouted over the sound of the storm. Carolla stopped, and turned back around, raising his arms slowly into the air. The two men stared at each other through the jagged, broken windowpane. Carolla looked pale in the room's electric light. The bulb hanging from the ceiling was directly above him, shining straight onto his face, casting the hollows of his eyes into cave-like shadows, giving his face the appearance of a death mask. Michael saw something in the man's expression that he'd never noticed before, a longing after something, a ravenousness. He wanted to ask Carolla if he thought all the death and misery was worth it. But then he heard a noise and looked down.

The man impaled on the glass was still breathing, making a gurgling sound as his throat filled with blood. Carolla, seeing that Michael was distracted, spun about and made to run out of the room. Michael jerked his gaze back towards him and time seemed to slow. His hand shook as he aimed his gun. For some reason he thought of the graveyard on Robertson Street, and with visions in his eyes of ancient tombs, stone angels and saints, he breathed deeply, and let off a shot.

57

After the men had dragged Lewis out into the corridor, Morval had turned and left through the door on the opposite side of the room. Ida guessed he would only be gone a few seconds. She twisted her hands, knowing her only hope was to grab at the knife in her pocket. Her fingertips could just about reach the edge of the handle, but she couldn't get enough purchase on it with her thumb. She shifted her body to the side, and her pocket turned a little, the knife sliding out of it towards the floor, but still she couldn't catch a hold of it. Her only chance was to turn her body so that the knife slid all the way out of her pocket, and to grab it as it fell to the floor. If she timed it wrong the knife would fall past her hand and she'd be lost. She thought again of Leeta, and of Lewis outside. She took a deep breath, and jerked her body. She felt the knife slip out of her pocket and she stretched out her hand.

She grabbed at air. She heard the knife thud against the floor and a panic-stricken sickness washed over her. She had missed. Her last hope had vanished.

She began to sob, waves of despair raking up and down her torso. But as her body convulsed, she felt something brush by her knuckles. Sniffing back her tears she opened her hand. She caught something between her thumb and forefinger. The very edge of the handle. The knife must have embedded itself by its point into the floorboard beneath her chair. She leaned her body down and pulled the knife out of the floorboard, then she crawled her fingers up the handle till she had it firmly in her grip. She turned it around, pressed it against the ropes, and began to shimmy the blade back and forth as quickly as she could. The rope was old and tough, and it would take her a while to get through it. She prayed Morval wouldn't return anytime soon, but a few seconds later she heard footsteps, and the door opened and he strode into the room, holding a black leather case in one hand, and a gun in the other.

Ida froze as he approached, too scared to continue cutting the ropes in case he realized what she was doing. He sat on a chair in front of her and put the gun on the table, pointing it her way. He smiled and opened the case. Inside was a collection of gleaming trapper's knives, complete except for an empty space about the size of the knife she had in her hands.

'If you harm me everything I know goes straight to the cops,' Ida whispered, feeling foolish even as she said it.

Morval jutted out his lower lip and thought for a moment. He picked up the whiskey glass on the table and took a sip.

'Well, that's not a threat unless I know what it is that you know.' Ida stared at him, and got the same feeling she had before – that he didn't really care what she knew, that the whole question-and-answer session was just a game, a preamble to the terror he had in mind. She thought that maybe she could work the game to her advantage, keep him talking long enough to set herself free.

'I know you arranged the Axeman killings on behalf of the mayor. Because the mayor wanted rid of Carlo Matranga. I got evidence at my lawyer's. Anything happens to me, it goes straight to the police.'

Morval thought for a moment, his small brown eyes gleaming and still. Then he shook his head and took a puff on his cigar.

'I'm just not believing you,' he said. He leaned over the table and took one of the knives from the case. 'If you had evidence you wouldn't be rooting around one o' my houses trying to *get* evidence, now would you? Seems to me all you got is theory.'

'I swear to God,' Ida said. 'I wrote a statement at a lawyer's, left it in his keeping. If anything bad happens to me, he's gonna send it to the police and the papers.'

Morval ignored her and stared down at the knife in his hand as if he had only just noticed it. Ida followed his gaze. The serrated blade sparkled, the pearl-effect handle bouncing the light in rainbow refractions. Morval smiled as he inspected it, a fondness to his look, as if it was a newborn in his hands.

'How you come by your theory, girl?' he asked suddenly, his tone flat, looking up at her, the smile no longer on his lips. 'Who put it in that pretty little head o' yours? Your boyfriend out there?'

'I figured it out on my own.'

'Well, ain't you a clever girl.' Morval smiled. 'I like clever girls. It's such a rarity to meet them in my line of work. Now if you telling the truth and you did dream this all up inside that pretty little head o' yours, then there ain't no reason in me keeping you alive, is there?'

He smiled, tossed the knife into the air, and grabbed it by the handle. Then he stood and stared at her, his eyes two pools of ice. He took a puff on his cigar and moved towards Ida's trembling figure. She waited till he was close, then she kicked out at him, using all the force in her legs to hit his ankles, hoping to sending him tumbling, to buy herself a bit more time. But she was weaker than she imagined herself to be, or Morval was stronger, and his feet stayed firmly locked in place. He stared at her and for the first time he showed some emotion, a glimmer of rage. His eyes narrowed, and he lashed out at her with the knife.

She was quick enough to see it bearing down and she shifted her body to the side. The knife missed its mark but she was not quick enough: it plunged into her torso just above her hip, and a pain tore through her so complete and consuming it felt as if time had frozen and all that existed was the agony coursing through her body. She gasped, the breath knocked out of her, and her heart began to beat at double speed.

Morval grabbed her by the neck and pulled her upwards, bringing her face close to his. He stared at her with his granite eyes, his breath warm and tinged with whiskey, his fingers like a vice around her throat. The tension of his grip was causing the ropes around her wrists – already frayed where she had sawn through them with the knife – to fray even more, and she prayed that the pressure would be enough for her to break free.

Morval placed his knife on the inside of her knee and dug its point into her flesh. Then he slowly dragged it upwards across her inner thigh, all the while holding her face in front of his. She took a deep breath and yanked her hands backwards and the ropes around her wrists tightened. She yanked once more.

And the ropes broke.

She swung her arm round in an arc, and with all her might buried the hunting knife in Morval's ribs. He wheezed and his eyes grew round, and he staggered back, and in a moment of instinct, he swung his own knife back towards her and caught her across her cheek.

But it was a death swing, a reflex. He stumbled back another step and collapsed onto the floor, rolling onto his back and choking, as the blood poured from the wound. Ida stared down at him, hyperventilating, shocked that she might have killed him, and scared that he might survive. But gradually his breathing became shallow, and his chest stopped moving, and the entire room became still, silent except for the muffled noise of the storm.

Ida wasn't sure how long she spent staring at his body, frozen with shock, as the blood pooled around him. Her mind was in some distant place, detached and withdrawn from the here and now. She heard a noise and looked up to see Lewis standing in the corridor. Her heart wrenched and she burst into tears and Lewis ran over and hugged her.

'It's OK,' he said. 'It's over.'

She didn't say anything, too shocked at what had happened, too disorientated by the pain coursing through her cheek, her torso and the inside of her leg. Lewis looked her up and down and his eyes rested on the spot above her hip where Morval had stabbed her. Ida saw the shock and concern on Lewis's face and she followed his gaze to see blood flowing freely from the wound, running down the length of her dress to the hem, from where it dripped to the floor.

'We need to get you out of here,' he said. Then he knelt, pulled the knife from Morval's chest, wiped it free of fingerprints on Morval's shirt and laid it on the floor next to the body.

'C'mon,' he said, and Ida suddenly felt a rush of shame.

'I can't walk,' she said, and she looked at him, panicked and afraid. He put his arm around her shoulders and, with half her weight on him, they limped out of the warehouse and into the yard, wondering how they could get her to a hospital in the middle of a storm.

58

Luca followed Baudet as he ran north into Marigny-Faubourg, somehow managing to move against the deluge of water pouring through the streets. The storm was dismantling the city, ripping loose fences, hoardings, roofs and trees. Smaller pieces of debris were being hurled along by the current, smacking into Luca's legs as he ran, making him stumble and drop to his knees every few seconds. He tried not to fall into the water completely, he had to keep the gun as dry as possible.

Baudet turned into a larger road and bounded all the way to the top of it, stopping abruptly in the middle of the carriageway, where the water-level was lower and a railroad crossed his path. Luca wondered what he was waiting for, and then he realized. He heard a roaring noise, then shuttering lights began to illuminate the dark, flashing off the water's surface. In an instant, the train was in front of them, roaring past. The *Smokey Mary*, the train that ran down Elysian Fields Avenue from the center of New Orleans, out to the pleasure district at Milneburg. Baudet had a ride all the way home.

Luca saw him jump, slipping on the wet metal, then getting purchase and swinging himself into the space between two cars. By the time Luca got to the tracks there was only one car left to pass. He put the gun in his pocket, jumped, and fell hard into the side of the train. He caught a grip on something, his momentum bouncing him outwards then smashing him back into the racing metal wall. He slipped a little and slid downwards, towards the hundred-ton wheels spinning noisily below. He swung his legs left and right, hoping to find some purchase, and after a few seconds, his feet came to rest on one of the running-boards protruding from the side of the car just a few inches above the wheels.

He took a deep breath, looked about him and realized he was two windows away from the end of the car. He levered himself up and grappled his way along the ledge he was holding on to, eventually reaching the pole that ran down the corner of the car. He grabbed hold of it and swung himself into the space at the end of the train. He stopped for a moment to catch his breath, and he noticed how fast his heart was beating, how the stress was pumping through him. He checked his pocket for the gun, took a few more deep breaths, unlatched the door, and stepped inside.

The car was empty, the lights switched off, and Luca guessed the line was sending its stock out of the city to avoid the flood. Beams from streetlights arced and rolled through the interior, shadows flying wraithlike in their wake. Luca made his way slowly up the aisle, holding onto headrests against the rocking of the train. He reached the front, opened the connecting door and stepped into the next compartment. It was just as empty, and as he reached its end, the last of the Elysian Fields lights flashed past and the car was plunged into even greater darkness.

He moved on to the next compartment, trying to remember how many cars had gone past him on the road. Five? Six? He checked each one, slowly, methodically, and finally, in the last car, he saw him. A shadow at the far end, barely discernible in the inky gloom.

'Baudet!' he shouted.

Baudet turned and stared at him, eyes glinting in the dark, the train clattering noisily over the tracks. He regarded Luca for a moment, then turned to look out of the window, fixing his stare on the swampland beyond. Luca paused, then stalked slowly up the aisle, the gun shaking in his hand.

When Luca was halfway up the car, Baudet opened the door in front of him and in a single, fluid movement, leapt into the darkness, his coat unfurling in the gale like a huge set of wings.

The sound of the storm roared into the car and Luca let off a shot that buried itself in the wood paneling by the open door. Heart racing, he opened the door nearest to him, and following Baudet's lead, jumped into the nothingness outside the car.

The freezing wind bit into his wet clothes for a moment before he crashed into the water. And then everything was silent, muffled and peaceful, no more storm or rain, just a beautiful stillness.

He felt he was floating upwards, then he came to the surface, and the world roared back to life. He looked around him and saw the train steaming off into the distance, taking with it the last of its light. There was no moon in the sky, just the storm passing overhead. He'd been plunged into absolute, terrifying, darkness. Slowly his eyes adjusted and he could make out where he was; a black water pool and, a little further away, a tree trunk. He swam over to it, leaned against it and hauled himself out of the water, taking a moment to get his breath back.

He cursed himself for getting caught up in the moment and jumping from the train. What did he think he could achieve, in a dark swamp, in the middle of a storm? A helpless dread crept over him, and the same mystifying emotion he'd felt when the man had attacked him in the bayou – an unexplainable impulse towards self-annihilation. He listened to the sound of the flood rushing through the blackness, the howl of the wind, the drumming of a million raindrops. He was alone in the watery half-world of the bayou.

He wasn't sure how long he stayed like that, lying against the tree trunk, letting the rain and wind batter him. Time passed, and he turned his head and saw a tiny shimmering dot of yellow in the distance, a lamp swimming in its own light. He pushed himself off the trunk and headed towards the light, falling into pools, tripping over roots, picking up ever more cuts and bruises as he went. Slowly the light grew large, broke into segments, began illuminating his way, and he realized it was an oil-lamp, its light emanating from the window of a hut.

He came to within a few feet of it and stopped a moment to

catch his breath. The hut was hidden in the midst of a dense thicket and it was built of branches and reeds that rested on stilts a few feet above the rushing floodwater. The eaves had been decorated with animal skulls, shining dully in the lamplight, and on the trees all around the hut, hung up by twine, were the rotting, skinned bodies of animals, swinging violently in the storm, smashing against the trunks and branches. Despite the wind and rain, he could smell the stench of the carcasses, putrid and decaying. And then he saw the dolls, tied to the trunks of the trees that surrounded the hut. Strange foot-high things made of reeds and covered in rags to look like people, with slanted eyes and screaming mouths painted onto their faces.

Luca took the gun from his pocket, praying it would still fire. He took a few steps forward, holding the gun in front of him, and then he saw Baudet. He'd been there all the time, crouching in the shadows thrown out by the lamp. Luca stopped and Baudet stared at him, a smile on his lips. He stood and approached and Luca saw he had a thick, heavy branch in his hand, sawn off at either end to make a club. If the gun didn't work, Luca was already dead.

Baudet stopped a few feet in front of him and tightened his grip on the branch. They stared at each other through the rain, both of them weather-beaten and sapped of energy. Luca compared the man standing in front of him to the photograph he had seen at Simone's. Baudet was still upright and broad-shouldered, well-built and imposing. But now there were scars and lines across his face and his hair had half turned to gray. Yet the biggest difference of all was in his look, in the set of his jaw and his narrow eyes. There was a focus in his expression, a determination so strong it made him look inhuman. Luca realized he was in the presence of a man who could be both meticulous and mad, a war hero and a murderer, a man who had coolly misdirected a whole police force, and had turned himself into a demon to avenge his parents.

Before Luca knew it, Baudet moved forward and swung the club through the air, catching Luca on the cheek, sending him into a spiral. Luca thumped onto the ground and the gun flew from his grip, disappearing into the darkness. His vision blurred, the earth beneath him rolled away, and as blood streamed into his eyes, he could just make out the tall shape above him swinging down. Then he sank into the soft, cool mud of the bayou, and as the rainwater washed over him, the music of the storm left the world.

PART SIX

The Times-Picayune

Wednesday 21st May, 1919

Local News

Clean-Up Progresses as Mayor Promises Change

At a press conference, City Hall, yesterday, Mayor Martin Behrman reported on the administration's clean-up efforts in the wake of the storm that ripped through the city last Wednesday night.

The Mayor stated that power and communication lines had been restored to most neighborhoods, although work had still to begin on fixing the city's broken pump systems and levees. With over three hundred coal barges sunk during the storm, the Mayor also outlined the city's plans for leasing space on barges from outside the parish to bring much-needed fuel to residents.

Also among the outlined plans was a plea to Washington for financial aid to help rehouse the many people left homeless after the storm. The Mayor stated that he would be asking Congress to extend the funds made available to the city under the Ransdell-Humphreys Flood Control Act of 1917 to help with levee reconstruction, and that he was in consultation to issue a series of municipal bonds to help with the reconstruction of the various railway lines and landmarks in the city that were destroyed, notably the collapsed Presbyterian Church on Lafayette Street and the collapsed St Anna's Episcopal Church on Esplanade Avenue.

The Mayor finished his report by promising residents

that this type of disaster would never befall New Orleans again.

After the Mayor, George Earl, General Superintendent of the Sewerage and Water Board of New Orleans, spoke on possible causes of the flooding. He stated that members of his Board who had been out checking damage to the city's infrastructure were theorizing that the storm caused an overflow of water from Lake Pontchartrain back into municipal drainage canals, which, combined with localized power failures, caused the pump systems in the center of the city to fail. Although he hastened to add that the above should be treated as supposition until the release of the Board's official report.

The Mayor concluded the press conference by praising the city's residents for the fortitude they had shown during these trying times.

STATEMENT

Statement: Miss Ida Davis
Date: Wed. 14th May, 1919
Location: Offices of D. F. Webb, Att., Lafayette Str., N.O.

The following statement is written in my own hand and has been placed for safekeeping in the care of Donald Webb, attorney, who assisted in its drafting. In the event of my death I have instructed Mr Webb to forward this statement, and facsimiles of it, to the New Orleans Police Department and local newspapers to do with as they see fit.

My suppositions are as follows:

1) The series of murders committed by the 'Axeman' in New Orleans these last few months were orchestrated by John Morval, who himself worked on the instructions of Mayor Martin Behrman
2) The aim of these murders was to destabilize Carlo Matranga as the head of the Matranga crime family so that Sam 'Slyvestro' Carolla would succeed him
3) The seed of this plan was the falling out of Carlo Matranga and Martin Behrman in the lead-up to, and aftermath of, the ordinance that de-licensed the Storyville pleasure district
4) John Morval was also personally responsible for the murder of Carmelita Smith of 1503 Robertson Street

For the avoidance of doubt:

I, Ida Davis, employee of the Pinkerton National Detective Agency, have spent the last few weeks investigating the Axeman murders, and although I have nothing but circumstantial evidence at present, I am certain, after speaking to some of the people involved, that the above is true. It is a well-known fact that before the Storyville district was closed down it was overseen for the most part by the Matranga crime family, with the blessing of the mayor. After the District was made illegal, the Matrangas carried on running their operations in the District, and this brought pressure to bear on the mayor from the War Commission. Unable to force the Matrangas to stop their business in the area, and facing censure from Washington if he failed to make them stop, Mayor Behrman employed John Morval to get rid of Carlo Matranga as head of the Family and install his number two, Sam Carolla, as head. Carolla agreed to close down the Family's business interests in the District in return for being installed as Family head with the mayor's protection.

John Morval hired a former soldier to kill people who paid protection money to the Matranga family to create a situation whereby Carlo Matranga would be forced to step down. The killer, who lived in the backwaters to the north of the city, was known to Morval from Morval's days as a trader buying furs from the trappers that lived in the swamps. At some point during the man's military service, Morval had lost contact with him, and had to track him down again, with the help of the Veterans Association partly run by former Brigadier General Samuel Kline Junior – a man Morval had previously blackmailed over his indiscretions. Kline was coerced into taking part in the scheme by Morval, who employed John Lefebvre, also an employee of the Pinkerton National Detective Agency, as his intermediary.

In return for his involvement, Morval had been promised the mayor's protection in relocating Storyville brothels to other locations around the city when the District was finally put out of business. To this end, Morval has already started buying properties in various citywide locations.

If any firsthand evidence is needed of the above, Samuel Kline Junior is available to testify to some of its truth. Having spoken to the same recently, I can confirm that he is willing to speak as to the veracity of these statements. In addition it may be worthwhile to seek out one

Daniel Johnson, an employee of John Morval's, who was tasked with cleaning up evidence of the victims' involvement with the Matrangas from the crime scenes. Lastly, it may be worth investigating John Morval's whereabouts on the night Carmelita Smith was murdered.

Ida Davis,
Wednesday 14th May, 1919

Mrs George Campbell,
3520 Salome Avenue,
Kenwood Springs,
St. Louis County,
Missouri

Patrolman Kerry Behan,
First Precinct Police Station,
Tulane Avenue & Saratoga Street,
New Orleans

May 8th, 1919

Dear Kerry,

I hope this finds you well. Needless to say your letter caused me great shock and joy. To know that you are so close by, and you undertook such endeavors to find me, fills me with upmost happiness. The offer of a place within our family is still open. Please arrange to visit at your earliest convenience — I will prepare a room for you straightaway.

I am glad that you have found work in the police force and I am glad you used the resources at your disposal there to trace us to our new home. We have been living in Missouri for two years now, and we find it a much more pleasant situation than New Orleans. I wonder why you had such difficulty tracing us; I left a forwarding address at our old residence for just such an eventuality; perhaps the old house changed hands more than once before you arrived?

I enclose a photograph of the family and me, and a photograph of our new house. To reach Kenwood Springs from St. Louis take any car to Wellston or Suburban Garden, then change to the car marked 'Ferguson'. It is just a three minutes' ride from Suburban Garden to our house.

Please let me know when you plan to arrive, any weekend is suitable.

Your ever-loving mother,

Mrs George Campbell

59

Michael had found the letter among Kerry's personal effects, in the green canvas sack the nightshift captain had given to him after the boy's death, remnants of a life, collected from Kerry's locker in the basement. Michael put the letter down after reading it and rubbed his temples. Along with the entries in Kerry's journal, Michael was able to reconstruct the story. His mother had given him up to the orphanage to save her family from some kind of scandal. Years later she had moved to America, and sent him a letter on his eighteenth birthday, telling him he was welcome at her new home if he wished to live there. The boy had spent his spare time in the records room trying to track her down.

Michael drummed his fingers on the desk and wondered why Kerry had never confided in him. He had been as fatherly to the boy as he knew how, and the revelation that he had lied clouded his memory of their friendship. But then Michael remembered he had not been honest with Kerry regarding his own family situation, and he guessed there were understandable reasons on both sides. He'd have to change trains in St Louis, on the way up to Chicago – a two-hour stopover, and he wondered if it was enough time to deliver Kerry's things personally. He shook his head as he thought how brokenhearted the woman would be when he told her what had happened. He put the letter back in the canvas bag with the rest of Kerry's possessions, put the bag in the cardboard box on his desk, and tied the box up with string.

Michael had handed in his letter of resignation the day after the attack on his home, and worked his notice from his desk, filing the reports, collating the evidence. He had gone to Hatener's funeral and had been asked to give a speech, where he praised the old man for saving his life, and going beyond the call of duty. He wasn't surprised Luca was absent. The men tailing him had lost track of him the night before the storm, and Michael guessed he had taken the opportunity to skip town.

The days passed easily, but during that time he hadn't had the heart to go through Kerry's things. It was only now, on his final day, when he had to clean out his desk, that he forced himself to sift through it all.

There had been a presentation by McPherson on the bureau floor. The other detectives gathered round and clapped politely on cue and Michael was given a carriage clock as a goodbye present. He smiled and McPherson gave him some fatherly advice, and the rest of the detectives joked with him a little as they tucked into the goodbye cake. He'd be back in New Orleans in a few months for the court hearings, but that was a long way off, and when it happened he wouldn't be an Orleanais anymore, just another visitor to the city.

In the days after the storm Michael, Gregson and Jones had filed reports and explained what happened in the most transparent terms; Carolla had been behind the Axeman killings; he had ambushed Michael on the night of the storm; Michael had killed Carolla in the shoot-out that followed, the shoot-out which had cost Detective Jake Hatener his life, the fifth policeman to die that night. The District Attorney had read their reports, listened to them eagerly, then ignored everything they'd had to say about Carolla's link to the Axeman killings, hinting that the mayor wanted an immediate end to the whole episode, for reasons unknown. The Captain had explained to Michael that if Carolla had been in charge of the killings, and he was dead, there was no point making the whole thing public and causing a Mafia war. Michael knew McPherson was right, but he also knew how the city worked, how corrupt it was, and in his spare moments Michael wondered just how high the corruption went. McPherson and the rest of the heavyweights at City Hall clearly knew more than they were letting on, but Michael didn't pursue the hunch – he'd be leaving the city soon, and the machinations of its hierarchy seemed less important than ever.

Since the hurricane no one had seen or heard anything from the Axeman, and with counting the victims of the storm, and the reconstruction efforts, the public had more pressing matters at hand. As Carolla was out of the picture, and the city authorities wanted so eagerly to draw a line under the matter, Michael guessed they'd never hear from the killer again. The Axeman had gone, washed out of New Orleans on the floodwaters, like so much other debris.

After the presentation, Michael said his goodbyes, picked up the box with his belongings in it and left the precinct. The Illinois Central Railroad was calling. He wasn't sure what he'd do in Chicago – he'd never been further north than Kansas City – but he felt happy about the idea of living where no one knew his name. He could maybe get a job with the Pinkertons, some kind of managerial position, if he was lucky. He didn't think about it too much; he had his family, and in Chicago they'd be safer than they were in New Orleans.

He trotted down the front steps of the building, a smile playing on his lips. Summertime was coming to the city, and the sun was beating down onto the street from a tender sky. He turned around and took a final look at the precinct looming up behind him, the stone glistening in the sunshine. He scanned the blank facade and the rows of dark windows. He felt no sadness for leaving it all behind. If anything, he felt like a weight had been lifted from him. He smiled to himself, until he passed the spot where Kerry had died and he suddenly felt guilty for his happiness, that he was somehow letting the boy down by enjoying his new beginning. He stared at the cracked steps where the bullets had hit and a sense of loss welled up inside him. He shifted the cardboard box and crossed himself. He hoped somewhere the boy was watching him and that he understood.

He took a moment, then stepped into the street, where he bumped into a chubby Negro boy rushing the other way. The box Michael was carrying fell to the floor, as did a gift-wrapped book the boy was carrying.

'I'm sorry, sir.'

'No problem. My fault,' said Michael, aware that he hadn't been looking in front of him. 'Got my mind on other things,' he muttered.

They smiled at each other and bent down to pick up their possessions. As they were kneeling down, Michael noticed Annette and the children approaching from the other side of the street, holding their luggage, dressed in their Sunday best. Annette smiled and Michael righted himself. The Negro boy looked from Michael to Annette and back again and Michael could tell what he was thinking. Then the boy smiled, tipped his hat and disappeared into the crowded street.

60

Ida heard footsteps echoing along the ward, and looked up to see the blue curtain around her bed pulled aside and Lewis being ushered in by a nurse.

'How's tricks?' he asked, smiling, and Ida grimaced. She had been reading the *Picayune* and she held it up for Lewis to see – a front-page headline about the mayor's attempt to secure reconstruction funds from Washington.

Lewis nodded sheepishly and sat in the chair next to her bed, and Ida guessed from his expression that he didn't want to discuss things yet again. In the days she had spent convalescing they had been over what had happened repeatedly, and what courses of action were open to them. Lewis wanted to let things lie, but Ida had wanted to see things through. In her mind she pursued every possible angle that presented itself to her, calculating its permutations like a chess player, trying to find a scenario that ended with the mayor being brought to justice. But eventually, when she had realized that all her options would result in dead-ends, she had come to agree with Lewis; short of going hunting through the swamps for the killer, there was nothing they could do. With Morval dead and no real evidence to link him to the murders, creating a case against the mayor would be all but impossible. The realization had made Ida feel powerless, and now the whole investigation felt hollow. There was no sense of victory, she hadn't put the world to rights. She was left with the feeling that all she'd done was prove to herself just how tightly the lines of power were drawn across the city, how strong the authorities' hold really was.

She noticed Lewis staring at the bandages wrapped around the side of her face.

'You look a lot better,' he said.

She curled her lip at him, knowing she was still bruised and swollen, and that her unsightliness was further increased by the fact that she was pale and hollow-eyed due to sleeplessness and morphine. Every night she dreamt of the storm, of Morval's factory. Her mind made her relive the events over and over. The weight of the knife in her hand, the resistance of the blade as it punctured his body, the smoothness of the metal sliding into place, the look in his eyes. In quiet moments, when there was nothing to anchor her mind to the present, the memories would float into her head and haunt her thoughts, making her heart race. Worse yet were those occasions when she didn't relive the events exactly as they happened – when the knife didn't connect, when the ropes around her hands didn't break apart, and Morval was allowed to continue with his cutting for as long as he wanted. That was when she woke up screaming and couldn't get back to sleep, and the nurse gave her an extra dose of morphine to help her drift back off.

'Anything about Morval?' asked Lewis, nodding towards the paper. She shook her head. She had been checking the papers every day but had found no mention of him. Lots of the buildings on the dockside had been destroyed by the storm, Morval's included, and as far as they could tell, he had been counted among the missing. Eventually the authorities would clear the remains of the warehouse and find his body, but that was for another day.

They sat in silence for a while, then Ida turned to Lewis, a frown creasing her brow. 'The whole thing was for nothing,' she said, gesturing towards the article about the mayor.

'I dunno,' said Lewis, 'we stopped Morval. World's gotta be better for that.'

She shrugged. He'd made the point before and she guessed he was right, but it didn't make her feel any better.

'*Chance put in our way a most singular and whimsical problem,*' Lewis quoted with a grin, '*and its solution was its own reward.*'

Ida brightened up and returned the grin. 'You've been reading,' she said.

'Yup. I figured I couldn't keep making up stories for Clarence, so I popped down to the bookshop.'

Ida nodded at him. 'It's a nice quote, but I ain't too sure about the "whimsical",' she said.

'No, me neither,' he replied, shaking his head. 'While I was there, I thought I'd get you a present.' He took a gift-wrapped book from his pocket and passed it to her.

Ida smiled, took the parcel and removed the wrapping to reveal a hardback volume – *His Last Bow: The Reminiscences of Sherlock Holmes*.

'It's the new one,' said Lewis. 'Just came out last month.'

'Thank you, Lewis,' she said, smiling. She turned and leaned out of the bed to give him a hug, then put the book on her lap.

'So what else has been going on?' she asked, and Lewis paused for a moment and looked bashful.

'I decided to take Marable up on his offer.'

'Lewis, that's great,' she said proudly. 'I knew you'd make the right decision.'

Lewis shrugged.

'Tell the truth, I'm kinda scared,' he said. 'I ain't never left New Orleans before, plus I won't be around for Clarence while I'm gone.'

Ida gave him a sideways glance. 'You'll be earning money, Lewis, to pay for doctors.'

Lewis shrugged again. 'What's your plans?' he asked, and Ida paused to think. She had been asking herself the same question ever since the storm. Amidst the nightmares and memories, she was also sensing something else – the possibility of a new dawn.

'I ain't sure,' she replied. 'I was thinking to ask for a transfer.

One of the big offices up north. Now I know Lefebvre was on Morval's pay-list, I reckon he'll write me a reference.'

Lewis grinned. 'Look at you,' he said. 'Getting all hard-boiled.'

Ida smiled bashfully, and then they lapsed into silence for a moment. Ida looked down at the book in her lap and ran her thumb over the embossing on the cover.

'Remember ages ago I told you that quote,' she said, looking up. '*There is no combination of events for which the wit of man cannot conceive an explanation.*'

Lewis frowned. 'I think so,' he said vaguely.

'I thought it meant it didn't matter how difficult a problem was, there was always a way to figure it out,' she said. 'Well, I ain't so sure anymore. I mean, everything kinda fell into place, right? I think maybe there was something else going on.'

'Like what?' asked Lewis, but Ida just shook her head. She wasn't sure exactly what it was, but she was bothered by a nebulous sense that what they had been doing wasn't really uncovering the truth, that some other process was at work, a process of construction, rather than discovery.

'I don't know,' she said at last, almost to herself. 'I was thinking maybe we didn't find the truth, maybe the truth found us.'

Lewis frowned at her, not really understanding, and Ida shrugged, dismissing the subject.

'I ain't got nothing to do for the rest of the day,' he said eventually. 'I don't mind spending it here with you.'

'Thanks for the offer, Lewis,' she said, 'but there ain't nothing to do here. You'll get bored.'

'Well, what was you planning on doing?' he asked with a smile.

She nodded to the book on her lap. 'Reading, I guess.'

'Then read out loud,' Lewis replied, still smiling at her.

He took a packet of cigarettes from his pocket, put one in his mouth and offered her another. She accepted and they lit up, and Lewis leaned back into his chair. Ida smiled and opened the book, flipping over the pages to the start of the first story, 'The Adventure of Wisteria Lodge'.

She took a drag on her cigarette before she began reading, and watched the smoke trace endless curves in front of the pale-blue curtain. From the window high above them she could hear the gentle lilt of the river. Soon enough the Mississippi would be taking Lewis north, and Ida would probably follow, pulled by its music, its unceasing flow as steady and freeing as the tumble of words on the page before her.

REPORT OF HOMICIDE

Department of Police

First Precinct, New Orleans	Fri. May 23rd 1919
Name of Person Killed:	John Riley
Residence:	552 Lowerline Street
Business:	Journalist
Name of accused:	Unknown
Residence:	Unknown
Business:	Unknown
Location of homicide:	Unknown
Day, date, hour committed:	bet. Mon. May 12th & Mon. May 19th (Coroner's Clerk initial estimate, see below)
By whom reported:	Mark Brennan, 750 Tchoupitoulas Street
To whom reported:	Corporal David Hall
Time reported:	8 o'clock A.M. Fri. May 23rd
If arrested, by whom:	Still At Large
Where arrested:	N/A
If escaped, in what manner:	N/A
Witnesses:	Mark Brennan, 750 Tchoupitoulas Street

Detailed Report

Capt. Paul Coman reports that at 8 o'clock this A.M. Fri. May 23rd, Mark Brennan, residing at #750 Tchoupitoulas Street, and a warehouse owner, came to this station and informed Corporal David Hall that a body had been discovered in the yard of the riverside warehouse he operates at North Peters and Marigny Streets. Corporal Hall immediately proceeded to the above place and on arrival discovered the body wedged into the underside of a storm-ditch.

Upon the arrival of Patrolmen James Faulks and Reginald Stevens, Corporal Hall successfully dislodged the body. He thereupon noticed the body was in an advanced state of decay, and that there was extensive bruising and lacerations around the victim's head. A wallet was found in the victim's jacket containing business cards that identified the man as John Riley, a reporter for the New Orleans *Times-Picayune*.

Corporal Hall notified by telephone Your Office at 9.15 A.M., and also the Coroner's Office, Clerk Paul Solomon. Whereupon Mr John Hunter, Clerk to the Coroner's Office, arrived up on the scene circa 10.00 A.M.

By order of Mr Hunter the body was removed to the Morgue at the Charity Hospital in the First Precinct Patrol Wagon, in charge, Driver William Godfrey and Patrolman James Faulks.

Mr Hunter's initial report (see attached, *ibid.*) was that judging from the levels of decomposition, the man had been killed at least two weeks previously.

Victim's clothes (one black tuxedo jacket, one pair of trousers, white cotton shirt, cummerbund, bow tie, and undergarments) were removed to the Coroner's Office. Also possessions: a notepad and pencil (jacket breast pocket), a box containing a small quantity of opium, a brass pipe, a book of matches from the Haymarket Cabaret (jacket inner right pocket), and wallet (right hip pocket), contents: three business cards, two dollar bills and a photograph of an unknown female.

Carbon copies of this report, attached Witness Statements, and Initial Coroner's Report have been sent to the Detective Bureau at the First Precinct Station.

> Very respectfully,
> Capt. Paul Coman
> Captain Comd'g Prec't
> J. Doyle, Clerk

EPILOGUE

Chicago, December 1st 1919

Chicago was a city of skyscrapers and snow, two things Ida had never before seen outside of a photograph. She had caught the sleeper train and had arrived at five o'clock that morning, bleary-eyed and a little dazed, the instructions in her purse. She had deposited her baggage in a station locker and whiled away some time drinking coffee in a diner on the concourse. An hour before she had to be there, she left the station and made her way to the Pinkerton offices on foot. She spent most of the journey craning her neck, dazzled by the beauty of the buildings either side of her that ascended like cliffs into the ice-filled northern sky. The snow on the streets came up to her ankles, and her feet were still half-frozen as she sat in the Pinkertons' reception area, waiting for her new boss to arrive.

The Chicago bureau was spread over two sprawling floors of a towering office block, and it bustled with people. There was a bank of four receptionists in the entrance hall, and a never-ending flow of men and women moving between the rows of desks that lay beyond a wall of glass screens. The front door opened and a tall man in a beige raincoat strode in, and one of the receptionists caught his attention. She smiled and gestured towards Ida.

'Your new recruit,' she said.

The man nodded and turned.

'Miss Davis?' he asked.

'Yes, sir,' said Ida, rising from her seat. The man held out his hand and Ida shook it.

'Welcome to the grindstone,' he said with a smile.

'Thank you, sir.'

'Now get your coat on. I only came in to pick you up.'

He grinned, turned and headed back towards the doors. Ida grabbed her coat from the chair she'd left it on and trotted out after him, back into the corridor and down a set of stairs.

'This is a crime-ridden city, Miss Davis, and prohibition's only making it worse.' They reached the bottom of the stairs and stepped out into an echoing marble hall. 'So we don't have time to sit still.'

'I understand, sir,' she said, as the man pushed through a set of revolving doors, another new invention that Ida would have to get used to. A couple of seconds later they were outside in the freezing wind, and they were both buttoning up their coats.

'You warm enough?' he asked, pointing at her thin Southern coat.

'Sure,' she said with a smile. The man smiled back and turned to look out over the snow-covered Chicago streets and Ida cast a quick glance at the scars on his face. He seemed happier than she had expected, warmer than his reputation had led her to believe, and she got the feeling she'd enjoy working with him.

'Where are we going?' she asked.

'I'm in the middle of a missing-person case,' he said. 'And I've been told to speak to . . .' He took a piece of paper from his pocket and consulted it, 'an Alphonse Capone.'

He returned the paper to his pocket and smiled at her.

'I saw from your profile you're a fellow Orleanais,' he said.

'That's right, sir,' she replied.

'You don't have to call me, sir,' he said. 'Michael will do.'

'Ida.'

'Well, Ida, let's see what you're made of.'

Acknowledgments

Thanks to Shem Bulgin, Nana Wilson, Dave Braga, Robert Long, Mariam Pourshoushtari, Tony Mulholland, William Culleton, Daisuke Tsubokawa, Robert Dupont, Sean McAuliffe, Jane Finigan, Susannah Godman, Juliet Mahony, everyone at Lutyens & Rubinstein, Sophie Orme, Maria Rejt, and everyone at Mantle and Macmillan.

Discover all four novels in Ray Celestin's
award-winning City Blues series

THE AXEMAN'S JAZZ

DEAD MAN'S BLUES

THE MOBSTER'S LAMENT

SUNSET SWING

The City Blues series begins with

THE AXEMAN'S JAZZ

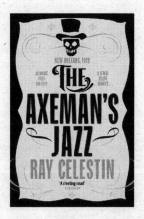

New Orleans, 1919.
As a dark serial killer – the Axeman – stalks the city, three
individuals set out to unmask him . . .

Detective Lieutenant Michael Talbot – heading up the
official investigation, but struggling to find leads, and
harbouring a grave secret of his own.

Former detective Luca d'Andrea – now working for the
Mafia; his need to solve the mystery of the Axeman is
every bit as urgent as that of the authorities.

And Ida – a secretary at the Pinkerton Detective Agency.
Obsessed with Sherlock Holmes and dreaming of a better life, she
stumbles across a clue which lures her and her musician friend,
Louis Armstrong, to the case – and into terrible danger . . .

As Michael, Luca and Ida each draw closer to discovering the
killer's identity, the Axeman himself will issue a challenge to the
people of New Orleans: play jazz or risk becoming the next victim.

OUT NOW IN PAPERBACK.

Discover the second book in the City Blues series,

DEAD MAN'S BLUES

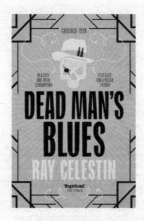

Chicago, 1928.
In the stifling summer heat three investigations begin . . .

Pinkerton detectives Michael Talbot and Ida Davis are
hired to locate a missing heiress. But it proves harder than
expected to find a woman known across the city.

After being called to a gruesome murder in Chicago's
violent Black Belt, crime-scene photographer Jacob Russo
can't get the dead man's image out of his head, and decides
to track down the culprit himself.

And with a group of city leaders poisoned at the Ritz, Dante
Sanfelippo – rum-runner and fixer – is called in by Al Capone to
discover whether someone is trying to bring down his empire.

As the three parties edge closer to the truth, their paths will cross
and their lives will be threatened. But will any of them find the
answers they need in the city of blues, booze and brutality?

OUT NOW IN PAPERBACK.

The City Blues series continues with the third instalment

THE MOBSTER'S LAMENT

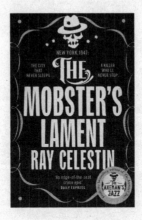

New York, 1947.
A gangster's last chance to escape the clutches of New York's Mafia,
and a ruthless serial killer is tracking his every move . . .

Mob fixer Gabriel Leveson's plans to flee the city are put
on hold when he is tasked with tracking down stolen Mob money
by 'the boss of all bosses', Frank Costello. But while he's busy
looking, he doesn't notice who's watching him . . .

Meanwhile, Private Investigator Ida Young and her old
partner, Michael Talbot, must prove the innocence of
Talbot's son Tom, who has been accused of the brutal
murders of four people in a Harlem flop-house. With all the
evidence pointing towards him, their only chance of
exoneration is to find the killer themselves.

Whilst across town, Ida's childhood friend, Louis Armstrong,
is on the brink of bankruptcy, when a promoter approaches
him with a strange offer to reignite his career . . .

OUT NOW IN PAPERBACK.

The City Blues series comes to an end with

SUNSET SWING

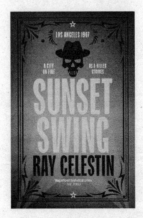

Los Angeles. December, 1967.

A young nurse, Kerry Gaudet, travels to the City of Angels desperate to find her missing brother, fearing that something terrible has happened to him: a serial killer is terrorizing the city, picking victims at random, and Kerry has precious few leads.

Ida Young, recently retired Private Investigator, is dragged into helping the police when a young woman is discovered murdered in her motel room. Ida has never met the victim but her name has been found at the crime scene and the LAPD wants to know why . . .

Meanwhile Mob fixer Dante Sanfelippo has put his life savings into purchasing a winery in Napa Valley, but first he must do one final favour for the Mob before leaving town: find a bail jumper before the bond money falls due, and time is fast running out.

Ida's friend, Louis Armstrong, flies into the city just as her investigations uncover mysterious clues to the killer's identity. And Dante must tread a dangerous path to pay his dues, a path which will throw him headlong into a terrifying government conspiracy and a secret that the conspirators will do anything to protect . . .

OUT NOVEMBER 2021 AND AVAILABLE TO PRE-ORDER NOW.